"You are my husband."

Raymond's head snapped up, his face pale. He stood, then sat down again. "Nay…she is but— you cannot be—"

"Why not? 'Tis not the person that is important, but the pact. If I do not please you, that is regrettable, but be assured I find the prospect of wedding you no more appealing."

"I did not expect you to find me appealing. I will force myself upon no one. Do as you will, go where you like."

His defensive attitude surprised Ceridwen. Not knowing what to think, she forged ahead. "Do I or do I not have your word that I might take up residence as your lady—in name only? You said you would not force—"

"I know what I said." Raymond rose to his feet. "Once we are wed, I care not what you do. Just keep out of my way…!"

Elaine Knighton grew up in California, riding her horse through the grassy, windswept hills and dreaming of romantic, heroic adventures. Now she lives in the misty and mystical Pacific Northwest and writes about romantic, heroic adventures instead of only dreaming about them. Elaine has roots in Poland, England and Scotland, a mixture in which there may be some hope of finding a balance between passion and reason, but she thinks she'll always be a dreamer at heart... You can visit Elaine at her website: www.elaineknighton.com

Mills & Boon® Historical Romance™
is proud to introduce this debut novel
from **Elaine Knighton**

BEAUCHAMP
BESIEGED

Elaine Knighton

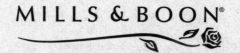

MILLS & BOON®

MILLS & BOON and MILLS & BOON with the Rose Device are registered trademarks of the publisher.

*First published in Great Britain 2004
Harlequin Mills & Boon Limited,
Eton House, 18-24 Paradise Road, Richmond, Surrey TW9 1SR*

© Elaine Knighton 2003

ISBN 0 263 83986 9

*Set in Times Roman 10 on 10½ pt.
04-1104-98551*

*Printed and bound in Spain
by Litografia Rosés S.A., Barcelona*

I have many people to thank,
but I particularly need to acknowledge:

Linda Abajian, who believed from the beginning.
Shannon Caldwell, whose medieval expertise and
beautiful longbows inspired me. Liz Engstrom,
Wes Hoskins, Deanna Mather Larson and Doe Tabor,
who taught me all about writing and to never give up.
Teresa Basinski-Eckford, Gwyn Cready, Sue Greenlee,
Sharon Lanergan, Evalyn Lemon, Laurel O'Donnell,
Ann Simas, Outreach International Romance Writers,
Rose City Romance Writers and many other members
of Romance Writers of America who offered me
unfailing advice and support. My agents,
Ron and Mary Lee Laitsch, and my editors,
Tracy Farrell and Jessica Regante, who gave this story
a chance. And James Pearson, who told me so…

Prologue

The Marches of England and southern Wales, 1180

"Slow down—*I* must lead!"

Raymond de Beauchamp ignored his brother Alonso's snarling command. As of today he was a full ten winters old. As of today he was one year closer to being a man—a true warrior. And even Alonso could not prevent that.

He galloped his stout cob through the forest, heedless of Everard the Fat's cries of distress at the pace. On a Welsh pony, little Percy bounced along behind, willing to follow anywhere if his three elder brothers let him.

Raymond gloried in the crisp air against his face. Golden leaves swirled and tumbled in the wake of the ponies' hooves. Ahead was an open hill, with crags of rotten stone that broke apart as they trod upon them. At the top lay the dolmen. A forbidden place, where evil spirits lurked and wicked lads might forever disappear. At least that was what old Nurse Alys said.

The stone slab seemed impossibly large and heavy. Raymond halted and stared, caught up in its mystery, in its implications of age-old, sacred blood.

Alonso strutted its length, a lock of gilded hair falling over his eyes. He challenged the two youngest boys with his gaze. Blue, gleaming, sharp as a blade. "Raymond and Percy! Let us make an offering, like the old ones, upon this stone."

Raymond stilled. So this was the price for winning the race through the forest. Everard, a chubby version of his older brother, stood next to his pony, twisting the reins around his hands. "Nay, 'twould be blasphemous to do such a thing."

Alonso narrowed his eyes at Everard. "Did I ask you, knot-head? It will not be if I say it is not. Percy. You will do, for you are the sweetest and the softest. The crones who come here to dance this eve will feast upon you with delight."

Grinning, he swung the child onto the slab.

The rosebud color drained from Percy's cheeks. Raymond's stomach tightened into knots of outrage. Percy was but a wee lad. Why, he still had creases of baby fat where his hands met his wrists. Loathing for Alonso filled Raymond, but he held himself in check, fiddling his sore, loose milk-tooth with his tongue. "Put him down, Alonso. He thinks you mean it."

Alonso merely bared his teeth and continued preparing to tie Percy up. Raymond clenched his jaw despite the ache. His brother's familiar, leering grin marred a face so fair that to all who did not know him, Alonso was surely a young man of nobility and honorable intent. But he had the heart of a carrion-eater, Raymond knew full well.

His blood pounded in a red wash of fury. He rammed his elder brother with his shoulder, fists pounding ribs. Alonso, taller, heavier, and more experienced, kneed Raymond in the belly, kicked his head, then dragged him upright by his hair.

"*Never* interfere with my pleasure, fool."

Staring into ice-blue eyes, Raymond struggled to draw breath and longed to batter that sneering face. But Percy needed him, he must hold back. The child sat on the stone, his straw-colored hair awry, rubbing his eyes with dimpled hands.

Alonso unsheathed his dagger. "Well then. Someone has got to be it. If not Percy, then who?" He cut a length of rope and started to wind it around Percy's wrists.

The lad turned a frightened gaze upon Raymond, who found it impossible to wink or smile in reassurance. He cleared his throat. "You desire a sacrifice? Let it be me."

Alonso smiled. "'Tis always more pleasing to the gods when the victim is willing. Get off of there, Percy."

The child stayed put, his lower lip trembling. "Nay. I will not let Raymie die for me."

Alonso simply tossed Percy to the ground. The boy scrambled up and ran weeping to Raymond, who brushed the gravel from his small palms. "Hush! I am not going to die." Raymond heaved himself onto the stone and hoped he'd spoken the truth.

"On your knees, Brother. We must do this properly."

Raymond's insides twisted as the cords bit into his wrists. "My hands are going numb."

"Get used to it." Alonso pulled harder.

Raymond began to struggle in earnest as his brother drew the bindings from his ankles around each thigh. Raw panic chewed at the last threads of his confidence, and sweat dampened his brow. "Alonso. I will not be hamfasted."

"You already are. Everard, help me get this knot right."

"Perhaps this is excessive." Everard's statement was more whine than protest.

Alonso jerked Raymond's feet and hands together for the final stage of his bondage. "Everard, hamfasting is an art. Do it properly—you are going to be a churchman, are you not? So, you must know how to persuade your flock to confess!"

Everard pushed Raymond's face against the stone slab. Now his wrists were behind him, lashed to his ankles. His heels were tight against his buttocks, and each ankle was bound to its respective thigh. The worst sort of criminals were hamfasted like this, before they were... Raymond fought down the terror welling within him. He would rather die than let them see it.

"Hurry up and be done, you swine!" He thrust his tongue into the painful socket of his tooth, which refused to let go.

"But, Brother, you are not in the true spirit of things." Alonso's eyes glittered in the lowering rays of the sun, and a new thought occurred to Raymond. Demons. It was the only explanation for Alonso's extraordinary cruelty. Something evil must have slithered out of these woods and possessed him.

The shadows of the forest edge grew and touched the rim of the stone, even as ravens spiraled in to roost among the half-clad tree branches. The western sky glowed pink, but in the east lightning already flickered amidst rumbling, blue-black clouds. Night would bring new horrors to this place.

"Now, for the shedding of blood." Alonso picked up his dagger and sighted down it, testing the edges with his thumb.

"You'll be sorry you started this. I will come after you." Raymond's words belied the churning in his stomach. The rough stone scraped his cheek as Alonso rolled him onto his back, and his thigh muscles stretched to the point of pain. The skin of his throat was exposed to the cooling air.

Alonso breathed against Raymond's cheek. "Father has not yet succeeded in drawing a single tear from your eyes, but mark me, it will come to pass. *I* have sworn to break you." He straightened and laid his knifepoint at the soft hollow beneath Raymond's jaw. "For what do we make this sacrifice, Brothers? Success in battle? Infidel's gold? The power of kings? Or the guaranteed salvation of our souls, so we never have to sit through one of Father Brenner's stupid catechisms again?"

Raymond's heart thundered. The dagger-tip trembled against his skin, a deadly point of heat. Alonso hissed, "Perhaps to be rid of a damned sight of trouble in future?"

"Finish it, then," Raymond growled.

"Nay!" Percy darted up and grabbed Alonso's elbow.

The older boy jerked free of the little one's grasp. The blade slipped into Raymond's throat. Percy screamed.

Raymond swallowed his tooth. He gasped and howled out his rage until he choked, his mouth full of metallic-tasting blood. Seeping warmth coursed around his neck. Alonso's gaze grew soft and liquid, as though he was charmed by the picture before him.

"We will leave him thus. 'Tis too perfect."

Raymond burned, a hot, malevolent pool of hatred swirling within him. Percy's cries grew into thin shrieks—high, piercing animal sounds that would not stop. Alonso wrapped one hand about his neck until the child was silent but for a few gurgling sobs. "Let us away."

Hooves clattered against the rocky ground, then a shroud of silence settled upon Raymond. At first he could not believe his brothers had truly left him behind. But the twilight crept closer, winding chill, blue-gray fingers about the dolmen.

The darkening sky wheeled overhead, faster and faster, until nothing existed but his unvoiced scream. Soon the wolves would come, and he would die. Alone. An offering, a human sacrifice, meant to stay the heavenly wrath Alonso was surely accumulating.

Then, unbidden, like a gift from some ancient spirit of the dolmen, a cold blade of resolve cut through Raymond's anguish. A new hardness permeated his heart, as if it were a piece of red-hot iron plunged into water. He welcomed the numbing calm, embraced its deadly resolution.

I will live. And one day, Alonso will not.

Chapter One

1196, sixteen years later, along the Marches

Already the battlefield reeked. Sir Raymond de Beauchamp wheeled his warhorse and arced his sword in a whistling blur of Spanish steel. The blade bit true and deep. He sucked in a great gulp of the stifling air within his helm, and watched the young Welshman topple from his small horse. The lordling died quietly, his blood streaming in bright contrast onto the spring verdure.

A hollow stab of regret pierced Raymond's soul. The fellow had fought well. But, there was no time to reflect upon the valor of one already dead. Raymond surveyed the chaos around him. His knights galloped in a disordered frenzy over the field, attempting to hack their way through the steadfast Welsh.

Inwardly he groaned. As ever, the horsemen allowed their courage to outstrip their discipline, and for that they could lose the fight. Too many of the rebel Welsh were still in the safety of the forest beyond, firing deadly volleys from their formidable longbows. The dreadful hissing made Raymond's gut clench even as he tried to calm his nervous horse. Neither his own mail, nor that covering the stallion would even begin to stop the penetration of a shaft loosed from one of those deceptively simple-looking weapons.

Raymond turned his head sharply at a sudden movement

along the field's edge. What he had taken to be a lifeless body jumped up and ran to the warrior he had just sent heavenward. A lad, barely old enough to be a squire, cradled the dead man's head and wailed his grief. Raymond's heart twisted in pity, despite his practiced detachment. So much blood, so many tears. The pitched energy he had summoned for the battle dissipated into a numbing weariness that spread through his limbs.

Hoofbeats thundered across the chopped turf of the meadow. It was his lieutenant, Giles. The boy would be cut to pieces and joining his master in a matter of moments. "Hold, Giles!" His friend could not hear him above the cries of fighting men and the keening of the lad. Raymond urged his mount forward and cut in front of Giles's horse at a run.

The boy stared openmouthed as the galloping chargers bore down upon him. Raymond leaned low and grabbed the scruff of the lad's tunic, throwing him across his horse's neck. He swerved to avoid trampling the slain Welshman and nearly collided with Giles's stallion. Even as Raymond improved his grip on the shrieking boy, a piercing, red-hot pain struck him. His prized destrier emitted a huffing groan and bolted, veering sideways. It took all his strength and skill to control the animal without letting go of the child, especially since he could not move his left leg. Searing torment flourished and spread with every movement. He clenched his jaw and broke into a sweat.

Then he looked down. An arrow had penetrated his thigh, his saddle, and mayhap even his horse. "Jesu—nay…" Raymond's voice faded as the sharp agony wormed deeper. He fought to hold onto his struggling burden as they cantered toward safety. Giles already pounded away in useless pursuit of the hidden archer, a blood-curdling roar echoing after him.

A fresh assault began, this time to Raymond's right leg. The boy, hanging upside down over the shoulder of the horse, swung his arm rhythmically with each stride of the animal, stabbing at his rescuer with a small dagger.

Raymond brought his knee up and gave the lad's head a solid knock. The jabbing ceased. Pulling his horse to a rough halt in the shelter of a hillock, he threw the boy to the ground. The ungrateful whelp landed hard, gasping for breath.

Raymond tried to slow the wild thudding of his heart. He relaxed methodically to combat the pain, and spoke softly to his trembling, sweating mount. It would be an ordeal worthy of an inquisitor to get free of the arrow. All because he had succumbed to pity. Always a mistake.

The boy began to push himself up from the ground.

"Halt." The curt order froze the lad, and Raymond stared.

Smooth cheeks beneath the mud, blood and tears. Long-lashed green eyes. A trembling body within a suspiciously full upper tunic. Holy Mary, if this was a boy, then he himself was a silkie from the sea. The horse took a deep breath and snorted. Raymond gritted his teeth against the jolt of fire that shot from hip to knee. "Take off that hood, damn you."

Tangles of wavy black hair spilled down about a charming, oval face. Raymond caught his breath. He was right. A girl, typically Welsh, and heart stopping in her fragile beauty. Except for the loathing that seethed from her eyes. He was used to hate-filled stares from his enemies, but this chit could not be more than fifteen years of age, the same as Meribel, his own beloved lady-wife.

The thought of a young woman on a battlefield fanned his anger as well as his longing to be away from this outlandish place. Welsh women were famous for the atrocious battle-harvests they reaped from fallen enemies. His leg throbbed as his destrier pawed at the soft earth.

"Idiot wench, what were you about? Be glad I do not beat you for my trouble." He forgot not to move in his saddle, and ground his teeth as the pain surged. A steady patter dripped from the underside of his stirrup.

"Just you try! Lord Talyessin's archer has pinned you to your horse quite perfectly," she said, grim triumph in her voice. "As you well deserve. I hope you die. Slowly."

Pretending to ignore her, he scanned the battlefield. The girl scrambled to her feet, her weapon still in her raised fist. Raymond turned his horse and a nudge of the destrier's shoulder knocked her flat once again. His mount shivered beneath him, and pain assailed his leg with unrelenting ferocity. Hot fury leaped in his chest at the maid's audacity. A girl-child gone to war. Hell and damnation.

Perhaps his lord-brother Alonso was right. These people were mad. Bereft of reason. He shook his head at the sight of the girl, sprawled in the grass, one delicate hand clutching her knife as though it were a talisman against him and his kind.

Her eyes filled with tears. "You misbegotten Norman bastard! You've killed Owain. Murderer!"

Raymond regarded her in silence. Sympathy crept up on his pain and anger, but he swallowed the will-sapping emotion. He had already suffered a crippling wound on her behalf. "I am a misbegotten *English* bastard," he growled. "And I would be your ally if your prince had any sense. Your friend Owain need not have died if you Welsh had the wits to capitulate." With an effort, Raymond softened his voice. "Let us go home. You to yours, and I to mine. Do you understand, *Cymraes?*"

The girl stared, apparently startled at his use of her language. *Welshwoman.* Perhaps he had mispronounced it. The little witch need not glare at him like that. Raymond bit his lip to stifle the moan that threatened as his restless horse shifted. Black spots floated before his eyes.

"I do, *Sais,*" she said quietly. "And *you* understand this: I shall come for you one day, when you least expect it."

Raymond felt the blood rise in his neck and was grateful for the helm that hid his face. *Sais.* Saxon. Anyone the Welsh considered beneath contempt, they designated as *Sais.* Coming from a Welsh mouth the word was synonymous with "pagan brute." She could have offered no worse insult. "So you will come for me. How do you plan to find me? Do you know who I am?"

The girl raised her small chin defiantly. "It makes no difference—you are all the same. Filthy, two-faced marauders who bleed our borders in the name of the English king. I will find you. I will follow the carrion crows to your lord's keep."

Raymond's helm muffled his humorless laugh. It was absurd to argue with this creature while he bled to death. "*Bon chance* to you then, my lady." He looked up as Giles crested the hill. The big knight's horse bounced to a stiff-legged stop before them, and Raymond blinked hard as his own destrier jigged.

"My lord, 'tis over. Talyessin's men are slinking back to their holes. Come away from this vermin and let me see to your wounds." Giles glanced briefly at the figure on the ground, then his steel-encased head swiveled back. "*Merde,* a lass? A bit bold for a camp-follower, methinks!"

"Meet my newest enemy, Giles. Sworn to see my bitter demise. Make certain she returns safely to her people. Oh, and find that pig-sticker she is hiding beneath her tunic. I would do it myself, but I am somewhat indisposed at the moment." Without a backward glance, Raymond turned his horse and rode away.

Chapter Two

1200, four years later, southern Wales

Ceridwen paced before her father. Plain rushes crunched beneath her feet, not fine herbs or lavender. Lord Morgan's hall at Llyn y Gareg Wen remained free of luxury. Firelight leaped on the stone walls, reflecting the gleam of lances, swords, and longbows, hung ready for retrieval at a moment's notice.

"Nay, Da, I will not be your bait. God intervened when I was but a lass to spare me marriage to a Beauchamp. Now you wish again to make alliance with those soulless wolves?"

Morgan gently set his goblet on the scarred oak table. That he did not bang it down warned Ceridwen just how angry he was. "Be quiet and sit, child." He turned his dark, sharp gaze full upon her. "For once you will do as you are told. You have disobeyed me in many things, but this shall not be one of them." His leather-bottomed chair creaked as he rose and took over the pacing where she left off.

Ceridwen flung herself onto a seat opposite her elder brother, Rhys. Her half-dozen siblings watched with great interest, from nearly every available perch in the hall. Little Dafydd climbed into her lap. She stroked his dark hair and held him close. The wee ones needed her more than ever now that Mam was gone. She gulped back the lump in her throat and tried to concentrate on what her father was saying.

Morgan paused before the hearth and stared into the flames.
"Old baron Beauchamp was wise to offer us peace once,
through his youngest son, Parsifal. And as you say, Parsifal's
death was the result of intervention, divine or otherwise. But the
remaining Beauchamp sons no longer have the counsel of their
father. They harry us without mercy, and I cannot keep up this
resistance forever."

"But—"

Her father silenced her with a severe look. "The next eldest
Beauchamp, Raymond, has a few more brains in his head than
the others. That aside, he is land-hungry. He had to sell his late
wife's domains to fund the defense of his keep at Rookhaven.
He chafes against the yoke his lord brother Alonso has placed
round his neck."

"And you wish me to act as the balm to soothe him?"

"I do!" Morgan's fierce tone punctured her show of bravery.
"Baron Alonso wields a vast fist of power. And Sir Raymond
is the well-honed dagger within that fist. Alonso suspects Raymond is near the breaking point. He has promised me, if I do
not find a way to thwart Raymond's revolt, I, and all who are
dear to me will suffer for it. And Alonso is a master of under-
statement."

Her father smiled in a way that sent chills down Ceridwen's
spine. She hugged Daffyd until he squirmed out of her arms.
Morgan's gaze followed his youngest child's search for a more
comfortable female lap, then he continued. "What Alonso does
not know is that I will control his brother by making an alliance
with him. Alonso will be held at bay by the threat of both Raymond and the Talyessin, and we will have Raymond under our
watchful eye. *Your* eye." Morgan took his seat once again.

"What if I cannot bear the sight of this man, nor the uncouth
sound of his language, nor his rabid touch? What would you
have me do, when Owain's blood is still unavenged?" Her handsome, fey Owain, both warrior and soothsayer. Ceridwen balled
her hands into fists, digging her nails into her palms.

She remembered the day of his death with agonizing clarity.
Owain had lain in the meadow as if asleep, but there was so
much blood—she could still see the evil gleam from the eyes

of the killer, within his shadowed helm. A knight under the Beauchamp banner had called her *Cymraes,* as though he thought her worthless and crude. And now she was being told to marry one of the monsters! Everyone knew what the English were like. They roasted their enemies over slow fires and ate them alive.

Ceridwen narrowed her eyes and searched her father's face for a sign he might relent. Finding none, she felt for her ivory flute, stuck through the belt at her waist. She twisted the warm cylinder in her hands and wished her mother were still alive. There were questions she could not ask Da, and even Mam had never fully explained the intimate details of what marriage meant for a woman. Now at nineteen—old enough to have borne several babes—she was mortified to admit her ignorance to anyone else.

Ceridwen caught the look her father exchanged with Rhys, who lounged in a confident sprawl on a bench near the fire. Her brother's head moved in a small negative shake. They always had secrets, those two. And kept them from her with great success.

Morgan casually unsheathed his dagger and picked up a whetstone from the table. "You think me heartless, Ceri, but I have not forgotten Owain. I believe Alonso would rather eliminate Raymond altogether than have him as an outright enemy. Once you are at Rookhaven, there will be many opportunities for you to set brother against brother. And if some unfortunate incident should result in Raymond's death—well, you are but a woman, and cannot be held responsible for your untoward passions." Spitting upon the stone, Morgan began to grind the knife blade against it in tight circles.

"Oh, Da!" How could he think her capable of cold-blooded murder? But a tiny part of Ceridwen wondered how far she would go to be free of the terrible ache that consumed her whenever she thought of Owain, dead in her arms. But it was no use bemoaning her fate. Whatever her feelings, her duty was clear.

Morgan paused in his sharpening and smiled at his daughter. "An innocent lass, yet woe unto anyone who crosses you. I doubt even the formidable Raymond will give a beauty like Ceridwen much trouble, eh, Rhys?'' He looked at his eldest son, who merely raised his brows and shrugged.

Ceridwen shifted uncomfortably on the hard bench and scuffed her bare foot on the rough wooden floor. Da always said she looked like her mother. She had the same shining, raven hair, the same eyes that changed color with her moods. But Ceridwen ignored her father's compliments. Beauty and innocence were their own kind of trouble. And Da was a shameless flatterer when the need arose.

''Has Sir Raymond agreed to this union?'' she demanded.

Her father stroked his sleek, black moustaches. Chuckling, he winked at Rhys. ''He will, sweet. He will.''

''You like dogs, do you not, Ceri?'' Rhys gifted her with a mischievous smile, showing his even, white teeth. ''Sir Raymond loves his wolfhound better than he does any woman. Be kind to the creature, and I'll wager the master will leave you alone.''

Ceridwen scowled at her brother. ''This is more shame than I can bear, to be held in lower esteem than a beast. How will I live with myself?'' She covered her face with her hands.

Impatience flickered in her father's tone. ''You will live with *him,* and stop thinking of yourself, girl. This is important to me, to the prince, and to the *Cymraeg.* Raymond is not one to take lightly. When he makes a promise—or a threat—he fulfills it. But once you have charmed him, he may learn sympathy for our cause. Perhaps some of his violence can be used to our ends. Or another solution may become necessary.''

Morgan's voice grew smooth, and Ceridwen recognized the cunning, silky inflection. ''I have every confidence in you, Ceridwen. After all, you are of my blood, and I am ever victorious. One way or another.'' He grinned, flashing the beguiling smile each of his children had inherited. Then he tested his honed dagger on a piece of leather. The blade slid through the skin in effortless silence.

Ceridwen's heart wrenched into a familiar knot. *You are of my blood.* Da had shed a great deal of it, keeping them alive. His own and English, too. She shuddered. The very thought made her feel faint. Peace was the only solution. Vengeance might be sweet, but it had no place in this situation. She paused at the expectant gazes of her young brothers and sisters. In truth she was no substitute for Mam. The best thing she could do for them would be to help keep the Beauchamps at bay, regardless of the personal cost. Ceridwen sat up straight. "Right, Da. If it pleases you and saves even one Welsh life, I will go to him."

"They have done *what?*" Raymond leaped to his feet. The bench crashed to the floor behind him, sending an echo through the cold solar. He leaned over the trestle table and grabbed the front of his lieutenant's linen surcoat with both fists. He'd spent the third day in a row combing the woods for his wolfhound and was in no mood for Giles's usual sideways approach to bad news.

"My lord, be easy. 'Tis a simple matter to get Hamfast back. All you need do is—"

"A simple matter! These Welshmen hold my dog hostage and you say 'tis simple? What if they don't feed him properly? What if he bites one of them, and they abuse him for it?"

Raymond took a deep breath to banish the painful image of his huge, noble hound in the hands of fierce Welshmen. He smoothed the creases he'd made in Giles's attire, then gave his friend's broad chest a thump to indicate he'd finished mauling him. "Where exactly do they have him?"

"At a deserted tower in Trefynwy." Giles dropped the joint he'd been gnawing, and it fell into his trencher with a sodden plop. He licked his fingers, one by one. For all his knightly virtues, Giles's table manners were abominable.

Raymond looked to his empty bed, where Hamfast usually slept. "They seek to draw me in, well beyond the border, and play me some trick. What ransom have they demanded?"

Giles cleared his throat. "Only you, my lord."

"Do not jest. Tell me truly."

"But I do. Lord Morgan has a comely daughter, one overripe for marriage. In fact, she was once promised to Parsifal, was she not?" Giles reached for his goblet and took a gulp of wine.

Raymond closed his eyes briefly at the stab of sorrow his long-dead brother's name still evoked. Percy, a brave knight of tender years and tender heart. Would that he had come home from the crusade and taken this Welsh maiden. Another marriage, be it to Helen of Troy, was a dread prospect for himself. "Nay. I will simply storm their defenses and retrieve Hamfast." Ever restless, Raymond fumed and paced, his hands clasped behind his back. Still, for the good of his people, he had to at least consider the idea. "What does Morgan expect to gain? How will Rookhaven benefit?"

Giles belched and carefully wiped the corners of his mouth with the pad of his thumb. "We are like lame wolves in a herd of wily sheep. Always hungry and never satisfied, worn out with constant moving from uprising to uprising. So, if there is peace between you, both will benefit. And the dowry she brings contains the crossroads of Llanmadog."

Raymond paused to consider. He had needed control of that area for years. With it in his possession, his western borders would enjoy security. He could better conserve his strength for the final push against Alonso—if it wasn't already too late. But there was no room in his life, nor in his heart, for any woman, much less a wife. He glanced at Giles. The handsome knight had tied back his thick, dark hair with a leather thong. He seemed able to accommodate any number of women, and his heart never became entangled with any of them.

Whereas with himself and Meribel…never had a lady been better loved, or caused more grief. Raymond pinched the bridge of his nose. "What does this overripe girl look like?"

"She is beautiful, of course."

It was as well Giles's hair was pulled back, for a hint of red crept into the curves of his ears. He was hiding something. Raymond crossed his arms. "Is that so? What good fortune. Tell me the color of her eyes."

"I did not get that close." The knight's cheeks pinked.

"Her hair, then?"

Giles bloomed a vivid, rosy hue and said nothing.

"You missed that, too?" Raymond's impatience waxed. "Is she short, tall, plump? Let me guess. You rode up to their gates and conducted the entire farce as a shouting match without ever dismounting. You saw no proof that Hamfast still lives!"

"I have it on good authority that the maiden resembles nothing so much as an angel, in both form and disposition," Giles said indignantly. "She is fond of dogs," he added, "and would never countenance him coming to harm."

"Whose authority? A shepherdess on her back with her skirts up to her waist, no doubt."

"Well, I…"

Raymond shook his head. "Giles, you will never change. We both know where your brains reside."

"Aye. How long has it been, Raymond? Is that why your temper is so short?" Giles speared a piece of meat and eyed it as though it were a tantalizing morsel of peacock, instead of tough, cold mutton.

Raymond stared at his friend. From habit his fingers tightened around his dagger hilt. Giles could needle him like no one else. Except perhaps Alonso. "Methinks you know me not at all, sir. Shall I bemoan my sad lack of romantic exploits and accept the offers of your leftovers? Or should we parley with these barbarians and rescue my hound in proper form?"

"I believe the latter would be for the best, my lord," Giles said with surprising primness. He actually sniffed, giving Raymond some small satisfaction.

"There is one other thing…." Giles began.

"Aye?" Raymond leaned down and set the toppled bench back on its feet with a loud crack.

"Her uncle is Talyessin." Giles sucked his teeth.

"So? Wales is full of Talyessins."

"*The* Talyessin."

Raymond blinked as this information penetrated. He had not been privy to the details of his late brother's engagement. At the time he had been profoundly absorbed in more important concerns, namely, staying alive on a battlefield in France.

The Talyessin. A mighty Welsh lord, maneuvering himself from the north to rule the whole of Wales. His kinsmen's expert archers had left Raymond with the near-fatal thigh wound that had cost him a full summer of recovery. The stench of the infection had kept Meribel away from him, had sent her looking for other, prettier amusements. He still favored that leg.

"Does he approve of this match, or is this an independent scheme of Morgan's?" Raymond knew he could not escape the marriage, if backed to the wall by both of the powerful Welshmen. Not alone, and not with his prized dog in their hands. Men far greater than he, condemned to death, had purchased their very lives with the likes of Hamfast.

"He agrees with Lord Morgan, that they are well served by persuading you to form an alliance." Giles wiped the grease from his eating dagger with the hem of his surcoat.

"An alliance based upon treachery. It goes against my grain. But, there is the happy thought that my righteous lord brother would find my new domestic arrangements intolerable." Raymond rubbed the carved stone head of a knight, sitting on the chessboard he'd had built into the table, and sighed. "I will do it. But if this girl causes any trouble, back she goes."

"Of course." Giles grinned. "But she'll be butter in your hands, I have no doubt."

A soft knock sounded at the door.

"Come!" Raymond frowned. *What now?*

His cousin-by-marriage, Blanche, peeked into the solar. As ever, her hair was modestly hidden beneath her head cloth. She wore an unadorned kirtle of russet wool, which lent her graceful form more elegance than any amount of finery.

"Forgive me, my lord, I did not know you were occupied." Blanche curtsied deeply and immediately turned to leave.

"A moment, lady." She lifted her head and Raymond could see in her silver-grey eyes that she was nervous before him. A penniless widow, Blanche and her daughter had been thrust into his care by her mother-in-law, his aunt Clarisse. A cunning old witch if ever he knew one. He would try to put Blanche at ease.

"Please, be seated." Raymond indicated his own place by the fire. She hesitated, then warily sat in the heavy oak chair. Giles followed her every move with his smoldering gaze.

"Tell me what brings you here. I am at your service." Raymond did not attempt a smile, but he did speak softly and avoided towering over her.

"Ah, well, 'tis but a small matter, perhaps best left for another time." She clutched the arms of the chair, as if readying herself to flee. As Raymond expected, the gallant Giles filled a cup with the unwatered wine he'd been drinking, and offered it to her with a courtly bow. Blanche was forced to let go of the chair in order to accept the wine.

Raymond cleared his throat. "Bree, again? She is the only small matter of concern at this keep." The child was a fair delight, but a constant vexation to her mother, and an endless worry to him. At times he wondered if Bree was a changeling. For all her guileless expression, the amount of trouble she caused made it more than a casual jest.

As if Blanche read his thoughts, she averted her gaze.

Raymond hastened to reassure her. "Never mind. As you say, let us speak of it later. In truth, I wish to have your opinion on the subject under discussion when you arrived."

Blanche looked up at him expectantly, her clear eyes reflecting a keen intelligence.

"Sir Giles believes I should marry again." Raymond watched in alarm as the color drained from her face. Giles jumped to retrieve her goblet as it slipped from her fingers. "I beg your pardon, Madame. I did not mean that *you* were the intended, er, bride." Raymond almost said "victim," but resisted the temptation. Sarcasm would not help.

Blanche's relief that she was not the focus of his intentions was immediately apparent. She took several more sips of wine and revived quickly.

"Explain, Giles." Raymond waved vaguely in his friend's direction and gazed into the brazier fire while Giles spoke. He did not enjoy being an object of terror. At least not to women. But all too often that was the case, and why not? They knew he'd been the death of Meribel. And Blanche knew it, too. But whatever she thought of him, he respected her. Anyone who had survived the intrigues of his family deserved as much.

Blanche listened quietly, occasionally murmuring an affirmation. Giles used the opportunity to full advantage. He sat beside her and took small liberties, touching her hand or leaning a bit too close. The young woman was visibly affected, for she started and blushed at each contact.

"I believe Lady Blanche understands, now," Raymond interrupted Giles. "What say you, Madame?" He did not desire her opinion so much as he did her participation, so she might begin to feel a part of his household. If Giles would but leave her in peace.

"Though celibacy is best," she began, throwing an arch look to Giles, "marriage is a necessary and proper state, for 'tis part of the divine plan. Of course in this instance there are many advantages, the safe return of Hamfast not the least of them. But have you considered the bride's willingness, or lack thereof? Has she freely consented, or is she being forced?" Blanche took a deeper swallow from her goblet.

"What difference does it make?" Raymond rubbed his upper lip with the knuckle of one finger. He did not want to be reminded of the possibility of a reluctant bride. "As you yourself point out, she is among the least of the advantages."

Fresh color flooded Blanche's cheeks, not entirely due to the imported Rhenish wine, Raymond decided.

"You will *feel* the difference, my lord. Every day." She glanced at Giles. "And mayhap every night," she added boldly, downing the last of her drink.

"I shall suit myself, whatever her position," Raymond said.

"My lord," Giles responded, "if I were you, I would succumb to whatever position she chose." He gazed in apparent innocence at Lady Blanche, who leaned back and returned his look with glazed eyes. She hiccoughed, blushed, and Giles laughed aloud.

Raymond clamped his jaw and frowned. Leave it to Giles to get a lady drunk at the earliest opportunity. And Blanche should know better. *Hamfast's return is all that matters. And the rest can go to hell.*

Chapter Three

"**D**id you hear that?" Rhys put a finger to his lips and halted his horse on the shadowed forest path.

Ceridwen's senses sharpened in alarm at the question, even as she shook her head "no." The remote forest through which they passed bore a tense and forbidding air, as though the mountains only waited to rid themselves of unwanted passersby.

Huge groves of beech trees rustled in the breeze, and even here they held a faint tang of the sea. In barren places, rough fingers of black, lichened stone stuck up at odd angles. The Black Mountains were notorious for the bands of outlaws inhabiting their craggy peaks. Such men had no qualms about murdering travelers, whether Welsh or English.

Rhys headed the dozen men escorting her to Sir Raymond's keep. The Englishman was supposed to have taken her back with him from Trefynwy. But upon retrieving his dog—and the pledge of her land—he had left as abruptly as he had arrived, without even meeting her. Ceridwen had been relieved at the time to be spared Raymond's attention, in spite of the insult, but now she feared for her company's safety.

"There it is again," Rhys murmured.

Heavily armed with both shortbows and swords, the other men of her guard twisted in their saddles to look about, and quickly flanked her. Ceridwen jumped as a flock of small birds burst from the canopy of the thick woods to their left.

"Wait…"

A whistling thud sounded. The horse between her and the forest screamed and began to go down, collapsing into her palfrey. Her mount lurched and lost its balance. She kicked her feet free of the stirrups as the animal careened onto its side. In a swirl of skirts she tumbled to the ground. Something hard struck her head and flashes of red and white exploded behind her eyes. Men shouted and horses whinnied.

"They have crossbows, Rhys! My lady!" Sir Dylan reached down for her hand, pulled Ceridwen up behind him and raced away. It was all she could do to hold on to him. Though her head spun and her heart was in her throat, she would gladly fight. The fear of waiting to be slain was worse than dying in action.

"Leave me, Dylan, I would rather help you than hide!"

Dylan galloped his horse a long way before he halted near a tangled growth of brambles, well out of sight from the lane.

"Do not be foolish, my lady. Crawl into that thicket. Do not make a sound. Don't move a muscle until one of us comes for you. Do you swear?" He swung her down and held onto her hand, looking into her eyes. "Swear on your mother's grave you will not follow me back."

Ceridwen hesitated and he crushed her hand in his grip. Wincing, she relented. "I swear, Dylan, but—"

Before she could protest, he was pounding back towards the fray. She cursed him for the stubborn man that he was and felt for her dagger, only to find an empty sheath. With a separate twinge of panic, she checked the slim leather case at her waist. Her stomach was queasy and her head hurt, but she breathed easier when her fingers touched the warm ivory of her flute.

Ceridwen crept into the shelter of the brambles and resigned herself to wait. Her legs cramped, but she could not move without thorns poking her in a variety of tender spots. Waves of dizziness swept her. A spider descended on a thread in front of her nose. As time crawled by with no sign of Dylan's return, worry gnawed deeper. Enough of obedience. She was a woman, not a mouse. Carefully she disentangled herself from the clinging vines. She abruptly stood upright, stars swirled before her eyes, and she pitched forward.

When Ceridwen woke, her head throbbed with a fierce ache. The day had waned. A fly buzzed around her nose, and she waved at it feebly. She had to find Rhys and the others. See that they were all alive. She wove her way back to the roadway. Dusk lay quiet on the forest, lending the air a smoky blue haze. A heavy stillness had settled, in ominous contrast to the faint clashes and shouts she had heard earlier. She walked along, ready to dart among the trees at the slightest sound of men.

Topping a rise, she looked at the site of the ambush. Nothing. Not a horse, nor a man, nor a piece of weaponry. She scrambled down the gentle slope and came to a skidding stop in the middle of the roadway. Frantically she searched the edges of the wood. Against her better judgment she shouted, calling out the names of the missing men, and even those of the horses.

It was as though they had been swallowed up into the fairy world and made invisible. She returned to examine the path, determined not to panic, not to weep. At first glance in the fading light, its muddy center yielded nothing but an unreadable maze of hoofprints. Kneeling, she touched the cold, wet soil. Her fingers were smeared with mud…and dark, red blood.

Ceridwen swallowed hard as the truth sank in. She had been left behind because Dylan was dead, or so badly injured he could not tell Rhys where he had hidden her. Perhaps they had searched for her and she had not heard them calling her name. In any event it was up to her now. But there was only one honorable way. East, towards the marcher lord's domains.

Days later, Ceridwen sat by the dusty road, her back to a tree. The blisters on her feet stung, but her mind and the rest of her body were numbed by exhaustion. At least the forest had proved itself a friend. She had found berries and nuts enough to survive. A blessed spring had provided sweet, clear water. A hollow chestnut tree had served as haven. But she had walked and stumbled and ridden in oxcarts until she was too tired to weep, much less marry anyone.

Her state of dishevelment had saved her, she supposed. No one had looked twice at her. She had pushed on, determined to finish what her father had charged her to do. Over and over again, she told herself that Rhys and the others were yet alive.

At the sound of hoofbeats and laughter, Ceridwen got to her feet. Cursing her nearsightedness, she squinted as a glittering cavalcade approached. Horses pranced, jewels gleamed, and a banner proclaimed a white stag, symbol of the house of Beauchamp.

An extraordinarily handsome nobleman sat his horse, a hooded falcon upon one fist. His golden hair, cut blunt and short, contrasted with his dark eyebrows and tawny skin. The wine-red folds of his mantle glowed with the sheen of velvet, and the ermine lining quivered in the gusting wind. He held the reins of his palfrey with casual elegance, not sparing a glance to anyone afoot. Nay, he could not be her betrothed. Could he?

The small crowd of spectators muttered his name as he passed, and crossed themselves. So, this was Alonso the Fair, whose knights routinely slaughtered her people. Ceridwen's eyes narrowed farther, and she tried to swallow against her dry throat. Alonso. Her future brother-in-law.

The baron and his retinue rode by, unheeding. If this was one of Alonso's villages, it could not be all that far to Rookhaven, where Sir Raymond was lord. Carrog Dhu, the Black Dragon, as he was known to the Welsh.

Perhaps he did not even expect her. But her only course lay in going to him and throwing herself at his dubious mercy. She must get word to her father that she lived and find out what happened to Rhys and the others.

Ceridwen's stomach rumbled and panged, interrupting her thoughts. Running her tongue over her lips, she tasted dust and salt. She watched as the villagers dispersed to warm cottages and hot food. A small boy stared up at her, his blue eyes wide. With a smile Ceridwen knelt to his level.

His mother ran to him and swept the boy into her arms. "Get away from decent folk, wanton. Go on with ye. Go!"

More people stopped to stare and whisper. The ill will they had summoned at the sight of Lord Alonso was now directed at her. A youth reached down and gathered a fistful of stones. To proclaim her worth would be a waste of time. These English needed someone to hurt, someone who could not retaliate.

Ceridwen eased her way through the villagers. She could feel their hostile stares, and sensed their restraint would be short-lived. She lengthened her stride, but something whistled past her ear even as a hard object struck her back. She flung her mantle aside, the better to run, and her pursuers might be satisfied with such a fine garment.

Ceridwen left the jeering villagers behind and tore across a fallow field towards the woods. For now, that was the only place to hide. The trees were old, majestic, their trunks thick and gnarled. As she ran scarlet and yellow leaves blew around her feet. Yew and ash, oak and linden rustled in the freshening breeze, beckoning her to take their shelter. A path disappeared into the dense array of trees.

Winded, she slowed and tried to focus on which way to go. But panic still claimed her. All the fear and pain and uncertainty of the past few days surged anew, bursting into a conflagration of emotions Ceridwen could no longer control.

She grabbed up her skirts and ran on. Brambles slapped at her, scratching her face and tearing at the green wool of her overgown. Her trailing hems, already soiled, grew heavy with mud. She raced against the heartbreak threatening to overwhelm her. Nothing mattered but to outdistance the pain.

Her breath rasped, and blood pounded in her aching temples. She would run until her heart burst and she was free of earthly bounds. Perhaps God would then forgive her for still harboring the wicked, unseemly passion of vengeance for Owain.

Ceridwen careened on, blinded by tears and her own short-sightedness. She collided with a solid object that had not been there a moment before. Thick arms engulfed her in a stink of rancid pork fat, sour ale and unwashed humanity.

"Oy! Hold on, what have we here?" A beefy young man swung her around, casually trapping her against a tree trunk.

Breathless, Ceridwen stared up at his sweaty face, too close to her own. Her heart sank. Wild beasts were one thing. Beastly men were quite another. She fought to free herself.

He grinned, snaggletoothed.

The tree bark dug into her back. "Let me go. I—I bear a message for my lady. You will have cause to regret delaying me." *She* regretted her lack of skill at telling falsehoods, not to mention her imperfect command of English.

"Your lady, eh? I doubt that, since there ain't none in these parts. Where's the message then? Where have ye hid it on yer fine wee person?" His hand plunged between her breasts.

Ceridwen ducked under his arm, but the man caught a fistful of her loose hair and slammed her back against the tree. She gasped in pain as her already sore head bounced on the wood, and for once regretted not cutting her hair short, as did most of her countrywomen.

"Don't be runnin' off now, pretty." His voice was congenial, his touch vicious. One greasy palm slid from her cheek to squeeze her throat. Deftly he pulled up her skirts with the other, climbing her thigh as she choked in his grip. She had the distinct impression he'd done this before.

"Ready for me now, wench? Hmm?"

Thick fingers kneaded her buttock. Pools of black flowed into her vision, spread, and merged. Ceridwen fought desperately to breathe, to knee him. She twisted her head. His hand slipped from her neck to grab at her breast. He laughed.

"Think yer too good fer me? Well, I'll make ye rue that pride, girl. I'll humble ye right proper."

Ceridwen inhaled deeply through her mouth. She lunged and bit down on his wrist. Tendons rolled beneath her teeth. The young man howled and began to throttle her in earnest. Her feet left the ground as he lifted her by the neck. She tried to kick but her legs would not obey. Ceridwen shut her eyes. She would die…she had to breathe…

"Come away, my lord. We have avoided Alonso thus far and there's no time for sport."

"Go on, then," came the curt reply.

The foreign, male voices barely registered as Ceridwen struggled for her life. A rumble of hoofbeats vibrated through the tree at her back. Faintly, through the roaring in her ears, she heard a hideous growl. Then her assailant grunted, and his hands fell from her body.

A searing pain lanced Ceridwen's abdomen, right below her ribs. She dropped to the ground like a sack of meal. Gratefully, she sucked in lungfuls of air. Never had the simple act of breathing been so sweet. Gulping air until the pain in her middle forced her to stop, Ceridwen lay in a heap and shivered, her eyes clenched shut, forcing back tears.

A hand slipped beneath her neck and gently raised her head. Ceridwen thrashed against it until another hand pressed hard on her stomach, right where it hurt the most. She moaned and opened her eyes to gaze into those of a stranger.

Flinty, cold, and blue. A wave of relief washed over her. It was not the same man who had attacked her. But…the accent of nobility, the hard expression. An Englishman. And no common one at that. She stiffened in renewed fear, and slowly, his features resolved into clarity.

What a face to belong to an enemy, she thought, in spite of her alarm. His hair was hidden beneath his mail coif, but his eyebrows and lashes were thick and dark. The clean line of his jaw was shadowed with stubble. He was blessed with a straight, unbroken nose and smooth skin. His mouth was wide, with a small bunch of muscle at each corner. It was a mouth made for smiling, but remained set in a grim line.

"Forgive me, 'demoiselle, for I have wounded thee." His voice was deep, rich—and devoid of warmth.

"What…wound? What do you mean?" Ceridwen looked down at herself in horrified disbelief. A dark stain seeped in an ever-widening circle from beneath the leather-gauntleted fingers upon her abdomen. "Oh! Oh, it hurts."

The knight took her hand and pushed it against the warm, sticky mess on her overgown as he slid his own away. She felt a hole in the fabric and another in herself. This could not be happening. Ceridwen watched in dread as he knelt beside her and unsheathed his dagger. But she refused to cry out at the wave of terror his act induced.

"Nay, do not do it. Not yet," she implored him in a hoarse whisper, her fingertips barely touching his knee. "I have not yet confessed."

"What? Speak French. Or English." He frowned and brushed

her hand away with an impatient flick of his fingers. He untied his belt, placed it to one side, then hitched a length of his surcoat up into his lap.

Ceridwen had not realized she'd slipped into Welsh. She tried again, barely able to form intelligible words. "The *coup-de-grace*. Am I mortally wounded? Will I die slowly unless y-you finish me off?" Rising panic urged her to run, but her head spun and her muscles felt like jelly, as though she had been fevered for days. Each breath moved her abdomen and caused fresh shards of pain. Perhaps he was right to put her out of her misery.

An odd look of sorrow flitted across the knight's face. But it vanished almost before she caught it, to be replaced by a stony, unreadable expression. With exaggerated care, he held the dagger up for her to see, the blade balanced between his thumb and forefinger. He then proceeded to slice a large piece of linen from the lining of his surcoat.

"You are not skewered nearly so completely as the knave. I misjudged his girth. From behind I thought him fatter than he was." He folded the cloth neatly and bound it against her wound with the woven belt.

Relief washed over Ceridwen as she realized the knight had not saved her only to kill her himself. "Mayhap the man was going to stab me anyway," she said, and flinched as the Englishman gave the binding a final tightening twist. Her glance strayed to the body of her attacker, sprawled on the reddened ground, his mouth gaping. Even as she averted her eyes her stomach lurched.

"He wished to run *something* into you, that is true." The Englishman unfastened his mantle and draped the thick gray material about her shoulders.

Ceridwen felt uneasy at these words, but their meaning escaped her reeling mind. She could not seem to stop shaking. Gratitude accompanied warmth as the knight enveloped her in the coarse garment. He scooped her up and, stepping around the dead man's body, carried her towards his horse. Afraid to look, she hid her face in the hollow of the warrior's sturdy shoulder.

The mail rings bit into her cheek despite his surcoat, which still smelled like the damp wool of his mantle. She touched her throat as she swallowed. It felt raw inside and tender on the outside. Harness jingled, and she heard the restless stamping of several horses. She peeked out of the corner of one eye.

At least five men waited. They did not appear pleased at the delay. She kept her forehead pressed against the Englishman. He was all that stood between her and the others. She hoped he could control his men. If he had wanted her for himself, she reasoned, he would be pawing her already.

"Let me take the wench for you, my lord," someone said.

Ceridwen trembled involuntarily.

"Nay." The knight plucked her arm from his neck and made her stand. "Can you ride pillion and hold onto me from behind?"

Clutching her middle, she looked up at him. At least his unsmiling expression did not belittle her weakness. But those eyes…dark blue, like the sea on a sunny day. Cold and glittering. She shivered. The very timbre of his voice increased the wobble of her knees. She didn't think she could hold on to *anything* for much longer.

"Right." Without waiting for her reply, he deftly unsaddled his horse. She realized he meant her to sit before him, for the war saddle would have left no room. Then, to her acute dismay, he reached down between her ankles. Gathering up the bottom of her skirts, he pulled the back towards the front and on upwards. He thrust the wad of fabric into her hand and boosted her onto the sweaty back of the tall, black destrier.

Astride the horse, Ceridwen wanted to double over in pain, but the snug binding the knight had fashioned for her wound prevented it. Her legs were not covered and she could not help but feel exposed before the foreign warriors. But she was in their lord's debt.

"I owe you thanks. I owe you my life," she whispered, and huddled miserably, clutching the horse's mane with both hands as the animal tossed its head.

"You owe me nothing." He swung up with ease to sit behind her. "Shift forward a bit. Do not expect me to keep you from falling. I may need both hands free, if we find more trouble." Thankful for his matter-of-fact tone, Ceridwen obeyed. She stifled a moan as the horse lurched into a canter. The knight slowed the eager animal to a brisk walk.

"Wace." His words carried despite their low pitch.

A young man's voice replied, "My lord?"

"Ride ahead. Send someone back for my saddle. And tell Alys to prepare for a belly wound."

The Englishman's breath disturbed Ceridwen's hair and warmed her neck. His resonant voice vibrated from his chest through her back, sending a ripple of sensation up her spine. But even as she felt it, he leaned away and broke the contact.

"Aye, milord." Wace galloped off, his master's shield bouncing at his back.

Ceridwen glimpsed the coat of arms. A white stag upon a split field of green, a black dragon coiling below. Her heart faltered and with her sudden intake of breath came a fresh stab of agony in her middle. She bit back a moan. God help her, she was already in the possession of men in the service of Alonso. A black dragon…she must know for certain the identity of the one who held her.

"What do I call you?" Painfully, Ceridwen twisted her head around to look at him. At this range, his features were perfectly clear. Glacial eyes stared straight ahead. His compelling face held no expression. He tipped his head to the side and lifted his chin, avoiding touching her. She saw an old scar in the soft area under his jaw.

Apparently he did not want to answer. Whatever his name, he was just another warring border-lord. But she was fooling herself. Deep inside, she knew exactly who he was.

"Raymond." He growled the name and still did not meet her gaze as he spoke.

Ceridwen's heart felt as though it curled into a tight, protective ball, and renewed embarrassment leaped to compete with her fright. She represented her people, and she looked like a ragged mendicant. It was shameful. Beauchamp had picked her up under the most undignified of circumstances. Her good intentions of carrying through with the marriage dwindled in the terrifying face of his physical reality.

She was afraid to tell him who she was. No matter what

reassurance her father had given, she had no reason to disbelieve the rumors. And she had heard them aplenty. Bards and wayfarers passing through her father's lands told tales. Lord Raymond's reputation was that of a ravening wolf, the worst of the pack headed by his elder brother, Alonso. A cursed, dark knight, folk said.

She stole another glance at his face. Stiff and grim. As though it were set in granite. He had barely glanced at her, and she was grateful for his disinterest. He had wed a lovely maid, so the story went, until one cold night her body was found floating among the reeds in his moat. It was said he caught her with a lover, and in his rage hurled her from the top of the keep. The dead girl had probably been close to her own age. A shudder convulsed Ceridwen and she pressed her arm against the rising clamor of her wound as the horse's motion rocked her to and fro.

Raymond wrapped his woolen mantle more closely about her body. She shrank from his touch and yet relished the warmth. No doubt he could be charming when he chose to be. Charming but so very wicked. When he gathered up the reins, she saw that the fingers of his gauntlets were soggy and dark. Blood-soaked.

Her blood as well as the villein's. Her heart protested, but there was no escaping the truth. This man had saved her life, and she was beholden to him. She also belonged to him, even if he did not yet realize it. But for a little time, she could pretend freedom.

For hours they wound through the hilly forest, climbing slowly. She tried to avoid resting against him, but it proved impossible. Her head fell back onto his shoulder when she was too tired to hold it up, and after the first few times he stopped shrugging her off. Her fear gradually eased with the soothing rhythm of the horse's walk, and her own exhaustion. She drifted in and out of wakefulness, watching the bright sky pale above the silhouettes of swaying treetops.

The daylight waned, and the thick smell of damp leaves gave way to a fresher crispness as they traveled higher. The wind sang through the rowans. If she had not been in such pain, or known who held her, it might have been a pleasant journey.

The harsh caw of rooks and the hollow thud of hooves on a drawbridge startled Ceridwen into alertness. Men shouted greetings. She looked up in time to see a corpse gently swaying. It hung in an iron cage from a gibbet on the outer curtain wall of what must be Sir Raymond's keep—Rookhaven, and well named. A row of ravens perched on the battlements above the body. Ceridwen covered her mouth and squeezed her eyes shut until they were past the gruesome sight. A prenuptial Welsh patriot, perhaps. A fitting adornment to the castle of a Beauchamp.

They passed beneath the spikes of the portcullis and into the main ward of a dark, crumbling edifice. Not what she expected of such a lord. Anxiety mixed with the dread already churning in the pit of her stomach. Like the tower before her, her promise to marry him loomed as an impossible monstrosity.

Men bearing hissing torches hurried to meet them and held the bridle of his restive animal as Raymond dismounted. He caught Ceridwen and carried her with long, rapid strides across the cobbled courtyard and up the narrow stairs of the keep.

Heavy, ironclad doors opened before them as servants and men-at-arms scurried to seek their master's will. There were bows and murmured welcomes, all of which he ignored. His attention, it seemed, was now fixed upon her alone.

Sir Raymond's arms were hard beneath her shoulders and knees, his steps sure and silent. A faint smell of roasted fowl lingered in the air above the reek of the hall, and despite her pain and weariness, Ceridwen's mouth watered. She looked up past Raymond's face, avoiding his frowning gaze.

The upper reaches of the large hall disappeared into gloom, and though a fire crackled in the center of the floor, it made little impact on either the cold or the dark. A stout, wrinkle-faced woman hurried over and touched Ceridwen's cheek with the back of her hand. The crone peered at her in the light of the fat candle she held.

"Welcome to Rookhaven, lass. 'Tis Alys am I, and who'll see ye to bed." The woman's gap-toothed smile vanished as she turned her attention to Raymond. "What have ye done? Her neck's purple. Her face is all bruised. Hmmph!"

The knight exchanged looks with the old woman. Hers was one of disapproval. His was unreadable, except for the unrelenting tightness around his mouth. He swept past her and took Ceridwen into a small chamber, fragrant with mint. Carefully he laid her on a narrow bed, but her relief was short-lived. Raymond threw down his bloodstained gauntlets and began to unbind her wound.

"You are overly familiar, sir. Take your hands from me," Ceridwen whispered, too drained to meet his eyes. Under the circumstances, he was not likely to believe her if she claimed to be his betrothed. But it was her duty to tell him the truth, and he had no right to manhandle the daughter of Morgan ap Madog.

Raymond paused at her objection, threw her a quelling look as she opened her mouth to reveal her name, then continued with his task. He gave up on her lacings and simply ripped the fabric, using the hole his sword had made as a starting point.

Ceridwen shrieked and tried to pull away.

"Jesu, woman! You're worse than any eel." Mercilessly he held her to the position he desired, using his knee on her thighs and his elbow across her chest. "I would see for myself what damage I have done. I do not trust the reports of others."

Ceridwen gritted her teeth as his fingers probed her wound.

"I am sorry to hurt you. But have no fear for your modesty. I look upon thee as I would any wounded creature."

"I am not a creature!" She squirmed and bucked in spite of the pain. "I am—"

"Tsk. My lord Raymond. 'Tis but a young lass here ye have. She'll not be understanding yer ways," the crone chided, her chins wagging.

"Nor has she any need to understand. Her only duty to me is to *lie still.*" He directed his last two words to Ceridwen, writhing beneath his hands.

"She has no duty to ye a-tall!"

"Alys, you try my patience." His eyes gleamed a warning to the old nurse.

She glared back. "Be that as it may, young master Raymond, ye're not needed here. In fact, ye're in the way."

Ceridwen marvelled at the woman's familiar treatment of her

sinister lord. She thought she heard a low growl sounding from Sir Raymond's throat, but her own pain distracted her. Abruptly his warm hands left her abdomen, and his knee lifted from her legs. The large bulk of Alys overshadowed her, clucking and muttering as she applied a pungent salve to the wound.

Ceridwen turned her head and fixed her gaze on the retreating back of the dark knight. The play of candlelight glanced off the mail covering his arms. The heavy, deep blue fabric of his surcoat rippled dully. As he reached the door, he pulled his coif from his head. With a small shock she saw that he was fair. Thick, brassy hair, with a tawny brown beneath the light outer layers, like an animal's pelt, tumbled past his shoulders.

Similar to Alonso, yet wholly different. Haughty, aye. But Ceridwen was surprised to sense no vanity in this Beauchamp. He was neither as tall nor as broad as his elder brother. But he commanded a powerful, forbidding presence that had nothing to do with size. *A fair-haired knight. A black horse. Bloody hands.* She swallowed as her memory stirred. Long ago Owain had told her a story, of a maiden who met just such a man. At the time, she had thought it a tale of his own imagining. But Owain had known of things to come, and saw things hidden—had it been a warning? Now she could not remember how it ended.

Raymond turned and regarded her over his shoulder. Their eyes met, and for an instant Ceridwen thought she felt compassion sing across the room to her. Then his handsome face shuttered, the light extinguished like a candle snuffed out by a cold wind.

She blinked, and Raymond vanished into the darkness beyond the door. Tomorrow. She would tell him her name tomorrow.

Chapter Four

"Damn. Damn. Thrice be damned!" Raymond cursed his way up a dank stairway of his ancient fortress, his wolfhound padding alongside. He had never bothered to improve upon the meager comforts of his keep, and drafts blew freely in the stone halls. Cobwebs were the only hangings to soften the chill.

The wench was trouble. A whole realm of it. A shudder of longing coursed through him at the remembrance of her fine features and delicate bones. Just as Meribel's had been. Raymond pushed his lady's visage back and it merged into that of the wounded maiden. She was exquisite, despite the fact she was dirty and bedraggled, her long hair all in rat's-nests.

It was the kind of hair he loved, soft and fine and black. And those upslanted eyes, deep with unspoken sorrow, shifting from sea-green to emerald. Eyes that sometimes glowed, lit from within by a pure fire, whether born of a fighting spirit or fever, he could not tell. Aye, a comely bundle, much too lovely for comfort. Why had he bothered spitting a perfectly able man to save her skin in the first place?

Perhaps it had been young Wace's look of anguish at seeing a girl about to be ravished. Perhaps because by saving the virtue of one maid, he could partially make up for the multitude of despoilings his brother perpetrated in the name of his rights as lord. A laughable thought. Who was he, Raymond, to pretend honor after what he had done to his own wife?

Her image leaped to torment him, as ever. Meribel, floating

in the noisome moat. Her eyes, once sparkling with both merriment and malice, now dull, open and staring. Heedless of the strands of green water-weed tangling in her long lashes. Beyond caring that her gown drifted up her white thighs, gleaming through the murky water.

Raymond groaned and with an effort that cost him dear, willed her away, his eyes tightly shut. Slowly she faded to a mere shadow on the periphery of his mind. Faint, but never fully banished.

The cur he had dispatched had not deserved such a clean, swift stroke. Raymond hoped he had not also ultimately killed the black-haired maid. He had seen no viscera emerging through her wound, and only good, red blood flowing, nothing green or foul-smelling. Hopeful signs, but it was too soon to tell.

"Wace!" Raymond reached the landing, kicked open the door of his solar, and the squire hurried to his side. "Disarm me and bring some hot water." He tossed his gauntlets and coif onto the bed, where his huge dog was already circling to settle down for the night. For some reason, the sight did not bring its usual satisfaction.

Silently Wace unstrapped his master's sword and dagger. He lifted off the flowing surcoat and sighed when he saw the ruined lining. Raymond ignored the small censure and leaned forward as if to touch his toes. The heavy mail hauberk slithered down over his head into Wace's waiting hands. The boy then untied the mail chausses, and Raymond shook them from his legs.

He should have gone to the armory to remove his harness, to save Wace the work of hauling it down, but it was too late now. Raymond started to unlace his haqueton, then hugged the padded under-jacket to his sides. "I will wait 'til the water arrives." Their breath plumed in the room and an awkward silence fell. Raymond stepped to the brazier to poke the fire back to life.

"My lord." Wace fidgeted.

Raymond looked at his squire. The rangy boy was new to his service, and still a bit shy of him. Wace's former lord had lived as violently as he had died, and the lad bore the scars to prove it. His auburn hair hung thick and straight about his solemn face, and his eyes were serious.

"Speak your mind, lad." Raymond sat on his bed, leaned back upon his elbows and stretched his wool-clad legs.

"I was wondering…what will you do with the maid?"

Raymond stroked his beloved Hamfast, and the dog raised an eyebrow and licked his hand. No woman could offer such devotion. "Do with her? I shall do nothing with her. Or to her, or for her. Does that answer your question?"

"Nay, milord."

Raymond responded with a mirthless sound, part grunt, part laugh. The boy looked displeased, if he was not mistaken. "I see. Are you concerned with the fulfillment of knightly vows? Do not be. She'll not starve." Not with a face like that.

"But is it not true, that once you've saved a person's life—even that of a woman—you're bound together from that moment forward? You have a responsibility to her now, and she owes a debt to you, does she not?" Wace insisted.

Raymond sat up, rubbing his scarred knuckles. "I hold her to no debt. She is free. The sooner she goes, the better."

Wace's brow creased into a frown. "She displeases you."

"Aye, so she does. I wish never to have sight of her again. She is a distraction, when I am bound to wed another." Raymond jumped to his feet. "Enough! By Abelard's ballocks, where is that water?"

The boy stepped back, his eyes wide. Raymond wiped his forehead with his palm and took a deep breath. "Wace, I shout a great deal. Do not take it to heart. Whatever ill-use you have suffered, you, at least, will never feel my hand in anger."

Wace nodded, and executed a slight bow before leaving the room. Raymond sank down again and put his head in his hands. *God help me.* Breaking in a new squire was like settling a high-strung colt. So much potential needing care.

He knew firsthand how best to encourage traits of value, and how to quell the rest without ruining a boy's spirit. It was a lot of work. And he already had a lot of work. To gather a body of trained men, arm them, and go forth to raze Alonso's keep to the ground. It would be a bitter disappointment to Wace, when he shattered the boy's idealism on the proper conduct of a knight to his lord. *But then, neither I, nor my lord brother are proper knights.*

Ceridwen knew she still dreamed, on the brink of awakening. Strong arms held her tenderly, featherlight kisses rained upon her face and neck. It was no one she knew, yet she had known him forever. He was warm, solid, and all hers. She kept her eyes closed, reluctant to break the fragile spell of pleasure.

But fingers of sunlight plucked at her lids, demanding that she wake. Her arms stuck damply to her sides and she was too warm. She slid the scratchy blanket down her torso. Pain stabbed through the drowsiness as her wound pulled, and she gasped. Someone next to her coughed. A deep, male sound.

She opened her eyes, and a small cry of dismay left her lips. From his seat beside the bed, Sir Raymond surveyed her. Ceridwen dragged the blanket back over her breasts and up to her chin. He was distressingly handsome in the morning light.

He had shaved, and wore a simple tunic of undyed linen beneath his sleeveless surcoat. The bland color accentuated his bright hair and healthy skin, though his fathomless eyes were shadowed with fatigue. She could not tell what he thought of her, and tried not to care.

"How do you feel?" The smooth voice was neutral.

"I am well, sir." She felt herself redden and clutched the blanket tighter. "I need no checking of my bandages, thank you," Ceridwen added, hoping to forestall any delicate ministrations he might have in mind. She shivered as a chill swept her body.

"Of course not. I have already done that while you slept. Unless you want Alys—" Raymond half stood.

"No thank you, my lord." He'd attended her while she slept? And what else? Ceridwen stared at him, willing his departure. He resumed his seat. His gaze lingered on her face, then he narrowed his eyes before looking away.

Ceridwen felt a surge of relief to be free of his inspection. But no one had the right to inspire such dread at the mere mention of his name, then be so…quiet. She had expected a bellowing, red-faced, brutish sort, and instead, she found him graceful, wasting none of his movements, with strong hands and a lean, muscular frame. Thus far Sir Raymond had impressed her with his air. Not one of contentment or ease, but of something powerful lying in wait, holding itself in check.

He returned his dark gaze to her. "What is your name?"

"Ceridwen." She bit her lip, awaiting his outrage at the poor bargain he'd made for the return of his dog.

"That explains it." His stare grew more intense.

She swallowed. No reaction. It dawned on her that he might not have bothered to learn the given name of his bride-to-be. That was how little he thought of her. Ceridwen's knuckles whitened on the edge of the blanket. "Explains what?"

"How you are so small and dark, in a land of fair Amazons."

Ceridwen looked at Raymond in bewilderment. What did her size or coloring have to do with her name…unless he meant she looked as many Welshwomen did? A spark of anger ignited within her breast as his cool eyes appraised her, then dismissed her. She would far rather be small and dark than some lumbering blond troll. Especially if the latter was his preference.

"How came you to be wandering in the wildwood? 'Tis no place for a man on his own, let alone a woman. There are things there, best left undisturbed," he warned her sternly.

"The wildwood is lovely in its own way, but aye, I wish I had not disturbed that man who tried to throttle me."

"I, for one, have only found trouble in those woods. That is why I race through them. I might easily have not seen you. Especially with that great lout blocking my view."

"I am sorry to have inconvenienced you."

"Think nothing of it. 'Twas my pleasure." Raymond stifled a yawn, and stretched his arms behind him.

Ceridwen's eyes widened. His pleasure? To kill a man, justified or not? He spoke of it so casually. Just another bloodletting—good sport. But what else could she expect? His fame had grown from the merciless fury he displayed, never accepting defeat at the hands of his enemies. Her people.

It was said he routinely destroyed farms and hamlets on his raids of acquisition. Rumor even had it that churches had burned by his command, to demoralize rebellious vassals. All to satisfy the greed and blood lust typical of his whole family.

She must not let his present mildness lull her into forgetting who and what he was. Ceridwen eased herself deeper under the covers. She had no defenses against him, in her weakened state. Why did he not go away and leave her alone?

Raymond spoke again, still not looking at her. "Who is your father, or husband? To whom do I return you?"

Ceridwen suppressed the leap of joy his words evoked. She could not go home, and he needed to be jolted out of his rude disregard. She glared at him, with what she hoped was an expression of fierce independence. "I am Ceridwen of Llyn y Gareg Wen. My father is Morgan ap Madog. And *you* are my husband."

Raymond's head snapped up, his face pale. He stood, then sat down again. "Nay…she is but—you cannot be—"

"Why not? 'Tis not the person that is important, but the pact. If I do not please you, that is regrettable, but be assured I find the prospect of wedding you no more appealing."

"I did not expect you to find me appealing. I will force myself upon no one. Do as you will, go where you like."

His defensive attitude surprised Ceridwen. She had feared once he realized she was his betrothed he would simply take what was his due. All the more frightening a prospect when she was not certain exactly what constituted…his due.

He continued, "However, Lord Morgan can count upon my good faith. I will marry his daughter, as promised. If in fact you are who you claim to be."

"My word is as good as yours, sir."

Raymond studied her, his blue eyes sharp and unforgiving. "You might have told me sooner."

"I tried. I kept getting interrupted—"

"And you fear me."

"Nay," Ceridwen lied, twisting the blanket in her fingers.

A rueful smile curved Raymond's lips. "If you do not, you would be wise to." He reached down and stroked the shoulder of a large, hairy dog snoring in the rushes at his feet.

"What is that?" Ceridwen peered in alarm at the great beast, with its tangle of impossibly long legs and rough fur.

The knight narrowed his gaze. "You did not meet, whilst he was your...guest?"

So this was the hostage wolfhound. Her rival. The Lord of Rookhaven's first love. The thought was so ludicrous Ceridwen had to cough in order to smother a giggle. Both actions hurt dreadfully, and she forced herself to be still. "Nay. I assure you I had nothing to do with that, sir."

Raymond returned his attention to the dog. "This is Hamfast. My wolfhound. He hunts with me, eats with me, and sleeps with me. He will not harm you."

His pride in the ungainly creature was evident.

Ceridwen nodded. "My brother, Rhys, cared for him with all due courtesy. But, sir..." She swallowed the sudden lump in her throat. "We had trouble in the beech-wood pass of the mountains, and I was separated from my people."

He arched one dark eyebrow. "You astound me. 'Tis a long way to come afoot and alone, milady."

"Mother Mary smiled upon me."

Raymond eyed her dubiously. "No doubt."

She fought the stinging behind her eyelids. "I am afraid they are lost. P-perhaps dead."

His perpetual frown deepened. "I will send a search party."

"I thank you for that, sir. And please, get word to my father that I yet live."

At this, a pained look crossed Raymond's face, and he gave her a curt nod. Not knowing what to think, Ceridwen forged ahead. "Do I or do I not have your word that I may take up residence as your lady—in name only?"

She shivered again, this time at her own audacity. If he did not want her, she'd not be used as a...a convenience. He could keep a—what were they called?—concubine for that. There it was again. She was not quite sure what *that* meant, or what concubines did. It was an area she must address, and soon. But for now... "Y-you said you would not force—"

"I know what I said." Raymond placed his palms on his knees and rose to his feet. "Once we are wed I care not what you do. Just keep out of my way. And do not have a mind to changing things. I am happy with my current arrangements.'' Hard-eyed again, he turned toward the door.

Ceridwen sniffed. ''You do not look happy to me.''

Raymond's back stiffened, and he reversed his departure. His gaze bored into Ceridwen as if he could see through her and liked not what he saw. ''Right you are, milady.''

It was not what she had expected him to say. He snapped his fingers at the hound. Hamfast woke and sat up next to her bed, one huge paw resting on the blankets, his brown eyes sorrowful. Tentatively, Ceridwen held her hand out for him to nose.

Halfway to the door, Raymond turned and spoke a quiet command. The dog's lips drew back as if in a smile, then he returned to his master's side. The door flew inward and Alys narrowly missed careening into her lord as she trundled through, her arms full of linens. After a last swift glance at Ceridwen, Raymond guided Alys back out into the hallway.

Ceridwen could hear the low rumble of his voice, but could not make out the words.

After a few moments Alys returned.

''Himself says yer poorly, and to take extra good care ye don't give up the ghost,'' the old nurse said bracingly.

''Did he, now? There's naught wrong with me. I am only a bit tired.'' Ceridwen tried to swallow the tendril of fear creeping higher within her. He must know, merely by looking at her, that the wound had gone bad. She could feel it too, though she did not want to face it. The fever, the chills, her clammy skin.

''Here. These are the finest linens anywhere's out of Ireland. You'll be more comfy swaddled with them betwixt ye and this wool. And now for my special hot compress, to draw the churl's evil humors from ye.''

''What's that you said?'' Ceridwen asked weakly, not sure that she wanted to know. English terms still challenged her.

''Sir Raymond said his sword carried the churl's evil humors, from his foul gut into yer own sweet body. I'm to draw them out, or he'll see my hide nailed to the barbican.'' Alys chuckled.

Alongside numerous others, no doubt. ''Oh. Ahhh!'' The steaming bag of herbs settled on Ceridwen's wound.

"If yer not better by the morrow, Himself'll send young Wace to find a physick, to bleed out the illness right proper."

"I will be better. I promise." No one would bleed her. *Himself's* plan must be to frighten her into wellness, to be rid of her faster. Would he be disappointed if she did not recover? That he might be pleased wasn't out of the question. He would have her lands without the trouble she herself represented. Had he not killed his first wife, once he had spent her wealth?

Ceridwen pushed the dreadful thought to the back of her mind. No Beauchamp would outdo a woman of the *Cymraeg*. She would leave only when it suited her to do so. After she found the knight in Alonso's pay who had slain her cousin, and made him dearly regret what he had done.

Perhaps as Raymond's wife she might achieve that end…if she survived. But right now she could not face the prospect of his hands on her again. His touch made her so very uncomfortable. Hot and cold and tingly. As though there was an emptiness within herself she had never known needed filling.

A cricket chirped from a corner of the candlelit sickroom. Raymond gnawed his thumbnail as he gazed at the sleeping girl. Her limbs twitched with fever. Her skin was translucent, and her body had wasted over the last several days. He had watched many a good man die slowly, and it never got any easier.

The pompous fool of a physician he had summoned from Chepstow had done nothing helpful. Alys's simples and balms had better effect. Now it was only a matter of time. Ceridwen's pain would cease, either through death or recovery.

But he could scarcely believe how he seemed to feel—as though he would shatter if he had to witness either her demise or her departure. And if she stayed, he would eventually destroy her. As he had his young wife.

Why was he drawn to this woman? Why had he sat here each night until the wee hours, guarding her sleep like some great oaf of a dog? She was no one to him. Of no concern at all. But if he did not follow through with the marriage the clever lord Morgan would plague him without end. Not to mention the fact he would lose the lands of her dowry.

Raymond winced at the memory of how Ceridwen had taken his clumsy description of her. Small and dark indeed. He had wanted to explain, to tell her the truth—that in his eyes she was perfectly formed, of ebony and cream. Spun of mountain mists and heather, so fragile she might break at his touch.

But he could not allow himself to become fond of her, or her of him. Even were it possible, she would only suffer for it. To love a Beauchamp was to court disaster. And a Beauchamp *in* love was a creature out of control.

If he had no feeling for her, and vice versa, it would not matter so much if they were wed. He might be a decent, dutiful husband, so long as his heart remained detached. But he was a mangler of love relations. Any small chance of happiness had been ground to dust by the circumstance of his birth into the noble family Beauchamp, where loyalty to one's lord rose above all other virtues and desires.

Raymond leaned his head on his palm and gazed at Ceridwen. Her lips were full, now pale, but when first he had seen her, the color of sunlit wine. In spite of his determination to remain aloof, he wondered how they would taste. How she would respond if he were to kiss them.

She sighed in her sleep and her dark lashes fluttered. Raymond closed his eyes. His head ached. At least he could do her the honor of carrying on a bedside vigil without lusting after her. He had to leave the chamber, before he did something he would regret.

Rising, Raymond entered the adjoining room where Alys slept. From there he took the stairs of one of the corner turrets above the main living quarters. He climbed them to the top and found the watchroom empty. The trees below cast black shadows over the moonswept land, and the marsh waters glittered as the breeze caressed them, their dark depths reflecting silver. An enchanted night. Like the one that had put an end to his foolish ideas about love and faith.

Inexorably his mind dragged him back towards the place he swore never to return to, and yet despaired of ever finding again. He took a cautious approach to the slippery remembrance of when his heart had loved freely, with no taint of suspicion poisoning each glance and touch.

The memory was hateful to him, because to love meant willingness to embrace pain beyond measure. To trust was to risk the loss of not only the beloved, but his own soul. He had loved his wife. Immoderately. Passionately. Wholeheartedly and without reserve. And his love had been rewarded by betrayal and death. Never again.

Raymond ran down the stairs. He could bear no more waiting. To hell with the land, to hell with Morgan ap Madog. Ceridwen was as good as dead, with or without him as husband. And once he openly defied Alonso, he himself would not be long for this world. He must do what was best for her—and that meant getting her out of Rookhaven.

In the women's chamber he searched for the nurse among the tangle of serving-girls she allowed in her bed to benefit from her warmth and protection. Nudging her awake, Raymond whispered to her, his voice fierce and desperate even to his own ears. "I must leave now. I will be away a fortnight. When I return, I want Morgan's daughter gone from here."

He heard an intake of breath. One of the maids—Shona, no doubt—was awake and listening. He turned his head in her direction and she vanished under the covers with a squeak.

"If—when she dies," Raymond continued, "take the silver from the small chest in my solar. Pay for her burial in a great church, in a place far from here, and for as many prayers as it will buy. If by some miracle she lives, give the silver into her hands and send her to the convent near Usk, where Morgan can find her. Provide her an escort. Someone from outside the keep, unknown to me. I want it to be as if I had never brought her here. Do you understand?"

"Aye, milord, all too well. Oh, Raymond, what happened to the sweet lad I once knew? You'll not wipe away the pain of Meribel this way." Alys's voice choked with tears. "This lass is the finest thing to come under your roof since—"

"What do you know, old woman? Keep your witchy words of wisdom for those foolish enough to listen. Do as I say or suffer the consequences."

"You'll be the one to suffer, Raymond. Mark my words."

A chill shuddered through him, for she spoke with the certainty of an oracle. "Your words are too late." Already he had suffered beyond endurance. Leaving Alys he wrenched open the door of the infirmary. He wanted one more look at his never-to-be bride.

She lay as though already dead, waxen and still. Raymond bent over her to reassure himself that her chest still rose and fell. His hand drifted toward her forehead, then withdrew without touching her skin. Why go through such torture, watching her fade? She hated and feared him like the rest, he had seen it in her narrowed eyes. He meant nothing to her but pain.

As Raymond lingered at the door, memorizing Ceridwen's face, her eyes opened and met his. Her lips curved into a poignant smile that tore at his heart. Without thinking, he retraced his steps to her bed. He knelt beside her, his hands on either side of her face, and his mouth came down upon hers in an aching, sweet caress. He gave her all the tenderness he denied in himself, all the caring parts he no longer acknowledged, distilled and concentrated into one potent kiss.

Ceridwen drifted in and out of her dreamworld. She had seen Owain, standing by the door, love shining from his eyes. He had come to tell her he wanted her to return home to her family—to him. She'd smiled to let him know how grateful she was. How happy she was to have him here.

He came to her, to hold her once again, to give her a kiss of peace and absolution. His face was a blur—she could hardly see it—but she caught a flash of dark blue eyes. How could that be, when Owain's were brown?

Instead of kissing her forehead, or cheek, or even the tip of her nose as he was wont to do when she was small, she felt his mouth upon hers. Warm and smooth. He smelled like freshly honed steel, and the oil to stop its rusting. Like horses and sheepskin. And something else, underneath it all, a rare, earthy aroma. It was intoxicating. His kiss burned like strong drink, heady and uplifting. She could feel it pouring into her, a humming vibration of weightless, light-filled energy. It was rich and pure and heavenly.

It was not Owain.

The realization hit Ceridwen as he rose to his feet and turned away. Her vision cleared and she saw his bright hair, his dark surcoat as he swept out the door. Raymond. Her enemy. Her betrothed. One of a whole fraternity of murderers and rapists. Her stomach lurched. She rubbed her lips, tried to wipe away the sensation of his kiss with her fingers.

But a part of him had already entered her, was one with her. He sang through her veins. He could not be expunged. And no matter what her head told her of his evil, her heart could only rejoice at how right his touch felt.

"There, there, pet." Alys appeared and patted Ceridwen's forehead and wrists with a cold, wet cloth. "Lie still, be easy. Himself's gone now, don't worry."

Ceridwen gazed at the woman's homely, comforting face. Her own hot tears spilled. They ran into her ears as she lay too weak to wipe them away.

"Now, now. You'll be well soon, and ye should be thinking on that, not on *him,* the wicked thing."

"But I was not—" Ceridwen began feebly.

Alys proceeded to ignore her own advice. "Y'know, he weren't always this way, so dark and broody. Once he was a good boy, a golden boy. You'd not find a kinder, lovelier lad."

"What happened?" Ceridwen whispered.

"That's not fer me to say. He'll be telling ye himself one day, no doubt. Then maybe he'll come right again." Alys stood. "I'll be sending in a nice brew for ye, and I'm warning the lassie to see that ye drink it all down. So make certain ye do this time, or it's *her* ears I'll be boxing."

"Aye, Alys." Ceridwen smiled through her dwindling tears.

The afternoon was frigid and clear. Watery rays of sunlight made their way through the narrow, parchment-covered window. Ceridwen sat wrapped in a blanket, mending the long rent Raymond had made in her overgown.

From the day he had kissed her, her recovery had been rapid. The fever left her weakened, but soon she had begun to eat more than gruel, and could totter about the sickroom. The wound closed cleanly at last, leaving a raw, tender scar the length of her little finger.

Sir Raymond had not visited once. But Ceridwen did sometimes wonder where he was. Wisps of memory, or dreams returned to her, of seeing him sitting by her bed, watching her, his eyes churning with the color of the cold, blue ocean depths. She tried to shake away the confusing feelings even the thought of him stirred in her. She had not yet fulfilled her vow to accommodate this man, and she would be a disgraceful coward to betray her father's trust. Somehow, she had to make it right.

Alys entered the chamber, holding a leather bag. "His lordship said yer to take this, and Godspeed." The old woman's hands shook a little.

"What is it?" The deerskin pouch was soft, and the weighty jingle of its contents answered her even before Alys replied.

"Silver coins, to see ye on yer way."

"On my way? Why would I want his precious bits? Is Beauchamp going back on his word? Does he think he can bribe me to leave?"

"It's been a good brace o' sennights since he left, and I daren't disobey any longer. If he finds the treasure still in his solar, there'll be the devil to pay upon his return." Alys wrung her hands and looked over her shoulder every moment or two.

Ceridwen had never seen the woman in such a state. Panic fluttered in her own stomach. She must stay. If she did not, Beauchamp had no incentive to keep the peace her people so desperately needed. He could claim she had run away from him. For Alys's sake, she tried to sound indifferent. "Then bury the coins, or give them to the poor. I do not understand what they have to do with me."

"What it has to do with ye is exactly what ye just said. I'm to bury ye with it, or give it to ye. Either way yer to be gone before his return and I expect him ere another setting of the sun."

"Why would he want his silver to be buried with me? I am not dead." Fresh apprehension filled Ceridwen, on top of her humiliation.

"Not *with* ye—for ye to be buried *with*. Oh, lass, I haven't the wherewithal to explain it. Ye must go. I've food for ye, and a pony, and Shona's best cloak. Now, old Nance will see ye safe to the village. He's deaf as a post, but a good sort. From there ye can hire a man to take ye to the cloisters nigh Usk. Then send word to your da.''

Hiding her dismay, Ceridwen reached out to touch Alys's arm. "I thank you for all you have done. I know 'tis your lord who forces you to this. I will not forget your kindness, but neither shall I take his silver, nor aught else I did not bring with me.''

"Please, lady, leave the treasure if ye must, but take the pony and the rest, to keep ye safe.''

The old nurse's pleading eyes swayed Ceridwen's proud heart. "Ah, Alys, I will come back soon and repay you.''

Alys wiped her cheeks and nodded in a resigned fashion before she hurried away. Wearily Ceridwen slipped her overgown back on. She could hardly blame Sir Raymond. What a disappointment as a bride she must be, under the circumstances.

But that was neither here nor there—too many lives were at stake. Willing or no, the arrogant marcher lord would simply have to make good on his promise to the *Cymraeg*.

And she was the only one who could see that he did.

Chapter Five

The fortnight had passed. Ceridwen was gone. Raymond launched the last of the glass goblets he owned towards a certain triangle-shaped stone in the wall of his solar. It struck dead center and burst into a thousand green shards. He had steadily shattered his precious glassware over the past few hours, each display of his deteriorating mood more vehement than the one before.

"Hey, what goes, my friend? Is this how you greet me?" A familiar, imposing figure lounged in the doorway.

"Giles. 'Tis good to see you." Raymond extended his hand and Giles engulfed him in a hug, slapping his back with hearty thumps before releasing him.

"'Twould appear you have been busy," Giles observed, dumping his sword, shield, helm and gauntlets onto the tabletop. A carpet of glittering bits lay on the floor and were liberally sprinkled over Hamfast's sleeping form.

Raymond remained silent.

"Oh, come, tell me what is on your mind. We have no secrets between us. At least none that I am aware of," Giles said.

Raymond refrained from rolling his eyes at Giles's deliberate obtuseness. "It would not be much of a secret if you were aware of it, then, would it?" Throwing his leg over the bench, he sat heavily and stared at the cracks in the oak planks of the table.

"Hamfast, what is wrong with your master? His tongue's

sharpened cruelly and he is sulking like a child kept home from the fair.'' Giles helped himself to a drink of ale.

Raymond groaned and put his head in his hands.

Giles eyed Raymond thoughtfully. ''You need help, my friend. What can I do for you?''

''Put me out of my misery.''

Giles asked knowingly, ''Who is she?''

Helpless in his grief, Raymond replied at last. ''Ceridwen. My betrothed.''

''Ah. Then what is the problem? Have at her!''

''She has gone.''

''What have you done?'' Giles gazed steadily at Raymond.

''When I departed she was dying.'' Raymond thought of Ceridwen, ill unto death—and by his hand. Guilt seared his soul anew. ''I ordered that she not be here upon my return.''

''Lord, you make things easy for yourself. But why?''

''She reminded me of Meribel. I could not bear it.''

''Then you should have plowed her and have done with it.''

Raymond's jaw tightened. ''You show me less respect than does Alys. Ceridwen is not meant for reckless plowing.''

''Oh, pardon me. I have yet to meet a lass who was not. But what will her father have to say?''

''I know not—nor even for certain whether she yet lives. Alys will not speak to me. But never mind all that for now.'' In an attempt to keep despair at bay, Raymond took back the jug briefly from his friend. ''How did it go, Giles?''

''Well enough. Robert of Dinsdale will send twelve men, two of whom are knights. Conrad Shortneck has promised twenty in all. Five knights, five horsemen, and ten men-at-arms. Another eight from Cruikshank, and Lucien de Griswold has graciously offered to come himself, along with ten of his best. He hates Alonso almost as much as you do.''

''Fifty-one, plus the twenty of us. We will need more.'' Raymond drummed his fingers on the tabletop.

''There are no more who can be trusted,'' Giles said.

Hamfast rose and shook himself violently, showering the floor with bits of glass. As the dog lumbered by, Giles reached out to scratch the animal's craggy head. The parting of black lips and a low growl made the warrior withdraw his hand.

"What is the matter with him?"

"He has been out of sorts lately." Raymond did not add what he thought—since leaving Ceridwen behind. Just like himself. "If there are no more, then we must hire mercenaries. What of those Teutons out Rotham way?"

Hamfast settled on top of his master's booted feet.

"That is a risky proposition. And expensive."

"I have a bit set by. God knows I have not spent a penny on this place since the fortifications." *And Ceridwen's burial.*

"What about arms?" Giles asked. "Do we have the spare lance shafts, axe heads and all?"

"Aye. Bruce and the armorer have seen to it. But for the most part everyone must bring whatever they can."

Wace knocked, poking his head around the edge of the door. At Raymond's nod he slipped into the chamber.

Giles raised a hand in salute. "Hey-hey, Wace! Are you ready for some warring and wenching?" Giles was ever jovial when a fight was imminent. The squire flushed and turned uncertain eyes to his master. Raymond merely raised his brows, as if he too wanted to know.

"I am ready for anything, sir." Wace straightened his shoulders and his expression grew fierce.

Giles laughed aloud and slapped the table with his palm.

Raymond tilted his head, coughed to mask the twitch of his lips, and recovered his stern demeanor. "Wace, take Sir Giles's gear and clean it. Make sure his mount is properly bedded down, and give the beast a hot bran mash. The icy weather tells on that one's gut."

"Aye, milord." Wace gathered up the gear and departed.

"Ah, would that I had the same careful attention you assure my horse," Giles sighed.

"What are you whining about?" Fitfully, Raymond ran both hands through his hair.

"You do need more women in this place, Raymond. A wife, to bathe your guests. And all the maids and ladies of quality that come along with a wife, to entertain and serve your friends."

"Serve, or be serviced, Giles?" Raymond unsheathed his dagger and began to carve the tabletop with a vengeance.

"Why not both?" Giles laced his fingers behind his head.

"Why not indeed? No woman in her right mind would have me apurpose, and 'tis for the best. You know what they say of me."

"Oh, I do, I do. The fair hero, Lord Raymond, whose valiant feats of yore are sung from north to south. The dark, wicked Lord Raymond, whose evil heart lurks behind his crumbling walls, waiting to devour passing maidens. Take your pick. The trouble is, no one knows 'tis the same Raymond."

"I hardly know myself."

"Then find this maiden who has bewitched you. Bring her back and get on with it."

"I must see to Alonso." Raymond brushed the wood chips to the floor. He didn't care to tell Giles of his decision not to subject an innocent girl to a short, unhappy life, tied to him.

"Well and good. But do you think it so very wise? What will you do once you've sacked his possessions? Kill him? You will have to, you know."

"I know. I have his demise planned, to the last drop." Raymond slammed his dagger's point deep into the oak, and the hilt quivered upright.

"You will regret it in the end. No good will come of it." Giles leaned back, ever at ease in his big, muscular body. "There is no guarantee he will not overwhelm you. You do not want to fall into his hands alive, once he knows what you are about."

"That will not happen. I do what I must, Giles."

"You drive yourself hard. I would but see you content."

"Thank you." Raymond looked into his friend's concerned eyes. "My happiness is in my own hands. And God's."

A rustle and slight clatter came from behind the door.

"Come here." Giles waved the serving-girl into the room.

Shona, the daughter of a knight who had died in Raymond's service, had no business doing menial labor. But she insisted upon earning her own keep, no matter what arguments he had presented. Neither gifts nor threats had changed her mind, so Raymond had resigned himself to accept her self-chosen role.

She was bright and lovely and of course Giles pursued her constantly.

"My lord, Wace sent me up with these things." Shona smiled at Raymond and glanced at Giles, as she set the trencher of bread, mutton stew, and cheese on the table.

Giles wasted no time on the food. He took the girl's hand and pulled her to his side, his arm snug about her hips. "Ah, sweet Shona, when shall we be wed, as I have begged for so long?" He gazed up at her, a grin threatening.

"When thou art true to me, sir, and love none other." She wound a lock of his sable hair about her fingers. Giles bent his head and rested his cheek in the curve of her trim waist.

Raymond averted his eyes from the sight of such comfortable familiarity. It only served to accentuate the terrible hole he felt growing in his own gangrenous core. Despite his bold statement to Giles, he was beginning to question his motives for waging war on his brother. How much was revenge, and how much simply a desire for annihilation? Was it Alonso he wished to destroy, or himself? Either way, it was a road straight to hell. But then, he was already there, burning.

He could not get the mysterious, black-tressed girl out of his thoughts. Ceridwen. He wanted her. Yearned for her. Dreamed of her midnight hair, trailing through his fingers. Her soft lips straining to meet his. He wanted to get his hands on her supple body, and bring a glow of passion to her white skin.

But even if she lived, she preferred the perils of the great forest to being with him. It was his own damned fault. Raymond retrieved his knife and pushed away from the table. Leaving the food untouched he left the solar, Hamfast bounding after him.

Giles sighed deeply and stood. Shona, with tousled blond hair peeking from beneath her linen head-cloth, came only to his shoulder. She tilted her head back to look at him.

"You are ever too great for me, my lord Giles." She cast her gaze downward.

"Not so great. And who is to notice, lying down?" He tipped her chin back up with his forefinger.

She batted at him with small, chapped hands.

Giles caught both of Shona's hands in one of his. Putting his free arm about her waist, he lifted her to eye level. "I am yours. Command me as you will." He moved his mouth nearer and nearer to hers, closing his eyes halfway.

Shona squirmed in Giles's grip. "Put me down. Nay, wait." Her lips met his in a girlish, chaste kiss. "*Now* put me down."

"That is a start, anyway." He set her carefully on her feet. "I must go after Raymond before he does himself hurt."

Shona paused as she reached to clear away the untasted food. "Help him, Sir Giles. None of us can speak to him. Not the way he needs to be spoken to."

"I will try, Shona-lass."

The dew had not yet dried on the grass, and the mossy, intricately carved cairn-cross rose like a tombstone at the side of the road. Ceridwen avoided its chill shadow as she sat astride the drowsy pony Alys had provided. Her escort, arranged by promise of payment from her father, was late.

Old Nance rubbed his bulbous nose and peered down the road. "Here ye'll be safe 'til Rory comes, lass. 'Tis a holy place."

Ceridwen frowned. "Aye, but how will I recognize him?"

"No matter, he'll find ye. There's no other maid waitin' here, God love and bless ye." Old Nance scratched himself in a resigned manner. "I'd best be on me way. The missus'll have me privates in the cheese press if I'm late to Mass."

"But—"

"That's settled, then. Godspeed and fare ye well, lady." With a wave Nance set off for home at a remarkable pace for his bowed legs. The old man wanted his warm hearth, no doubt.

Ceridwen hoped the crossroads was indeed a safe place, but the stout dagger at her waist offered reassurance. Rookhaven lay quiet with the master and most of his men at large, but it seemed Raymond's commands were obeyed whether he was there or not. How she was to return, Ceridwen did not yet know. Meanwhile, she would do her best to sort out a plan.

The pony raised its head, swiveling its shaggy ears forward. Ceridwen tightened her fingers around the knife-hilt as two men crested the hill. Both were stocky, with similar heads of stiff, red hair, and were armed with short swords. Freemen, and brothers as well, she would warrant. But they carried themselves boldly, and their stares made her uneasy.

The taller of the two spoke up as they neared. "Good morrow, lady. Me and Sam here was just telling Old Nance how Rory's still too drunk to be of any use this day."

Ceridwen woke her mount with a squeeze of her legs. "Aye?"

The man smiled. "Even sober, Rory couldn't find his way across the village square to save his own life. We'll be your guide and guard, and won't charge much." He eyed the bag hanging from her saddle. It had bread and cheese in it, but he obviously envisioned something more valuable.

"I will go after Nance and speak to him myself. I have naught with which to pay you until I reach home." Ceridwen hoped she sounded convincing. The men exchanged glances. The one who had done the talking stood by as Sam took a step closer to the pony. Ceridwen's heart thudded and her stomach muscles tensed.

The talker smiled again. "Naught? But you've just been Beauchamp's…guest." He winked at Sam. "When it comes to women, Lord Raymond is generous to a fault. Gives them their due, he does." Casually, he reached for her pony's reins.

"Nay!" Ceridwen kicked the sluggish animal forward and whipped her dagger from its sheath. "Back off! I have taken nothing from Sir Raymond. He can keep his filthy blood-money."

The men hesitated, then shrugged and stepped aside as she brandished her blade. Urging the pony past them, Ceridwen managed to put it into a canter. She pounded down the road. There was but one, and as long as it led away from the ruffians, she was satisfied.

"'Tis a poor bargain you've struck, girl! A maid's innocence is worth a pretty penny to a Beauchamp!"

The guffawing men were soon left behind, and Ceridwen did not look back. It was broad daylight, after all. She would appeal to the parish priest when she found him, to help her find shelter until she knew what to do.

* * *

Raymond rode his courser west, cursing the lateness of the day, the glowering clouds over the hills, the stubbornness of Welshwomen, and most of all, his own idiocy. He had thought he could accept not knowing Ceridwen's fate, but the wondering had been unbearable. Upon his return Alys had given him a look that would have curdled milk, and refused to tell him anything.

But that in itself spoke aloud. Surely if the girl had died, Alys would have shunned him entirely, and made his life a much greater misery than she was doing now. So here he was, searching a dozen sheep tracks and byways, every glen and wayfarer's resting spot, hope dwindling with every step. Hamfast too scoured the hedgerows, only to follow endless false leads.

Perhaps Ceridwen was lying in a ditch, or wolves had devoured her. Raymond's fist tightened on his reins. He should have been with her, seen her home himself, or seen her body home, either way. He was a feckless wretch to have abandoned her. It was his duty to see her safe. It did not have to mean he cared.

There was one thing he could still do for her, though. Raymond looked up toward the bruised, purpling clouds, swollen with unspilled rain, and made a promise to God. *While I yet live, I will honor Morgan's request for an alliance. Even without a bride to seal the pact.*

The sun had vanished into the gathering storm, and Ceridwen took a path leading into the shelter of the woods. A quiet dell would provide grass for the pony and a haven from the road. In a meadow deep amidst the trees the pony grazed, and Ceridwen leaned against the bole of a hoary oak.

She was tired, and could not afford to give way to fear. The oak sighed in the wind, and her fingers sank into the moss growing thick and cool upon it. Listening to the whisper of the boughs overhead, she watched as red squirrels scampered up the twisted trunk. She felt faint, light-limbed, as though if she released her grip she would float up and away towards the scudding clouds beyond the treetops.

It was as though her will had been drained along with the poison of her illness. Or perhaps her sanity. She was an utterly pride-addled fool to have left Rookhaven. But what choice had Beauchamp given her?

A rattle of chain and the pony's high-pitched whinny startled Ceridwen into alertness. A huge dog bounded toward her through the grass, a horseman loped after. Her first instinct was to run and hide, but Rhys had warned her not to try to outrun dogs. It was better to curl up in as small a ball as possible. She might have done, had the hound been alone, but even as she realized the beast was Hamfast, so did she recognize Raymond.

There was no mistaking the dark, brooding air that seethed about him, even had his person and horse not been so distinctive.

"What do you want, sir?" Ceridwen swallowed the lump that seemed to grow in her throat as she met Raymond's chilly gaze.

"Get on that pony. I am taking you home." His voice had a ragged edge, unusual for him.

He expected her to protest. He wanted her to resist, she could feel it in her bones. Why, she was not so certain. But if it would please him to drag her back to Rookhaven behind his horse, she would not provide such pleasure, when honor required her voluntary return. She stroked Hamfast's head and replied, "Aye, milord, as you will."

Ceridwen hid her satisfaction at the look on Beauchamp's face. A mixture of surprise, and aye, dismay. He had thought to be rid of her, and hoped to blame her for his own failing, no doubt. Without hesitation she caught the stout pony, who reluctantly gave up its munching in order to be led toward the great courser.

Offering no assistance, Raymond leaned on his saddle-bow as Ceridwen climbed onto her mount. "You seem fit enough, lady," he said, rather carefully, she thought. Her wound still ached, but never would she admit that to him.

"Perfectly, sir. Let us be off."

"Right." With a creak of leather Raymond turned his horse and led the way back to the road. But instead of going toward Rookhaven, he continued in the direction she had been headed earlier.

Ceridwen had to make the pony trot to keep up with the black horse's long strides.

"I thought we were on our way home."

"You are." Raymond flashed her a glance, firm in his apparent course towards Llyn y Gareg Wen.

Anger kindled in Ceridwen's breast and she drew rein.

"I have given you no reason to shame me, to put me aside. I will not be returned like a castoff you have changed your mind about. We have a pact. You must honor it, as will I."

Raymond halted his horse and addressed the road, his back to Ceridwen. "You know not of what you speak. You know nothing of the peril my proximity holds for you. 'Tis far better that you return to your father's care."

"'Tis wrong to deny me the chance to fulfill my duty!"

Ceridwen gasped as Raymond swung his fierce gaze to her. He seemed aboil with rage and anguish and regret.

"Do not speak to me of duty, of right and wrong. I will not dishonor you again by forcing you to go. I thought it would be your preference. Do you refuse to return to your people?"

Her throat ached. Oh, how she wanted to go to them. But silently she commanded herself to reply as she must. "I do."

Raymond's low voice and calm manner only served to intensify his words. "So be it. One more mark on my soul's tally of disaster won't matter. Perhaps it will to you, but not to me."

He swung his horse's head around and Ceridwen urged her pony to fall in step beside him. Gazing upward, she did not believe his statement. The lines of pain on the Englishman's face bespoke the truth. The "tally" did matter to him. 'Twas not likely that she was the cause of his distress, but something gnawed at that soul he claimed to have, however black it was.

As they neared the lane's entry to the woods, Ceridwen thought she saw Raymond take pause. His horse tossed its head as if to confirm her suspicion, but Beauchamp shook the reins and reclaimed the animal's obedience. The knight sniffed the breeze. "Rain will soon fall, we will be caught out. I know a shortcut, but we must take a steep path. Can you manage?"

"Aye," Ceridwen replied. Come what may, she would stick to her pony like a burr. She followed Raymond's mount as the black courser bolted through the woods, nimble despite his size.

The Englishman rode lightly but the horse seemed out of control. A madness had possessed him as surely as it had his master.

Ceridwen was hard pressed to keep up, but Raymond hurtled on anyway, the faster to get through the forest he hated. Tree trunks sped past in flickering alternations of light and shadow. He let the horse take him, share with him all its wild power.

Leaning over the animal's neck, Raymond's hands left the reins, and he rubbed his palms down the pounding, sweat-slickened shoulders of his mount. He did not want to think or to feel. For a little while, he simply wanted to be.

But his momentary peace was shattered as a flash of white burst into the path before them. Grendel whinnied and shied and reared all at once. Raymond kept his seat until his mount headed irrevocably for a low branch. He dove off, landed wrong, and lay still for a moment with his eyes closed.

A jingle of harness and the receding thud of hooves told him of Grendel's desertion. Hamfast licked his cheek and whined. Moist breath warmed his face as Ceridwen's pony arrived and nuzzled him. God grant that she was still upon its scruffy back.

"Are you injured, Beauchamp?"

"Nay." Raymond picked himself up and tried standing. Too quickly, but he managed to avoid her proffered hand. His right knee throbbed. As he tested it, a soft whuffle of sound caught his attention. Raymond stared down the curving path.

Standing there was the stuff of legend. A white stag, living and breathing. Heretofore an insubstantial animal of his imagination, from tales told him by Alys when he was a boy.

Raymond blinked and looked again. It remained, its nostrils flaring gently with each inhalation, deep brown eyes staring at him. A faint blue light seemed to flicker about its antlers and along its back. It snorted and pawed the earth.

He glanced at Ceridwen. She looked unperturbed, as if magical deer were an everyday occurrence. The stag leaped away between the trees. Raymond could not help himself. "Come on!" he shouted. The great dog at his heels, he ran after the beast, drawn like a moth to flame.

A white stag. Emblazoned upon his shield as befit a man of Beauchamp. He could no longer make that claim. He had gone through the motions, followed Alonso's orders. But his heart was not in it. His ideals of keeping a united front, standing by his brothers no matter what, now seemed as vaporous as the creature he pursued. The stag was a creature purely of myth. It did not exist, except in the minds of superstitious old women. Perhaps all that he had lived for was as much a phantom as the beast. But it looked so real. He had to find out.

Chapter Six

Raymond ran on, limping, his breath coming in ragged gasps. He cursed. Men who owned horses had no business on foot. He pursued the stag through the bracken. It led him higher, pausing now and again, mist swirling at its feet, only to dart away as he approached.

As if from far away, Raymond heard Ceridwen calling. But he could not stop to explain and let the stag escape. The air took on an opaque quality, as if a layer of thin cloth had dropped before his eyes. The wind died and the terrain grew steeper.

Raymond's heart pounded, until it beat in his ears and neck and belly. His knee felt on fire. The old thigh wound, from the Welsh arrow, ached like the bad memory it was. He climbed the last craggy steps over the rotten, crumbling rocks of the tor. Wisps of fog gathered in the open space of the summit, gray fingers reached to meet each other in a silent entwining. Leaning over to catch his breath, he looked about. The stag was nowhere in sight, and Hamfast too had vanished.

"Sir Raymond!" Ceridwen's clear voice echoed.

"Keep off! 'Tis unsafe." Infested with demons, it was.

She tied the pony to a shrub and marched toward him. "What in God's name are you about? Have you gone mad?"

Raymond kept silent, for in that moment he did not know. A long dolmen was before him, a horizontal slab of stone that had no doubt lain there since the beginning of the world. It rested upon two smaller stones, like a tabletop. The dolmen was waist high, but once it had seemed gigantic. Dread knotted in his stomach. He tried to swallow and could not.

Ceridwen stepped closer, brushing past his arm with the lightest of touches. He kept still until she was out of reach.

"What is this place? Has some enchantment taken you, sir?"

He stared into her clear, innocent eyes, then shook his head. She was the only thing capable of enchanting him, and that he would not allow. A pang speared his gut and the unwelcome past burst upon him, vivid and intense. "An evil remembrance."

Ceridwen nodded sagely. "Bad memories are like infected wounds. They must be allowed to drain."

Her knowing words surprised him. But never had he told anyone what had happened here. Not even his lord father, who had made an earnest attempt to beat it out of him. To speak of it might give power and substance to Alonso's act of betrayal. Raymond rested his hands upon the bench of stone, its surface rough and gritty beneath his palms.

He rubbed his scarred wrists, the legacy of scraping his bonds against the stone to free himself that night. He had survived, but poor Parsifal had never been the same, ever at Alonso's mercy, or lack thereof.

"What happened, then?"

He jumped at Ceridwen's question. There she sat, still waiting for him to speak. He cleared his throat and looked at the sullen, brooding sky. "I had a—small disagreement with my brothers here, long ago."

Ceridwen raised an eyebrow. "You do not care for the truth. Its lack will haunt you."

Raymond scowled at her impertinence and climbed onto the stone. He lay back, touching the rough, lichen-covered dolmen with his fingertips. The events of that night still burned at the bottom of all his hatred for Alonso.

Ceridwen clambered up to sit cross-legged on top of the dolmen. "You had best tell the tale before the storm breaks."

"I do not want to speak of it."

"Are you afraid of my judgment?"

Raymond smiled grimly. "God is my judge, not you."

She studied him, her eyes grave. "We all have fear. Or regret. If one keeps it always at bay, one never heals."

"I have healed. Many times. I am covered in scars."

"That is not the sort of healing I mean."

Raymond shifted uncomfortably and glanced at the young woman beside him. She was like a stick poking a raw wound. "Here is the truth, then. I spent an uncomfortable night here once as a boy. I woke at dawn, warmed by a great dog. The original Hamfast, as I named him, the great-great-grandsire of all that have since followed." Never had he been so glad of another creature's comfort. God only knew where he had come from.

The girl made no comment. The stone bit into his shoulder blades. The sky wheeled overhead, as though the slab he lay upon revolved on its own axis. Here he was, on the brink of war, of fratricide, no better than Alonso. He wanted to cover his face with his hands, but not with Ceridwen looking on. He was glad he had not revealed the sordid tale of his humiliation to her.

His life was a hell of his own making, and no amount of talking could ease the burden. "Where has that damned hound got to?" he snapped. He could face Ceridwen's probing green eyes no longer. "Hamfast!" His shout rang through the woods.

"You should not curse the one thing you love. And mayhap the one thing that loves you." Ceridwen rested her chin on her palm.

"Woman, when I want your opinion, I shall ask for it." Raymond was about to add that she would have a long wait, when Ceridwen's face turned white. He followed her stark gaze toward the edge of the clearing.

Gradually, out of the mist, the faint figure of a man appeared. Bare legs showed from beneath the ragged edge of a dark-stained tunic. His hair fell past his shoulders in tangled ropes. Bearded and gaunt, he stood in silence.

"A ghost...?" Ceridwen whispered.

Guarding his knee, Raymond eased down from the stone, the hairs on the back of his neck on end, his heart battering his ribs.

The wraith seemed familiar. Was it someone he had slain, long ago? "Begone!"

The apparition backed away and vanished into the forest.

His pulses still pounding, but satisfied the thing had departed, Raymond turned to Ceridwen. "'Tis high time we left."

"What was it?" she insisted, eyes yet wide, walking with him toward the tethered pony.

"I know not. It looked like…" He shook his head. It was impossible to nail down. "Probably some poor wretch so thin we could nearly see through him."

"Perhaps. But 'tis unusual enough to see a white stag."

Raymond rubbed his jaw, relieved that he was not alone in having seen the beast. "Never mind. I must find Grendel before he gets lost any farther. He is a great goose of a horse."

Apparently content with his change of subject, Ceridwen held out the pony's reins. "You are hurt. Do you want to ride?"

"Nay. I shall lead you."

Ceridwen snatched the loop of braided leather from Raymond's hand, flung it over the pony's neck, and gave the animal a swat. It squealed and trotted off. The girl stood defiant, her face pale but radiant with unbowed spirit. "If you walk, so will I."

He wanted no kindness from her. "Do as you like." His beleaguered heart thudding in protest, Raymond turned his back upon Ceridwen and led the way from the dolmen. There was no point in bemoaning his choice in allowing her to return with him. He would keep his distance, as any prudent man would when confronted by something as unpredictable and desirable as this Welshwoman.

Raymond gave silent thanks when, before going a mile, they came upon horse, pony and hound. The equines shivered, head-to-head, contrite, but Hamfast sat guard, princely in his bearing.

Ceridwen trudged to a halt near the animals, and her slight form swayed as she rubbed her arms. Of course she was still weak from her wound, cold and hungry. Stroking Hamfast's head in greeting, Raymond glanced from Ceridwen to the growing darkness, forming all too quickly between the trees.

"If you ride with me upon Grendel, we will make better time. Or do you need to rest first, a fire to warm you?"

She shook her head, her hair shimmering in black waves. "We had best push on with ghosts about, don't you think?"

Raymond did not reply. It was difficult to converse with her calmly, to look at her without staring, to pretend he did not want her on her back, then and there. That aside, he did not care to spend the night in the woods.

To make matters worse, big drops of rain began to splash earthward, pocking the dust of the trail and making the fallen leaves bounce beneath their impact. With the opening of the clouds, a shudder seemed to go through the forest.

The back of his neck prickled. Danger. Close by, and more than he could handle alone, Raymond was certain. He caught a shadowy movement between the trees and straightened, hand on sword hilt. "Get behind me, lady. Hamfast, stay with her!"

There, from the deepening twilight of the forest, a group of men emerged. With silent footsteps and menace in their faces, they advanced, bearing lances. Pikes. Swords and axes. Without warning, they charged, yelling like demons.

Raymond's furious reaction was lightning-fast. Shrinking away, Ceridwen watched in as much astonishment as terror. His sword whistled clear of his scabbard quicker than her eye could follow. He roared and swung it in great arcs, cleaving wood and bone alike. The attackers regrouped and set upon him afresh.

Beauchamp fought as one possessed, spun and ducked and sliced until four of the surviving men brought him down from behind. Hamfast stood between Ceridwen and the fight, quivering with the apparent effort of not joining his master.

Well hidden behind a tree, Ceridwen peeked through her fingers, horrified at the savage blows showered upon the knight, until he no longer moved. She quaked at the sight of so much blood, and was ashamed she could not aid him.

"Hah! Who would've thought it'd be so easy? He's no such a dragon after all." A big man grinned down at Raymond's body, now being bound, hand and foot.

"Speak for yourself, you great ox." Another man cradled his bloodied arm, and looked mournfully at his fallen comrades.

"Where's the lass, then?"

"What lass?"

"Never mind, she's hared off. The warden'll get her and the other on the morrow, when it's light. But this black is a grand horse, indeed! Need we show it to his lordship, do you think?"

Relieved that for the moment they were more interested in Grendel than in herself, Ceridwen waited, biting her lip. The magnificent courser, so easily frightened by apparitions, greeted the attentions of the strangers with even less grace.

He reared, snapping his lead, and struck out at them with his front hooves. Whirling, he plunged into the gloom of the forest, leaving the now captive pony to whinny after him.

Ceridwen watched as the men dumped Raymond facedown over its back. They left, carrying their dead, with Beauchamp in tow. An unexpectedly vast and painful emptiness yawned within her as he was taken away. Englishman or no, it was terrible to see someone she had thought invincible, defeated by lesser men.

She knelt and threw her arms about Hamfast's neck, hugged him and wept into his rough fur. Was Beauchamp alive? What had the brigands meant, they would get her and "the other" tomorrow? What other? And, "his lordship" could be any of a number of warring barons along the Marches.

Her tired muscles ached and she shivered as the pelting rain began to soak through her clothes. She would have to find her way to Rookhaven and get help, following the path. But Raymond had said this was a shortcut, not the way he had brought her the time before. Nothing looked familiar.

Fighting down her panic, Ceridwen took a deep breath, and decided to follow the outlaws as best she could. As she took her first few steps, a soft trilling met her ears. The notes ran up and down, now sounding the song of a woodthrush, now the chirp of a sparrow. She must be dreaming. Small birds did not sing thus, so late in the day, and certainly not in a cold downpour.

Hamfast barked and a shriek left Ceridwen's throat as a man seemed to materialize out of the air before her. The fact that he was doing the whistling, not the birds, stopped her flight for an instant. In that time she beheld the rough-bearded face of a young man, browned both by the sun and an abundance of dirt.

His blue eyes were placid, his presence benign, and her fear melted away, leaving confused exhaustion in its wake.

To her relief Hamfast merely nosed the man, then sat down, apparently unworried. The fellow stood quietly, his wild tangle of fawn-colored hair replete with leaves and twigs.

Ceridwen caught her breath. This was none other than the ghost himself. No wraith, she was now certain, but a human, filthy, barefoot, and older than she had first thought, for there was white mixed in the dark-blond hair. She found her voice.

"My name is Ceri. W-who are you?"

He shrugged in answer and did not meet her eyes. Clustering the fingertips of one slender hand, he put them to his mouth. The wrist exposed by his motion was circled by scars, like those left by manacles. Perhaps he had escaped some dungeon, but the poor wanderer must be hungry.

"I have nothing for you to eat. I am sorry." Ceridwen showed him her empty hands. He looked down at her white fingers, and his lips tightened in an expression akin to pain. As though it were treasure he beheld, not the hand of a fellow creature, alone in the woods. "I must go after my—my betrothed, he is sore beleaguered," she said.

The man gazed at her, his expression flat and empty, as if his spirit had been quenched.

Ceridwen's heart ached with pity. "Come with me, if you will. When next I speak to my father, he will give you a place at Llyn y Gareg Wen. You'll be warm and safe there."

The man's eyes flickered in apparent understanding, and he fell into step as Ceridwen started down the forest path, following the pony's hoofprints, an eager Hamfast nosing his way along. Her companion walked silently, and at times seemed to almost disappear, so well did he blend into the background.

"You need a name. How does 'Awyr' suit you? It means air, for you are nearly transparent, yet make yourself felt."

He made no objection. They passed through great beech groves, and misty dingles where ferns all but choked the trickling streams. A herd of does raised their heads at their passing, then turned tail and disappeared into the trees.

As darkness fell, they reached a ridge, and from that vantage saw the encampment of Raymond's captors, at the base of a cliff. A large cookfire snapped beneath a joint roasting on a spit. Whispering reassurance to Hamfast, Ceridwen gripped his collar firmly to stop him from roiling down to seek his master.

She squinted and strained to see. There sat Beauchamp, now conscious, still bound, but his rage and defiance were evident even from a distance, as his keepers thought it necessary to kick him every so often. At finding him alive, a great knot within her chest loosened. The extent of her relief was unexpected.

A whisper of steel sounded, and Ceridwen turned to find her strange companion had drawn a sword, apparently from a scabbard at his back, and now stared intently at the scene before him.

The pommel glinted in his trembling hands. She saw it bore a crystal, which she knew must have embedded within it the relic of some saint, to render its bearer all-powerful. Where had Awyr gotten such a valuable weapon? And why did he not sell it, that he might live a while in comfort? Whatever the reason, he must not use the sword now.

"Nay! Don't go down there, you will only be killed. See, he is not—" Ceridwen stopped. This man might desire Beauchamp's death, not his rescue. "Do you know him?"

Awyr turned to her, his face as blank as before, then eased back to a sitting position, his sword resheathed. She tried again to communicate. "We can but wait. If there is a chance to slip down unseen, we may, else try to learn where they will go, and inform the garrison at Rookhaven how they might retrieve their lord." Ceridwen did not know how to accomplish that, without help or sustenance. The rain had stopped, but she crouched, shivering in her wet clothes, and her teeth chattered.

Suddenly, from behind, Awyr slipped his arms around her and drew her against his chest. Fearful of his touch but more afraid of alerting the men below with noise, she struggled in vain. For all his thinness, the mute was strong. He tightened his embrace and at the same time laced his fingers through hers, making a soothing sound through his teeth all the while, as one might to a child. "Shhh…shhh…"

As her fright waned, Ceridwen relaxed by degrees, her trembling eased with the warmth he provided, and his grip lessened. With the strangely intimate communion, she was reminded uncomfortably of Raymond's hands on her bare skin in the infirmary. It was as though both men brimmed with the pain of memories that could not be set aside. Or perhaps in Awyr's case, memories that had been so well hidden that everything else had been lost with them.

But the one who held her began to gently rock, and as his heat seeped closer, she dozed, Hamfast curled before her.

"On your feet!"

Ceridwen woke with a yelp at the harsh command. Someone kicked her legs. She sat up, momentarily confused, then scrambled like an animal at bay, frantic for escape. In the morning light, four men surrounded her. Her mysterious companion of the previous night was gone. The men were well-clad in wool and leather, and carried thick wooden staves.

Their leader kicked her again. He was stout, bearded, and she read no mercy in his face. It had to be the Warden.

"I said get up." He jerked her to her feet by one arm.

"Don't touch me. I have done nothing wrong." She tried to pull away. His fingers bit into a sensitive spot above her elbow and pain shot to her shoulder.

"Oh, that's rich. You and your fine friend, poaching and living off his lordship's land."

"What friend? I am alone." Perhaps Awyr had been able to get away. She did not see Hamfast, either.

The Warden back-handed her face with a blow that nearly knocked her down. "That's your second lie. Don't let me hear a third." He took her dagger and clamped a fist on the scruff of her neck. "Let's be off."

A shove at her back propelled her forward. She stumbled several steps and when she looked up, there stood Awyr, bound and bloodied. One of his two captors had put the crystal-hilted sword through his own belt.

The leader addressed the prisoners. "I'm Tom Forester, Warden here. Remember that name, for 'tis me who keeps Alonso's woods free of vermin like you. Especially this one." He indicated the captive man. "We've sought the murderer of young Nat these last weeks. And this lunatic bears a sword finer than most. Both he and it fit the crime." Tom pushed Ceridwen along the path, and the others followed.

Nat? Oh, could it be the same rogue who had attacked her? "You're wrong!" she protested. "This man never hurt anyone. A beastly swine, it must have been that Nat—he laid hands upon me. And—and—" She stopped before blurting out that it had been Sir Raymond who had killed him. If they believed her, it would not help matters, if this Nat was so precious.

The forester guffawed. "Hah! A woman who shuts herself up! Who'd've thought it possible?"

The other men joined in the laughter, but all Ceridwen could think of was the forester's words…Alonso's woods. A bolt of icy fear shot through her. They had come much farther than she realized. She looked back at Awyr. For an instant their eyes met, and she saw his abject apology. He must have tried to lead the Warden's men away, to give her a chance to escape. But he had not known there were two groups of them.

"Enough of your mooning, there, girl. You'll get plenty of lovin' at the castle." Tom and his men hooted, and Ceridwen's cheeks burned.

Chapter Seven

Ceridwen's gaze traveled up the walls of the accommodation provided to her and Awyr at Alonso de Beauchamp's castle keep. Rusty iron rings were set into the stones, at extraordinarily inconvenient heights if one were actually chained to them.

She rubbed her arms against the chill, and grimaced at the stench of the dungeon. Straw more filthy than that forked from a cow byre littered the floor in clumps. A noisome bucket was the only furnishing. Already she was beginning to itch in places she did not want to scratch within sight of any man.

Air and daylight penetrated through a windhole leading upwards to the ground level, as did rain and other liquid run-off. She had quickly learned not to stand below the opening. The entrance to the cell was a small wooden door with a hatch through which their food, or what passed for food, was shoved once a day. Three meals in three days. It was not enough fare with which to fight the cold. Or the other inhabitants.

A small skittering sound was followed by something tugging at the thin leather of her shoe. She looked down and stifled a shriek. A rat dangled as she tried to shake it from her foot. It held on with long yellow teeth, its hind legs flailing for a purchase. The mute reached over and enclosed the struggling brown body in his hand. After a moment the creature relaxed and released its grip.

"Is it dead? Has it fainted?" Ceridwen peered at the animal. Its whiskers twitched. She could not understand why it hadn't sunk its teeth into her friend's fingers. "You have a gentle way with vile things."

Awyr smiled and shook his head as he stroked the rat's belly. He seemed completely at ease. She shivered and sat huddled in the corner, as far from the rat as possible. Awyr pulled out a bit of the moldy bread they'd been served and fed it to the creature. Holding the tidbit in its front paws, it rapidly consumed the crust. Once again on its feet, the rat hesitated, then made a run for its hole.

A rattle of keys sounded, and the rough voices of the jailers grew louder as they approached. The lock groaned and the door opened. "You there, wench. Get your skinny arse up."

Ceridwen swallowed hard and looked at her friend, who with a small motion of his head encouraged her to obey. She set her jaw and took heart from his calm fortitude.

"Hurry it up, woman!"

She slipped past the guard's big stomach with as much dignity as she could summon, even as he gave her bottom a painful tweak. She craned her neck to see Awyr one last time in the wavering torchlight. His eyes burned after her.

The guard cuffed the back of her head.

The mute leaped up, put his hands to the jailer's throat and his knee to his groin faster than the fellow could shut the door. The guard screamed, doubled over, and grabbed one of Awyr's legs at the knee with his free hand. They fell together, and Awyr's skull hit the stone floor with an ugly thud.

Ceridwen yanked on the guard's hair in an attempt to pull his bulk from atop Awyr, and he rolled away, flailing at her with beefy arms. The second guard burst into the cell. "What goes, Will? Damn the wench, what has she done t'ye?"

"*He* did it, Dirk!" Will regained his feet. Ceridwen knelt to protect her friend's head while the furious jailer kicked his inert body and rained a stream of curses upon him.

Dirk snatched Ceridwen by the hair. "Filthy bitch." He dragged her out into the corridor, and Will staggered after them, pulling the door shut. He held her from the front while Dirk tied her hands behind her back.

"What d'ye think?"

The rear guard's voice held a sly note that sent fresh ripples of fear coursing through Ceridwen. He slipped his big hands to her breasts and cupped them. She jerked and tried to pull away until he snaked one arm all the way around her, crushing her against his chest. His elbow dug into the tender scar beneath her ribs, and his breath was hot against her ear.

"I'll hold her for ye, Will," he offered softly.

Ceridwen held her breath. Will wheezed and frowned and shook his head. "Nay, Dirk. Now won't do, thanks to that scum down there. And what I don't get, nor shall ye. Fair's fair."

"My missus'll thank ye for your sense of justice, Willum."

"Shut up and let's be rid of this little witch."

Ceridwen's legs nearly gave way with relief. Flanking her on each side, the men hauled her up the torchlit stairways. The sweaty walls were riddled with cracks seeping green and brown muck. The guards barely allowed her to get her feet on one cold step before bumping her into the next, and her ankles were sore and bruised by the time they reached the door.

The trio emerged into an open courtyard, and the broad light of day made Ceridwen's eyes ache. Dwarfed by the burly men, she squinted up at a tall shape before her and it resolved into none other than the impressive person of Lord Alonso.

To his right was a lady, tall, fair and elegantly gowned. She emanated a flowery scent, making Ceridwen all too aware of her own sad state of uncleanliness. The woman sneered. Their eyes met, and Ceridwen felt the stab of the lady's ill-will.

The baron laughed, circling what his men held fast. "This? This miserable creature is what gave you such trouble? We heard your shrieks all the way up here, William."

"'Twas the other one, milord. He near to killed me."

Alonso leisurely donned a pair of fine leather gloves. "He will hang from the southern gibbet, Monday next. There will be more people to take heed, during market. And as for the girl, if she behaves, Cook needs a scullion, otherwise, give her to the garrison. But…wait a moment." He paused and turned to face Ceridwen, and as he gazed at her, his visage grew pale.

She stared back at him with all the hatred she could summon in her eyes, holding her back stiff and straight. No more cringing before sadistic Englishmen. It was the least she could do in Owain's memory. She was her father's daughter. He should be able to remember her with pride.

"Who are you?" Alonso demanded, sweat beading upon his upper lip. He wiped it away, staining his gloved finger.

Ceridwen saw that the blond lady seemed to swell, like an angry cat. "A Welshwoman, is all."

Apparently indifferent to the menace building in his consort, Alonso continued to stare. "You look so alike." He tipped her chin up and turned her face this way and that.

Ceridwen did not understand his distress, why he swallowed hard and then, to her complete bewilderment and dismay, tenderly stroked her cheek with his palm. She jerked away.

As if he had woken from a dream, Alonso released her face with a hard wrench. "Watch yourself, *ma petite*."

"I would advise thee the same, my lord," Ceridwen replied.

Alonso slapped her. The blow whipped her head to the side and brought tears to her eyes. He followed it with a savage kiss, more humiliating than the guards' manhandling.

"I look forward to seeing you again, little girl," he whispered, smiling at her with the false, devastating charm that had undoubtedly doomed many an unsuspecting maid, and then strode off, his outraged lady firmly in hand.

Ceridwen shuddered, as much with revulsion as with anger. She spat the rich taste of Alonso onto the ground and scuffed it into oblivion with her foot. She wanted to rub the sting of his palm away but her hands were still bound behind her back.

To think she had been close to feeling the first tender shoots of affection for Alonso's brother. But they were all alike. Raymond was cast in the same mold of noble brutality. She thought of the body she had seen swinging from the wall at his keep. Left to rot, ravens pecking at his eyes. That would be Awyr's fate, in but six days. She had to save him, somehow.

"Well, what'll it be?" The guards eyed her hopefully.

"Take me to the kitchens. Please," she added, as Will and Dirk began to grumble their disappointment. They hurried her across the wide bailey and past the armorer clanging at his forge, and at last to the kitchen sheds.

"Cook! You've a helper, says his lordship." The guards untied her hands and quickly abandoned her.

Cook replaced a tong in a hanging rack and turned to her with a scowl like burnt meat. He circled Ceridwen's arm with his forefinger and thumb and lifted it. "A wee pullet. They've brought me a scrawny, *black* pullet." He dropped her arm in disgust and wiped his hand on his tunic. "Rose!"

A russet-haired girl hurried over at his summons, her cheeks pink beneath a dusting of flour. "Aye, sir?"

Ceridwen returned Rose's curious gaze even as she inhaled the enticing aromas of the kitchen, wishing they could ease her hunger pangs.

Cook jerked a thumb at Ceridwen. "Wash her in the yard."

"Thank you, sir," Ceridwen said, forcing a smile.

Cook gave a start, as if surprised the "pullet" was capable of civil speech. "Hmmph."

"Come along, lassie." Rose led the way to a watering trough outside the stables and handed Ceridwen a bucket. "There. Take your time." With that Rose sauntered over to the saddling area. An idle groom watched her, his gaze ravenous. He intercepted the lissome girl and they were soon lost to sight. An assortment of squeals and giggles flowed from around the corner.

She had a fair idea of what was going on, but all she knew for certain was that when men got too close to women, babies resulted, and sometimes the women died.

Ceridwen dunked her hair in the bucket and the cold water snapped at her scalp. Scrubbing her head, she longed to strip off her overgown and sit in the deep horse-trough in her shift. At least that would loosen the crust of the last week.

Perhaps no one would notice if she did. She peered about. Not a stableboy in sight. It would take but a few moments. The sounds from Rose and her lover were dwindling into long sighs, moans, and barely discernible murmurs.

Ceridwen yanked her loose gown off over her head, and shook it as hard as she could before laying it aside in the cobbled yard. In her shift, she put a foot over the side of the tub, and the water came up to her knee. Then the other foot.

With a shriek she slipped on the green slime at the bottom.

Her rear end landed in the water with a whumping splash, and the back of her head hit the wooden edge. Stunned, she sank below the surface, wishing she had been content to stay dirty.

From a narrow window in a little-used chamber of Alonso's keep, Raymond watched Ceridwen go under. He held his breath for her, counting the heartbeats of her submersion, each one an agony, an eternity. How had she come to be here?

And did Alonso know who she was? At last she spluttered up, gasping. Relief battled outrage that she should be in such circumstances. He had to get her far beyond Alonso's reach.

As she swept her hair from her eyes several young servants gathered round the trough in raucous laughter. Ceridwen put her elbows together in front of her chest, with her knees drawn up. One of the boys pushed her head underwater again.

Raymond lunged against his chain, and his powerless state enraged him as much as witnessing Ceridwen's ill-treatment at the hands of boors. Searing pain in his wrenched knee brought his futile reaction to a halt. Wood scraped against stone, and warily, he looked toward the heavy door. He did not expect Giles, or anyone else who might aid him, and indeed it was not.

"Greetings, good-brother!" Reeking of jasmine, Alonso's mistress, Gwendolyn de Lacey sidled into the chamber and closed the door. "Watching the peasants play?" She glanced out the window. "Look at that little blackbird, see how they prey upon her! But, if she is stupid enough to disrobe in a sta-bleyard, 'tis all she deserves. I shall have her whipped and thrown out, for causing so much trouble and tempting the grooms. And mayhap tempting you as well, the Welsh bitchlet!"

The venom in Gwendolyn's voice made Raymond's stomach churn. She could only be so angry if Alonso had taken notice of the girl. And if either one of them got hold of her...

Abruptly Gwendolyn turned and approached him, her violet eyes luminous. "Ever the silent one, my dragon-lord." She reached under his tunic and drew a sharp fingernail up the con-tours of his naked ribs. "I have ever been fond of you, Ray-mond. Would you not like me to amuse myself with you? And in return...I might help you to escape."

Raymond stared at Gwendolyn, willing her to self-immolate in the flames of her own unnatural desire. It was hot enough to burn anything, her appetite unquenchable, he knew, though not through his willing participation. "Surely you have learned by now, Madame, that I am no one's plaything. Your unique and abundant charms cannot sway me, incapable of feeling as I am."

"Incapable?" She dug her nails into his side. "No feeling?" She raked them upward. "Ah, nary a flinch can I provoke. Why, Raymond? What is it about me that displeases you?" Daintily she sucked his blood from one fingertip, while working to untie his braes single-handedly.

"Lady, I am not my brother. I prefer to be master of my woman in all things, not her private beast of burden."

"Oh, and that attitude was most successful with the Lady Meribel, was it not? So meek and biddable was she, beneath your masterful hand? Like this?" She knelt before him.

"Damn you, Gwendolyn. Take your wretched paws from me." A blinding urge to throttle her swept him. It was her good fortune that his hands were bound behind his back.

"As you will, sir. See, I don't need my paws to take you."

"Gwendolyn! So swear I, I will break your fair white neck betwixt my legs, I warn you."

"Oh, my! I do tremble before your show of temper!"

Raymond brought his good knee up and cuffed her temple hard, then planted his foot between her ample breasts and shoved. She landed in a pile of dusty sackcloth, screeching obscenities. He hobbled to the window and leaned out.

"Alonso! I demand a parley, forthwith!" His shout drew stares from all in the courtyard, including Ceridwen, who appeared to be brawling with a red-haired wench for possession of a filthy overgown.

"You!" Raymond directed his bellow toward the groom. "Bring your lord, tell him his lady requires assistance. Now!" The young man leaped to obey, and the others scattered like pea hens to their respective duties. All but Ceridwen, who clutched her muddy gown to her bosom, looking upwards to him.

"What are you gawping at? Get to work!" Raymond snarled. For her own sake he did not want Gwendolyn or Alonso to discover that she knew him, even less that she was important to him. Only for her lands, of course, and her father's goodwill.

But that look of hers! As narrow-eyed and cutting as any Meribel had ever given him. Ceridwen made a good job of politeness when face-to-face, but at a distance, her true feelings showed. It was just as well.

A jerk on his chain made him spin to face Gwendolyn. She glared at him, nursing the side of her face, though he could see no mark. "You will rue the day, proud Raymond, so superior, so aloof. Alonso shall make you suffer in ways I cannot. Mark me, it shall be so. I promise you!" She spat the words at him, breasts heaving, gentian eyes brimming. As she reached for the door, Alonso burst in, dagger drawn.

"My dearling, what has he done to make you weep?"

Gwendolyn winced as Alonso touched her cheek. She buried her face against his chest and cried all the harder.

"For God's sake, Raymond! My lady comes to comfort you and this is how you repay her? With blows?"

"Aye. If I could, I'd take a strap to her backside. Except she would enjoy that too much, I trow."

In an instant Alonso had the tip of his blade nestled at Raymond's throat. "You, brother, must needs learn the folly of your impudence. Gwen, unlock his chains. Raymond has been our honored guest, but has now fully abused our hospitality."

It would not do to provoke his brother further, Raymond thought. With the dagger now discreetly at his back, Alonso pushed him along. Down and around they descended the tower stair, until they emerged into the bailey below. Gwendolyn clung to his right arm, Alonso stayed close by his left. From the corner of his eye, Raymond watched as Ceridwen slipped into the shadow of the stable door.

"Now, when he comes looking for you, I shall tell your bastard friend Giles St. Germaine that you are here to make peace with me, and if he has any intelligence he will depart while he may. But you shall not. Nor shall you wed the daughter of the barbarian, Morgan, in this fiendish plot of yours. Nay, when you apologize to me, repledge your fealty, pay a fine, *and* I believe you are sincere, I will send you home. Until then, only a goodly ransom will bring your freedom. What say you?''

Raymond turned a baleful eye upon his elder brother. ''Too late, Alonso. I have already wed her. The pact was sealed in sight of God and man. I have all the might of the Talyessin at my back, plus that of my other allies. 'Tis not worth your while to detain me, neither in silver nor in blood.'' Raymond consoled himself that the lie about his nuptials was one he could easily turn true. If he lived.

''Ah, but you wound me, Raymond! To marry and not invite us? What an insult. Nay, you must learn some manners. Where is that reeve?''

By now, a small but bristling crowd of men-at-arms had gathered, among them the stout shire reeve, who swaggered forward, his arms crossed against his massive chest. He had a distinctive sword at his hip. Its crystal pommel caught the sun's rays and bounced rainbows off Alonso's creamy wool mantle. ''Milord?''

''My brother, here, wishes to inspect my dungeons.''

Raymond swallowed. The idea of being chained, alone in a pitch-dark cell, drowned all rational thought in waves of shameful panic. With an effort at calm that cost him dear, Raymond met his brother's glare. ''Alonso, do yourself and your men a favor and offer me no hindrance. I am not alone in my weariness of your greed. I have half a thousand men at my command, awaiting my return.'' This in fact was yet another barefaced lie. He had fewer than one hundred.

''They are not here, though, are they? And still days away, no doubt.'' Alonso dug his dagger point harder against the base of Raymond's spine. ''A great deal can happen to a man's morals, in a few hours, where flesh is involved.''

Raymond heard a small gasp, from the vicinity of the stable doors, but no one else seemed to take note. Without looking in Ceridwen's direction he responded to his brother. ''Giles will come, not alone, and, bastard or no, his father is a duke. He is better-born than you or I, so have a care as to his welcome.''

If Gwendolyn had had pointed ears, this information would have pricked them upright, Raymond thought. The arrival of a possible new conquest was ever her delight. But St. Germaine could take care of himself. And, hopefully there would be no time for dalliance. If he could contrive for Giles to remove Ceridwen from this place, he could better concentrate on his own survival.

Alonso threw a black look to his lady. "The Norman loves you, though, brother, and that will ensure his cooperation."

"That is beside the point. Hear me well, Alonso. I refuse any longer to pay you tribute. I refuse to bear arms for you against a people who only fight to keep what is rightfully theirs. I refuse to starve my villeins in order to afford the exorbitant revenues you demand of me. I remove my fealty to you."

Alonso rubbed his chin, while the reeve stood openmouthed, as did everyone else but Gwendolyn. "Impossible," Alonso said at last. "You expect me to agree to this? To give up the income just like that? To allow you to flaunt the law of the land and celebrate your disloyalty to me?" He motioned to the reeve, who came to attention.

Raymond straightened his shoulders and tried not to sneer. If he was going to be in gaol, it might as well be for something worthwhile, rather than by Alonso's whim.

"This is perfidy. Base treachery. 'Tis treason." Alonso's voice broke, and two big tears rolled down his cheeks. "You know the penalty for treason."

Raymond knew. To be hanged, but not until dead. To be drawn, and one's insides removed for one's own inspection. To have one's limbs tied to four strong horses, and…he had seen the rest, and did not care to dwell upon it.

"Aye," he replied, shaken, but unimpressed by his sibling's display of feeling. Alonso had ever been able to weep at will. "Call it what you like, 'tis still not high treason, for you are far from princely, brother."

"Raymond, truly, I owe you an opportunity for reflection, that you might contemplate this grave error upon which you are about to embark. You will thank me in the end." Alonso made a graceful gesture with his hand, as though he were a cleric bestowing a benevolent blessing upon a misguided sinner.

Raymond's demons rose in a deafening chorus within him, scattering what little prudence remained. "No doubt your dungeons provide that opportunity for all those you seek to improve. I thought you would prefer knowing where I stand, and allow an unwilling sword go its own way, rather than turn against you!''

''There! You heard it, all of you. As my witnesses before God this day.'' Alonso waxed triumphant. ''I name thee traitor, Raymond de Beauchamp. Your life is forfeit if you are not ransomed in a timely manner. I want five hundred talents of silver. One from each man of your assembly. That should not prove too difficult.'' Alonso began to laugh.

Raymond's heart sank. The sum was impossible. Even had there been five hundred men, no one had silver in such quantities. Most folk paid what they owed in eggs, or wool, or their own sweat. Giles would no doubt damn him for another of his ill-conceived schemes not shared with the one person who knew better—Giles.

From habit, he scanned the faces of Alonso's soldiers for signs of weakness, and the surrounding bailey for any avenue of escape. But he could not go, even were he free to do so, not with the Welshwoman still trapped within these walls.

Even as Raymond came to that conclusion, Alonso increased the pressure of the blade at his back. Gradually, it pierced his skin. Little by little, it drove deeper. A small twist, and sweat drenched Raymond's tunic. He bit his tongue and closed his eyes. He would not run. He would not make a sound. Over the years Alonso had made many such attempts to break him. The devil could claim his soul before he allowed that to happen.

Alonso sighed, and withdrew. ''Some other time, Raymond, have no doubt. Take him down, reeve.''

Chapter Eight

With a final grind of the key, the reeve locked the irons around Raymond's wrists. The knight went quite pale as Ceridwen watched, aghast. The Beauchamps were as vicious to each other as to their enemies. When they turned toward the great door leading to the bowels of the keep, she winced at the sight of a bright bloodstain across Raymond's lower back, and wondered if it was from his fight of the previous day. But it looked a fresh wound.

With a queasy lurch of her stomach, she realized Alonso must have been busy as they stood talking. Never had she considered that Raymond might need her aid, but in the space of two days he had fallen from his horse, been beaten senseless, stabbed, and was now on his way to a dark, noisome hole indeed.

As the reeve unlocked the door, Raymond bent his head to the older man and spoke to him. Ceridwen decided a bold approach was in order. Slinking about would only make her look as if she were doing something wrong. She dashed to the nearest kitchen shed, grabbed the first basket she came upon, stuffed it with straw and ran after the reeve and his prisoner.

"A handsome piece, that blade of yours," Raymond was saying. He glanced at her without a glimmer of recognition, and the shire reeve ignored her completely.

"Aye, it is, it is." The man rubbed an appreciative hand over the sword belted at his paunch.

"Did you win it in a wager? Or capture it in battle?"

"Nay, milord. I took it from a prisoner we have below."

"Has my brother dealt with this prisoner in person?"

Raymond asked the question casually, but looked as though every nerve in his body hummed. Except, Ceridwen thought, he often looked that way. Tense as a drawn longbow.

"Nay, he's never laid eyes on the scoundrel."

"May I see the blade before we go below and 'tis too dark?"

The reeve looked at him doubtfully. "On your honor, you'll play me no tricks?"

"I swear. Upon my honor. I wish to look upon one last thing of beauty."

Raymond's gaze flickered to Ceridwen and she felt herself blush. The reeve slid the ribbon of steel out halfway. No spot of rust marred its smooth length. The groove that served to decrease its weight was immaculate.

Raymond gave a low whistle. "'Tis magnificent. Draw it the rest of the way and turn it over."

Awyr's blade gleamed in the sun as it revolved.

Ceridwen saw that it was engraved, but could not read the inscription. Many swords, her father's included, had prayers and good-luck symbols etched into the metal.

Raymond swayed slightly and shook his head. "Forgive me. It seems I am overwhelmed by the day's events."

The older man responded gruffly, "Never mind." Sliding the sword back into place, he noticed Ceridwen at last. "Oy, lass, what do you want?"

Ceridwen had practiced a good deal of mummery with Rhys, to entertain the mobs of cousins and other children each Yuletide at Llyn y Gareg Wen. She fell into one of her more successful roles, gulping and rolling her eyes. "Puh-p-p-puhleese, sir, I have muh-muh-m-m-m-meeyorders, sir." She dangled the basket and tipped her head toward Raymond, then winked broadly at the reeve.

He raised bushy red brows. "Very well. But mind you cause no trouble, or I'll take it out of your pretty little hide."

Ceridwen nodded in spite of Raymond's scowl. She followed as the reeve took his charge beyond the metal studded gate that opened to the dank tunnels and cells below Alonso's keep.

The clean air and bright sky surrendered to must and gloom. Water trickled down the walls, leaving trails of slime. Their footsteps echoed, and fear seemed to ooze from the cracks of the stone, like a disease left behind by doomed men.

A pair of guards glanced up from their game of dice, and Ceridwen ducked her head as she recognized Will and Dirk.

"Here. I'll give you a place to yourself, Sir Raymond," the reeve offered, stopping before an empty, rough-hewn cell. "If this were your lord father's day, you'd be chained comfortable-like, upstairs in the solar. Never did he put a noble prisoner down here. 'Tis shameful, what the world's come to." The man shook his head.

Raymond gave him a withering look. "That is not your concern, but mine and Alonso's only. I have no desire to be in his solar, nor in a cell to myself. I want to see this fellow, and what manner of man he is to have such a weapon."

"I daren't put you in with poor Nat's murderer. That one's a lunatic, and best left undisturbed."

"I care not. I'd as soon have him handy, to taste the food before me. Who was this Nat, anyway?"

"A stout lad, and popular in the village, if a bit brash. Tom Forester found him, run clean through. 'Twas only a sword such as this one could have done the deed so slick. That was the damning evidence, the prisoner's possession of it."

The reeve chortled and patted the treasure hanging from his belt. "And the jest of it is, milord, they said the churl's conniving wench claimed poor Nat's attentions were unwelcome! Most like he'd not the coin she'd demanded once the sport was over, and her partner took care of it, the wicked sod."

Ceridwen shuddered at the remembrance of the lad's "attentions," even as renewed concern for Awyr's plight furrowed her brow. In truth the jest was upon that poor wretch, here for a killing Beauchamp had committed—on her behalf.

Raymond cleared his throat. "What a tale. But in truth, I was the one who spitted that miserable oaf."

Ceridwen stared, surprised by his ready admission.

The reeve's mottled cheeks turned a dusky red. "Nay!" He put his palm possessively over the hilt of the exquisite sword.

Then his brow cleared. "One charge more or less'll not matter. Hanging's still the penalty for poaching."

Raymond narrowed his eyes. "I take my own consequences, reeve. You have orders, follow them."

The reeve sighed. "Willy! Bring the ring, man." He flicked expertly through the tangled mass of huge keys handed to him and selected one. The wavering light of the torches added some illumination to the small space as he shoved the door open. The smell of old urine, rat dung and rotting straw wafted through to the corridor in a pungent flow.

Ceridwen peered between the men. Awyr lay quite still on the floor, his nose bloodied and distorted, his eyes nearly swollen shut, the rest of his face a patchwork of cuts and bruises. Raymond glanced back at the reeve, then at Will the guard. "Someone started early on his punishment?"

"Resisting, milord. Needed subduction." William swelled with importance. "I bear the painful proof of it." He flexed at the knees slightly, and his hand strayed toward his crotch, as if to make an adjustment.

"Aye, Willy's not the same, is he?" The reeve laughed out loud, and William's brow grew a pair of deep creases.

Raymond's expression turned feral. "Bring me ale and a lamp."

"Aye, milord." The reeve hesitated, then removed Raymond's irons. "D'ye want the girl left with ye?"

Raymond eyed Ceridwen and her basket. "What have you got there?"

"Muh-m-m-med-meh… Bandages, sir."

None too gently he pulled her into the cell. The reeve and Will bowed, shutting the door as they left. Raymond's hand tightened around her wrist. "What the devil are you up to, creeping about in a place like this?" His eyes gleamed with unexpected ferocity.

Even as she opened her mouth to protest such rudeness, he forestalled her objection with a swift, thorough kiss. It left her gasping, as much with indignation as with the heady splendor of his touch. Even Beauchamp looked stunned.

"I—I didn't mean to do that."

Ceridwen still trembled from the shocking burst of his passion. Unable to look him in the face yet, she turned to Awyr. "He needs attention. As does your back. And no doubt the rest of you, after the beating you took yesterday."

Raymond rubbed his brow. "'Tis of no import. Let me see to him." He knelt on one knee beside the still form on the floor, and carefully lifted the man's head. "Have you indeed bandages?"

"Nay, I wish it were true."

"Then help me take off my boot."

Wincing, he eased his leg around, still cradling Awyr's bloodied head. Loosening the laces, Ceridwen worked the soft leather down and slipped the boot free. Raymond folded its top and slid it beneath the man's skull. "I felt no fracture. Mayhap 'tis just a bump."

Ceridwen wondered at his concern. "Do you know, Sir Raymond, that here lies the 'ghost' we saw?"

He stared at her, and even in the dim light the windhole afforded, his eyes were intensely blue, like the heart of a flame. "Surely not." He fingered a tattered scrap of red cloth clinging to Awyr's threadbare tunic.

"Aye, they are one and the same. He is quite harmless."

"Not so. The reeve took an excellent and lethal blade from him. I want him to wake up, so I may ask him whence he got it."

"He is mute."

"He will tell me, especially if he's a grave-robber."

"Nay! You will not bully this man, he is my friend!"

Raymond raised a dark brow. "You should be more careful whom you befriend. And what of Hamfast?"

"He ran away at first light, before we were arrested."

"Grendel?"

"He fled, too, after you were brought down."

A smile curved Raymond's lips, or what passed for a smile with him. "Good. One or both of them will find their way to Rookhaven, and Giles will be warned." He turned back to Awyr, who breathed noisily through his broken nose.

Ceridwen drew herself taller. "To answer your first question,

sir, I am here to rescue him. I had not thought at first you would
be here too, but—"

"Rescue him! *You* need rescuing, from yourself, as well as
from this place. As you say, I am here, so don't trouble yourself
with any more of your plans. I will get you out. Both of you."

"Did you truly intend him to be your taster against poison?"

He looked at her as if she were an idiot child. "What do you
think?"

"I think your arrogance is beyond all reason! But I can't
believe you would let him die for you in that manner."

"Not him. Not anyone." Raymond straightened as the lock
rattled and William entered, bearing the promised brew, and a
small oil lamp. The tiny flame made the guard's shadow loom
huge on the wall, as he shuffled from foot to foot.

At the deadly look in Raymond's eyes Ceridwen shrank back,
and the guard, noticing it at last, stammered, "My lord?"

Raymond nodded towards Awyr. "What will happen to
him?"

"Monday's 'is hanging day. He needs to get better, afore he
gets worse, if ye take my meaning. His lordship wants him kicking and screaming. To set an example."

"Aye. Well do I know the power of example, Will." Raymond bared his teeth in anything but a friendly way.

The guard began to stumble backwards. "Aught else you
need, just call out." Hastily he withdrew.

Raymond poured some of the ale onto his under-tunic and
washed the man's face, cleaning the blood from cheeks, chin
and forehead. "Will is a filthy swine to beat a defenseless starve-
ling." He turned to Ceridwen with a glare. "And he struck you
as well!" His voice trailed off into a guttural snarl.

Not appreciating the reminder of her own aching bruises, Ceridwen watched as Beauchamp smoothed back Awyr's matted
forelock. Then a chill ran through her gut. The skin on his brow
was scarred, deep and red, impressed with a brand in the shape
of a small, precise crescent. "What is that?"

"The work of Saracens," Raymond said slowly.

"Holy Mary…" Ceridwen crossed herself. "Have they come,
then? How did they cross the sea in secret? I—"

"Lady, the Saracens are not here. This man went to their lands, I trow. He must have been a crusader."

Ceridwen's jaw dropped. "Then why does his family force him to live in the wild, like an animal, after such service?"

Raymond gave no reply, for his heart was beating wildly within his chest, his mind racing with possibilities. The fumes from the drink seemed to have some effect, for the injured man awoke, and peered intently at Raymond's face. The bruised blue eyes welled, and to Raymond's dismay, the fellow began to weep. Helping him to sit up, he put the jug of ale into the man's hands and urged him to drink. "It will make you feel better."

The crusader took a long swallow, then wiped his puffy lips and eyes with the back of his wrist. He looked from Ceridwen to Raymond, saying nothing.

"He whistles marvelous well," Ceridwen offered.

"Does he?" Breathing was now becoming difficult, and Raymond grew restless under the man's relentless gaze. Patience. He must sit and wait for the truth. Thirsty work. He took the jug from his silent companion's unresisting hands and drank deeply, tilting his head back.

Cold, clammy fingers crept across Raymond's throat, like the delicate feet of a salamander. He choked and almost dropped the heavy bottle, checking his impulse to clout the fellow in the head with the earthenware jug. The fingertips traced the scar Alonso's dagger had left under his jaw, so long ago.

Gently, Raymond reached up and pulled the questing hand from his neck. "What are you doing, my friend?"

"R-Raymie?"

That utterance of two syllables, barely audible through the man's cracked lips, made Raymond's heart take pause. Joyous, aching disbelief flooded him. There was indeed a God in heaven, who listened and heard and answered prayers, even those of a monstrous sinner like himself. No grave-robber could know him, or his pet-name.

"Percy?" Raymond whispered past the closing of his own throat. "Parsifal?" He reached out and touched the man's hollow, tear-streaked cheek. "You always did weep too readily." He pulled his brother to his chest and held him tight, rubbing his hand up and down Percy's knobby spine to soothe his shivering, as he had done so often, a mere lifetime ago.

A faint moan told him he was squeezing too hard, and he eased his grip. "They've kicked you as well as used their fists, have they not?"

Percy nodded slowly. Raymond's face contorted and his body tensed. All his considerations of reform vanished before the onslaught of rage rushing through his veins. Percy cringed at the sight of him, and Ceridwen remained frozen in her place.

"Alonso will pay for his crimes against you, Parsifal. I shall drag him naked to the dolmen. I shall lay him down and cut out his heart. My falcons will rend his flesh. My hounds will dine upon his entrails. Alonso the Fair shall lie as carrion, until his bones are dust and his name is forgotten."

Raymond glimpsed Percy's horrified expression and stopped his tirade. His brother winced and shook his head vehemently. Ceridwen had covered her face with her hands. Raymond fought down his temper. "I'm sorry, I'm sorry to frighten you two. But why do you not speak, Percy? Have you forgotten how?"

The younger man mouthed the word "nay." He coughed and cleared his throat. "I hid."

Raymond caught the hoarse words and nodded. "You hid from your enemies. Where?"

Percy raised his hand to his forehead in an eloquent gesture. "I went inside, and once there I could not find my way out." The effort of a full sentence seemed to drain him, and he opened his mouth slightly to take in a breath.

"Don't worry, lad. All will be well. I will get you out of here, and you'll come and live with me. I shall buy you a snow-white palfrey, and we will go hunting, and hawking, and..." Raymond's voice died away as he saw desolation creep into his brother's eyes. The once-handsome face closed in on itself, as if the thoughts of normalcy and happiness were too much to bear.

Raymond stood and looked around in desperation. Cold stone walls. Rusty shackles. He clenched his fists. No way out. A plump brown rat came scuttling up and boldly sniffed at his boot on the floor next to Percy. Ceridwen gave a small shriek.

Raymond kicked the rat with his still-shod foot, throwing his weight-bearing knee into agony. He cursed and the rat squeaked shrilly as it flew. It struck the wall and fell down dead. Raymond sat heavily to rub his limb. "Filthy nuisance."

A shuffling sound caused him to look up. Percy crawled over to the rat. Raymond's heart plummeted as his brother picked up the limp body and cradled it in his hands. Percy stroked the rough fur, and rocked to and fro with his eyes closed. Raymond choked as memories flooded in, of little Percy and his obsession with small pets. Field mice, sparrows, hedgehogs, kittens.

Raymond grabbed fistfuls of his own hair and tugged. His eyes burned and his chest ached. "Oh, God. Percy, I beg of you, forgive me, I did not know."

Ceridwen caught his weeping brother into her arms. Her offering of comfort seemed as natural to her as killing was natural to him. Raymond turned away, clutching his agony to himself. He too mourned, for yet another life wasted.

Chapter Nine

Ceridwen huddled in a corner of the cell, still stunned by the turn of events. Parsifal, alive! A shell of a man, indeed, but breathing nonetheless. After her impulsive embrace, he had fallen back into a fitful sleep.

Staring at his brother, Raymond's only movement was the irregular tensing of his jaw. A few remnants of light still found their way down the windhole, but they were fading fast. Ceridwen dreaded the prospect of spending a night in the dungeon again, and with Raymond, even more—at least that was what she tried to tell herself.

Apart from that, what if she could not help Parsifal to freedom? What if they decided to hang Raymond along with him? Along with the dark, fear crept closer, winding around her throat in a stranglehold.

Her skin tingled and she looked up to see that Beauchamp was now regarding her. To what purpose, she did not know, but his gaze felt predatory, as though she was pinned in place. Taking up her basket, she stood. Somehow that seemed more proper than squatting on the floor. When Raymond returned his attention to his brother she leaned against the cold wall and closed her eyes.

"There lies a knight slain 'neath his shield, his hounds they lie down at his feet, so well they do their master keep."

A lament, sung in perfect pitch and control, shimmered softly through the prison. Ceridwen listened, entranced. The dark, rich beauty of the singer's voice sent chills of appreciation surging through her body. It was both heartbreaking and inspiring to hear such a melody in such a place. She kept her eyes closed, the better to hear each nuance of sound. But all too soon, it ended.

She opened her eyes, half expecting to see a fourth person locked up with them. It was so unlike him, but… "Sir Raymond? You can sing thus?"

He glanced her way, blinked once, but did not reply. For an instant she wondered if she had dreamed the song. Parsifal had not stirred, but fresh tears glistened in his lashes. Then, abruptly, Raymond got to his feet, approached her, and everything vanished from her mind but his physical presence.

Even as the light waned, her awareness of him grew. She breathed in deeply. Up close, he had such a comforting smell, of ordinary things. Animals and work and warmth. He was still a Beauchamp, but at the moment that did not seem so important. Anyone who could sing with such feeling definitely had a heart. Even this Englishman. And that he loved his younger brother was painfully obvious.

"You've made Parsifal weep, even as he slumbers. Now when he wakes, his sorrow will be eased," she said.

"Only a Welshwoman would conclude such nonsense," Raymond growled, revealing no trace of that other, velvet voice. "Come to me." He caught her arms and drew her towards him.

"What are you doing?" Ceridwen stiffened in resistance. He was tall, commanding, he knew…everything, and she did not. "Why must you be so beastly?"

He tugged on the handle of her basket, pulling her yet closer. "Because, lady, I am so glad you are here, that if I did not maintain my angry edge, and thus provoke yours, I might disgrace myself before you." In silence he ran his fingertips down her arms, raising gooseflesh.

His confession touched Ceridwen and eluded her at the same time. "Your words confound me."

"I would have you rolling on the floor with me. Is that plain enough?"

"Why would anyone want to roll on the floor of this stinking midden?"

"You're such a child."

"I am a woman." Of that much she was certain.

"Are you? Show me." Warm hands slipped around her waist.

"You have seen far too much of me already. And even were it not so dark I would not allow you sight of me again."

"Ah, well, I have no need to see, after all."

To no avail Ceridwen wriggled to free herself from his encircling hands. Her body warmed of its own accord, in spite of the chill air. "My lord, leave my virtue intact, for pity's sake. I am but flesh and blood, just as you are."

"And you wish my flesh to remain apart from yours."

"Nay. Aye. I'm not—"

"What, not ready? Not excited? Not in love?"

Ceridwen determined not to let him make her angry. "You badger me, my lord."

"And you tempt me."

His quiet words surprised her with their intensity. His fingers pressing along her back made her want to lean against him, to take refuge in his strength, but some instinct restrained her. He *was* perilous, as he had warned her. Now his powerful hands drifted again to her waist, and he rubbed along her ribs with his thumbs.

He drew her closer, until his hips touched hers. A delectable and surely forbidden sensation flared, deep within. A bright image of him came to mind. His unruly hair with its layers of light and dark. The sharp, blue gleam of his eyes. The habitual side-tilt of his head. The criss-cross of scars on his knuckles.

But now he seemed unfamiliar. A shadowy being of the night. Heat radiated from his body. She craved his warmth, and something else. Arms at her sides, Ceridwen's grip tightened on the handle of her basket, but she did not pull away from Raymond's embrace. His palms followed the contours of her hips and waist upward, making her muscles tense and recoil at his touch, even as she pressed closer.

"Ah, sweeting, you bubble and boil, beneath that tight lid of yours," he said.

His intimate handling of her was shameless, and she relished it. His hands lingered at her breasts, quickening them in a way she had never before experienced. Long fingers slid up to her temples, crossed her cheeks and then trailed down and around her throat to rest upon her shoulders.

"You are a beauty." His voice held reverence.

"I am not. You mustn't say such things."

"I will say what I like." Raymond's breath was warm upon Ceridwen's cheek, and his lips brushed her face on their way to her mouth. He wrapped her up against his lean body.

"Please, no." Her heart tripped and the basket dropped to the floor. Her hands found their own way around his waist and up his back. She crushed the raw, nubbed linen of his surcoat in her fists as Raymond's lips, haloed faintly with ale, covered hers. His tongue slipped into her, caressed her, fanned the embers of desire she had denied.

Ceridwen pulled back, then found herself returning each thrust he made into her mouth. Her thigh climbed his, and his hands squeezed her against him. An aching tingle sparked to life, in a region far below her mouth.

To feel such things was wrong. Truly wicked. Even were Raymond already her husband she would surely burn in hell for it. But his touch felt so right, so good. His kiss was intoxicating, full of restrained passion, like the prayer of a kneeling priest. And she was the altar before him.

An unwelcome voice in her mind warned her—this was the path down which lustful men led innocent lasses, to an end always hinted at, but never yet revealed. She must resist him and her own wanton inclinations. At last she began to understand what the parish priest meant by temptation. But, even if it did mean going to hell, then so be it.

She clung to Raymond, basked in his confident embrace, returned his kisses with a passionate abandon that let her spirit soar. Slowly and slowly, he brought her down from the mindless and all-too-brief flight she had taken, easing his mouth from hers until only their foreheads touched.

"Sweetness pours from you, like a balm to my weary heart," Raymond whispered, and smoothed back the hair from her face. He gave her lips a final, soft brush with his.

"Oh," was all Ceridwen could say. Perhaps being wed to this man would not be such a bad thing, after all.

"Well, milady, I must congratulate Percy." Releasing her, he bent down and rummaged through the straw.

"Why is that?" She swayed without his solid support to steady her.

Raymond straightened, and wrapped her fingers around the willow handle of her basket. "He is fortunate to have a bride like you to look forward to."

Ceridwen choked. "What?"

He narrowed his eyes, as if a phantom sun pained them. "Had you forgotten? You were promised to him once. Now he is here, so that troth must be honored." Raymond's voice was flat.

A wave of emptiness enveloped Ceridwen. She felt dizzy without him holding her in the dark, and staggered backwards.

Raymond was with her in an instant. "Are you ill?" He held her waist, and with that contact the silence between them grew taut as a bowstring. "What is wrong?"

"Nothing," she said at last, anger tightening her voice. How dare he warm her like that, only to abandon her into an icy desolation? Parsifal needed sanctuary, not a wife.

"I see." Raymond's tone was bleak as a windswept moor. "'Tis just as well."

Why did she feel overwhelmed by grief and guilt, when she should be rejoicing at the miracle of a man's return from the dead, Beauchamp or not? And why did Raymond sound so bereft?

"You're his. I had no right to kiss you. I will not do it again." He gave her upper arms a squeeze. "Help him, Ceridwen, *ma cygnette noire*… Look after him for me. He needs someone like you, someone gentle and innocent."

Ceridwen was surprised at how much she enjoyed the sound of soft words rolling off his tongue in Norman French. And she still found it hard to believe that such a man, with so much blood on his hands—Welsh blood, she reminded herself—could express such tender concern for his brother. Not to mention how he made her feel. She forced her voice into lightness. "Surely once we find a way, you will escape with us and see to him yourself?''

"I cannot. I am honor-bound to remain as Alonso's hostage until my ransom is paid. He does not truly want the silver, though he'd take it gladly enough. 'Tis the game he enjoys, as ever. When he tires of the play, he will set me free.''

"I do not understand you or your rules of chivalry.''

"That is because my brothers and I bend and twist them until they are unrecognizable.''

"That much is true. But the idea of my wedding, of anyone wedding Parsifal now is absurd. My father has made it clear—''

As if she were not speaking, Raymond picked up the small oil lamp and placed it carefully in her basket. "Do not drop that, and don't smother it.'' He stepped over to the door and banged on it. "Oy! Will! I have finished with this smelly wench. Come and take her off my hands.''

Unreasoning panic seized her. "What are you doing? Do not let them have me, please!''

"Percy, wake up! Time to go.'' Raymond hauled his brother to a sitting position and patted his cheeks until he opened his eyes. "Hold his hand, lady, and follow me out.''

With no other choice, she did as he commanded. Percy yawned, then winced. "Who are you?'' he blurted, staring at her much the way she had when she'd mistaken him for a ghost.

"Pull yourself together, Percy. You know her, she is called Ceridwen.'' Raymond hopped a bit as he pulled his boot on.

"I know her. I do.'' Percy stood and swayed. "Let us go.''

"He is not used to strong drink.'' Beauchamp steadied his brother. "Here comes Will. Stand aside.''

"Has the wheesh not been satisfact'ry, milord? There's allus Rose, I'll wager she'll come down if ye promise her a ha-ha-ha'penny.'' From his hiccoughing speech, Will was well on his way to passing out.

The door creaked open. Raymond's fist smashed between William's eyes and the man dropped like a stone. With Percy safely through, Raymond grabbed the guard's torch and tossed it into the cell they had left. A blaze erupted as what dry straw there was caught fire.

Under cover of the billowing smoke, he led them to what looked like a dead end.

"Oy! What goes there?" Heavy footsteps echoed from an upper level.

"Quick, over here." Raymond showed them to a low door, hidden behind a turn of the rock. With Percy's help he unbarred it and they entered a narrow tunnel. They wound their way through dripping rock and over chunks of rotting timbers, climbing steadily. The men had to crouch to avoid hitting their heads on the support beams, and the tiny oil lamp did little to combat the darkness.

"This leads to one of the posterns. To an open field beyond the walls," Percy said.

"You remember well, brother."

"Sir Raymond, you're hobbling," Ceridwen observed.

Ignoring her remark, Raymond halted. "Once out, run hard to the cover of the woods. Follow the brook to the River Usk, then go north. With luck you will meet Giles and Wace. Tell them not to come here."

They reached the door that led to the outside, lifted the bar and pushed. A bitter wind swept through the opening, instantly snuffing the lamp. The trees across the field were hidden in darkness, but their sighs and creaks were clearly audible.

"Go, go!" Raymond urged them through, holding the door.

Percy faced his brother. "How can I leave you again? How will you forgive me?"

"I'll not forgive you unless you get out of here." Raymond gave Percy a thump on his back. Percy stood his ground. Raymond addressed Ceridwen. "What are you waiting for?"

She turned to him, unable to simply walk away, even to save herself. Though staying was his own choice, he might never see freedom again. She could not force him to come away, but she could give him something. "Kiss me again."

"Oh, woman, I cannot. I dare not."

"Then I will kiss you." A gust whipped Ceridwen's hair across her face as she put her hands on Raymond's broad shoulders. He swept the silken mass aside. Standing tiptoe, she hesitated, her lips a whisper away from his, and in that instant the postern slammed shut.

"Damn!" Abandoning her kiss, Raymond tried the door. It would not budge. A powerful leap shook Ceridwen's heart at the thought he would not re-enter that hole. His fingers bit into her arm. "I will see you safe to Giles, then return myself."

Ceridwen shook her head. "Nay!"

Percy touched his brother's hand. "'Tis better to come away, Raymond. God has a purpose in everything."

Raymond looked heavenward. "Why must I suffer such fools? Come on, then!"

Ceridwen ran and stumbled her way over the tufted grass, Raymond tugging and half-dragging her when she fell behind. She could not understand him. Why, when he was free and had friends to escort him home, would he insist upon returning to Alonso's custody? But when did men make sense, especially lords?

Besides, how had her own heart made the treacherous shift to caring for a Beauchamp? She understood her compassion for Parsifal. He was an innocent at heart, and had befriended her unquestioningly. But there was no excuse for the bewildering morass of feelings Sir Raymond aroused in her.

She could not begin to describe them, so unfamiliar were they. And some felt very good indeed. His hands on her waist. His lips on her neck. His tongue in her mouth.

Ceridwen shivered and sucked in a breath of cold air. Icy drops began to fall, and a flicker in the sky was followed by a low rumble. They reached the forest as the rain increased to penetrating intensity, blown horizontal by the wind.

"I can't see a damned thing," Raymond snarled.

The lightning flashed more frequently, and every accompanying rumble sounded louder than the one before.

"But the storm lights the way for us." The wild night filled Ceridwen with exhilaration, and the sense of heaven speaking to earth thrilled her. She wanted to run, gulping up the clean, raw air, but Raymond was limping more since the dash across the field.

Parsifal was of little help. He wandered, stopping here and

there to touch the trees, or to simply stand looking upward, letting the rain fall into his mouth. At this rate dawn would catch them still miles from the river.

But finding the way was not as easy as Raymond had made it sound. The song of the brook was hard to catch as long as the thunder rumbled. Then she saw a faint flicker ahead, as though a little piece of lightning had been left behind. "Lord Raymond. Look, what is that?"

Raymond stared. "Jesu! That accursed stag has come for me again!" He began to run toward it, heedlessly crashing through the brambles. "Demon beast! You will not lure me and lead me to unholy places. Come here and I'll slit your throat for you!"

"Nay, Raymond, do not!" Parsifal cried out as his brother floundered through the undergrowth, the eerie light ahead of him. "Leave it alone! It brought me to the dolmen, and you, as well!"

At this a sudden chill ran through Ceridwen. "Sir Raymond, stop! Wait for us!"

She took Parsifal's hand and together they caught up to him. He stood in a small clearing, holding his hands over his face, his hair hanging in sodden strands. He whirled around fiercely as they approached. "I hate this."

Parsifal looked stunned. "He made me leave you, Raymie."

"I know, Percy. I would have made you leave, too, had you tried to stay."

Parsifal's hand hovered over Raymond's shoulder as if he was not certain it was solid. "D-did you die, too? I did not mean to kill you. Or was it only me who died?"

Ceridwen stared. Had they both gone mad?

"Nay, Percy. You didn't kill me, 'twas an accident. There was a lot of blood, but you have seen for yourself that the wound has healed. And you, Percy, are here with me again. Right, Lady Ceridwen?" Raymond caught both of his brother's hands and shot her a pleading look.

"Oh, aye, of course."

"Ceridwen will be your bride, Percy. She was promised to you long ago."

"But I do not want to marry. I know nothing of women." Parsifal returned from his dazed state.

"Who does?" Raymond countered. "But you need not know much. You will quickly learn the bits that count."

Parsifal's face wore a strange look, of consternation, as though he were trying to remember something. He crouched into a ball and hugged himself.

"The contract is null and void, Sir Raymond," Ceridwen said in an urgent undertone, and knelt to comfort Parsifal.

"*He* does not know that. A promise was made and it shall be kept. He needs you. Can you not see that? Look at him!"

"Then I will be his good-sister, and care for him. Why must I marry him? He does not want to, and you cannot make me." Ceridwen heard the childish tone in her voice but could not help it. She helped Percy to his feet.

"We shall discuss your marriage at a more convenient time, Mademoiselle." Raymond whipped his head around and his hair flung strings of water into Ceridwen's face. "Where did it go?"

"Where did what go?"

"The stag. I must find it. There! Damn, that jailer yet has my dagger." He headed into the trees beyond the clearing and she had no choice but to follow.

Parsifal jogged by her side. "Do not worry, Lady Ceridwen. He gets wild like this sometimes. It usually happens when he doesn't get his way. Or wants something he cannot have."

Ceridwen ached from the cold, and her wool skirts dragged, heavy with water. What could Raymond possibly want that he couldn't have? A man like him simply took whatever he desired.

Just as Alonso did.

Chapter Ten

Shafts of misty sunlight pierced through the trees, and twigs caught on Ceridwen's soggy skirts as she brushed past. She had survived the wettest night of her life. And nearly the coldest. But the chase after the stag had brought them to the river, and Raymond and Parsifal had sheltered her between them when at last they stopped to rest. Their protective embrace had warmed her heart as much it had her body.

They pushed on, and the river guided them with its rushing voice that changed with every boulder and tree-fall it met. Ceridwen caught the tang of drifting smoke. The sound of an axe echoed as it struck wood, and a horse nickered.

"I will see if 'tis Giles." Raymond motioned them to stay back while he went ahead. He nearly hopped on one leg instead of walking. Ceridwen had not dared ask him to let her check his knee, or the wound in his back. She stopped with Parsifal in a copse of trees and resigned herself to wait.

"Oy!" Raymond called out. "St. Germaine!"

"Hey—hey! His lordship lives!" After a few moments, Giles appeared, retying his braes, his usual robust glow intact.

"Too much ale last night, eh? Not that this forest needs more watering." Raymond received Giles's customary back thumping with good grace.

"Raymond, thank God you've made it safe. Hamfast brought Grendel, then the storm delayed us, and the Usk's flooding must have cut Lucien off. We were about to come after you."

"I am going back, Giles. As soon as I've eaten, I will be away."

"Nay! I will not have it!" Giles's face turned several shades darker, and though there was not much difference in their heights, he managed to loom over Raymond. "You may command me, you may berate me, even threaten me, my lord, but you will not return to Alonso's care."

"Giles, 'tis a point of honor, and you know as well as—"

"Damn your honor. Damn your pride! Look at you. You're half starved, lame, and soaked to the bone. They will break their fast with you, and have but a scrap left over for supper."

"Get the hell out of my way, so I can find a man who will yet obey me." Raymond shouldered past Giles, who was left staring into the faces of Ceridwen and Percy as they emerged from the shrubbery. He smiled pleasantly at them, and bowed as if he were at court, greeting expected guests.

"Giles St. Germaine, at your service. My lady Ceridwen, I have awaited you with great anticipation. And you, sir…?"

"Parsifal de Beauchamp." Percy turned to Ceridwen with a questioning look. "Should I know him?"

Giles stood frozen, his mouth open, his hands extended to Percy. "Good lord…where did you come from?"

"Well, I was born in the château of my grandfather in Rouen, and as I understand it—"

"Forgive me, my lord. I meant of late. I cannot tell you how pleased I am to see that you live. You must relate all your adventures to me. And to think—well, never mind. Come along, the both of you. We'll get you warm and you can help me talk some sense into Raymond. He has gone beyond the pale again, with his stubbornness."

Later, Ceridwen closed her eyes and savored the spicy stew she'd been served. It burned her tongue but the pain was worth the sensation of heat in her stomach. She huddled by the small fire, wrapped in Giles's scratchy woolen mantle. Her wet overgown was spread over a rope tied between two trees.

"Cruikshank. Have you a moment?" Giles addressed a thickset man to Ceridwen's right. "Come take a look at Raymond, eh?"

The man grunted and nodded. Wisps of colorless hair emerged from beneath his woolen hood, and his florid face bore many scars. As he followed Giles, she could see from his rolling gait that one leg was shorter than the other. A man of experience. She might learn something. Setting aside her bowl, Ceridwen tucked the wrap snugly about herself and trailed after them.

Throughout the encampment, dozens of warriors of varying rank stared as she wound her way past. She grew increasingly nervous under their combined scrutiny. Some of these hard-eyed men, English, Scots, Franks and Danes, made her father's seem almost gentlemanly by comparison. Whistles and kissing noises followed her passage. The mercenaries grinned and leered and punched each other's arms.

With relief she neared a pavilion of heavy blue-and-white striped cloth. Inside, Raymond lay as if in state. One brawny, bare leg was exposed, and his knee rested on a rolled-up pelt. Ceridwen could not help but smile. He was helpless as a babe.

"Cruikshank, welcome," he said. "Giles here will not allow me to get up. Tell him to stop this foolishness and let me go, as I must." Raymond peered past Cruikshank's bulk to Ceridwen.

Emboldened, she stuck out her tongue at him. He scowled and spoke to Giles, who shrugged and approached her deferentially.

"My lady, Sir Raymond desires that you enter his sanctuary, sit beside him, and hold his hand while we attend his injuries."

"I damn well desire nothing of the kind!"

"You cannot stop her, though. Come, Lady Ceridwen, he may behave if you are present." Giles led her by the hand into the tent, to a folding seat. "Parsifal allowed us to patch his face without complaint. We need you whole, so do not be difficult."

Raymond crossed his arms over his chest and refused to look at Ceridwen. "I'm naked."

"Nonsense."

"As good as. Ahh…"

Cruikshank wrapped Raymond's swollen knee with linen and handed the bucket and ladle to Ceridwen. "Soak him. Every tenth breath. Cold, straight from the river." Then, to her astonishment, he patted her on the head. "This one'll do, Beauchamp," he said with a wink, and departed.

"Nay. Lady, get you gone." Raymond's baleful glare skipped Ceridwen to rest upon Giles. "Wace shall do all the tending and pouring from now on."

Giles made no effort to fetch the squire.

"'Tis a conspiracy! All of you are in collusion to impress this woman upon me when I cannot…help myself."

Raymond met Ceridwen's gaze at last, and his eyes gleamed, like the bottomless reflection of the sky in a forest pool. A pool overlaying quicksand. The footing around him was so very treacherous, and here she stood, right beside him. She paused, brimming ladle in hand, and to her dismay felt her eyes well up.

Raymond looked about with an air of panic. Giles and Cruikshank were gone. "Now you know me for the coward I am, when it comes to women," he said matter-of-factly. He raised his hand to his mouth and concentrated on gnawing his thumbnail.

"I know you for a fool." Ceridwen wiped her cheeks.

He looked up sharply. "Your manners are atrocious. Did your mother not teach you to respect your elders, to say nothing of your betters?"

"I am sorry if the truth is painful. You spurn the love of Giles, Wace, everyone. They do their best to help you find happiness and you push them away. What a stupid man you are, to throw aside such riches in order to wallow in your own misery."

"Who are you to speak to me thus? You do not know me. I do not need them. And I do not need you."

His callous words cut into her. She had overstepped her bounds, but she had meant it for his own good. "I have a task to complete," she said softly.

"Oh, lady, I warn you…remain at your peril. If you had any sense you would run. Away from me. Even away from Percy. The same bad blood flows in his veins as it does mine."

"I know." Ceridwen carefully poured the water over his beleaguered limb.

Raymond tilted his head back and covered his face with the

crook of his arm. "For God's sake. What do you want from me?"

"What gives you thought that you have anything I might want? Or need, for that matter?"

"I have plenty of what you need," he growled.

"And what might that be?"

"You do not want to find out," he snapped, uncovering his eyes. "Leave me. While you still can."

"No." She pulled the mantle tighter around her shoulders and went back to sit by the head of his bed.

"Why do you stare?" he demanded.

"I find you…interesting."

"As a fawn finds the grin of the hound, I suppose."

"Nay, in truth I might compare you to a crystal. Dreary and colorless apart from the sun. But once before it, it sparkles and spreads rainbows all around, in an endless whirlwind of light." Ceridwen realized she had leaned toward him, and sat back.

Raymond grunted, an abbreviation of a laugh. "You could not possibly see that in me."

"Not yet, Lord Raymond. You are half dead. Still in the dark, black and buried."

"How can you tell? You're but a child." He stared at the pattern of sunlight dappling the tent fabric.

"I am an old child. Older than you are." Ceridwen spoke with the confidence of absolute knowledge.

"Now you speak in riddles. I have thirty winters. What have you, all of sixteen?" Raymond challenged her with his look.

She merely smiled at him. "Nineteen. But I have lived with my heart open all my life. You locked yours up ages ago, and no one can get in. So for those years, you were not alive."

Raymond frowned at Ceridwen, then went back to studying his ragged thumbnail. "You shame me with the clarity of your vision. I have no way to respond. But you are right. I died, as Percy said. Long ago. I was brought back to life, for a little while, before I perished yet again." He narrowed one eye at her. "This time, I do not think I can come back. The way is too painful, too long. And the ghosts…"

He dropped his gaze. Ceridwen felt no triumph that he looked away first. "I have one as well."

"A ghost?"

"Aye." She picked an invisible bit of debris from his bandage. "My dearest friend. He was slain four years past. Sometimes I think I feel his spirit near me still. I want to set things right for him somehow, but everything has changed."

"I do not follow you."

"Vengeance, Sir Raymond. You understand that, well do I know. I was going to extract the *galanas,* a high honor-price for his death, from the man responsible for it."

Raymond shifted to lean on one elbow. "Hmm. Was the culprit some cuckolded husband?"

"Nay! How dare you say such a thing? Not everyone is like you." Ceridwen looked straight at him.

He did not protest her implication, but merely tipped his head and closed his eyes partway. "Why have you not had your revenge?"

"I have yet to determine exactly who committed the atrocity. Then, someone got in the way, and I was diverted from my quest."

Raymond's eyes opened fully. "Who?" His voice died to a whisper.

"Can you not guess?"

He paused, studying her face. "Perhaps, for so has someone come between me and my desire for vengeance." His fingers twitched. He lifted his hand, as if to reach out to her, then curled it into a fist.

Ceridwen's insides constricted. Raymond's small, aborted gesture hurt. With a jolt she realized she wanted the contact, the feel of his skin against hers. But why? After all, she had intended to be a martyr to her father's cause, to sacrifice herself in a loveless marriage on behalf of her people.

But the thought of marrying Raymond did not fill her with the same horror it had at first. Her feelings had been far from noble purity when he had held her in his arms and kissed her. Did he not sense it too? Was he but playing with her? Or did he simply lust after her? She stood, her heart sore and bruised.

Every encounter with him ended in pain. She dumped the contents of the bucket over his leg. "I will send Wace back to attend you." Leaving him with a bewildered look upon his face, Ceridwen ran from the pavilion, desolation licking at her heels.

The tattered clouds fled, but the moon set and night fell thick and black upon the encampment. Raymond shivered as darkness crept from between the trees, sought him out, covered him in a breathless void. The deep woods. They hid things which never saw the light of day. Evoked memories that refused to stay buried. He hated lying awake for hours, alone amidst the whispers and moans and flutterings of the forest at night.

He had ordered all fires banked. Neither light nor smoke could reveal their presence in the event Alonso's scouts were out searching for him. He had decided to see Ceridwen safely back to Rookhaven, and Giles could take her to her father from there. Then once his knee was better he would return to Alonso on his own, not bound and led by a fat, greasy reeve. And when it was all over, Parsifal's sword would be restored to him.

But now she was here, in his tent, on the floor. His squire had been forced to drag her back from where she'd gone to pout at Cruikshank's fire circle, claiming she needed to dry her soggy overgown. Here was the safest, warmest place for her, surrounded by Wace, Percy, Giles and himself. Or would in his arms be even better? Raymond gripped the edges of his bed.

This was torture, pure and simple. He followed in Alonso's footsteps in spite of all his efforts otherwise. Lust for his little brother's betrothed plagued him. Murder still flickered on the edges of his mind. Revenge was the bitter poison in his blood. He would never be free of the dark passions consuming him. They were the threads that held him together. He had borne them so long he had forgotten any other way of being.

That very morning he had stared into Ceridwen's sea-green eyes, seeking relief from his own burning heat. Her gaze was clear and cool—she was insufferable when she was right. But he had provoked her into anger, and enjoyed the resultant smolder of her temper. And provoke her he must, in order to crush any heart-grown feelings toward him. She belonged to Percy.

But time and again she came too close to the truth. She understood him better than she ought. This day, for the first time, he had looked beyond the beauty of her form, past the fact she was a woman, to the essence of Ceridwen. He saw innocence and wisdom, compassion and fire, love and loyalty. Admirable qualities which made him feel even blacker by comparison. If only he could stop thinking of her lying within arm's reach.

One of the tent's occupants snorted in his sleep. From closer by came a sniffle. Then another, and another, until Raymond was sure it was the sound of Ceridwen weeping. The one soft spot in his heart began to ache. He raised himself on his elbow to peer down toward where she lay. He couldn't see her in the dark. The sniffing grew more pronounced, punctuated by half-smothered sobs.

Raymond reached out, thinking to find her shoulder, and over-balanced. The planks of his makeshift bed teetered and slipped from the trestles they straddled. He clutched at air and cursed, then slid and rolled, landing half on Ceridwen, and half on the dank matting of the floor, cold and wet from the water poured over his leg. She gave a little shriek. Raymond stifled a moan at the acute twist of pain in his knee.

"Shh—" He held his breath and finished his groaning in silence. The snores of their companions continued unabated. "'Tis only me," he whispered.

"Should I find that reassuring?" Ceridwen asked in a tear-congested voice.

"I merely fell out of bed."

"How convenient for you."

"I beg your pardon?" His knee throbbed. He should be making himself hateful, not offering solace to the sharp-tongued wench. Every time he acted on one of his infrequent inclinations to kindness, he got abused in the process.

"I said, how inconvenient for you." Ceridwen sniffed again. "Are you hurt?"

"Of course I am. What of you? I hope I have not squashed anything precious." Raymond put his hand out again and it met with something soft, tipped by a firm little nubbin. Ceridwen jerked away almost as fast as he did.

"I see you are damp and cold." He swallowed convulsively and stretched out gingerly alongside her, propping his head on his palm. He threw his blanket over her, careful this time not to touch her. "What were you blubbering about, anyway?"

"Oh, I do not wish to disturb you with that, my lord."

You can't help but disturb me. He was going about this all wrong. He should wake Giles, and have him help him back to his pallet. He should tell her to move down next to Percy—it was uncomfortable being this close to her. Increasingly so. *I should take her in my arms and kiss her silly.* "Go ahead. I cannot sleep with all this snoring. Percy's nose is swollen so he keeps breathing through his mouth."

"I noticed."

"Do not worry. By the time you wed him 'twill be healed."

Ceridwen made a strangled sound. "My lord Raymond. You have come right to the crux of the matter."

"What matter is that? You have nothing to be concerned about. You are secure in our hands. Or is that what bothers you?"

"You know what bothers me, sir."

"Do I?"

"If you do not then you are thicker than you pretend to be."

Raymond ignored Ceridwen's rudeness to continue with his own. "Very well…let us assume we both know of what we speak. Ours is a situation requiring great self-control. If that presents too much difficulty for you, being a lusty Welshwoman and all, then I shall remove myself immediately." He could hear her breathing quicken as her temper started to sizzle. So reliably inflammable.

"Please do. You would not want to put yourself in jeopardy, in such close quarters with a half-savage like me."

She was burning now. All he had to do was to feed the fire, and make certain she thought of him only with revulsion, then her heart would naturally turn to Percy. "I was just thinking the same thing. How would I fend off your advances, in my present state? 'Tis a sobering thought."

"Has it occurred to you that I may not find you the least bit attractive? That enduring your presence is a trial for me?"

"Nay, it has not. But it does not matter, because I know what you really mean to say." *Keep pushing, until she admits she hates me…how is it she always smells like rosewater? It must come out of her very skin.* Raymond moved closer, until he could make out the white of her face and throat against her black hair. "Say it again."

"What?" Ceridwen sounded annoyed.

"My 'presence is a trial for you.'" Raymond leaned toward her. His own breath came faster. Ceridwen gave a little gasp as his hand touched hers. His senses began to swirl in the disembodied feeling the darkness evoked. Giles was right. It *had* been a long time. "Ceridwen…"

"My presence is a trial for you," she whispered at last.

"'Tis indeed." Raymond breathed out a small sound, as one in pain might make.

"What ails you, my lord?"

"Nothing."

"As I have learned to lie, so have I learned to spot a liar. And you are such," Ceridwen said flatly.

"My body does not lie."

"Nor shall it, at least not with mine."

"You order me about as though I were one of your villeins—you call them *y taeogin*—right? Aye, and without a thought for the cost." Raymond slid his fingers up her arm.

"Cost of what?"

Ceridwen waxed indignant, but despite that, Raymond felt her shoulder relax beneath his hand. "Your disgraceful impertinence. Even young pages, eight-year-olds, know they should only speak when spoken to, and then with a bowed head. Your father has spoilt you. No wonder he is so anxious to marry you to me."

"My father loves me." Ceridwen shrugged off Raymond's hand.

"Of course. But he is not here, is he? What makes you think I will not put you in your place? Use my *droigt du seigneur?* Break you, so Percy will not have to?" His fingers found hers and tightened around them. So small, so delicate…

"Just you try." She met his grip with equal force.

It was useless. He did not wish even to pretend to bully her. "You truly believe me an animal, don't you?" *Was that not the point?*

"You are the Carrog Dhu. Everyone knows that."

"To merit such a name, I must breathe fire. Are you not afraid of being singed?"

"Hah! Your fire is out. You are a cold worm."

Worm indeed! "I have killed men for milder insults."

"That does not surprise me."

Raymond shifted into a more comfortable position—closer to Ceridwen—and farther from the soggy floor mats. "You bandy words with the ease of a royal courtier. But I will wager you have never been a day's ride away from home before, have you?"

"Nay. I was happy there…I never wanted to leave."

"Ah-ah—no more sniveling." He hated himself for his cruelty. He wanted to hold her close, to smell her hair…and soothe her with his presence, so that she might feel safe. But to treat her thus would be as bad as an outright lie. He would never let her in. Not her. Not anyone.

"My lord?" Her voice was small and watery.

"Aye?"

"Have you sent word to my father that I am well? Did your men find no sign of mine?"

"I am afraid they did not. Nor did I wish to tell your father you were well or ill when I was not sure which was true. I will get word to Morgan as soon as we reach Rookhaven. But why did you attempt to come to me on your own in the first place, Ceridwen?" Raymond realized he still held her hand, and fought the impulse to pull her towards him.

"'Twas my duty."

"And now? Do you still think only of duty?"

"Oh, how I wish it were so!"

Raymond tensed and his pulse leaped. A silence ensued, brimming with Ceridwen's effort to contain her need. Then, it spilled from her in a hoarse whisper.

"Hold me."

He could not. As much as he would like to, he could not. He

well knew the effects of warmth and darkness and loneliness when a woman like her lay so near a man like him. Only disaster and heartbreak could come of it.

He reached for her anyway. His lips brushed her mouth before she could pull away. One hand slid to her nape and the other around her waist. With a soft cry Ceridwen wrapped her arms around him and kneaded his back with her small hands. He buried his face in the fragrant luxury of her hair. Her touch was like a miracle, driving every thought but her from his mind. Slowly, Raymond parted her lips with his tongue. He reveled in her clean taste. In the aching sweetness of her tentative response. In the burgeoning strength of his own desire as she grew bolder in his embrace. She ran her tongue over his teeth, then nipped the bunched corners of his mouth. Given time and encouragement, her passion could equal his—he knew it.

He pressed her against the hard length of him and captured her thigh with his leg. He thirsted to possess her. Was thick with wanting her. Ceridwen's soft moans made Raymond smile around her kiss. He held her tighter, closer, and she slid her fingers into his hair, grasping handfuls of it.

She arched toward him, and he freed her breasts from the damp gown to warm them with his mouth. Her clinging arms and legs belied her small protests.

Raymond ignored the wrench of pain in his knee and rolled to cover her with his body. His breath grew ragged as he skimmed his hand down to find its way beneath Ceridwen's skirts, then up and up to touch the satiny skin of her hip. She stiffened and sucked in her stomach as his palm rubbed there, and a bit lower…she clamped her thighs, trapping his fingers.

What in God's name did he think he was doing? "Shh, little one…don't be afraid." Carefully Raymond withdrew his hand. She was untouched. And he was a beast. "Forgive me—"

He sat up and brought her with him. Ceridwen tucked her head beneath his chin. Her hot cheek lay against the bare skin of his neck, where his pulse still throbbed, as it did throughout the rest of him. She clung to him, all womanly curves, and the trickle of her tears slid into the hollow of his throat. He was sorry he had taken advantage of her vulnerability. Sorry he was so prone to her charms, with her rightful lord so close by.

Jesu, what had he done? The exact opposite of what he had intended. Perhaps it was not too late to undo the damage. Raymond took a deep breath and pulled away from her. "Why the tears? I took nothing you cannot spare. You were easy to breach, but other men might not be so patient with your teasing—"

Her palm struck his cheek with a loud slap. A righteous, well-aimed blow, even in the dark.

"I hate you, Beauchamp. You and your dead, lying heart. I felt something—'twas true and pure! I felt it and so did you. But you are a coward—hiding behind Parsifal—and a liar and a filthy hypocrite besides."

There. *I hate you.* She had finally uttered the words. He would hold them close and remember them, every time he found himself wanting her. "Hush now, say your prayers like a good girl and go to sleep. With the morning comes hope, to those who believe." *But not to me.*

"I should not have asked you for comfort," she said. "I will try to be more like you. Perhaps it *is* best to feel nothing."

Her low voice carried the words, like silver arrowheads. They pierced Raymond with cool, unerring aim, barbed and polished. He let the agony burn, farther and deeper inside than it had ever gone before. When at last he had willed the pain down to a faint twinge, he spoke. "It is, at that."

Chapter Eleven

An unusual quiet lay over the land as they approached Rookhaven. The fields, striped in chaff and dark, wet soil, lay deserted. Even the birds in the trees had stilled their voices. The group drew rein in the village, where every window was shuttered. Unease prickled up Ceridwen's spine. All was not well. Neither here, nor where any Beauchamp resided.

Wace hopped down from his horse and pounded on the local wheelwright's door. A portly man emerged, his bald head gleaming damply in the afternoon light.

"What goes here, Master Aelfson?" Wace asked.

"Oh, my lords, we've been taken by a terrible wicked bunch of cutthroats." The good fellow wrung his hands and rolled his eyes as he stood, surrounded by tall horses and a small army of bristling men. The various lords, knights and men-at-arms had gone home, but two dozen or so of Raymond's mercenaries remained.

Raymond nudged his mount forward. "Go on."

"They took my precious Annabelle, and had her all in pieces before ever I could stop them," Aelfson sobbed into his sleeve.

Wace drew his sword. "Where did they take her? I will kill the wretches!"

Ceridwen had never before heard the squire speak in anger, and realized he was no longer the shy, quiet lad he had been when first they met. Such was the Beauchamp influence—a peaceful boy turned avenger. Just as she had been influenced.

Raymond shook his head. "Easy, Wace. Annabelle is, or was, his favorite heifer. A regrettable loss to be sure. But not one worthy of murder," he drawled. "Pull yourself together, Aelf-son. Are they still without the gates, or have they gained entrance?"

"They are lolling in the meadows yonder, filling their faces with my Annie and using John Tapman for target practice."

He seems less concerned about poor John Tapman than his cow. Ceridwen patted her palfrey's neck as she listened.

"With what are they practicing?" Raymond's tone was sharp.

"Bows, my lord. Great long bows, gnarled and evil as can be. Their commander looks like the devil himself—short and dark, with black moustaches. He smiles constantly, baring his teeth. Unnatural they are, white as the bones of dead men."

Ceridwen's heart leaped. "Da!" She urged her horse forward. Raymond's hand on the bridle brought her up short.

"You are not going anywhere."

"I am. Get out of my way."

"You know not for certain who awaits us—"

"It can be no other." Ceridwen struggled to free her horse's reins from Raymond's grip.

"Stay here with Wace. Giles and I will go and greet this…visitor. If he offers us resistance we shall make shorter work of him than he is already."

"Nay. You Beauchamps have already killed too many of my people. I will not stand by to watch it happen again," Ceridwen said hotly.

"I will not stand here arguing with you. Be quiet and stay put." Raymond cantered away at a leisurely pace, Giles at his side.

Ceridwen stared after them. Her da was close by. And no Englishman was going to stop her from seeing him. She turned her palfrey abruptly and put the horse into a gallop. Raymond had provided her with a fleet mount, and Ceridwen wasn't particularly heavy. She passed Giles and Raymond with ease. The palfrey splashed mud behind her as she raced up and over a gentle rise.

Ceridwen glanced over her shoulder and saw no sign of Raymond or Giles. But Wace and the others were cresting the hill in pursuit. Ceridwen gritted her teeth and returned her gaze to the way before her. A column of smoke rose beyond the thick stand of trees ahead. She stood in her stirrups to get a better look. Then Giles raced out of nowhere to flank her on the right.

"Lady Ceridwen!" He grinned.

She frowned at him and tried to veer away. Then a hard arm drove the breath from her. Raymond grabbed Ceridwen's middle and swept her off her horse from the left. He threw her across his horse's withers, between its neck and the front of his saddle, and cantered on. So easily tricked—like a child.

Ceridwen wanted to scream in frustration, but her position was too painful and precarious. This was a horribly familiar situation—the old battle with the English knights rushed back in vivid detail. She pounded on what she knew was the already sore knee of the knight now available to her. Ceridwen feared she might get sick, so much violence was being done to her stomach.

Raymond cursed, and halted his horse. "Confound you, woman! Do you want to be tied and dragged behind me?"

"Aye!" She kicked and struggled to right herself. "Then shall my father see you for the beast you are. Put me down!"

"I will not. I have acceded to your idiotic demands before, and look where it got you—bare-arsed in a horse-trough!"

"Demands? Hah! Nor was I bare! My shift covered me."

"And a lot of good it did. I could see right through it."

"Why then did you look? A decent man would not have let his gaze linger. I will bite your leg if you do not release me this instant." Ceridwen made ready to carry out her threat, for the blood was pounding in her temples from hanging upside down.

"Ceri, be still. You two quarrel as if you are already wed."

Ceridwen froze, her open mouth poised above Raymond's thigh. She turned her head, and saw the hairy underbelly of a Welsh cob. There were the elkskin boots she had cleaned and oiled so often that she knew their every stitch. "Da?" she said weakly.

She felt Raymond's legs tense and the next thing she knew he was rapidly backing his horse away from her father. Ceridwen fought Raymond's restraining grip. His hand grasped her firmly by the leather girdle at her waist. Another looped under her arm and suddenly she was upright, sideways before him, perched in even greater discomfort on the curved edge of the saddle bow.

Ceridwen was dizzy and her hair flowed in a mass over her face. She flung it aside, and Raymond had to spit the strands out of his mouth. His horse stamped a hoof in irritation.

"Do you want her back?" Still wiping his face free of hair, Raymond addressed her father.

Morgan grinned. "Lord Raymond, I have already asked you to take her, with my deepest gratitude and heartfelt thanks."

Despite her father's statement, Ceridwen smiled through tears of relief. Rhys was here, safe and whole. As was Dylan. He winked at her, then shook his head and shrugged.

"Thank you, my lord, but I cannot accept," Raymond said flatly. "By rights she belongs to my younger brother, Parsifal."

A shadow crossed Morgan's features. "That was no part of the bargain. 'Twas with you, and you alone we contracted."

"There is a prior agreement that voids mine. Parsifal is alive, returned from the east at long last." Raymond's voice was low and even. But his arm squeezed Ceridwen's waist so hard she could take only a shallow breath.

"I see. 'Twould appear there has once again been a divine intervention." Morgan met Ceridwen's eyes.

A maelstrom of emotions surged within her. Joy at seeing her father—with Rhys and Dylan and the others at his side. Fear that a fight would erupt between the two groups of armed men, so recently deadly enemies. Anger that she was passed from one man to another as chattel, part of a contract. And beneath it all, a sense of devastating loss.

Morgan continued, "I do not recognize any prior claim of your brother's. I dealt then with your father, and you, Sir Raymond, are not the man he was. But you are the focus of this plan, like it or no. I expect you to honor your promise."

"As I would expect you to honor yours. Must young Parsifal be denied this woman, who is not mine to withhold from him?" Raymond's neck veins bulged.

"Excuse me, I—" Ceridwen began.

"Hsst!" Raymond gave her middle a short, hard crunch. She jabbed her elbow into his stomach, but his muscles were so tense the blow had no apparent impact. "Perhaps I *should* keep you instead of inflicting you upon poor Percy," he said.

"Of all the overbearing, bloated, arrogant men! Think you I am not good enough for your brother?"

"That is right. He needs a proper wife. Someone to wait upon him and manage his household."

"He *has* no household!"

"He shall."

"Truly? Where, then?"

"One of Alonso's border castles. As soon as I capture it." Silence fell and the grins of the onlookers on both sides faded as the implications of Raymond's statement sank in.

Morgan's face darkened. "You would violate our agreement and break the peace?"

"He has sorely wronged Parsifal. It was by Alonso's report we thought Percy dead. Now I wonder what really happened on Richard's crusade, for Alonso to return wealthy and Percy not at all. He has not yet spoken of what took place."

"Why were you not there?"

Raymond's expression was grim. "One must have either a pure heart or a blood lust for killing Saracens to be a crusader. I lack both of these qualities."

"Your pursuit of vengeance is understandable," Morgan said. "But 'tis also a wicked thing, that will cost you much in blood and men. If that is your choice then I must take my daughter back. I will not have her widowed and left to Alonso's care."

"You assume I will be defeated."

"I do not assume. I am certain of it."

Ceridwen's heart sank. Her father was rarely wrong. She wriggled as Raymond flexed his hand against her waist, and his thumb brushed the undercurve of her breast. For a moment she wondered what it would be like if they were not at odds, and she could relax into his arms, and a secure future awaited them. But it sounded as though there would be no future for Raymond.

"I cannot lose if you fight alongside me, Morgan," he said.

"My purpose here is to protect the *Cymraeg*, not to become involved in some endless fraternal conflict," Ceridwen's father replied. "I want safety for my people. But as you are a young hothead, 'tis impossible for you to understand that, I suppose."

Da sounds so bitter.

"Good fortune to you, then, my lord." Raymond turned his horse and began to ride away with Ceridwen still before him, his arm now cushioning her bottom. Giles cantered ahead. Ceridwen struggled to see her father and brother over Raymond's shoulder.

"Where are you going with her?" Morgan's shout was nearly drowned by the sound of Raymond's men rushing up to surround him.

"Nay, Rhys!" Ceridwen cried out as her brother whipped his sword from its scabbard. He broke through the men-at-arms and came after her and Raymond. Wace burst forth in pursuit of Rhys. Like a nightmare reenacted, she saw in her mind's eye Owain riding after the English knight, and that terrible warrior spinning his horse about and with one fell stroke, forever putting an end to her friend's youthful exuberance.

She pounded on Raymond's chest and arms. He nearly dropped her as he put his horse into a flat gallop. Over his shoulder she saw Wace catch up with Rhys, then they were lost to her view behind a rise. Raymond pushed his mount to reckless speed, and she was forced to hang on with all her strength.

The curtain wall came into sight, and with it the dangling remains of the hanged man, what little was left of him. Ceridwen's revulsion caused her to cling all the more tightly to Raymond, even though he was the cause of it. She felt like a child, who, after being beaten by its mother, cries into her skirts, having no one else to turn to.

They clattered across the drawbridge, following Giles. Chains rattled and groaned as the porter cranked furiously to lower the portcullis behind them. As soon as Raymond came to a halt, he ejected her from his horse with a shove to her rear. Ceridwen caught Giles's outstretched hand and he slowed her descent to the uneven stones of the outer ward.

"You have angered him, my lady," Giles whispered.

"*I* have angered *him?*" Ceridwen stood on shaky legs. "What of me? What of my father and brother? They may already be dead!''

''Nay, my lady, for Raymond gave no order to that end. Wace is hardly a match for your brother, and as I am sure—Rhys, is it not?—is a man of honor, the lad will come to no harm. And your father has his entire encampment at his back. I will lay odds that his men and ours will all soon be companionably drunk.''

''I pray you are right.'' She glanced at Raymond, who was giving a series of rapid orders to his mercenaries. ''But I am still angry.''

Giles shrugged. '''Tis of no account, where he is concerned. His fury overrides everyone else's. So for your own sake stop provoking him.''

''Why? Will I wind up like the poor wretch outside?''

''What poor wretch?'' Giles looked puzzled.

''The one on the wall.''

''There is no one there.''

''The gibbet, Sir Giles.'' She was so exhausted by his thickness she hadn't the energy to remain vexed.

''Oh, him. That is one of the local freemen.''

''What was his crime?''

''It is not a pretty story.''

''How pretty would it have to be to make the sight of a dead man palatable? I wish to know what might provoke his *lordship* to take the law into his own hands, put a man to death, subject his body to such indignity, and not even give him a Christian burial.'' Ceridwen waited beside Giles as he saw to his horse.

''My lord does not deny *every* guilty party that courtesy, Mademoiselle.'' The knight paused for a long moment, his brows knit and his mouth tight. ''Except in the case of this fellow, over whom you demonstrate such concern. He had a winsome daughter. She was fair, and her name was...''

Giles scratched his chin, and Ceridwen thought she heard a catch in his voice. ''Anyway, he had a mind to sell her, for he wished to buy a piece of land.''

Ceridwen's stomach turned. ''How could he do what is forbidden by God and man?''

"Many forbidden things are done every day. Even you must know that, my lady."

Ceridwen was stung by Giles's rudeness. He had no cause to speak to her thus. But she resolved to remain quiet, and allow him to tell the story without further interruption.

"He discovered she was with child, and of course the buyer had agreed only to a virgin. So her father took a rod to her."

Ceridwen's resolution to keep quiet failed as she guessed the outcome. "The girl died."

"Aye."

"The babe, too?"

"Of course." Giles looked away.

"What of her lover?" Ceridwen asked carefully.

"There was no lover."

"How can that be?" She did not understand his reluctance.

"It was Alonso. He abandoned her when he was through."

At this she felt positively ill. "I am sorry, Giles. It seems I am questioning events I have no right to query." Ceridwen put her hand lightly on his arm.

Slow applause sounded behind them. She whirled around. Raymond's face was pale and drawn. He looked as though he needed a hot meal and a week's sleep. "Sweet silence, at last. Have you any idea what it is like to have one's every action and motive examined? To know that people will always think the worst?" His gaze bored into her.

Ceridwen avoided his accusing look. She did judge his every action, past and present. "I have no personal knowledge of such prejudice, my lord."

"I thought not." He limped back toward his horse. Giles and two or three others hurried to his aid. It struck Ceridwen how accommodating his people were. For such a reputedly harsh lord, he certainly inspired devotion. Or was it fear? They might be simply courting his favor. But from what she'd witnessed, he treated everyone much the same. With barely enough civility to get by.

"I am going back for Wace and Percy. Giles, see that Morgan's daughter is comfortable." Raymond nodded to the porter to open, and he and his mercenaries exited the bailey.

* * *

Night had fallen by the time word came of Raymond's return. Ceridwen waited with Giles in the hall. It was as she remembered, except dirtier, if possible.

The straw and rushes were broken into small grease-laden pieces, liberally mixed with the detritus of months of meals. Well-gnawed bones, feathers, even the shriveled crescents of horse-hoof trimmings strewed the floor, dragged in from the farrier's by the dogs. At the smoking firepit in the center of the hall, Shona fed the flames with sticks of wood.

Ceridwen heard the rumble of men's voices. The curtain at the doorway between the hall and the forebuilding parted. Raymond's bright hair flashed against the blue of his surcoat. It reminded her of when she lay wounded, and how she had watched as he revealed his blond hair in the doorway. He had kissed her then…her first. She still felt an odd quiver in her stomach when she thought of it.

Hamfast leaped to greet his master and his paws reached Raymond's shoulders as he licked his face. Ceridwen saw a glimmer of what Raymond might look like should he ever be relaxed and content. His expression softened at his hound's greeting, and though he still did not smile, his frown disappeared. She felt a sharp twinge of regret, that a dog could evoke a response from him, where she could not—except for his lust.

But why should it bother her? He had made his decision, and she must get back to her father and Rhys. She cleared her throat, and Raymond immediately turned his head toward her.

"I would see my father safe, sir."

"He is safe. He is free to leave." Raymond rubbed Hamfast behind the ears.

"Take me back to him, please. Or let me go."

"Why? Do you tire of our company at this fine keep? Do you find our hospitality lacking, when you are used to being waited upon, and served up sweets, and having baths?"

"My lord…" Giles began.

"Nay, let her answer. I would know what it is about us that she wishes to flee."

Ceridwen's hand crept to her flute, still at her waist, hidden in the folds of her skirts. What did make her want to leave? Raymond was foreign. He frightened her. He was unhappy and rude and often cruel. But he had saved her life. Twice. Alys had helped, but it had been his kiss…she remembered how his power had surged and raced through her veins, bringing clarity to her mind. It made no sense, yet here she stood.

Where was that Raymond, who could give of himself with such generosity? She preferred the memory of the man she had felt in her dream to the reality of the hard, demanding one now before her. Ceridwen met his mocking gaze.

"I flee your hopeless pride and endless rage. Why should I stay, if you refuse me as your bride? I will not marry Parsifal. So it is best that my father take me back, as he told you. Though it will cost him dear."

"He will have your lands still."

Ceridwen chewed her lip. "He needs your help. We are hard pressed by Alonso. Together we might stand a chance."

Raymond narrowed his eyes. "These matters are not your concern. I will decide what to do with you, once I talk to Percy."

"You make it sound as though I am a hostage!"

"Look at it any way you like."

"How dare you!"

"I am lord of this place, that is how. Daring does not come into it. I have the will and the strength. Do not question me, or I will soon teach you a lesson about who is in authority here."

He loomed over her.

"Oh, so that is the secret to your people's cooperation. Threats and intimidation." Ceridwen tossed back her hair in a defiant gesture. "How do you intend to carry out this so-called lesson, Englishman?"

"As I would for any misbehaving wench who presumes to call herself a lady."

"I will not stand for it."

"Nor will you need to. You will be bent over my—"

"Stop this. Both of you should be ashamed." Giles stepped between them, hands on hips. "Vicious as a pair of London Towne whores—especially you, Raymond. You bring out a side of this young woman that I had no idea existed. It is not becoming."

"Giles, you are like a mother and father both," Raymond said. "How proper of you to rebuke me." He looked down his nose at Giles, and crossed his arms.

"Oh, I weary of your sarcasm, my lord. Do you not grow tired of your own anger?" Giles looked to be near the limits of his patience. He paced and shook his head.

"I do indeed, Giles. Forgive me, lady. I am unworthy even of your scorn." Raymond swept her a bow, then threw himself back into his chair and glared at no one in particular.

Ceridwen rubbed her thumb along her flute and said nothing. The man had no room in his heart for anything but his own bitterness. She was fortunate he did not want her. Her life would be spent in the shadow of his pain, or alone, as he went off to plunder the countryside. She should go home, with or without his permission, the first chance she got. Gathering her skirts, she rose to leave the hall.

"Come here," Raymond growled, looking into the fire instead of at her.

She stopped before turning away but made no move toward him.

"I can see your mind working on a plan of escape, Ceridwen. Do not bother. I can make it as difficult to get out of this keep as it is to get in. Tomorrow with Percy we will settle this once and for all." He got to his feet, winced, and motioned for her to precede him up the winding stair that led to his solar.

He did not force her into his chamber as she expected, but led her down the corridor to a narrow stair leading up to a side-turret. "I cannot manage any more steps tonight. Go up and knock on that door. There resides someone who might be glad to meet you. But if you attempt to leave, Wace has orders to detain you with as much force as you make necessary."

Without waiting for a response Raymond turned his back on her and limped away. Ceridwen looked from his retreating back up into the dark stairwell. He left her little choice. At least until everyone was asleep.

She climbed upwards until she stood outside the heavy door. Whomever awaited her, she preferred to be in a room, rather than in the drafty halls at the mercy of the rough soldiers who occupied them. She rapped on the door.

"Friend or foe?" a feminine voice called, the sound faint from behind the thick oak planks.

"I am Ceridwen. Lord Raymond has sent me to you."

After a few moments the door opened to reveal a big-eyed young woman, wearing a gown too large for her, as though she had lost weight. Was the brute starving the unfortunate lady?

"Come in, please do." Her smile was quick and charmingly dimpled.

Ceridwen entered the small, square chamber, and the woman bolted the door after her. Ceridwen's first impression of a timid creature was soon amended as she caught the sharp gleam of the young lady's gray eyes.

"I suppose he has not told you who I am, any more than I have been told of you. I am Blanche, Sir Raymond's cousin. Please sit here before the fire, and have some wine."

Ceridwen lowered herself to a stool and looked at her hostess expectantly. She was delicate and blond, but with a strength to her chin and nose that saved her from insipidness.

"Are you prisoner here?" Ceridwen asked.

Blanche laughed. "My own cowardice makes me captive. All those hired men he keeps frighten me. As does Raymond himself. Or did once."

"He is daunting," Ceridwen agreed. "But I am beginning to wonder if he is not more bark than bite. Have you been here long?"

"Nay. Just since Lammas. I arrived in desperation, hoping to escape my husband's lady-mother's plans for me. I am a widow… Sir Raymond's aunt Clarisse is a weaver of plots so intricate, I feared I might end up as some horrible old duke's plaything." Blanche smiled wryly and looked down at her hands.

"I could not subject my daughter to such a scandalous environment. But 'tis not much better here. At first I was grateful to be given refuge, but then I heard so many tales, of murder and revenge…I have been in this tower ever since."

"That explains why we did not meet, during my stay here before." Ceridwen wondered at Raymond's sheltering Blanche and her child. Yet another inexplicable surprise on his part.

Blanche sighed. "I had no knowledge of you. He never mentioned you."

"I am somewhat of an embarrassment to him, I think," Ceridwen admitted. "He is supposed to marry me, but seems to have changed his mind." She took a sip of wine and to her surprise found it both delicious and unwatered.

"That may be for the best. There are those who say he should be banned from such a sacrament, after what he did to his first…oh, I am sorry. I should not speak out of turn."

"I have heard the story. Do you believe it true?" Ceridwen shifted uncomfortably. She did not know what to think of him, anymore.

"'Tis true enough she is dead. And Sir Raymond himself admitted his guilt. But no one dared charge him with murder. People fear him for fifty leagues in any direction." Blanche paused and leaned forward confidentially. "You are Welsh, are you not? 'Tis a bold match for a marcher lord. Tell me, do you think him handsome?"

Ceridwen blushed. "Well, he is much different from the lads at home."

"I find him uncouth, untidy, and unfashionable. He never smiles, and he and that hound are inseparable. And, he thinks too much." Blanche's eyes looked speculative.

"I would have to agree with you," Ceridwen replied.

At the sound of a small sigh, Blanche glanced over her shoulder to a thick pallet on the floor. "There is my Bree, still sleeping, thank goodness."

Ceridwen saw that the pile of bed rugs in fact contained a flaxen-haired little girl. She changed the subject with relief. "Oh, Madame, you are blessed, to have such a child. I fear my path is a barren one, leading to a convent, or to be my father's spinster chatelaine."

Blanche looked at Ceridwen with an appraising eye and reached out to touch her hair. "Mmm, lovely. Has Giles been bothering you?"

"Nay, he teases, but has never made bold with me. Why?"

"I but wondered. He fancies himself quite something. And so do a great many women, I hear. But he is much too confident."

Ceridwen smiled. "Are you friends?"

"Aye, but Sir Raymond has forbidden me to see him. He says Giles is too lusty, and that I would be sorely offended by him. 'Tis quite true he is brash. Impious, too."

"I have not yet met a pious knight." *Except perhaps Parsifal,* Ceridwen thought. "Lord Raymond's concern is surprising when he is so offensive himself. Tell him you will teach Giles to behave properly."

"As a matter of fact, one reason I am here is to do just that, but to benefit Squire Wace, not Giles. Sir Raymond has high hopes for the lad to make his way up in the world. And he is an apt pupil in the social graces."

"He is certainly absorbing his master's lessons of violence." Ceridwen reached out and took Blanche's hand. "Come down from this tower, Madame. The two of us together cannot come to harm, and should you have concern over her, little Bree can sleep with old Alys, as does every other maid of the keep." She wondered at herself, speaking as though she would stay on at Rookhaven.

To Ceridwen's surprise Blanche threw her arms about her shoulders and hugged her close. "I am so glad you are here," the young woman whispered. "Ever since my lord died, I despaired of having a true friend, someone I could trust."

"I too have longed for a companion my own age. My sisters are much younger. I did have a friend, once." Ceridwen thought of Owain and the familiar, aching shadow fell across her heart. But she did not want to share her pain with Blanche, for fear of offending the lady, as she could not help being English.

"Let us go see Lord Raymond, then, and show him we are a united front." Blanche's eyes sparkled.

"At this hour?" Ceridwen was dubious.

"'Tis better now than after he has had a chance to rest and garner his will against ours."

"What are our demands?" Ceridwen began to warm to the idea of a confrontation.

"That he give us rein to make this a civilized place, fit for women to set foot in. I could show you things here that would make a Beguine weep, so disgusting are they."

"I have no doubt," Ceridwen agreed.

Chapter Twelve

After making sure Bree was sound asleep, Ceridwen and Blanche made their way silently down the stair, candles in hand. At the bottom a guard dozed with his arms crossed. Carefully they stepped around him.

Blanche smiled at Ceridwen, who felt more trepidation with each step nearer Raymond's solar. By no means would he be pleased to see either of them. Their feeble lights revealed Wace, already asleep outside his lord's door. Ceridwen was loath to disturb the exhausted boy, but it could not be avoided.

She was about to knock when she heard a series of deep groans and sighs from within the chamber. Blanche's eyes widened and simultaneously she and Ceridwen put their ears to the door.

"Nay, not there—ahh…quit—ohh…nay! Please, Shona. Giles, make her stop!"

Ceridwen and Blanche stared at each other.

"This I must see." Blanche reached for the latch.

"Oh, Lady Blanche, this does not seem the most opportune moment to invade a man's privacy, especially this particular man." Ceridwen put a restraining hand on Blanche's arm.

Wace struggled up, floundering amidst their skirts. "Mesdames, pray get you back to your quarters." He stood a hand taller than either one of them, and dark red whiskers glinted on his chin and upper lip. Not such a boy after all.

"But Squire Wace." Blanche tucked her arm through his.

"We will see to your lord's comfort. Can you not hear his distress?"

"Em, I am not sure what that is, my lady, but I am certain he wants no audience. I shall escort you back to your chamber."

"Nay. Do that and I will scream," Blanche promised.

Wace frowned. "'Twould be most inappropriate."

"You must learn to handle the most delicate of situations, young man. Here is a golden opportunity to display your worldliness and *sangfroid*."

Ceridwen was impressed by Blanche's audacity.

Wace tugged down his tunic and adjusted his dagger. He patted Blanche's hand. "As you will, my lady. But I will go first." He cracked the door open and got as far as, "Lord—" when Blanche pushed it wide and dragged Ceridwen in after her.

Throat-high, a blade fully four feet long barred their path. Giles towered at one end of it.

"I told you I should go first." With one finger Wace pushed the sword aside, inclining his head to Giles as he did so. The knight shrugged and resumed his place at Raymond's bedside.

Ceridwen had been ready to avert her eyes at whatever scene of intimacy presented itself, but all she saw was Raymond seated on his bed, fully clothed, and the maid Shona next to him. A pile of captured chessmen lay on her side of a wooden board. Hamfast snored next to his master, his head on a pillow.

Raymond looked up at Ceridwen in annoyance, his hand at his brow. "What are you doing here?"

He frowned and his long fingers relaxed to run back over his head. Ceridwen found herself wanting to do the same, to once again sink her fingers into his thick, brassy hair.

Giles studied the chessboard rather too intently, and bit his lip. Shona's cheeks were flushed, her hand poised to make her next move. Lady Blanche looked from the one to the other, a crease forming between her pale brows.

"We were conversing, my lord," Ceridwen said. "Then when we heard the odd sounds we thought something was amiss."

Raymond quirked an eyebrow. "What sounds were those?"

"Em, you seemed to require a bit of rescuing, my lord."

"Indeed. Is there anything else you think I might require?"

He asked this with such a feral gleam in his eye that Ceridwen opened her mouth only to close it again without speaking.

Raymond laced his fingers behind his head. "Right. Now that you are here, and have witnessed my humiliation at the hands of Shona, what do you want of me?"

Want of him? Ceridwen did not know. Confusion crowded out rational thought. It was odd to see him in such a relaxed setting. He looked at her from the shadowy bed, and his eyes shone with a cold color brighter than anything else in the room. They struck her as somehow familiar....

Suddenly she felt like running away, and yet she wanted him to send everyone out so they might be alone. She wanted to slap Raymond's face for his treatment of her before her father, and at the same time gaze into his eyes, to see if she might find anything there beyond a casual disregard.

"We have come to ask permission to remedy the brutish state of this keep. If we are to stay here, we might as well make ourselves useful, and it liveable," Blanche said.

Shona bristled, and Giles neither spoke nor smiled.

"Things are fine as they are. Why do you not busy yourselves mending the holes in my mercenaries' clothes, instead? Or better yet, get to weaving so they might have something warm for the winter. But do not meddle with how my people manage this keep. We have purpose behind our slovenly appearance."

"Oh, to make your enemies run before the smell?"

There was a snort from Giles.

"Why, Lady Blanche, please be forthright, do not spare me. What have you done with the wan, forlorn widow of a few weeks back?" Raymond asked.

"She has seen through you at last, my lord. Perhaps you are but a man after all, not a monster," Blanche replied archly, glancing about the sparsely furnished solar.

"Do not be too quick to that conclusion, my lady." Giles resheathed his sword.

"I have to agree with Giles, Lady Blanche. You think yourself a sophisticate, having survived the intrigues of Aunt Clarisse's household. But in my world subtlety is as nothing compared to speed and brute force. When it suits me to feign weakness, I do so. When heads must roll, I see that it comes to pass. Do not question my methods. You have no idea what goes on here, what it takes to keep you and all the others safe. But Ceridwen does.'' Raymond turned his icy gaze upon her. "She has had a glimpse of the truth. Nor did she find it comely."

Ceridwen returned his look through half-lidded eyes, and without conscious intent rubbed her abdomen where her scar still stung. He was reaching out to her with his words, but she did not want to acknowledge his effort. "I must say that I see Lady Blanche's point. The reek of your hall is stifling. And, it takes a stronger man to withhold a blow than to strike one.''

Raymond's face darkened ominously. Now she had done it. Her father had warned her—her tongue would be her doom. She began to back away from Beauchamp's smoldering look.

"Giles, take Shona with you as you go. Wace, remove Lady Blanche.'' Raymond did not stop looking at Ceridwen as he spoke, in a quiet voice that demanded unquestioning obedience. "And take Hamfast as well. What follows shall not be for his ears."

They left, Blanche and Wace avoiding Ceridwen's gaze, and Giles casting her pitying looks. The door shut behind them with a hollow finality. She stood alone before Raymond.

Her limbs trembled, and she wished she had never set foot outside her father's hall. She closed her eyes, prepared for the worst. Added to her anguish was the fact she was not sure what *would* be worse—to be abandoned by Raymond, or possessed by him. He stood right in front of her. She could feel his heat, smell his smoky scent.

He spoke in a low voice. "You think you can judge the worth of a man's withholding, of his restraint? You believe I have no self-control—that I am just another Alonso?''

Ceridwen opened her eyes. "You are Beauchamp bred and born. That name equals excess, whether of violence or greed or lust.''

He was too close. The gleam of his black-lashed eyes pierced her. Their blueness was unlike any she had seen before, and yet something in them echoed from the past. They reminded her of a deep mountain lake, or the sky on a winter's eve, before the stars emerged. He breathed softly, in and out, slow and even. His blood throbbed a pulse in his neck, mere inches away. That dark-gold hair, within reach at last. His mouth, arrogant and unforgiving…she wanted to turn around. To hide her face. But he held her with his gaze.

"I am not touching you, sweet." Unnecessarily Raymond showed her both hands. Strong and shapely, with calloused fingertips. "Here is the question of restraint: if I wanted to touch you, could I stop myself?" A peculiar, almost pained look passed over his face. "Or, is the question rather, if you wanted to touch *me,* could *you* stop yourself?"

"I see no point in touching you, my lord." Ceridwen put her hands behind her back and wove her fingers together.

"There we go again. You expect me to believe that? Of a Welshwoman? Of you?"

"I expect nothing. You are the most rude, cruel bully I have ever come across."

"Ahh…she speaks her mind. In sooth, I prefer that bitter medicine to a mouthful of poisoned honey. Tell me another truth." He bent his head so his cheek almost brushed hers, and his mouth was close by her ear. "Do you truly want to go home with your father? Shall I have Giles take you to him?"

Ceridwen's heart fluxed with a tumult of conflicting emotions. Her mind could not concentrate when he was so near. The surging warmth he elicited bewitched her to the point where it was all she could do not to take his face between her hands and kiss him, just to see what happened next.

But he had challenged her self-control. It was not fair. She had little experience of desire, so how could he expect her to know how to hold back? A well-bred maid should not be in such a position in the first place. Not alone with a man in his bedchamber. Especially Raymond de Beauchamp.

"I do not want to leave this minute, if you please…." she whispered. What had taken possession of her tongue, to make such a reply?

He looked at her then, and she saw pain and shame and sorrow all clouding his face. He stepped away from her, leaving an empty space that flooded with cold air. "You and Percy are two of a kind. Complete innocents. You will make a good match."

"You have forfeited the game, my lord."

"Nay, Shona was victorious. I fought to the death."

"Not that game. The one just now. The contest of wills. You have walked away."

Raymond grunted a laugh, without smiling. "Ah, well, that is something I need to do more often, Ceridwen. I tend to destroy the very things I most desire. I am ravenous, all the time. But nothing satisfies me. And when I find what I truly want, it turns to dust in my hands."

His grim, bereft tone scraped her heart. "Perhaps the fault is in the thing, not your hands."

"You are far too generous, lady. You had best leave now, before I wax any more melancholy."

"To see my father?" Ceridwen could not disguise her hope.

"To await Percy. Soon he will be strong enough to wed you. 'Tis late." Taking Ceridwen by the arm, Raymond pulled open the door and thrust her through to his squire. "Wace, show her to her bed, and see that she stays there."

The handsome Wace flushed a deep red. Ceridwen turned toward Raymond, ready to deal him a scathing remark, but the raw look on his face brought her up short—he'd meant nothing scandalous. By the time she recovered, his expression was hard once again, and he shut the door in her face.

"I am sorry to have disturbed your rest, Wace. I can find my own way."

"Nay, lady, I must obey his orders. Believe me, I do not mind." The squire flashed her a grin and Ceridwen smiled back. To her, Wace felt more like an accomplice than a warden, so she allowed him to do his duty without hindrance. *There will come better opportunities for rebellion,* she thought.

Ceridwen swung her bare feet back and forth, her thighs clamped around the rough, dry bark of the branch she straddled. The freedom she had enjoyed over the past few days while Raymond's knee healed was an intoxicant better than wine. It was not hard to slip away from Wace, for he could not be everywhere at once.

Beauchamp had stayed abed, and had not yet made her speak to Parsifal. The crusader was slow to recover his mind, though from Alys's reports, he improved daily. With a pang Ceridwen remembered her father, still waiting beyond the oakwood for Raymond to come and parley. Soon she would find a way to go to him. He would take her home, away from this maddening place.

She wiggled her toes at the thought and breathed in the crisp air. At the movement of her abdomen, her scar ached, biting into her like a bad memory. As though Raymond's sword had pierced more than skin and muscle.

He himself was like an itch that would not go away. Of late she had tried to hate him, to dislike him, to regard him neutrally, all to no avail. He was so irritating. So confounding.

What sort of man would wish to kill his brother, then surrender himself to that same brother, who could on a whim then have him put to death? What kind of man played with a woman, switching from hot to cold and back, then insisted someone else should have her instead? He could be as kind as he was cruel.

Apart from his chess games, his animals and Giles, he had no enjoyment. Yet Alys said that once, in high spirits, Raymond had ridden his destrier up the stairway, into the hall and jumped it over a trestle table, nearly decapitating Giles in the process. *A golden boy*…Ceridwen could not sort him out.

Male voices sounded nearby. Ceridwen scooted in reverse along the limb, until her back rested against the oak's wide trunk. Peering down the lane toward the keep, she drew her feet up beneath her skirts and tried to make herself inconspicuous.

Raymond and Giles, out walking. How unusual. Then she remembered Alys's insistence that Raymond stretch and use his leg, whether it hurt or not. "'Twill stiffen and shrivel!" she had warned him, against his bitter resistance. Apparently her nagging had finally penetrated, though he still limped.

The men approached, engrossed in an animated conversation. A contrasting pair. Giles, smiling, tall, big all over. Raymond, more compact, tightly knit, with the narrow hips and long legs of a born horseman. And that hair. Even now he scraped it back from his forehead with a careless gesture, each finger track showing the dark roots below.

She remembered the sensation of running her own fingers through it. Thick…wild…soft as an otter's pelt. Hurriedly she quelled the thought, and held her breath, wondering if she should make her presence known.

"My lord, your plan to return to Alonso is outrageous. I would be remiss in my role as advisor if I told you otherwise," Giles said, coming to a halt beneath Ceridwen's perch.

"Since when have I listened to your advice?" Raymond asked.

"Rarely."

"Then do not trouble yourself giving it. Your concern is to keep me alive, I know. But that is not my first priority." Raymond leaned over and rubbed his knee, then slid his back down the tree trunk and sat on the ground. He gazed out over his land. "This is one of my favorite oaks. I like the way it reigns the hill. Dominant and yet offering shelter."

Like you, Ceridwen thought.

Giles sat cross-legged before Raymond. "Must I chain you in your solar, and post guards over you for your own protection?"

"You are worried if I die you will lose your chess partner." Raymond flicked an acorn at Giles.

"Sometimes, Beauchamp, I can see myself thrashing you, and it would give me such satisfaction—"

"You would not."

"You think not?" Giles asked.

"Come now. A duke's son, stooping, literally, to the level of a minor knight's chastisement?"

"Nay—a duke's bastard, who but for that knight, would be crow's bait on a battle plain in France. Given that, I have every right to beat the living—"

A squirrel chittered loudly, scolding the human intruders. Giles looked up. "Well I'll be blessed. Lovely fruit your oak grows, Raymond."

Ceridwen nearly succumbed to the urge to pull her skirts over her head and hide her face. She would have, except for the view it would have afforded them of her backside.

"Like a bloody corbie!" Raymond scowled up at her. "Get her down, will you? She is the one who needs thrashing, not I."

"You will have to do it, then, for I could not lay a hand in anger upon one so fair."

"Not without it landing somewhere it should not, you mean."

"Oh, aye. That goes without saying." Giles grinned and winked at Ceridwen.

Her cheeks were blazing, she knew. "Pardon me, my lords, I was merely taking the air."

"And felt compelled to climb a tree? You may breathe as much air as you like, but kindly refrain from taking up residence in my oak-wood. There are enough nymphs and spirits here already. This was the hanging tree, before I built a gallows." Raymond indicated the scarred bark along one stout limb.

Ceridwen nearly leaped into Giles's arms in her haste to descend. The knight swung her down with one arm about her waist. Raymond's scowl deepened, and with surprising grace he rose. Ceridwen brushed her skirts and attempted to smooth her hair. "I might have known it would be your favorite, then."

"'Twould appear our tastes are similar, since it was your choice as well." Raymond stood before her, his head tilted to the side, his arms crossed.

"It chose me."

"Ahh. A woman of distinction. 'She was chosen...by the wild oak, the hanging tree, where my true love once sang to me...'" Raymond's song trailed off in a series of soft, bittersweet notes.

Ceridwen's breath caught. His low voice demonstrated a rare perfection of tone. It was much more difficult to sing well softly than loudly. Everyone in Wales sang who could. And many who could not. It did not matter. The song swelling from the heart was the important thing. She searched Raymond's eyes and caught a fleeting glimpse of heated emotion. "A singing voice is a wonderful thing to possess," she said.

He looked away and made no reply.

Ceridwen persisted. "Your voice is rich and smooth. Why do you keep such a gift secret?"

Raymond's mouth curved into a half smile. "I only use it on rare occasions."

"And those are…?" She took a step closer to him.

"When I am moved, to either joy or tears. But most of the time I feel nothing, as you have pointed out." He stared at her for a long moment, then turned and limped after Giles, who had discreetly slipped away.

Ceridwen trotted after Raymond. "But you sang in Alonso's dungeon!"

Raymond replied without halting or turning around. "Aye. And poor comfort was I to Percy."

"Why will you not talk to me? What is it you cannot express?"

"Some things are best left unsaid. I try to amend my way of thinking, but old habits die hard."

"What habits?" she asked his back.

Raymond swung around to face her. "What do you want to hear? What do you expect me to say? I am used to mayhem. Spurting blood. Screaming women and crying orphans. Men dying for no good purpose. Crops burned and livestock slaughtered in order to teach someone a lesson."

"I do not believe it."

"Why not? Everyone else does."

"Then why do your men love you, and your people respect you?" Ceridwen clenched her fists, and Raymond followed suit.

"Who says they do?"

"I do. I see it in their faces."

"You are a child, as I have said before. No doubt you believe in fairy tales as well."

Ceridwen shook her head in frustration. It was useless to talk to such a one as he. Obstinate. Jaded. Cynical.

"Do not look at me like that, my girl."

"Like what?"

"Like you just took a mouthful of verjuice." Raymond's blue eyes narrowed dangerously.

"I am sorry." Ceridwen dug her toe into the soft earth.

"Do not say that unless you mean it."

"Stop ordering me about. I never say what I do not mean. Unlike some people." Ceridwen shot him a defiant look.

Raymond took a step towards her. She started to move away but trod on the hem of her gown and came up short. He reached out and kept her from falling backward. He pulled her up to his chest, one hand about her waist, the other still holding her hand, trapped between them.

They looked at each other. She forgot their argument as she marveled at his face. The dark brows and lashes over brilliant eyes. High, flat cheekbones and a firm chin, with the hint of an indentation in the middle. His hair, a burnished fawn against his neck, while the pale outer layers spilled to his shoulders and beyond. Her gaze fell to his surcoat, frayed and stained with old blood someone had not properly washed out.

"You need a woman," Ceridwen whispered, fingering the worn fabric.

"I know." Raymond's eyes darkened. His hold on her tightened with an unmistakable possessiveness. His hand slid to her back, his fingers spread.

"I—I did not mean it that way—"

"There is but one way. And you just said, you never say what you do not mean. Are you so unreliable? Must I drag the truth from you?" He put his thumb on her chin and played with her lower lip.

Ceridwen turned her head. "The truth is I am embarrassed, standing here in broad daylight, in such close proximity." More than embarrassed. Her legs wobbled and she had an urge to bite his neck. Not hard, just enough to make him pay attention.

"No one thinks anything of it. And if they object, they will have me to answer to." Raymond drew her face back to his. "You are blushing!"

Aye, she felt consumed by a blush, from head to toe.

"I beg your pardon, my lord," Giles said from behind Raymond, "there is a matter of some urgency in the keep."

"There is a matter of some urgency right here."

"'Tis an emissary, from the bishop."

"Oh?" Raymond looked up from his examination of Ceridwen's mouth. "What do they want?"

"To excommunicate you."

"Jesus God."

"Indeed."

"Forgive my trespass upon your person, 'demoiselle." Raymond released her. "I was carried away."

"You need to be carried away," Ceridwen replied, as his limp grew more pronounced.

"Giles, please find this creature some worthy occupation, to keep her hands busy and her mouth shut." Raymond jerked his thumb at her over his shoulder as he made his way down the path.

"Ah. I know what I would have her do." Giles looked at Ceridwen fondly. She turned and hid her face against a tree until the men continued on. Then, silently, she fell into place behind them.

"Are you sure 'tis I who is in trouble with the church, and not you, Giles?" Raymond halted briefly to fiddle with his boot. He put one hand on Giles's arm for balance. When he leaned down, the motion emphasized his muscular taper, from shoulders to hips.

Ceridwen bit her lip.

Giles began waving his free hand. "Do you realize how serious this is, Raymond? If you are excommunicated then so in effect is everyone within your manor, and the whole village will be cut off from the sacraments. The churchmen will demand your reform. Or a penance."

"They probably want something for their coffers, and will leave happily with a few gold pieces."

"Not this time, Raymond. 'Tis your brother, Prior Everard who will soon arrive, with grievances from Lady Meribel's family as well as a whole list of other charges."

Raymond straightened and stood stiffly. "So they are coming at last. They threw her to the dragon for their own convenience, and now they want blood money."

"'Twould seem so."

Raymond stroked his jaw. "I will not receive them."

"What? Do not be a fool."

With a dreadful fascination, Ceridwen watched Raymond

grow before her eyes, the way she had seen animals make themselves appear bigger before a fight. He spoke softly to Giles, who had already backed away a step.

"Giles. My nobly-born friend. My older, wiser friend. My friend who knows what is best for me when he should be thinking of what is best for himself. Do not, ever, call me fool again."

Raymond glanced at Ceridwen, then returned his attention to Giles. "Reserve that title for the next arriving gleeman, whose lute strings shall resound with your inner beauty, as they will be made of your guts, should you deign to name me thus. Now get the hell out of my sight, and tell those bastards to hike up their skirts and begone!"

Ceridwen was shocked to see the big, bold Giles slink away in the face of Raymond's fury. If he felt that was the wisest course, perhaps she had best depart as well.

"Where do you think you are going?" Raymond's voice cracked like a lash at her back.

"Nowhere, my lord. I would but keep out of your way." She turned to face him. His pupils constricted. His expression was flat. Its deadness terrified her. What had shifted his mood so swiftly? Lady Meribel, Giles had said. It could only be his late wife who fed the darkness within him....

Raymond interrupted her conjecture. "Do me a favor, Mistress. Go to Percy and see that he is happy. Alys has cared for all his hurts, she will allow him some relief from her constant meddling now, I think. They are in the south tower, you know where it is." He turned, leaving her standing in the lane.

"I will go and say goodbye to him."

He rounded on her. "You will what?"

Ceridwen did her best to return Raymond's glare, but wilted beneath his practiced animosity. He was not one used to being countered in his wishes. "If you will not have me, I want to go home and make peace with my family. I am...weary, my lord."

"Weary or no, your duty is to my brother. I am constantly forgetting that, but you should not."

"But my father awaits me."

"When it suits me, I shall return you to him, and you may reacquaint him with your betrothed. Until that time, I expect you to remain within the keep and out of my trees, not wandering hither and yon. There are too many mercenaries about for you to roam safely unescorted.''

Ceridwen raised her eyes to meet Raymond's. He had no right to tell her what to do, no right to keep her. He muddled her mind, stirred her heart, made her lose sight of her purpose, the pursuit of justice. She had not thought of Owain in at least three days. All she could think of was Raymond. Of his kisses, of how his skin felt against hers, in the dark…

This foolishness must stop.

She could no longer believe that a union with him would curb his bad temper or make him more malleable for her father's purposes. Whatever Raymond had in mind, she would rather go into a nunnery than marry either him or Parsifal. Would she not?

Her heart struggled against her attempt to thwart its shameful hunger for the wicked Carrog Dhu. Right now she had a chance to escape the brothers Beauchamp. To escape facing the truth of her own passion. All she had to do was run.

Ceridwen gathered up her skirts and raced down the lane. She passed a startled shepherd. Dodged sheep. Rushed headlong into the trees that skirted the common. Raymond could never catch up with her, not with that knee. She paused to get her bearings and catch her breath. She glanced over her shoulder. At the sight of him a twinge of panic caught Ceridwen's throat.

He came after her. Slowly. Painfully. Relentlessly. With a grim determination even she could read from a distance, by the set of his shoulders, and the measured strides he took, though marred by discomfort. Something about the picture he made evoked a tender response in her.

She imagined him as a boy, walking small and alone through the deep forest, a big, ungainly dog at his side. Stubbornly putting one foot before the other, dreading his destination, refusing to give in to fear…the vision slipped away as softly as it had come.

What had Raymond to fear from her? She reminded him of something, or someone. That much she had gathered, from the curtain that always fell between them. She had grown to count on him to stifle the sympathetic resonance that sprang up whenever they were together. It absolved her of responsibility for her own inexplicable tangle of feelings.

Raymond drew closer and came to a halt. He stood with his hands at his sides and stared mutely at her. She could feel his battle. Detachment struggled against a longing for intimacy. Anger fought desire, buried deep within. His fingers flexed and his gaze broke from hers. He was poised to turn and walk away.

Ceridwen's heart pounded, close to breaking. She emerged from the shadows of the great oaks. Her bare feet sank into the cool, damp earth as she went to meet him. She could not help it. She was drawn to him the way he was drawn to the white stag. She did not know why, or what needed to be done. When he stood before her like this she simply could not leave him.

No words passed between them. He held her with his gaze, no longer cold, and carefully linked his little finger with hers, as was the fashion for lovers. As if it were the most natural thing in the world. They walked in silence, back to the keep.

Chapter Thirteen

"Good morning, my lord."

Raymond looked up from where he sat by the fire circle in his hall. Ceridwen approached, wearing the ancient overgown he had once torn. He stared at her. A modest veil covered her neatly bound hair and draped about her shoulders.

So proper. So maidenly. He felt an urge to rip it off, and the rest of her attire as well. To test the wild heart he knew lay beneath all those coverings. Instead, he rose from his chair and stood in a formal posture, his hands behind his back.

"Have you visited Parsifal yet today?"

Ceridwen met his gaze. "Nay, he needs me not."

Raymond strolled nearer to her. "You are foolish to resist having him. Of all of us he will do you the least harm."

"Of all the men in your family? Or just the brothers Beauchamp? Are there any more I should know about?"

"Nay, we are enough. There are too many of us as it is. We breed like mice."

"Not you, apparently," she replied.

He thought he heard a smile in her voice, and lifted her chin to see. If there had been one, it was gone. But her lips were as sweetly burnished with pink as the sky at dawn. "I do not because I am reserve stock, sweeting."

"Reserved? For whom?"

Ceridwen's linen head cloth covered the side of her face and Raymond squashed it back to see her better. He saw a tremor run through her, and his hand flexed, wanting to stroke her cheek. "Someone special, with a subtle palate, and a tongue that aches for my taste…someone who can drink me all night long, appreciate every nuance of my body and flavor, and yet be able to stand the next day…"

"Oh, my lord." Ceridwen gave him a bewildered look, then closed her eyes and took a deep breath. Her full lips parted and Raymond's heart gave a treacherous lurch. He was a hairs-breadth away from taking her up the stairs, two at a time, bad knee or no, the betrothal be damned.

"Shall I go on?" he asked softly, and stepped back from Ceridwen, whose paleness had given way to bright spots of color in either cheek. "We will settle this now." He made sure Ceridwen followed as he limped toward the chamber where Percy recuperated.

Percy sat at a table, playing draughts with old Alys. He looked up, blinked, then smiled at his visitors. "Hullo. I am winning." He returned his attention to the game.

"Parsifal, I have something important to say to you. Put the gamepiece aside." Raymond pulled Ceridwen close. His arm curved about her supple waist as though it was made to fit. When she tried to pull away, he did not release her.

"Here is Ceridwen. She is betrothed to you in marriage, Percy. Do you understand? 'Tis time you faced the fact that you are alive and started acting like a man." As it was time for himself to rise from the dead, and live. But without Ceridwen, he did not believe he could. And *with* her…?

Percy hopped his draught over Alys's with three resounding thumps. Clear-eyed, he gazed at Ceridwen and Raymond, rose from his stool and stood before them. "I thank you, for all you have done for me, for your protection and care." He picked up Ceridwen's hand and kissed the back of it. "If I ever were to marry, my lady, I would choose you over all others. But, I am going to take my vows with the Cistercians, at the abbey."

Raymond stared at his brother, then turned to Alys. "What have you done to him? He has lost his mind."

"Nay, Master Raymond. 'Twas ever little Percy's wish to enter holy orders. The rest of ye, your father included, trampled over his yearnings 'til he forgot them himself. Now he has re-membered his calling.''

Percy took Ceridwen's hand and placed it in Raymond's. Her slim fingers could be as easily crushed as his heart had been, before it petrified in the aftermath of Meribel's death.

"To you, Raymond de Beauchamp, do I give over the care and loving of this woman, Ceridwen, Morgan's daughter. Keep the troth, marry her in my stead. Let me go freely to my heart's desire, with no burden of worry nor fear of honor unmet.''

The last two words echoed in Raymond's mind. There was something about Percy's smile that made him uneasy. It was brittle. Like Meribel's smile, before she went over the edge.

"But—" Raymond cut himself off.

"Nay," Ceridwen responded.

Raymond saw his own dismay mirrored in Ceridwen's eyes. She still feared him, like the rest. As he feared himself. But he could not spoil Percy's tenuous dream of peace. The lass was his to give up, after all. He swallowed, hard. "As you will, Percy. I had thought to see you settled. But if this is what you truly wish, I will not stand in your way. Have they accepted you?"

"They will, Raymie. Father Torwald told me, long ago, to come to him should I feel the call. Now my strength is returning, and I have no doubt I can stand up to the demands of the brotherhood.''

"The question, then, is can I stand up to the demands of matrimony?" Raymond muttered.

"Never fear, my lord," Ceridwen said. "You shall not be put to the test. I release you from any obligation you may feel on your brother's behalf. I will not be some…some second choice over a dog or a falcon or whatever it is you prefer.''

He heard the edge of pain in her voice, but steeled his heart. "You are most kind, trying to spare me, lady. Be assured I would prefer you over any number of animals in my keep. But in truth, had I a choice, I would not marry. For me 'tis an all consuming thing. I cannot long keep my fellow wolves at bay when a beautiful woman is constantly distracting me.''

Raymond gazed into Ceridwen's green eyes, through the black fringe she hid them beneath, and felt a surge of desire. He wished he could hold her close, have her naked heat pressed against him in the night. To glory in her warmth, and lose himself in the discovery of her body, her heart and soul, to gain respite from the burdens of what he had become.

But he could not indulge in such fantasy. With Percy's defection he was honor-bound to marry Ceridwen whether she liked it or not. He would take advantage of the strategic lands her father offered, and help Morgan resist any onslaught of Alonso's. But that was as far as he would go. Never again would he put himself or a woman at risk, by falling in love.

In the evening Raymond rode alone toward Morgan's encampment. The air smelled of smoke and damp, dead grass. The Welsh cookfires glowed and bubbling stewpots hung from iron tripods. If he and Morgan were to be allied, he wanted to see firsthand how trustworthy the man was. The fact that Ceridwen's brother had held Hamfast for ransom still rankled. But he needed control of that pass. It was an escape route, should his people ever have to flee Alonso. They could melt into the mountains as the Welsh did when pressed too hard.

"The Carrog Dhu approaches, my lord," a sentry called.

Raymond winced to hear his nickname. But he had worked hard for it. Morgan rose from where he sat by his fire. He was flanked by two men, the one called Dylan, and the other bearing a striking resemblance to Ceridwen. Rhys. Dark and handsome, with flashing eyes and a white, wicked grin like his father's. Unnatural, as Aelfson had said.

"Welcome, Sir Raymond. Sit with us and eat."

Raymond was surprised to meet no challenge. If it were his daughter held in the keep, he would not greet her captor so casually. But perhaps it was a ploy, to put him off guard. "My thanks, sir." He dismounted and tossed his reins to the sentry, hopping a bit as he landed. His knee still throbbed and buckled unexpectedly, despite Alys's ministrations.

"So. What think you of my fine girl? Has she been behaving herself?" Morgan stretched expansively, as though he were at home in his own hall.

Raymond sat next to him. "As far as she is capable, aye."

"You must have a steadying influence upon her."

"I doubt that is possible. But more to the point, will you stay to see us wed?" Raymond rubbed the stubble on his jaw and watched Ceridwen's father carefully. He looked the sort of man who might smile at his enemy and knife him at the same time.

"You have changed your mind about fighting Lord Alonso?" Morgan asked.

"Do you not wish to be rid of him?"

"Aye. But he has close ties to the crown. If he dies, more of his kind will be sent to subdue us. At least he is a known quantity. My decision still stands. Keep the peace or I take her home."

"How confidently you speak. What makes you think I will give her back?" *Why do I balk at freedom? Let him have her and be done with it.*

The white smile gleamed. "What makes you think you still have her? Ceri!"

A slight, veiled figure, all too familiar, emerged from Morgan's tent. Raymond jumped to his feet and regretted the movement. "How did you get here?"

"Sir Giles is most accommodating, when he wants to speak to Lady Blanche."

Ceridwen's sly smile infuriated Raymond. He strode over and grasped her hand. "Have you no concept of honor? Of what is expected of you?" He pulled her to the fire circle.

"Father, what did I tell you? Do you see how he treats me? Worse than a wife! What a specimen of chivalry."

"Lord Morgan, I am beginning to believe you are getting the best of this bargain," Raymond said. Ceridwen squirmed against him, most provocatively, damn her. Giles would pay dearly for his assignation.

"Muzzle her, my lord," Rhys suggested cheerfully.

"If I did not think you were up to the challenge I would not have let you take her in the first place, Beauchamp." Morgan rubbed his hands before the fire.

"Why does everyone insist upon speaking as though I were not present?" Ceridwen jerked ineffectually against Raymond's hands.

He pinned her arms to her sides and whispered in her ear, "Cease this unseemly wrestling, my lady. Save thy contortions for thy wedding night."

"Oh!" Ceridwen's heel came down hard on his instep. Raymond twisted his other foot around her ankle and swept her off her feet. He threw her over his shoulder, rump skyward, and took a deep breath.

The wench was but one more fetter of responsibility staring him down. In his youth he had assumed a wife was not to be taken too seriously. But when it came to Meribel, how quickly he had discovered he had absolutely no capacity for detachment. She had torn him apart. Slowly. And *this* one...

Raymond's hand crept along Ceridwen's thigh as though it had a will of its own, and for a moment he forgot his purpose. But he was older now, in full control of his emotions. He could take what he needed and leave the rest. He came to an abrupt decision. "As long as your daughter remains willingly within my care I will refrain from any assault upon Alonso that he does not first provoke. If that satisfies you I would take my leave now, sir. Before I change my mind."

Ceridwen's hard little knee caught Raymond off guard as it rammed his midsection. He forced his free hand down, barely resisting the impulse to smack Ceridwen's bottom for her temerity. If she struck him once more, he would, whether her father saw or not.

"As you will." Morgan bowed. "By the way, your man is yonder. Sleeping off several tankards of ale."

"Tapman?"

"Aye, he held up the archery butt for us these many days. No one else cared to come and try. He is a stout fellow."

"I was not prepared to overlook his death, Morgan, so I am glad you spared him. As regards this hellion, have I your permission to do with her as I see fit? I cannot promise to love her, nor even to be kind. But I will be fair." He clamped down hard on Ceridwen's legs as her struggles renewed, put her on her feet, and backed away a step. He rubbed the spot on his shoulder where her small teeth had nipped through his tunic. "Do not bite me again."

Rhys snorted his laughter. "Already she takes after your hound, my lord."

"My hound has far better manners."

"But infinitely more fleas!" Ceridwen jerked her mantle into place and whirled to face her brother. "Rhys, do not shame me before this Englishman. Despite your jest I have no doubt he treats his dog better than ever he will me. Father, I will not disgrace you by refusing your wishes. I will do what I must to help protect our people from these English, and to please Uncle Talyessin. But, I tell you one thing, Raymond de Beauchamp."

Ceridwen faced him, hands on hips, her green eyes snapping with anger. "Hamfast shall not be our bedmate!" She swept away to his horse and climbed into the saddle.

Raymond stared after her. What had he committed himself to? She was already trying to change him. She would have to learn the hard way. Or better yet, he would sleep alone. He looked at the stubborn set of her chin and saw nothing but trouble awaiting him.

Morgan and Rhys went to stand at her stirrup, and spoke softly to her in their own tongue. The proud carriage of her shoulders drooped for a moment, then she sat stiffly upright.

"Will you come to the hall, Lord Morgan, and be my guest?" Raymond asked as he took his reins from the sentry.

"Thank you, no, sir. My own domains call me back. But I would leave Rhys with you for a while, as my representative."

"By all means. Adieu, then."

"Farewell, Carrog Dhu. You may find yourself growing fond of her, in time."

"That remains to be seen." Ignoring the pain in his knee, Raymond vaulted up behind his future bride. His arms slid around her waist to take the reins, and his chest tightened. All his carefully constructed barriers bent beneath the strain of her nearness. Her soft skin, the faint scent of rosewater.

He could see the swell of her breasts rising and falling with each indignant breath. He must not let her lay siege to his heart. But it already suffered the first pricks of feeling, as if it woke from a numbing sleep.

As they entered the bailey Ceridwen saw that the doors of the great hall were flung open. Servants scurried with chests and coffers from carts and wains. Raymond kept Ceridwen close by his side, and looked neither to the left nor right at the assemblage of dignitaries, richly garbed and overfed.

The most imposing of the group stepped forth and blocked Raymond's passage with his bulk. His tawny hair, perfect skin, and piercing blue eyes were a combination of traits possessed only by Beauchamps, to Ceridwen's knowledge.

Could this be Everard, the cleric? She frowned. He wore sumptuous clothes, even to the point of affecting a sword, boots, and spurs, as befit a knight. He also swelled with his own importance, as befit a brother of Alonso.

"You, Raymond, flaunt the laws of man and God alike. You are a disgrace to the memory of our lord father, God rest him. We are here to set you back on the path of righteousness, at Alonso's behest. He is most concerned about you. As am I."

Raymond tilted his head and his arm squeezed Ceridwen's waist. "In other words, Everard, he has sent you to do his dirty work. Are you not here to collect the monies forfeit for my ransom, and perhaps ensure that I roast in hell into the bargain? To fill your purse in the name of God and the lost Meribel?"

The prior's jowls trembled in indignation. "I do not—"

"Do not expect a farthing from me, nor my obedience. Giles?"

"Aye, milord." Giles stepped forth, tall and grim, and Everard's group of lackeys cringed.

"See that these good people find lodgings in the village. I have a mind to sleep well tonight, not stay awake wondering if my throat will be slit." Raymond turned toward Everard and his retinue. "If 'tis Meribel's dowry you are after, I have already sold those lands. And spent the money on men and arms. Did you see them, outside? Make sure you count them carefully, so you can report back without error." He gripped Ceridwen's hand, and headed for the circular stairs leading to his solar.

"You see, a new courtesan, as they said."

The whispered comment carried up the stairs, and Ceridwen burned with humiliation.

"Not another word from the likes of you!" Raymond roared down at them. "This woman is Beauchamp betrothed and shall be married within the week. And I will not be inviting you to the wedding, so make haste to depart.''

"Our lord King has been warned of you, Raymond. This keep is adulterine. It shall be confiscated, for His Grace never authorized its fortification.''

Ceridwen's eyes widened at this disturbing revelation.

Everard's voice filled the hall. "You will be charged with the murder of that man hanging outside, the serf in the wood, and your poor lady wife as well. For all your arrogance, you have no right of high justice. Add to that your aiding the escape of the poacher, and your plots against Alonso. By the time we have finished there will be nothing left of you to hang, much less to rot in hell.

"Beware, Raymond. You and all who stand by you. The archbishop will carry out your excommunication and you will be banned from the church and from the company of any decent human being. An outcast, to be buried in unconsecrated ground, like an animal.'' The cleric spat on the floor.

Ceridwen's heart convulsed, but Raymond did not flicker an eyelid at his brother's condemnation. Raymond's high-handedness was beyond belief. But she despised these officious men who came only to make threats. It did not seem fair, and it made Raymond act even more like a bear with a sore head. In spite of that, his hand around hers felt good and warm—nothing like the outer impression he gave. Indeed, his body seemed to tell its own story altogether....

Ceridwen swallowed hard and her breathing quickened. A queasy mixture of dread and anticipation filled her at the thought of being wed to Raymond. Something from him called to her despite his resistance or her reluctance. Her heart ever answered with a leap over which she had no control.

Passion. Raymond had that in abundance, and he poured it into everything he put his mind to. And he was about to put his mind to *her*—and his body too, she supposed. But at the rate he made enemies, she could easily be a widow before she became a mother. Then she would be completely at the mercy of Alonso, Everard, and any number of others she knew nothing about. Not to mention the possibility of meeting the fate of his first wife. She jumped when Raymond spoke again.

"Come." Her arm ached and her worry grew as Raymond dragged her upstairs to his solar. The heavy oak door was marred with innumerable small indentations a foot or two up from the floor. He swore as he kicked it open, making yet another mark on the wood. Inside, atop her perch, his prized gyrfalcon ruffled her white and black speckled feathers.

Ceridwen looked in surprise at the elegant bird, her anger and Everard both forgotten. "Is she ill?"

Raymond began to stroke his falcon back to calmness. "I think she is better. I should not have made such a disturbance."

Ceridwen crossed her arms. "You do that with great regularity. Why have you brought me up here?"

"I would keep you safe, until these clerics leave."

"Surely they would do me no harm?"

"Being relatives of mine, they might," he replied. "Stay put. I will send Alys to you." He slipped out the door before she could respond.

"What do you think of all this, Mistress Hawk?"

The gyrfalcon merely blinked at her. Ceridwen sighed and gazed about the room. Several chests lined the walls, and one had its lock undone. Besides herself and the bird, what other sorts of things might he want to keep safe up here? It was wrong to pry, but if she could find any clue as to what went on in his head…she eased open the lid of the trunk, and her eyes widened. Not jeweled daggers, nor gold. Nothing she might have expected.

She lifted out a carved wooden horse, cleverly painted. A doll, with long hair of black wool, wearing a red linen kirtle. A small flute. A stuffed leather ball. Ceridwen was mystified. Surely these were not relics of his boyhood. Putting her hand deeper into the chest, her fingers met silk. She hesitated. She should not rummage through his things. But curiosity won over propriety.

Carefully she drew out a flowing, pale yellow shift, with tiny rosebuds embroidered around the neck. The material could only have come from the Saracen lands or beyond, so fine and soft was its weave. Ceridwen held it up, and saw that it was small, even for her. She bit her lip. There was no excuse for invading his privacy. The door opened.

"Alys will be along presently. I must deal with—" Raymond stopped short. He stared at her, stricken.

Ceridwen hugged the forlorn garment to her breast. "Forgive me." Alarm hurried her forward. "My lord, you are so pale...." She backed away a step as the truth struck her a hard blow. "Meribel. That is who I remind you of, is it not?"

Raymond's fists clenched and his jaw muscles tensed. He took a breath. "Aye, 'tis true, Ceridwen. That is why I cannot abide the sight of you, nor can I bear to look away. For in you I am ever forced to see her."

Ceridwen lowered her head in shame. So, his kisses, in the dungeon and in the tent had been for the desire of a dead woman, who had betrayed him. "What are you doing, then? Do you seek to punish her, using me as a substitute?" She raised her chin and her eyes brimmed. "By leading me on, then repulsing me? By wanting me, only so long as I remind you of her, as she once was, perhaps, so you can destroy her again?"

"Nay..." Raymond's voice was a raw whisper. "Never was she as you are now."

Ceridwen winced at the pain in his face, then fear replaced her sympathy as his expression changed. She had wanted to believe the horrible tale of murder was the malicious rumoring of his enemies. But the hardness creeping back into his eyes filled her with unease. "Oh, my lord, I do not know what to—"

"There is a great deal you do not know. And, I hope, never shall." He turned to the door. "I must go see that Giles has come to no harm. Ah, Alys. Just in time." Raymond ushered the elderly woman in with a sweep of his arm. He backed out the door, then stopped and fixed Ceridwen with a deadly look. "Do not touch those again." He indicated the chests with a jerk of his chin. "Be ready for me. On the morrow." Then he was gone.

Ceridwen felt adrift and alone, in spite of the old woman's presence. "What did he mean, Alys?"

The nurse grinned broadly. "You are a lucky lass. He means to wed you come the morn."

Chapter Fourteen

In less than an hour's time she would be a married woman. Ceridwen could not stop the tremors that coursed through her body, every time she thought of it. The imminent prospect of wedding Raymond made her limbs grow numb and her skin cold.

"Tsk—Ceridwen. What do you do with this hair—stay up all night tying it in knots?" Blanche struggled with the comb. "The sparrows shall all be grateful for the soft lining you provide their nests." She shook several strands from her fingers and they floated out the window.

"Blanche, what am I to do? I cannot go through with this. I hate him. I—"

"What rubbish. Of course you do not hate him. 'Tis the idea of being tied to a big brute of a man—any man—that irks you. You will get over it. All it takes is one good, em…the right sort of handling—well, you will find out soon enough."

Ceridwen twisted the white silk ribbons meant for her hair around her hands. "Tell me what to expect, to ease my mind."

"Alys? What shall I say?" Blanche rubbed her fingers with rose-scented oil and stroked Ceridwen's hair into smooth, gleaming waves. "I do not want to raise her expectations too high. Nor frighten her."

"You young people. I know not what to think. In the old days there weren't none of this skipping about the subject. But the lass is delicate, I can see that. Best not to say too much.

What's done in the dark <u>ain't</u> so dreadful if yer not thinking on it all the livelong day beforetime.''

''Now that is most reassuring, Alys. Look at her! She is shaking so I can hardly finish her hair.'' From behind, Blanche put her hands on Ceridwen's shoulders, and bent to her ear. ''Not to worry, love. The Beauchamps may be ruthless in battle, and scheming liars at court, but from what I have heard, and what I know, in bed they are the most extraordinarily—''

To Ceridwen's relief Wace poked his head into the room and interrupted Blanche. ''My lord awaits you. And a lovely sight you are, my lady.''

Ceridwen smiled shyly, but within moments the ripples returned to assail her stomach. She felt like a small, trapped creature as they escorted her down to the great hall, Blanche and Alys at one elbow, Rhys at the other.

Her damp palms stuck to the silken red damask of the borrowed overgown. The skirts were so long she had to gather up fistfuls of cloth to keep from tripping as she walked. On her head she wore a wreath Alys had woven, of wheat stalks and dried flowers. To make her fertile. She trembled.

Raymond was so—physical. So powerful and dominant. Here she was, about to be bound to him and his whole clan of stone-hearted killers. At least she still had her own family.

Ceridwen looked up at Rhys. ''I am so glad you are safe.''

Rhys smiled down at her and squeezed her hand. During the chaos in the mountains he had chased the robbers far afield. Dylan had been struck down—no one knew where to find her, she had not responded to their calls. They had searched frantically, but the men's wounds needed attention, so at last they had given up. By the time a fresh search party was organized, the River Usk had risen to impassable levels, and they were cut off. It had all worked out, but whether for the best remained to be seen.

Rhys's attention shifted and he stared over Ceridwen's head at Blanche, who looked pointedly forward, her cheeks turning ever more pink. Ceridwen nudged her brother in the ribs. He winked at her and nudged her in return. Her brow creased. He found it easy to enjoy himself—*he* would not be under Raymond's command. Then, but a few paces ahead, she saw her bridegroom, as she had never seen him before.

His shining hair hung neatly down his back. Elegantly attired in black from shoulders to heels, Raymond looked like a prince—in mourning. Silver gleamed, from a dragon brooch on his shoulder to sword-hilt to spurs. He stood tall, surrounded by his doting minions, his presence regal and forbidding.

Raymond appeared every bit the Carrog Dhu—except for his eyes. He did not blaze them at her, nor wither her, nor even try to freeze her marrow. They were wide open, blue as a kingfisher's wing, frankly staring. *Afraid.* He was afraid, *of her.*

The knowledge came to Ceridwen with the certainty of a divine revelation. What could he possibly have to fear from her? He should be afraid of his own dark self instead. Then the problem was driven from her mind as they entered the chapel, and the brilliant colors of a high window dazzled her.

The sun shone through it and scattered jewels of light to the floor. A wonderful fragrance filled the air. The nave was thickly strewn with musk roses. Her favorite. She was touched that someone had taken so much care, and amazed that such flowers were to be had so late in the season. Then her hand was thrust into Raymond's, and the ceremony proceeded, in a hazy blur of censer smoke.

What struck her most was the sight of Prior Everard, scriptures in hand, stammering over the words, Giles's dagger point tickling below his ear. That, and the presence of Hamfast. He stood guard on the other side of the portly cleric, growling softly all the while.

At the designated moment Raymond kissed Ceridwen's mouth briefly, perfunctorily, and it was over. She was his—and there would be no escape. Down in the hall a raucous cheering began. Lutes and tabors clamored. Laughter and voices raised in good humor. Men and women she did not know offered her congratulations. Why were they so happy? What was there to celebrate? Giles loomed before her, ready to claim a kiss of the bride.

"Nay, St. Germaine. You will frighten her."

Raymond's warning jarred Ceridwen out of her dazed state. "If the prospect of you does not frighten me, how can he?" She blithely raised her face to Giles, for a symbolic peck. She was not prepared when he swept her off her feet, took her in a bone-crushing embrace, and kissed her in a manner so bold that for a moment afterward she could not draw breath. She tottered.

Raymond pushed her aside and stepped up to Giles. His fingers quivered at his sword-hilt. "Never again, St. Germaine. Do you hear me?" His tone was deadly quiet.

"Aye, milord. You are a blessed, fortunate man, milord." Giles's grin was just shy of insolent. He bowed his way backward, out of reach of Raymond's sword, but not his baleful glare.

"What was all that about?" Rhys whispered.

"I know not why Giles would provoke him so." Ceridwen wiped her mouth with the back of her hand. She could guess why. It was Giles's way of making Raymond want her. If not out of love, then out of possessiveness. But part of her knew the lieutenant had also done it for himself. He had enjoyed that kiss—every lingering, wine-laced moment of it. She would have to let him know she did not appreciate his intervention.

A hard hand gripped her elbow. "If he ever touches you again, my lady, *he* shall dangle next from the curtain wall," Raymond growled. "And should you ever encourage him, you will be right there alongside."

Ceridwen's heart chilled. He would do it. She had no doubt. "Giles will receive no encouragement from me." She met Raymond's menacing look from beneath half-lidded eyes. "Nor shall you." She pulled away, and left him standing amidst the sea of revelers as she hurried up toward Blanche's tower room.

"Nay!"

Ceridwen looked back in alarm. Raymond bounded after her, showing no sign of pain in his knee. Before she reached the door, he had her fast, and her heart was in her throat. She should have stood her ground, shown him she was as brave as any English maid, that the *Cymraeg* did not run in the face of danger.

"Do not embarrass me in front of my people, Ceridwen. If you wish me to leave you alone when in private, that I will gladly do. But you will keep up appearances. And you will not take a lover. Do you understand?" He gave her a little shake.

"I do. Unhand me."

He released her as though she had burned him. Ceridwen wished she had. Raymond cleared his throat. "Come back down now. Have something to eat. I am supposed to feed you, I believe."

"Have you washed your hands?" she demanded, vastly relieved that he had calmed in spite of her outrageous behavior.

Taken aback, he glanced down at them. "When the basin is brought to me, I will."

"Good." Ceridwen swept past him and hid her smile. At this point even tiny victories were quite satisfying.

The moon was a sliver of light in the sky, and through the embrasures of the battlements the fitful wind cooled Raymond's face. Below, the noisy wedding guests had spilled out into the bailey. A group of young men attempted to sing together in a circle, without falling down.

Giles leaned precariously, his back to the stone wall.

Raymond crossed his arms over his chest. "What in God's name possessed you to risk a taste of my sword?"

"'Twas well worth the risk, my lord." Giles sighed, as if in remembrance. "Do not get angry again—I did it to test you."

"Aye. I nearly tested my blade against your neck."

"I thank you for substituting your fist in my face." Giles delicately put a knuckle to his split lip.

"'Tis the least you deserve. Swine."

"Why do you not stop feeling sorry for yourself and take her to bed? 'Tis the usual thing, on one's wedding night," Giles said reasonably, and hiccoughed.

"And I suppose you and a half-dozen others will want to attend, to see that I do the job right?"

"Well, then give us assurance we will not be needed."

"St. Germaine, you have had too much to drink."

"And you have not had enough."

"I have had enough of *you* for one night."

"But not of *her.*"

"Shut up, Giles. You are so full of—"

"Do I lie? Tell me to my face that I am a liar." Giles heaved himself to an unsteady, but standing position, and leaned toward Raymond.

"She does not want me." Raymond avoided looking at his friend.

"Ah, but you are wrong, Beauchamp. She fairly shouts out her desire, with every move she makes when you are near."

"What theory of seduction are you trying to stretch to fit me now? Just because you think you see it does not make it true."

"Raymond. Accept the fact that you are ignorant of these matters. You know horseflesh, and I know women. I am telling you, if you let her slip away, you are a bigger foo— I mean, milord, you would be wise to make the most of the situation, instead of doing your damnedest to push her away."

Raymond chewed his lip. "'Tis hard for me. I want to get close to her, I think about it, then when she is before me it all falls apart and I end up saying something revolting. At first I did it to keep her safe for Percy. But, I seem to do better with her in darkness. She does not remind me of Meribel then."

"That is something, at least. You have about five hours until dawn. Plenty of time to fulfill her wildest imaginings. In the dark." Giles warmed his hands over the coals in the brazier of the watchtower.

"I do not think she has wild imaginings, Giles. I do not believe she knows anything of carnal relations."

"Try kissing her and you will think otherwise."

"Damn you! I *have*. That is how I know she is innocent. Her passion springs forth, fresh and sweet and spontaneous. But she has no idea where it will lead. I must protect her, so she will not find out." Raymond challenged Giles with his look.

"Are you *that* inept in bed?"

"To hell and back with you, Giles—one day you will go too far!" Raymond closed his eyes and took a deep breath before reopening them. "Do you not understand? My heart is not whole. How can I give her only the burned bits of it Meribel and Alonso left behind? 'Twould dishonor her."

"You miss the point, Raymond. Ceridwen is the one who will pull you back together and heal you. If you let her, she will keep Meribel at bay—in her sarcophagus, where she belongs!"

"I would that she could."

"Give her the chance." Giles tossed back another swallow of honey-scented mead.

"She will not have me. She told me as much before I came to beat some respect into you." Raymond flexed his sore hand.

"You are not trying hard enough."

"I do not want to try! If it did not mean going back on my word I would send her home tomorrow."

Giles shook his head. "You are infatuated with her, and you don't even know it. If I were you, I would go down on my knees before her, beg her forgiveness, spout poetry, whatever it took."

"You are *not* me—and you can thank God for that. You do not have to put up with having a bloody satyr for a lieutenant."

"'Tis plain to see you are still jealous." Giles offered his chin to Raymond. "Take another swing at me, if it will help."

"Do not tempt me, Giles."

"As you wish. And now that you are wed, there will be no more talk of you returning yourself to Alonso, will there?"

"It is too late for that, I think, my honor aside. But now I see I dare not leave Ceridwen alone with you about, so the point is moot." Raymond turned to go. "And Giles, stay away from Lady Blanche. Find your pleasure elsewhere."

"You are a cruel master, my lord. But the choice is not always up to me."

"I do not want to hear any excuses of being helplessly ravished by her. Just make certain you keep out of reach."

"Aye, milord." Giles sank back to the stones of the walkway, and the tower guard ambled over to him, flask in hand. Raymond paused at the head of the stairs to look back at his friend. Giles needed someone to steady him, keep him away from an excess of wine and eager women. A formidable challenge. But not as great as the one he himself faced now.

Ceridwen sat in a small alcove along the curtain wall, below an arrow loophole. Hamfast had followed her from the hall after the feasting had deteriorated into informality, and he rested his craggy head in her lap. She held her flute in her hands, warming it and turning it slowly. She had not played it since her mother died. Two years or more.

"I do not know if I yet have the heart to blow life into it," she whispered to the dog, and he heaved a sigh as though he understood. But she raised it to her lips to try.

Like a small miracle the notes emerged. Hesitant at first, they flowed and rippled into a bittersweet song that both eased her sorrow and kept it fresh. Ceridwen played as softly as she could, but as if of its own accord, the music swelled. It echoed against the stones and flew out into the night, carrying her heartache with it. Gradually it slowed and dwindled, until the melody was but a whisper on the wind. She lowered the flute. Hamfast lifted his head and growled.

"You have turned him against me."

Raymond's silhouette filled the opening to her hiding place, backlit by the fires the guards burned in their braziers. Ceridwen's heart bounded. There was no eluding him. Her husband. "Hamfast does what he wills, of his own accord."

"As do you. How did you manage to escape Alys and Blanche and Shona? I would have thought it impossible."

"I am chatelaine now. They do as I command. Does that surprise you?" It had surprised *her* mightily when Blanche had addressed her as "Madame."

"Nay. 'Twould seem everyone is ready to fall at your feet."
Except you. But I must be very, very careful now.

Raymond sank to his haunches, then to his knees. "What do you wish of me?"

His action startled her as much as his words. Never could she have imagined Raymond de Beauchamp on his knees, for anyone. He had even refused to kneel during the wedding. But he was doing it now, and she had best honor him with the truth. "Time, my lord. I need time above all else."

"Take all you need, then."

His voice was low and even. She could detect no trace of either sarcasm or disappointment. Ceridwen waited for an insult, a last cutting word. But it did not come.

"You play like a troubadour." He reached out to pet Hamfast. The beast licked his hand as if in apology.

Ceridwen was bewildered by Raymond's mildness. "Thank you, my lord."

"You should entertain us in the hall some time."

"I would like that."

"I had best get back to our guests, before the place is torn down." He rose, overshadowing her once again.

Our guests. Not "my" guests. Something was going on that made her uncomfortable. It was much simpler when he made himself easy to loathe. "I would accompany you, my lord, but the women will accost me and—"

"You cannot hide from them all night. Let them bathe you, and dress you, or undress you, whatever. No one has to know what you and I do, or don't do afterward."

Relief flooded Ceridwen and she had to stop herself from sounding too happy when she replied. "Guide me then, for I am unused to such crowds."

"Come." Raymond offered her his hand.

Ceridwen accepted it and got to her feet, whereupon he gently withdrew his fingers from hers. Feeling a sudden hollowness, she walked with him back to the hall, to merriment and laughter in which they did not share.

Raymond's bed was big. Cold and empty, but for her. After what he had said about appearances, Ceridwen had no desire to anger him by making a point of sleeping elsewhere. She trembled in spite of her best efforts to remain calm. She had only his honor to rely upon, that he would leave her alone. Blanche and the other women had primped and perfumed her until she could hardly stand herself. She felt like a sacrificial offering.

They had left moments before, upon hearing word that Raymond approached, propelled by a gang of young men headed by Giles and her brother. But at least Raymond had forbidden the usual custom of the revelers tossing the bride and groom into bed and undressing them for all to see.

Just outside the door, they made crude jests and ruder noises. She tugged on the bedcurtain to close any gap. Despite her care, it billowed apart as the door opened. She jerked the covers up to her chin, amidst lusty whoops of appreciation.

"Nay, get out—even you, Wace. I need no assistance. And take that stinking dog with you." Raymond slammed the door shut after Hamfast and leaned his back against it. "Jesu."

A giggle was quickly stifled. Ceridwen started. She certainly did not find the situation amusing. Raymond jerked the curtain fully open and surveyed his bed, without taking particular note of her. He dropped to the floor and after a few resounding thumps reappeared with a lad in each fist. Ceridwen's gasp of dismay at the black look on Raymond's face turned to mirth when she saw the impish, identical grins of the young men.

"Scoundrels. Heathens. To whom do you belong?"

"Why, we are your cousins, my lord." They spoke in unison. "We came from London Towne with our lady-mother Clarisse."

"See that you return there. Soon. Do not let me catch you in here again. My lady is Welsh—she has wicked skills for dealing with the likes of you." Raymond ejected them bodily out the door and barred it. "Meddling old woman. Who does she think she is, spying on me with her cretinous offspring?"

"Are we alone now?" Ceridwen forced herself not to clutch the bedclothes.

"Aye. Does that worry you?"

"My father said you are a man of honor."

"That still does not tell me if you are worried or not." Raymond leaned against the bedpost.

"Should I be?"

"Aye." Raymond began to take off his clothes.

Ceridwen swallowed. "You promised."

"Did I?"

Frantically she thought back. He had implied, he had offered, but he had promised nothing. "But I understood you to say, that is, I meant for you to understand that I—"

"Shh...I know. You are not ready, nor do you love me, and I am a motherless, wife-killing Beauchamp. Does that sum it up?" He sat on the edge of the bed and pulled off his boots.

"Perfectly." She averted her eyes as he removed his hose.

"Well then. Beds are rare in this keep. This one is mine, and I intend to sleep in it. If you do not exercise the privilege of joining me, the floor is yours—I will not touch you. And if you can refrain from touching *me,* you will remain a virgin until hell freezes over, if you like.''

The gall of the man! He should be so fortunate that she might deign to touch him—and as for the floor, even Hamfast did not sleep there. But there was something in his voice....

As Raymond slid between the linens Ceridwen finally dared look at him. In the light cast by the fire his skin gleamed golden. She had caught a glimpse of his narrow waist, and the taut muscles of his buttocks. His shoulders were broad, and the contours of his chest were sprinkled with hairs the same dark color as his beard.

Apparently the blond of his head was not reproduced elsewhere on his anatomy. Not that she cared. Without his clothes, he appeared younger. But their lack made no difference to his behavior. He was completely unselfconscious. And as offensive as ever.

'''Tis rude to stare,'' he said.

''Pardon me.''

''Good night, Madame.'' He turned his back to her and pulled the sheet up under his arm.

She had seen it again in his eyes. That small edge of fear. ''My lord?''

''Mmm?''

''You need not have dismissed Hamfast, if he is used to sleeping here with you. There is room.''

He turned to look at her, over his shoulder. ''You ever surprise me, my lady. But sometimes, even I cannot stand him and his fleas. The bedding is clean, and I had a bath today—he did not. He will survive the night with Wace.''

Ceridwen cleared her throat. ''My lord—Raymond—this is very awkward. You have taken me to wife as a favor to Parsifal, and to satisfy my father. I know I asked for time, but I have a...a duty towards you, whether we are enemies or not. I am not sure what it is, exactly, but—''

''That much is painfully obvious.''

Raymond turned over to face her and raised himself on his elbow. His cool gaze traveled over her features, her hair, the dips and mounds of her body beneath the covers. In a nervous motion at odds with his look, he wiped his face with one hand. The ripple of muscle across his upper arm, the flexing of his strong fingers did strange things to her stomach.

"Duty. What an inspiring concept on one's wedding night," he drawled.

"As long as *she* is between us, duty is all that I can offer." Nay—that was not what she had meant to say! She did not want to offer him anything. If he took something from her, that was his right, and she must endure it. But she had no business offering herself to a Beauchamp. Especially not one who seemed as tense and ready to pounce as this one.

"You are clever, Ceridwen. You manage to say the one thing that will absolutely ensure I will not profane you. But right you are. *She,* as you put it, is here. She once lay where you are lying now. Her hands gripped the bedclothes, even as yours do at this moment. Her scent filled the air…her laughter broke the silence. She is dead, but she is still stronger than you are."

"Stop it! Don't." The strain of the day had worn Ceridwen down to her last few ragged threads of composure. If he made one more cruel remark, appearances be dashed—she would go sleep with Alys. Before she could prevent it a hateful tear slid down her cheek. Before she could say no, Raymond took her into his arms and kissed her face, her neck, her shoulders.

"Forgive me," he whispered.

Bewildering, delicious new sensations racked her body at his touch. Heat poured off his naked skin. He was hard and angular, so different from her…but even as his fervor surprised her, so did his gentleness. Her heart cried out for her to relax into his embrace, but she could not. To enjoy him would be a sin, against her people and her own honor. She stiffened in his arms. A low moan escaped him, a whisper of sound…

"Meri…"

Like a splash of ice water, the name separated them.

"I am sorry," he said, his face gone white. Until that moment Ceridwen had not fully realized what word he had uttered…merry? Marry? She knew better. He had asked Meribel's forgiveness—for touching her, Ceridwen. Fresh pain lanced her above her old wound. But the ache was nothing the arts of medicine could remedy. ''I never thought to hear myself say this, Raymond, but, so am I.''

Chapter Fifteen

W eeks passed, and with each day Ceridwen felt more like a ghost herself. She moved silently about the keep, from the hall to the kitchens, and from there to the turret where she, Blanche and Alys spun and wove wool to make clothes for the men-at-arms. She oversaw the laying by of stores for the coming winter, grain and ale and barrels of venison soaked in boiled fat.

Raymond was rarely about. He rode far into the hinterlands for days, returning exhausted and looking grimmer each time she saw him. He did not tell her what he did on these trips. They spoke only of practical matters, their personal feelings submerged, as beneath the awful weight of an impending disaster.

Rumor had it that Alonso was making ready to lay siege to Rookhaven. Besieged. The thought struck terror to Ceridwen's heart. She had not experienced it herself. But she had heard from survivors who came to throw themselves upon her father's mercy. It would seem exciting at first. Banners and challenges and expectations of a good fight. But the veterans knew better.

They spoke of the slow, grueling descent through boredom, fear, starvation, and worst of all, thirst. If there was no well within the keep, or if it had been poisoned, it was only a matter of time. There would be no need for the mangonels and trebuchets or other engines of destruction.

There was another danger. Someone could slip out in the night, and in exchange for his life, or some other reward—hand over the keys, and make sure the gate was left unbarred. It had happened. Many times. Then the defenders, having forfeited their lives the moment they first refused to surrender, weeks or months before, would be put to the sword.

Thinking of this, Ceridwen walked through the village, Blanche and Bree at her side. No doubt the situation was one of the "opportunities" her father had spoken of. But she could see no honor in putting the people of Rookhaven in harm's way. If Raymond suffered, so did they.

"Good morrow, Master Aelfson." She nodded to the man.

"Bless you, my lady, and many thanks for the loan of the cart." He beamed at her, his high forehead shiny even in the crisp air of November.

"Bring all the fodder and wood you can glean. Make certain everyone knows they are to be within the walls well before nightfall on Friday next. I want no headlong rush at the last moment. 'Twill be inconvenient, but I will not take chances, with so many children about."

"Aye milady, I will see Sir Raymond's orders is carried out."

Ceridwen did not bother to advise him that Raymond had given no such orders. She acted on instinct, on the cold prickle of fear that crept between her shoulder blades when the wind blew from the east—from Alonso's demesnes.

"Madame—"

"Do not call me that, Blanche, please." Ceridwen strode farther afield, toward the oak grove.

"You are too stubborn. You have a position—use it to full advantage. Why do you not leave all this to Raymond?"

"He already has his hands full."

"Doing what? Nothing but running about—like a capon who thinks he is still a rooster."

"He is—" Ceridwen put her hand to her mouth as unexpected laughter welled up. She amended what she had been about to say. "—ready to be plucked—"

"Stuffed," Blanche offered.

"Basted."

"Stewed."

"In his own juices," Ceridwen finished. She laughed out loud, and for a moment felt as she had at home, when she and

Rhys had poked merciless fun and mimicked Englishmen, play-acting for the benefit of their siblings.

A rumble of hooves vibrated the ground beneath her feet. Ceridwen lunged and jerked Blanche out of the path of six horsemen as they crested the hill at a gallop.

He had returned.

In a smooth maneuver, Raymond peeled away from the group and cantered back to where the women stood. His prize charger, Orpheus, heaved and snorted, spraying them with flecks of foam. Raymond's hard-eyed glance barely touched upon her, but came to rest on Blanche.

"Do you wish a ride back?"

"No thank you, my lord."

"What of you?" Raymond's gaze shifted to Ceridwen, and she was dismayed at his state. Mud-splattered from the waist down, his clothing was torn, his face wind-burned and crusted with dried blood from a deep cut over his eye. She looked to Blanche.

"Go ahead, Ceridwen. I see the others there. Bree, take the basket and start looking for chestnuts." The child ran off, with Blanche following at a leisurely pace.

"What the hell are you doing out here, gathering pig-fodder?" Raymond leaned down and extended his arm, curling his fingers impatiently. There was no refusing him. Ceridwen put her foot in the stirrup he freed for her and he hoisted her up to sit pillion behind him. She put one arm around his waist, then slipped her little finger through her skirt's hem-loop to prevent her gown from draping too far down the horse's flank.

She relaxed her tense stomach muscles as Orpheus moved forward at a sedate walk. "I am preparing for a siege. Is that not my responsibility, as well as yours?"

Raymond did not reply, but sat his horse stiff-backed and silent. Anger sparked within Ceridwen. She was tired. Of his long absences, of his surliness, of feeling all alone even when he was with her. "What say you, man? Am I not speaking English?" She gave him a thump between the shoulderblades.

He surprised her with a chuckle. "You are, barely. But 'tis improved a hundred-fold since first you came." He twisted around, with a crooked grin on his face. "I must tutor you in French, next."

"I look forward to it. What happened to your brow? That is a gaping wound."

"I ran into one of Alonso's scouts. His lance, rather."

"Oh, dear."

"'Twas worth it. He told us Alonso has taken to his bed, and the lady Gwendolyn attends him night and day."

"How do you know 'tis not a ruse, to put you off guard?"

"It is the truth."

The look on his face, the brief, predatory gleam in his eye, told Ceridwen the scout had not suffered long. She hastened to change the subject. "Who is Gwendolyn, after all? I met her once, and she liked me not one bit."

Raymond returned his gaze forward. "She likes no one but herself. She is the sister of Alonso's lady-wife."

"What? He has taken his own good-sister as a lover?"

"Are you surprised? You have much to learn about my brother."

"Is his wife dead, then? Even so, how can he spout piety, along with Everard?"

"His lady is quite alive, in a convent. She is well rid of him. And you should know by now, that when the wealthy sin, 'tis looked upon as high spirits, or eccentricity."

"I see." She did not, but had no wish to pursue the topic. "Why is it, my lord, that we can speak intimately of others, but not of ourselves?" The weary horse stumbled and Ceridwen gripped Raymond's middle harder. "We did before, on occasion."

"That was ere I knew you too well. Or, when we are in the dark, and I can forget…"

Who I remind you of. Ceridwen shifted up, as the motion of the destrier's rump tended to work her slowly arrears.

"Do you wish to sit before me?"

"Would that be wise?"

"Probably not."

"All right." What had her treacherous mouth agreed to now? Raymond halted his horse, and grasping her about the waist, swung her onto his hip, the way a mother carries her babe. "Come on, slide your leg over, I cannot hold you all day."

"Facing you?" She was aghast. "Astride?"

"Aye. 'Tis the only possible way to fit you in." He grinned at her, a wicked, slow grin that spoke more of lust than of humor. "We are married, after all." He settled his hands on her bottom in a most familiar manner, lifting her thighs to ride over his. "Perhaps it is time we got to know each other better."

"What I know of you is quite enough, my lord."

"I cannot say the same of you."

She shivered. "I had best get down and walk the rest of the way. Orpheus is tired."

"Nay, he does not mind. Let everyone see. Let everyone think you are soft and willing…that I can charm you, and you are not burnt to ashes at my dragon-touch."

Raymond's mouth was too close to hers, as was his body, between her parted legs. Dizziness swept Ceridwen as she looked upon his chiseled features. Of late, he had not been near enough for her to see him clearly. It was a gift, to have him but inches away. She bit her lip at the sight of the gash in his brow. Without thinking, she stroked the clean line of his jaw.

"Does your wound not hurt?"

"Oh, aye, it does, it does…" Raymond breathed, and slid his hand up her thigh. Ceridwen squirmed and sighed. He blinked, then his eyes opened wider, and stayed that way. She smiled. He looked innocent—almost. She slid her fingers behind his ear, into the thick, dark undercoat, and was lost.

"Not now…not yet," he whispered. "Wait."

Raymond's head tipped back and her mouth hovered above his. Then he straightened and his arm tightened at her back as he looked past her. Ceridwen released the breath she had been holding, and disappointment bumped her heart as a horseman raced toward them. It was Wace, and something was very wrong.

"My lord—'tis Hamfast, he is in a bad way."

"What has happened?"

"They have brought him in sorely injured from the hunt."

Raymond's face paled beneath the blood and grime. "Excuse

me, lady, I must take my leave of you.'' He boosted himself backwards over the cantle, giving Ceridwen room to draw her leg up and slip down to the ground, with his support. As soon as she was clear he vaulted back into the saddle. He touched his spurs to Orpheus's sides and the charger sprang away, leaving her and Wace alone in the lane.

Ceridwen swallowed a lump in her throat. Why did he exclude her from the rush to aid his dog? She too loved Hamfast. If he was hurt she should be there. ''How bad is he?''

''Bad enough that if I could avoid my master for the next week, I would. And that only if Hamfast lives.''

''Let me get up behind you, Wace. Perhaps there is some way I might help.''

''I pray that you can, lady.''

''Ahh, Bruce. How came this to pass?'' Raymond knelt beside Hamfast. The dog lay on a litter by the central fire in the hall. Raymond rubbed the hound's great head and Hamfast whined and licked his hand. The huntsman had bound the wound, but a red stain spread through the bandages on the dog's belly. Raymond knew there would be no hurrying Bruce's telling of events. ''Has he taken any water?''

''Nay. No' yet.'' The Scot shifted uncomfortably and hunkered down. '''Twas a stag that done it.''

''Truly?''

''Aye. Never in all my days did I witness such a sight. Hamfast had the one stag at bay. When the rest ae' the hounds cut loose, he was caught when the thing swung its head. Then a *white* stag appeared, and engaged t'other. Shinin' pale, it was. Like a fair maiden's throat.''

''And?'' Raymond's mouth went dry.

''While they fought we were able tae bear away your poor wounded beastie.'' Bruce shook his head.

''A white stag…'' Raymond wondered if it was *his,* ethereal white stag, or some other. But there could hardly be more than one. ''What was Hamfast doing out with you, anyway?''

''Och, milaird, he's been that restless. I couldnae deny him, ye've been gone sae much. Forgive me.''

Raymond rubbed his forehead and sighed. "Be easy, man. 'Tis not your fault. Did you bring down either stag?"

"Nay, we abandoned the chase when Hamfast was felled. Such a strange thing. 'Twas an omen—a warnin' tae do the right. So we all agreed."

"Perhaps it was, Bruce. Do the right, come what may. Get some rest. I will watch over him." Raymond glanced up as Ceridwen and Wace entered the hall. God bless her for the lovely sight she was. The hair…those eyes…her skin. He shook himself mentally. Since when had he ever allowed a woman to distract him from his dog? He was breaking his cardinal rule. Over and over. He stole another glimpse of her.

"How is he?" she asked, crouching close by Raymond's thigh. Her clean scent quickened his pulse.

"'Tis too soon to tell. He could go either way. Perhaps he will be lucky, as you were."

"Something other than luck saved me, my lord."

Raymond slanted his gaze to her. "Oh?"

Ceridwen's cheeks pinked. "Do you not remember?"

"I recall Alys torturing you with a bag of hot, putrid herbs. I recall your shouts when she made you drink yet another of her noxious brews." He recalled bathing her with cool water as she twitched with fever…he recalled the ache in his heart when he had looked upon her face and thought he would never have sight of her again. That was when…

"You kissed me. And afterward I got better."

"Shall I kiss Hamfast then? Or should you? Perhaps all of us should take turns. I know—get Giles. He is the kisser *par excellence*. Fetch him, Wace. Let him deal with this." *Oh, God, let me stop this fruitless denial.*

"Why do you ridicule me?"

"I do not. I am but acting upon your recommendation."

"You have no heart, Beauchamp. Why did I ever think you might? You are right. Alys cured me of my wound. I would that she could cure me of you as well." Ceridwen rose and headed for the stairs.

Raymond jumped up after her. "Wait, Ceridwen."

She faced him, and the confusion of pain and sorrow he saw

in her eyes added another hundredweight to his guilt. "About what happened, on our wedding night. I did not do it a-purpose, nor to wound you. I—I seemed to slip into another place."

Why did he even try to explain? It was useless. How could an innocent girl like Ceridwen understand what he himself could not? He had loved Meribel. He had hated her too, for what she had done. But mostly he hated Alonso, with a burning passion that spread and overflowed until it had begun to consume all else.

"You are staring at me, my lord."

"Am I?"

"I would like to consult with Alys. Perhaps she can advise us on Hamfast's wound." Ceridwen stood with her fists full of overgown, ready to flee him.

"Nay, sweeting. There is nothing to be done for him beyond giving him time, and—love." Good lord. Was not that what she needed as well? She had asked for time, so he ignored her. She had never asked for love. But then neither had he. He could not afford it. Could he? "Ceridwen—"

"Excuse me, Raymond. I have business to attend." She curtsied and swept away. He was left in the damp gloom of the hall, chewing on his thumbnail as he watched her depart.

"Woman trouble?"

Raymond bit his tongue. "Hell, Giles. Can you not desist from sneaking up behind me? Are you planning to take over, when I drop dead from one of your frights?"

"Well, now. Not a bad idea, at that."

"My hound is dying, Giles. Does that mean this farce of a marriage will end when he goes? After all, they bought me with him." Raymond sank to the floor and drew Hamfast's blanket up to cover the dog more securely.

"Oh, Raymond, you cannot give up on him. Look, his nose is damp, his ears are cool. He is doing better than you did after we got that arrow out of you." Giles squatted next to Raymond.

"Such helpless waiting tears me apart inside." Raymond smoothed the wiry hairs of the dog's brow with his knuckles.

"Then do something. Go practice your swordplay with Wace. Or find someone who needs a good beating, and give it to him."

"I am surprised to hear you make that suggestion."

"'Tis but one of many. Now, the best way to bury one's sorrow, is between the legs of a—"

"I do not want your suggestions, Giles. What I want is for you to watch over Hamfast in my place. And if even a whisker of his muzzle looks awry, let me know."

"Where shall I find you, milord?" Giles settled down next to Hamfast, and Shona slipped from the shadows into the knight's encircling arm.

"In the chapel, Giles, where else?" Raymond allowed himself a small grin at the look of surprise on Giles's face.

"I am sorry you believe his condition that grave."

"'Tis my own as much as his. Shona-lass, do not let Giles's hands wander. Have you the dagger I gave you?"

She nodded.

"And you remember how to use it? Upthrust, always, when you are disadvantaged by height." Raymond demonstrated.

"Aye, milord, and many thanks." She beamed triumphantly at Giles, whose benign features had compressed into a scowl.

Raymond nodded. "Good, then." He strode away to the stair leading to the chapel, where he had seen the trailing hem of Ceridwen's gown disappearing upwards.

Evening blues and reds glowed faintly from the round window above the nave, still littered with the crushed, dried petals of the roses he had obtained with such difficulty for the wedding. He had wanted to give her joy that night, in the only way he knew how. But she was not ready for him. Perhaps she never would be. And he had failed her miserably.

His wife knelt at the altar working at something, apparently so engrossed she did not hear him behind her.

"Ceridwen."

She started and gripped her forefinger with a little gasp.

"Let me see it."

She pulled away, as a three-year-old might. "Nay."

"Ceridwen, we do not make blood sacrifices at this keep, no matter what you may have heard. Tsk—that is not so deep. Nay, do not put it in your mouth!" He cut a bit of the altar cloth and bound her finger with it. "What are you doing?"

"Trying to help."

"I see." Raymond picked up the chunk of beeswax. She had chopped off the end of a large candle. It was preciously wrought, considering how short a time she had had to carve it. The figure of a dog, standing tall and strong. A wax replica of the sick person or animal on the altar would effect a cure, so the pious believed. Keep God's attention on them. God knew he needed it—he and Hamfast both.

Raymond found himself sinking down next to Ceridwen. Gently, he slipped his hands around her waist. She did not pull away, and he looked into her shadowed, sea-green eyes. "Thank you, for caring. He is but a beast, after all."

"Less so than are many men."

"Myself included?" His fingers flexed, and her hip bones were too sharp beneath his palms.

"I—I cannot believe that anymore, Raymond. You are too many things at once. You have befuddled me."

Ceridwen touched his forearm lightly, and a chain of unbidden desire tightened between his loins and his heart.

"I know the feeling," he replied. "But sometimes I too start to disbelieve that I am wholly a beast. Shall I be honest with you?" He stroked the back of her hand, and her black lashes veiled her eyes briefly before she met his gaze again.

"I would have it no other way."

"There is something that strikes fear in me."

"That I already know. But what?"

Raymond took a deep breath. "When a man like me falls in love, there is no turning back. Neither for himself, nor for the object of his devotion. Either both will soar, or both will be engulfed in flames. And there will be no rising phoenix from those ashes, I can tell you. I fell once before, Ceridwen, and I fear to fall again. I am fighting it. And it is killing me."

She winced and he loosened his grip on her.

"But *why* do you fight it? It must be liberating, to have such a feeling. Why must it become dark and dangerous?"

Raymond's hand strayed to trace the pure line of her cheek, contrasting against the jet of her hair. "You have not experienced it then, to ask such a question."

"I have too. And my love remains true, even though the one I love is dead."

Raymond's heart twisted at these words. But he had no right to feel jealous. He could not expect any love from her. Even if he never again let Meribel come between them. He was nothing to Ceridwen. Why did he lay his feelings out? She was a woman. She would store them up and use them against him later, when he was most vulnerable.

Ceridwen's cool fingers rested on top of his and stopped their fidgeting. "Raymond, I will not mock you for having a heart. I did not mean what I said earlier."

"I deserved it."

"You cared, Raymond. Enough, at least, to do for me what I would do for your dog. You should rejoice and nurture the spark of warmth you find within yourself."

"'Tis a bit more than a spark."

"Is it?"

"Aye." It had grown into a blaze. Hot and perilous.

Ceridwen met his gaze fearlessly and moved closer, still on her knees, as was he. She put her palm to his chest, over his erratically pounding heart. "Show me."

"You want me to cut it out?" His voice cracked.

"Nay. Show me, Carrog Dhu…breathe your fire into me. Let me feel it." Ceridwen's voice was like a whisper of silk, inviting him to touch her.

"I cannot."

Her hand slid upwards to skim his throat. "Why not?"

He swallowed. "We are in chapel."

She smiled at his excuse. "Then let us go elsewhere."

Raymond looked about. "I will feel guilty."

"Hamfast will not mind. He is happiest when you are pleased, as is everyone else at this keep."

"Truly?"

She nodded solemnly. Raymond sighed. "Then I owe it to them all, to make up for the misery I have reflected."

"You owe them, and you owe me."

Raymond smoothed his lady's hair back from her face. "I have treated you shamefully."

"Aye."

"Everything between us will change, Ceridwen. But you have not seen me when—you do not know—" *He* knew what he was like. And Meribel had been a spitting cat in the bedchamber. But for all her willfulness, Ceridwen was yet a tender, sweet morsel of a woman. Perhaps it was not such a good idea to bed her. But his body begged to differ, and the ache was becoming unbearable.

She squeezed his hand. "I have faced quite a few terrifying sights, my lord. I do not expect you to be the worst of them."

Raymond increased the pressure of his fingers around hers. "I must see to the men, and finish my rounds. We will continue this discussion…later." He helped her stand, and carefully set Hamfast's image at the feet of the Virgin Mary.

Ceridwen placed a kiss on the head of the wax figurine. "I will settle him for the night."

Shadows wavered against the soaring arches of the chapel, and candlelight danced, picking out red highlights in her hair. Raymond shivered, part from the cold and part in nervous anticipation. "I hope not to be too long. Bruce wishes to see to my wound, since Alys has gone to her daughter's croft."

"Let me try. I will not have you scarred by his clumsy hand."

"Nay, he will be sorely offended if I do not let him do it, he feels so badly about the dog."

"He will have me to answer to if he makes a shambles of it."

Raymond raised her chin with his finger, and looked into her glittering eyes. "My, my. So proprietary. Perhaps I had best stop by the kennels and put on a collar and leash."

"Do that." Ceridwen smiled at him, with a mixture of hope and longing and what he knew was false bravery. She saw too much, and yet she knew not everything. He wanted to kiss her then and there. But once started, he would not be able to stop. He touched his fingers first to his lips then to hers. "To bed."

She skipped away, throwing him a mischievous look over her shoulder. "I will give Lord Hamfast some broth first."

Raymond tried to return her smile, but his face felt like it would shatter with the effort.

Ceridwen hurried from attending Hamfast, who had dutifully lapped up the bowl of rich meat juices she had warmed for him. He was safe, for Giles dozed by the fire, his head pillowed on one arm. But what had she started with Raymond? How much time did she have to prepare?

Once in their chamber she was not sure what to do. They had not slept in the same bed since their wedding night. Ashamed to go to Blanche and confess her failure, she had kept to a pallet of straw in the corner, refusing Raymond's offers to share his bed, even undisturbed.

Someone rapped on the door. Was he back for her already? Deep inside, she hoped so. "Enter."

"Ah, Ceridwen—I am glad you're still awake—but what is the matter?" Blanche hurried to her side.

Ceridwen felt herself redden. "Tonight he will, em, I think we are going to—oh, I am so afraid of making a fool of myself!"

Blanche stared, wide-eyed, and her hand went to her mouth. "You mean to say Raymond has not yet fulfilled his duty toward you? But that is scandalous!"

"I have not exactly given him the chance." Ceridwen was surprised to feel she must defend him.

"He desired it?"

"I do not know. But his wife—"

"*You* are his wife." Blanche's lips compressed into a line.

Twisting the end of her belt in her hands, Ceridwen sat upon Raymond's bed. "He still loves her."

"Then make him love you more. Make him forget her."

"How do I do that?" Ceridwen searched Blanche's kind eyes.

The lady sat beside her and took her hand. "Dearling, he is but a man and all men are the same."

"I do not understand men. I know not what to do."

"You do not have to do anything. Just let him get a good eyeful of you, then douse the lights if you wish."

She would not douse the lights. What if he imagined her to be Meribel in the dark? "You mean, make sure he knows it is me?"

Blanche smiled. "'Tis more complicated than that, but that too is wise, considering the family we are dealing with."

"Oh."

"Listen." Blanche's gray eyes gleamed in earnest, and Ceridwen paid her full attention. "When he comes to you, do not be coy. Do not hold back. Give him everything of yourself, all that you feel. Do not try to hide it."

"You are telling me to trust him."

"Never be dishonest in bed. Only whores are thus."

Ceridwen was silent for a moment, absorbing this. Her eyes burned. "'Tis wrong of me to love him. I am weak-willed. He is the enemy of my people."

"Nay. He is your husband before all else. It is God's will that you are his. Abide by it." Blanche rose and went to the door, then turned. "'Tis no sin to love him. And if you do, then pray he will not be taken from you." She bit her lip, and when Ceridwen started to go to her, Blanche shook her head and smiled fiercely. "Nay, stay you there, and have much joy this night."

Ceridwen sat in bed, awaiting Raymond's return, wearing her flimsy shift. Her insides fluttered with a sort of dreadful excitement, the same way she felt seeing a falcon stoop to its prey. She loved the beauty, and hated the blood. Whatever happened the truth would become apparent. Prove whether there was anything of value between them, or destroy it forever. She could not go on being torn in two. But Alys had been right about one thing. The waiting and wondering were awful. She scooted under the covers.

Do not be coy, Blanche had said. Well, she never slept in her shift normally. She had best be brave and dispense with it now. She wriggled out of the garment and tossed it over the side of the bed. The candles burned lower, her eyelids dragged, and still no sign of Raymond. Perhaps he had changed his mind. Disappointment battled relief. She wanted him. But she was afraid of giving him control...of her body, of her life. He would hold it in his hands. Bloody, Beauchamp hands.

How could she reconcile the parts she knew of him into a whole she could accept? A man who loved his animals with as much tenderness as most men gave their children. One who killed with ruthless efficiency, who hated with a violence that had poisoned his whole being. And who loved so furiously that even death could not dim his passion. Where did she fit in, except as a minor distraction as he went about the larger, darker things of his life?

If the night was a disaster it might be just as well. She could bury the pain in her heart—the leaping ache when he was near, the sharp longing when he ignored her. She could return to viewing him as the enemy. But it would not be easy.

In spite of everything, Ceridwen yawned, and lay back on the pillows. If he did not come in soon, she would bar the door, and he would have to *ask* her permission to enter.

Chapter Sixteen

Raymond was drowning. The sun shimmered faintly above him, far beyond the surface of the cold, heavy water of the moat. He reached for it, his arms extended. His fingers closed on nothing. His lungs were bursting, aching to draw breath.

He was doomed. The air, the light, all goodness was beyond his grasp. Any instant his mouth would open, and he would inhale a great breath of dark, foul liquid. No one would ever find his body, weighted down with guilt.

Then he saw her. She floated facedown above him, her dead eyes stared into his. Meribel…Raymond gasped as he woke, bolt upright. A draft chilled his wet skin. Shivering, he slid down between the sheets, rough and damp against his back.

What a hellish night. Just as he had steeled himself to go up and see to his bride, one of the grooms had arrived in a panic—Orpheus, his most cherished destrier, had colicked. He had had to walk the horse himself for half the night, as the stallion would quiet for no one else. Once that crisis ended it had been all he could do simply to drag himself to bed.

He had found the door unbolted—thank God—and upon seeing that Ceridwen had fallen asleep waiting for him, had not had the heart to disturb her.

Raymond peered into the shadowy space beside him, illuminated by the great candle that still burned near the bed. For an instant he had forgotten that Hamfast was downstairs and not in his usual spot. Instead, Ceridwen lay there asleep, curled into a warm ball, like a cat. He rubbed his face with his hands and stole another look at her.

It was hard to believe she was real. Waves of black hair twined across her pale, slight body, like that of an elfin woman who might only exist on the borders of the physical world. Perhaps he should test her solidity, as was his right. But the old, poisonous fear churned in his stomach.

Once having tasted her, merged with her, he might begin to love her. And once he loved her, he would be consumed by her. She would own him, body and soul, and his life would never be the same. But it was useless to deny the truth. He loved her already.

Raymond lay back and tried to will away the growing warmth threatening to melt his icebound heart. He was her enemy. She was trouble. His head turned again in her direction as if of its own volition. His hand slipped toward the black skeins of her hair, and his fingers delved into the pool of it swirling around her as she lay. He bent his head and lifted the fistful of silken strands to his nose, inhaling their scent, hers alone.

Would losing himself to her be such a tragedy? Surely it was better than his current slow involution toward nothingness. He did not live, after all. He merely existed, awaiting death.

Raymond slid down until he was on a level with Ceridwen. He flexed and extended his fingers to stop his hand from shaking. Even if his mind was not ready, his tense body fairly shouted its refusal to retreat. He ran his palm up her slender arm, to her shoulder, and then around her back, even as he eased his other arm beneath her. She sighed and burrowed her head against his shoulder.

He squeezed his eyes shut and hardly dared breathe as he drew her close. Even if it went no farther, she was more sweetness than he had ever hoped to find in this life. He let himself drift farther into the rising heat that made his blood burn and surge through his body. He would bring her pleasure, joy, and the certain knowledge she belonged only to him.

"Mmm…" Ceridwen floated a notch nearer to wakefulness. This was like her sickroom dream, so long ago. Strong arms about her. Comforting warmth and the musky smell of a man.

So familiar. He was hers, a lover all her own. That was how the dream went…she did not want it to end. She tried to snuggle tighter to him, their closeness nearly complete, but her body yearned for something it lacked.

Ceridwen ran her hands up his muscled back, along his neck and into the thick, soft hair on his head. Her dream and an image of Raymond merged, of his animal undercoat that she longed to touch. Now she could touch him anywhere, any way she liked, in her mind. Her dream lover moaned.

"What is it?" she murmured, sleep still thick in her voice.

"Tu. Tu seulement," he whispered, and his warm lips kissed her neck. He had her locked in his arms, and one heavy, hairy thigh covered her legs. Ceridwen opened her eyes wide and stiffened. Her breath came in quick little gasps as the dream dissolved. Here was no biddable lover. This was Raymond. In the flesh. She had no idea what he expected of her. And the last thing she wanted was for him to discover her ignorance.

His kisses had given her body a hint of something he withheld. The nibbles of the feast with which he tantalized her were no longer enough. Now that she was here with him, she could not imagine what prevented him from revealing to her what she missed, but she was too embarrassed to ask. It might be some fault in herself that she could not remedy.

Why was he breathing so hard? His chest rose and fell against hers in rapid, shallow swells. His mouth moved over her skin with a heated urgency that cried out for her to soothe him, and her fear slipped away. She felt an unfamiliar sense of power, and a peculiar humility.

Her lord was vulnerable. He revealed his need, in secret, to her alone. She ran her fingers back through his hair and down the tight muscles of his shoulders. His lips found hers and he filled her with his tongue and the taste of wine and what was uniquely himself.

Ceridwen melted inside, like honey in the sun. She rubbed her breasts against the crisp hair of his chest and arched her back. Raymond groaned. His silken hardness increased along her belly, hot and blunt. This was where the mystery began. Instead of the anxiety she had expected, a thrill pierced her and her body throbbed in response to his.

His hands whispered on her skin, he was exquisitely gentle. She had not thought him capable of such tenderness. He trembled with the effort of his restraint, and that evidence of his courtesy warmed her heart as no amount of fair words could have.

He bent his head and kissed the peaks of her aching breasts. His mouth closed gently around one nipple, and as he sucked, her flesh grew hard. A tightening, deep within. She caught his shoulders, her need fierce. "Kiss me again!"

This time he took her mouth as hungrily as she did his. They met as equals. Her joy in him took flight, her hands slid along his ribs and on around his back, holding him close—yet not close enough. She rubbed the calf of his leg with her foot and rocked her hips. He caught his breath.

"Open to me, Ceridwen...let me in." Raymond's voice had lost every vestige of authority, every overtone of command. It was a raw request, man to woman.

"Raymond, you need not ask for what is already yours. Please, show me what to do."

He hesitated only an instant before he slid his hand between her thighs. His intent became clear, and she tensed in spite of her willingness to learn. He kissed her throat, murmuring against her skin. "'Tis all all right, Ceri. Believe me, God help us, it will be all right."

He explored her depths with one finger, and stroked her expertly until she writhed against him. Her senses whirled from the overwhelming, delectable assault. "Raymond, I cannot bear it. What is it? *Do* something!" she begged.

"I will, love. We will do it together."

He shifted above her, his heat and weight satisfying in themselves. His hands ran up her thighs and around her hips. What was he waiting for? Ceridwen grew frantic. This was excruciatingly lovely, but there *had* to be more.

Blanche had said he must fulfill a duty. What was the word? *Consummation.* A choked cry came from her throat. "Raymond, discharge thy obligation to me, this instant!"

He paused in his nibbling and chuckled. "Nay, love, not this instant. You would not like that, believe me."

Raymond continued his infuriatingly slow, sensuous caresses. He kissed every part of her he could reach, until she was ready to scream. At her core was a heavy, full throb of desire. "Oh, my lord…" Ceridwen was utterly swept away. He might have asked anything of her, and she would have complied, just to obtain relief.

"I believe you are ready, sweet." His knee parted her thighs. "With my body, I do thee worship," Raymond whispered, and with his most intimate touch Ceridwen knew what *it* was all about. The sly looks and sleepy smiles and blazing eyes, everyone, from Rose and the groom to—aye, even her parents.

But that thought did not quell the surging demand her body made upon his, her need to have him plunge into her, and fill her, to match her perfectly in opposition. He met her desire so fully she barely felt the pinch of pain at the start, and she bit his neck and scratched his back and cried out to God.

Raymond kissed her again and rode her harder, through every buck and twist she made. His thrusts jolted her, each one taking her higher, faster, until her ecstasy exploded into shivering streams of pulsing sensation, shooting up into her belly and down her thighs. To Ceridwen's surprise it seemed his experience was akin to hers, for he shuddered and groaned as if he were about to die of pleasure.

He slid in sweat to her side, and she clung to him. Tears streamed down her face and into his hair as she nestled her face into the warm hollow of his shoulder. Ceridwen felt his throat convulse as he swallowed. He put his arm around her.

"I have made you weep." Raymond's hoarse voice was full of concern.

Ceridwen sniffed and smiled. "Aye. It was—you were wonderful. I had no idea a man could be so—oh, 'twas simply the most glorious thing. Why have you kept this secret from me so long? Make the magic again, Raymond, please." She stroked his rough cheek, and ran her fingers once more into the thick, soft strands of his hair.

He kissed the top of her head and held her close. "It takes a little time, sweeting. For the potion to replenish. Time and wine. Happily we have plenty of both.''

Ceridwen could hear his grin.

The moon had passed them over and sunk long since. Ceridwen dozed astride Raymond, her cheek on his chest, her knees clamped at his ribs. She listened to his heartbeat, to the life flowing through him, and was glad. Never had she felt so close to floating away, for sheer happiness. Nothing had prepared her for this incredible, miraculous joining of two bodies. Of loving a man, heart and soul, and giving him everything of herself.

Now she understood. It was wonderful and overwhelming and holy. She was thoroughly grateful she had not gone into a convent as she had once said, rather than marry a Beauchamp. She was worldly, through and through.

Ceridwen sighed in contentment and placed a kiss on Raymond's salty neck. He had done his best, and it was better than anything she had ever dreamed of in all her girlish imaginings. The mighty Carrog Dhu had worn himself out.

He stirred beneath her and she found herself displaced as he rolled in his sleep. Raymond sprawled facedown and lay diagonally across the bed, one arm flung across her chest. Turning onto her side, Ceridwen pulled the covers back over them and hugged her joy to herself. Everything would work out between them, and she would ask her father to send help. Surely they could stand up to Alonso if they did it together.

The full light of day filled the curtained bed with a white radiance. Ceridwen heard voices below, of chattering women and the cheerful shouts of men. Dogs barked and cattle lowed. It was late. She woke slowly, without fully opening her eyes, and stretched, in a state of happy, tender exhaustion. Now she was a wife in deed as well as name.

Her foot rubbed against another warm body. Her heart leaped. Raymond was with her still. She peeked at him. He slept on his side, his blond head cradled on one arm, his long legs tangled in the bed linens. She had expected him to be gone, off and about his usual duties. Love was not to get in the way of what needed doing.

But this was an opportunity to take a closer look at him, unencumbered by either clothing or formality. She raised herself on one elbow and let her eyes drink up his male beauty. In sleep he lost the half frown that was his most frequent expression. He was even more handsome with his dark brows not drawn together, and his mouth relaxed.

Raymond had a truly exquisite nose, she decided. Long enough to look dignified, but refined and straight. Ceridwen smiled. His lips looked as bruised as hers felt. Strands of sun-lightened hair swept his cheek. She did not dare touch him to push them aside, for fear of disturbing him. And it seemed that Bruce had done a fair job of plastering Raymond's brow, for the bandage had not come loose, in spite of the strenuous night.

Her gaze traveled down. His shoulders were broad for his height, and she loved the way the muscle and bone blended into the complicated dips and rises that she had buried her face against. She had explored every part of him in the dark, every bunched muscle and taut sinew he possessed. Now she wanted to see what heretofore she had only touched.

Ceridwen followed the contours of Raymond's lean torso with her eyes, and quickly passed over the scratches her nails had left on his back and hip. Certain details of their second encounter sprang to mind, and her cheeks flushed.

She caught her breath at the sight of an incomplete circle of small indentations on his flank. A bite-mark? She had no recollection of the point at which she had made *that* particular impression upon him.

Ceridwen chewed her lip. What must he think of her? Her glance strayed lower, to that part of Raymond which had amazed her so in the night. In repose it did not look the way it had felt. There *was* some magic at work here. How had he done it? Changed himself into an instrument of such proportions? But her excursion of his body while he lay unaware was discourteous. Much too revealing. She grasped the edge of the blanket to pull it over him. He shifted his left leg and turned onto his back.

What that small movement revealed triggered the cascade of

a myriad of small bits and pieces in her mind. His eyes. His voice. Even the feel of his hands.

Ceridwen stared at Raymond and knowledge crashed down around her, like a tower collapsing into rubble. She struggled to breathe. Her stomach clenched with fury and crushing disappointment and disbelief. Raymond and Alonso. Similar and yet so different, or so she had thought. She had been blind. Stupid. Gullible. Why had she not put it together before? Ceridwen twisted away, her face hot, and lurched toward the bed's edge.

Strong fingers closed around her ankle and brought her to an abrupt halt. ''Where might you be going, my love?''

''Do not spew any more of that talk upon me.'' Ceridwen's voice was tight and sharp. She kicked Raymond's hand free and turned her back on him.

He sat up, wide awake, his heart thudding in his chest. What had he done wrong? The night had been wild, but Ceridwen had been a party to it at least as much as he himself. Her cries of ecstasy had been genuine, he would bet his life on it.

But his love must lack potency, for the thaw in her to be so short-lived. The worst of it was the growing, somehow familiar look of hatred in her eyes when she met his gaze again.

''Why do you turn from me?'' Raymond swallowed, and waited for Ceridwen's reply. When it came, it was not as he expected.

''Murdering English bastard. *Sais.*''

''*What?*'' Her words snatched his breath away.

''You heard me.'' She scrambled out of his reach, the sheet clutched to her breasts. ''Look at yourself. Look at that.'' She pointed to his thigh, to the entry and exit scars the Welsh arrowhead had left on its way through to his destrier.

He followed her gaze. ''I know not what you mean.'' They were the same as ever, no uglier than most of his other scars.

''Do you not? So casually do you strike down hapless young men? You forget so easily whose blood you spill? Think you harder, my lord.'' Ceridwen's eyes flashed and brimmed.

Raymond stared at her. He blinked as recognition seared him like a hot poker. ''*You* were that vicious, beautiful idiot of a girl?'' He gulped and broke into a sweat, searching for the name. ''And I—I killed your Owain.''

''And I will never, ever forgive you. Even once you are dead.'' Ceridwen ran from the chamber, heedless of her state of undress.

Raymond roared after her. She glanced over her shoulder. Serving-girls scurried out of his way as he blazed closer, with nothing but a linen towel about his waist. ''Where do you think you are going?''

It was not the first time he had asked her that question. ''Anywhere, so long as it is far from you!'' Tears blinded her beyond her already imperfect sight, and she hesitated, not sure which way to turn.

Raymond caught up to her and took her arms in a rough grasp. ''Running away is your answer to everything, is it not? Well, I have not the luxury of that choice. And neither do you.''

''I hate you!'' Ceridwen tried to twist away, but it was impossible to escape Raymond's hands. She beat her fists against his chest and sobbed, lapsing into Welsh and naming him every foul creature she could think of.

He held her close even as she twisted and shook her head. When she found him difficult to pound she tried to knee him. When that effort was thwarted by his legs pinning hers, she sank her teeth into the flesh of his shoulder.

Her head jerked back as a big hand grasped a fistful of hair at her scalp. Not Raymond's hand, but Giles's.

''Release her, St. Germaine.'' Raymond's order was curt.

''Aye, you brute! Turn loose my lady or you will feel *my* teeth in your backside!'' Shona tugged on Giles's surcoat.

Adding to her misery, Ceridwen wanted to sink into the floor and disappear. Here she was, behaving like an animal, reinforcing these Englishmen's already low opinion of her people. Wace appeared at his master's side, full of concern for Raymond's bruised shoulder. A few guards trickled into the walkway to see what the noise was about. Giles's hand slid from her hair.

'''Twas a nightmare only. I will see her calm.'' Raymond glared at the immediate group of would-be saviors, and firmly escorted Ceridwen back to his solar. He thrust her into the chamber and she whirled to face him, still clutching her sheet.

"You cannot force me to stay!"

"Can I not?" He stood between her and the closed door.

"You would not dare."

"You do not know me very well, do you?"

"I know you for what you are and have ever been. A murdering, lying Beauchamp!"

"You would dismiss all that passed between us in the night?"

"It meant nothing. You took your pleasure. And I took mine." Nay!—her heart shrieked in silent protest. It had meant the world to her. Her throat burned and ached as she tried to swallow.

Silence fell like an icy fog, smothering even the heat of their anger. The look on Raymond's face would have frozen the heart of a berserking Dane. Ceridwen took a step backward.

Raymond moved forward. "You *took* your pleasure? Nay, wife, *I gifted you with it*—I alone." He half turned away, as though finished, then spun back to face her. "I told you once before, my body does not lie. What I express with it is the honest truth, whether 'tis dealing death or making love."

"I am sure many a killer is sincere in what he does." She tossed her head, creating a rippling curtain of ebony silk.

Raymond rubbed his hands over his temples, then caught his towel before it fell. "I have no time to quarrel with you, nor to wait 'til you come to your senses. It hurts, I know, to lose someone close to one's heart. And believe me, the pain never goes away, no matter how much blood is spilled in vengeance."

He looked at her, and his cold, sea-blue eyes softened to the color of a summer's eve sky. "I took your friend's life in battle, Ceridwen. Honorably, not out of hate. If I could bring him back, he would tell you he died well. You can be proud of him."

"I am. But Owain is just as dead, whether your so-called honor made you do it or an argument over a meaningless wager did. I cannot forget. I cannot let go." The old, tired memory engulfed her in a fresh wave of anguish. Mixed with her rage, it made her want to tear her hair. Or Raymond's. That thick, luxurious pelt she loved—nay—he must pay for his crime.

But…last night had been matchless in its passion and tenderness. Ceridwen closed her eyes and clenched her fists and bowed her head. Her sheet slipped to the floor, but she did nothing to retrieve it. She stood there and shivered, her hair spilling about her like a black shroud.

Raymond suppressed a shudder of anguish. She was so small. So fragile. He could break her so easily. With his body or with but a few well-chosen words. He leaned down and picked up the linen, drawing it back up around her shoulders. She did not move or look at him.

''I will go elsewhere to sleep from now on. Have no fear for your person.'' Raymond looked about for his clothes. The commonplace, everyday motions of putting them on only served to accentuate the disaster that ravaged him. This was the end. He had no more capacity for pain. Perhaps this was how Percy had felt, when the Saracens had finished with him. Empty. Hollow. Only a silent scream echoing in the dark hole of his heart.

''My lord, you understand, do you not? How it is impossible for me to be with you?'' Ceridwen asked, looking up at him.

He understood. He read it in her eyes, filled with tears, narrowed against the sight of him. It was not only Owain. It was all the people, of her family and hundreds like it, who had died during so many years of oppression. A sea of Welsh blood. The conflict would never end. At least not with her.

''What is your plan, my lady? Should I expect a blade in my throat, or poison in my ale? A loose stone upon my head, or the girth to my saddle cut through?'' He pulled on his boots and fastened the lacings.

''Those are my father's methods, not mine.''

''And what are yours?''

''I sought to…I thought—'' Ceridwen raised her hand to her mouth, and her fingers trembled.

''Tell me now, for I will not stand before you again like this and allow you to abuse me.'' Raymond's heart thundered against his ribs as he strapped on his belt and dagger. He had come back to life only to find torment waiting to engulf him.

"A part of me thought to c-conquer you, with l-love. But it is too late now...." she whispered.

Raymond exhaled the breath he had been holding and stepped toward the door. "It has always been too late, sweeting. You never had a chance in hell of conquering me."

Chapter Seventeen

"What did you say, Giles?" Raymond asked.

Ceridwen looked up from her needlework in time to catch him looking at her instead of Giles. She gave him no hint of her true feelings. Her heart lay like a red-hot stone in her breast.

Raymond's gaze bored into her, challenging her, as it had every day in the week since she had discovered his guilt. Her rage had turned inward. She was a coward, unworthy of her father's faith. And Rhys had probably already reached home, bearing witness to that fact.

Love thine enemy. She had certainly done that. Even from the first moment of knowing the hideous truth, she had seen that she could never avenge Owain by physically harming Raymond. To inflict a wound upon him would be to inflict it upon herself.

There was a better way to hurt him. If she managed to escape him, to run away, it would break his heart, she was sure of it. Just as she was sure it would break her own. It was what they both deserved.

Giles made a small sound of impatience. "I said, the south gate pilings are rotting where they enter the ground, and the keystone of the old tower foundation has a crack as wide as your hand running through it. Alonso, bless him, is making ready to lay siege to us, while you sit here and glower!"

"Ah well, I have as much a mind to cut and run as defend this crumbling death trap." Raymond rubbed his half-healed brow, stood, and paced the floor. Hamfast, still weak but slowly improving, followed him with his head, back and forth. "Why should I remain in this worthless keep? For my honor? A siege costs too much for that sort of indulgence."

"Raymond, you bolster no one's courage by such talk."

"Forgive me, Giles. I have a cruel streak, which needs curbing. Does it not, Madame?"

Raymond turned back to Ceridwen, and she felt her cheeks pink beneath the gazes of the men in the hall. "I cannot understand your cruelty, my lord, so I am no judge of it." Cautiously, Ceridwen awaited his reaction.

"Perhaps you need more experience of it, then."

Giles groaned. "For pity's sake, Raymond. She is an innocent."

"No one past the age of ten is innocent, Giles."

Hamfast whined and Raymond gave him a questioning look. The dog laid his muzzle between his front paws and blinked his ale-brown eyes.

Blanche cleared her throat. "Innocence can be regained."

Raymond gave a short bark of laughter. "Nay. Some things are long gone, and can never be again. Like faith in man. Like virginity."

"Faith can renew. And virginity is a state of mind as much as body. Man can be cleansed. Purged of fear, and doubt, even of hatred."

"And how, pray tell, does this miracle take place?" Raymond walked over and sat on the bench, next to Blanche.

"Aye, lady, tell us, for Shona ever awaits the return of my innocence, so she can take both it and me home to her auntie." Giles tugged on the apron-strings of the dimple-cheeked girl, who passed unnecessarily close to him.

"I am serious, sir. I speak of love, naturally. It heals the deepest of wounds." Blanche glared at Giles.

Ceridwen, her heart pounding, looked up at Raymond from her needlework. *"Amor vincit omnia,"* she offered.

Giles sighed and Blanche smiled archly. Raymond tilted his head and half closed his eyes, as he ever did when he wanted to appear nonchalant—a gesture now utterly familiar to her.

"So, in spite of everything, you have not entirely given up.

will have to do something about that.'' He spoke for her ears alone.

Ceridwen lowered her gaze, sorry she had entered into the conversation. What did he mean?

"'Love conquers all.' What a feeble-minded sentiment,'' Raymond continued. "Only fools and women would find such a statement worthy of consideration.''

Blanche sniffed and looked down her nose at him.

"For those who would listen, we are about to be struck down by an enemy with ten times the men we have.'' Giles leaned forward on his elbows at the table.

"Aye Giles, we hear. You, my friend, must remove my lady. Immediately. Assemble an escort and take her to Lord Morgan, who is yet mourning the loss of his daughter, no doubt.''

"What of the other women?''

"For now they are safer here than in the mountains. Bree is too small to make such a ride at speed. Besides, Ceridwen can see to herself.'' Raymond rubbed his shoulder.

Ceridwen set her jaw. She would not go at Raymond's command. When she left, it would be against his will. "You cannot send me away. It would be disgraceful to leave now and sit in safety. I will not go.'' The embroidery needle poked her finger, and a spot of blood welled up.

"The decision is not yours.''

"Then I will find a way around it,'' she countered, and put her wounded finger in her mouth.

"You will do nothing of the kind.'' Raymond strode to her, grasped her face and forced her to look at him. He pulled her hand away from her lips. "Get this into your head, and hold it fast: there is no future here for you, Ceridwen. None. Not with me. I want no mewling girl underfoot. I have not the time, nor the patience. I do not love you. I never have, and I never will. You cannot replace Meribel.'' Raymond's hand left her cheeks with a rough twist of his fingers and he pivoted to resume his pacing.

Silence fell across the hall. Raymond's men-at-arms looked at each other, or down at their hands. Anywhere but at her. Even Blanche averted her eyes. Ceridwen struggled to breathe, to keep the tears at bay. And beneath the scalding anguish, her anger seethed.

"What are you waiting for? Ready yourself!" Raymond bellowed. He bore down upon her, until Ceridwen flattened back against the wall. His eyes were like blue flames, searing her heart with merciless heat. Then, as if a puff of air had extinguished them, their light vanished. They went cold and dead. His fists relaxed and his voice dropped to a hoarse whisper. "Begone, *Cymraes.*"

Ceridwen stared back into the chill blue of his eyes, and fought for control. He had won. Damn him, the dragon had slithered back into his dark cavern of impermeable numbness. A place that would be the death of her should she try to follow. He had robbed her of victory. Dismissed her. Discarded her.

"With pleasure, Carrog Dhu." Ceridwen summoned all her will not to strike his face where he stood. She let her embroidery fall from her fingers. Straightening her shoulders, she left the hall attended by Blanche, leaving an icy wake.

Raymond watched her go, and tried to forget her look, the way her green eyes narrowed in the old, familiar loathing he inspired so readily. "Giles, have Wace go in your stead. I need you here."

Giles stood. "You did not have to break her heart."

"Did I not?" Raymond stopped short in his passage across the hall. "Would you rather she weeps a few days and forgets me, or that I allow her love to grow to full blossom, and she spends the rest of her life mourning my loss?"

"You are not lost. And you possess a colossal ego to assume she would mourn if you were. But I believe it is already too late to spare her grief."

"So think you. I plan to fight Alonso to the death, since he gives me precious little choice. And 'tis much more likely to be my death than his. I will not risk condemning Ceridwen to what I have gone through since I—since Meribel died. 'Tis far better if she hates me. Hate sustains, and gives one the strength to go on. The lovelorn sit and weaken, caring for nothing." Raymond's voice trailed away. He clenched his fists and looked down at Hamfast. The wretched dog covered his eyes with one foreleg.

"I know not where you get these ideas, my lord. You, who are supposed to be an example of chivalry, make a mockery of all I hold dear. I have had enough of your self-indulgence. I would fain part with you, so painful do I find your present state."

"Part with me? Say you this, as we perch on the brink of war?" Raymond's head whipped up and he could feel his neck veins bulge. "Then get you gone." He lunged after Giles, his dagger drawn quicker than the eye could follow.

The knight skipped backwards and put up both hands. "I am going, I am going. I will take her home."

"Aye, do that. Perhaps she will fall in love with you on the way, and I will have seen the last of you both," Raymond snarled, feeling smaller and smaller inside.

Giles gave Raymond a look of long-suffering and left the hall. Shona glared at him too, and flounced out in Giles's wake.

Raymond took a deep breath. "Now that is settled, let us make ready for battle." He sank back into his great chair, his head aching fiercely. His men rallied to him, all of them speaking at once.

Ceridwen sat her horse in the bailey, and tried in vain to swallow. Her nose tingled. She should have known all along that he would turn on her. Like the vicious animal he was at heart, sprung from a pack of curs. Breeding told—especially bad breeding. He had warned her, and she had ignored him. Love conquers all but Raymond de Beauchamp. Waves of pain boiled through her, making her clutch her stomach with one arm.

Wace stood at Ceridwen's stirrup, and she touched his hand as he held up a mazer of wine. "My thanks, Squire Wace. You have ever shown me kindness. I hope we shall meet again."

"Aye, milady. 'Tis not my place, but I apologize for my lord's behavior. He has not been himself since he stabbed you."

"Truly? I thought he was quite as his reputation led me to expect. I wish him well with his swords and dogs and the dry bones of this keep.'' Ceridwen bit her lip. She had no right to pour her frustration upon the head of the boy.

Wace's soft gaze dissolved her discomfort. ''In his heart he loves you, though he will not admit it to save his life.''

''His love is of no value to me if he cannot share it. He is like a ragged, starving man carrying a locked coffer full of gold, who never looks for the key that is hanging about his own neck.'' She sipped the wine and passed the mazer to Giles, who leaned over the withers of his horse to take it.

''His temper trips him up, every time,'' the warrior observed. ''That and his melancholy. 'Tis best you leave, my lady. Only sorrow awaits you here. He will never change.''

'''Tis no matter to me, anyway. He murdered my dearest friend, a man of my blood, and that I will not forgive.'' Ceridwen gathered the reins and clucked her mount forward. ''Farewell, Wace. Watch over old Alys for me.''

Wace grinned. ''If she will allow it. Have a safe journey to your father's care.''

The small group of riders crossed the drawbridge and headed west. The sky was clear and deep blue, but for a few puffy clouds scudding overhead. Villagers nodded farewells and glowing, breathless children dashed up to watch the riders pass.

From the start, Raymond's people had not looked like they belonged to a tyrant. Few were thin or ragged. The fields were well tended, the sheep plentiful. As they reached the open road Ceridwen's heart roiled with emotions she could scarcely sort out. Raymond was like a selfish, spoiled child. He used people to his own ends, surrounded himself with fawning retainers, but never rewarded them, as far as she could see.

Why did they stand by him? And yet he had nursed Hamfast back to health with the tender care of a mother to her babe. He had nursed *her,* too. She shook her head in bewilderment.

''What is it, my lady?'' Giles asked.

She sighed. ''I do not understand Raymond. How can he be so kind and so cruel, all at once?''

'''Tis simple. He is a double-cheeked ass.''

''Giles!''

''Nay, I know him, better than most. Raymond has the

strength, skill and intelligence to be a great lord, yet he resides as his brother's vassal in this backwater. Alonso has taxed him into poverty, extorted land and monies from him, forced him into warring for profit and revenge. And Raymond has put up with it out of family loyalty.'' The knight paused to scratch at his chest with an apologetic smile.

''Pray continue,'' Ceridwen said.

''Now my lord decides to revolt. Alonso is tired of playing, and will crush him under his heel. All the refugees Raymond has gathered under his protection are now at risk. And when the one appears who would save him from himself, he drives her away.''

Giles spoke matter-of-factly, but Ceridwen could see the pain in his face. He had not mentioned his own forced departure. ''What was that you said—he has gathered refugees?''

''Aye, 'tis Raymond's way of making amends. When Welsh folk pass through, starving and beleaguered, he allows them to stay and recover their strength. If they work hard and look to be honest, he sends them to his lowland meadows and gives them what they need to raise their sheep and build their crofts.''

Ceridwen was amazed. ''How can he afford such charity?''

''You have seen his keep, how he lives. He has sacrificed a great deal of comfort on their behalf. And of course in time they give him a share of their wool and all. It infuriates Alonso that Raymond refuses to bleed his people dry.''

''But why the secrecy? At least it seems a secret to me.''

Giles smiled. ''Ah, that is where Raymond's true nature is revealed. He forbids the peasants to speak of his generosity. In fact he orders them to spread the lies of his ferocious cruelty, and to complain bitterly to strangers. Thus he discourages other lords from attacking him. The worse his reputation, the more they think it will cost them in blood to take his keep. And the less he need spend on his defenses.''

''My God. So that is his way. He did not mean all that he said to me then, did he? Was he trying to push me to leave, for my own safety—is that it?'' She could not hide her hope.

''I have already said too much, milady. If I allow your return he will have me strung up on the wall.''

"He is your greatest friend, Giles, is he not?"

"Aye. I can never stop loving him. But Raymond is teetering like a rock on a cliff-edge. I will not stand by and see him slaughtered, if that is your concern."

"'Tis not mine, but God's only." *A pathetic lie.* Ceridwen turned in the saddle as her horse ambled. She swallowed hard and looked back, squinting, for a last glimpse of the place she had thought to make her home. But it was now out of sight.

The dark edge of the great wildwood lay ahead, and they aimed for the entrance to its murky depths. Ceridwen welcomed the dank smell of rotting leaves, the sharp whiff of danger. The forest floor muffled the clatter of the horse's hooves and the stagnant atmosphere enveloped her, as though the wood held its breath, with her caught in it.

Ceridwen's heart ached. Within her the hatred she bore Raymond had dwindled to nothing, like a prisoner slowly starved to death. A prisoner of love. But her anger still simmered, an anger that she never should have tried to abandon.

The tiny village of Llanmadog nestled in the pass, a few slate-roofed cottages gleaming dark green with the recent rain.

"These are—were your lands, were they not, milady?"

"I suppose so. I have never been here before."

Giles drew rein in front of a brew-house that churned with laborers, slate cutters arriving for a draught of ale on their way home. "My lady, go with the escort to the edge of the verge. I will bring some food and drink while they build a fire."

"We are not staying here?" Ceridwen looked up at the wattle and daub house. Its small, sheepskin-paned windows glowed a warm yellow as evening fell. Laughter and Welsh voices rose in song within and she yearned to join them.

"Have you ever slept at an inn, my lady?"

"Nay…"

"'Tis an experience to be avoided, for a woman like you, at least. And this place cannot even be called an inn."

Ceridwen sighed. "I will take your word for it, then." Dutifully she rode away with the men to a nearby field. Mist already rose from the damp soil beneath the hay stubble as the cooling air settled. When she dismounted one of the men bowed and took her reins. Ceridwen thanked him with a small smile, and over his objections walked out to where the field met the dark woods, to look for kindling.

She missed Blanche, and little Bree. Hamfast had grown to expect the treats she surreptitiously fed him when he nosed her hands under the table. And Alys needed her, especially now.

The old nurse had confided her fears of a siege. "'Tis the reason I am so fat," she had said, pummeling a lump of bread dough in the kitchen shed one afternoon.

"Whatever do you mean?" Ceridwen had smiled. "You are soft and comfortable—just right."

"I am fat, and no mistake about it. I have been so, ever since I was a young girl, your age. I have worked hard to gain this much, and 'tis a cowardly thing, too."

"You were hungry once?"

"Aye. Three months we sat under siege, trapped. None of us that survived was more'n skin and bone when the surrender came. I have been eating ever since. My Raymond's indulged me all this time, though he disapproves."

Her Raymond. Ceridwen shook her head at the memory and stomped through the barley stalks, oblivious to the shouted protests of the men-at-arms that she was going too far alone. She snatched up fallen branches at the edge of the wood. *Her Raymond* was a deceitful, lying Norman. A dastardly rogue. A warmongering, dog-besotted madman who had fooled no one but her.

Tears stung her cheeks. Ceridwen flung down her armload of sticks to run headlong across the field. Raymond's words taunted her…*running away is your answer for everything.* Curse him! He made it the only choice, he was so hateful.

Then, an unbidden memory of his strong, golden body joining with hers jolted deep in her belly. She had believed their hearts had been joined as well. But the truth was inconceivable. She had lain with Owain's killer. And enjoyed it, more than anything she had ever known. Was she any more honorable than Raymond, when she had accepted the marriage as a means to keep her father informed of Beauchamp plans and ambitions?

"Lady, what is wrong?" Giles trotted up, his horse's nostrils blowing white vapor in the chill of the evening.

She turned her back on him and hugged herself, cold in spite of her wool mantle. "Oh, Giles, I am so torn inside, I do not know what to think or feel or do."

"Tsk, I know your pain. My heart has been broken a hundred times or more." The knight dismounted to stand beside her.

Ceridwen was glad he could not see the small smile that sprang to her lips at his avowal. "Have you a good remedy?"

"Well, what remedies me would be most unsuitable for you, Madame. Come, eat now. You will feel better once you have something in your stomach."

"'Tis good of you to take such trouble." Ceridwen turned to face him.

"'Twas no trouble."

"Have you charmed the innkeeper's wife for our supper?" She should not tease him.

Giles narrowed his eyes at her. "You think to take Raymond's place in goading me? Indeed, the meat and bread and ale you will enjoy tonight depends upon my breaking my fast in the morning with the goodwife's daughter. Be grateful."

"I will warrant *she* will."

"I blush to hear such inference from you."

Ceridwen sighed. "I beg your pardon. You are right, I am not suited for scandalous talk."

"Never mind. Soon you will be safe in the bosom of your loving family. They will be overjoyed to see you, I expect."

Ceridwen knew better.

Chapter Eighteen

"R_{hys!}"

The volume of her father's voice echoing through the hall set Ceridwen's teeth on edge. She cringed in her seat, but her brother remained relaxed before Morgan's tirade, as always.

"I charged you to see your sister safely installed in Beauchamp's keep, and she is home within two months!" Morgan strode the hall, and stopped abruptly before Ceridwen, his eyes accusing. "And you—what have you to say for yourself?"

She had endured many of her father's rages, but this one leaped to fresh heights of fury. Though he had never before struck her, she felt he was not far from it now. But he had best know the truth. She stood, and looked straight at him. "Da, Raymond is the knight who slew Owain, right before my eyes."

"Oh, for the holy Rood's sake! You left him for *that?*" Morgan's dark eyes sparked in anger and he thrust his face to within inches of hers. "If you had obeyed me the day of the battle and stayed home, Owain might not have tried to impress you by engaging Beauchamp in the first place. Have you thought about that?"

Ceridwen stared at her father. Horror seeped into her heart, like cold, bitter poison. "Nay! It cannot be—oh!" She hung her head, and dry-eyed, gazed upon her folded hands. The truth carried with it more pain than she imagined possible. "You are telling me that *I* am the reason Owain is dead?"

"I am telling you that there are consequences to your foolish, headstrong behavior."

She drew a quavering breath. "I did not leave my husband. He sent me away."

"That is even worse. 'Twould have been better had he taken a strap to you and locked you up."

"Da!" She sobbed.

"Do not 'Da!' me. 'Tis a remedy *I* should have given you myself, long ago. And perhaps it is not too late to do you some good." Lord Morgan appraised her, fingering his belt. Then he crossed his arms over his barrel chest and turned his back on her to face the glowing fire.

"Giles." Rhys stepped neatly in between Ceridwen and their father. He sat her down, sliding his arm protectively around her hunched shoulders. "Where is the lady Blanche? My sister has come all this way with no female companion?"

Morgan turned, glowered first at his son, then at Giles. "Aye. What is this disgraceful state of affairs? The Englishman is alone with one of his own kind—this other woman, of whom Rhys has not stopped babbling since he returned."

Ceridwen looked up at Rhys, and watched in surprise as his color rose. She smeared her wet cheeks with her wrist.

"Madame Blanche has a small child who could not withstand the rigors of the journey," Giles said. "But the lady has no designs upon Raymond. Far be it. In fact she—"

"Gave me this." Rhys produced a length of white silk which Ceridwen recognized as part of Blanche's best veil and barbette, the ones she wore to chapel.

"What were you up to while I was suffering through the wedding, Rhys?" Ceridwen asked softly.

"Nothing more than establishing friendly relations between Welsh and English."

Giles's eyes darkened and his brows drew together. "If you have laid a finger upon that lady, who is so far above you in station that you are not fit even to step in her shadow, I will see you run from here to the River Usk—"

Rhys jumped up, his hand hovering at his dagger hilt. "By deeming me unworthy then so do you insult my sister. You are a fine one to talk, sir. I will warrant I saw you in the arms of a half-dozen maids—two at a time on occasion—during the course of that wedding feast. You cannot have any claim to honor the lady Blanche with your forbearance.''

''I had to try and keep them all happy. You know not what it is like, to have jealous females clamoring night and day.''

''Oh, do I not? What do you know of the demands made upon me, as the eldest son of my lord father?''

''Shut up. Braggarts and liars both.'' Morgan pointed at Ceridwen. *''This* is the problem—not the lady Blanche.''

''Nay.'' Ceridwen sat up taller. ''The problem is the Carrog Dhu and the Welsh blood on his hands. What is to stop him from keeping my lands, telling Alonso he will take his side and launching an assault against us? He might, if it meant sparing his people.'' But even as she spoke, the words rang false in her heart. Her guilt was greater, and not a matter of honor or war.

''Indeed he might.'' Morgan turned to Giles. ''I have no quarrel with you, sir. I do not think it fitting that you should be subjected to this frank discussion of your lord. Unless, of course, you no longer consider him thus.''

''There are many indefensible things of which Sir Raymond is guilty. But the chance of him making an alliance with Alonso is as remote as that of Rhys here besting me in a joust.''

''Damn you for the Norman bastard you are!''

Giles turned slowly from Morgan to fix his gaze upon Rhys. ''Why, how did you guess, young man? My own father does not know who or what I am. Lady Ceridwen, I meant no offense.'' Giles left the hall with long strides, his sword rattling at his side.

Ceridwen rose, thinking to go after him and soothe his hurt, then stopped. ''Rhys, you risk more than you know, speaking thus to Giles. This is how battles are lost. In the wasted breath of idiotic men who cannot see past their own pride. If none of you will address the situation, then I shall.'' She started for the doors and looked back at her father. ''I will ask the Talyessin for help against Alonso.''

''Stop, girl. Go no farther.''

''What will you do, Da?'' Ceridwen raised her chin.

"If you bear even the slightest feeling for Raymond, do not approach the Talyessin with any news of his vulnerability."

"Why not?"

"Talyessin would bring Rookhaven to its knees, and its lord to the gallows. He would support Raymond only enough to provoke Alonso into extending himself too far. Then he would set upon them both, while they were busy at each other's throats."

"How know you this?" Ceridwen's voice dropped at the look on her father's face. His jaw was set in a hard line, and his dark eyes gleamed fierce and bright.

"Because, Daughter, 'tis what I myself plan to do. You think you hate the Beauchamps? Nay. *I* will scatter the dust of their bones to the winds. The Afon Usk will run red with their blood. Not one man, woman or child will be left alive to breed. Their name shall be nothing but a reminder of our victory."

The hideous ache in Ceridwen's heart burst into agony at her father's words. She clutched at his surcoat. "How could you? Oh, you are clever, my lord, and have the instincts of a fox, but never, never did I think you capable of such a dishonorable scheme."

"That is because you are young and foolish. Why do you think I gave you to him, Ceridwen? To make him happy? To bring him joy?" Her father took her by the shoulders and held her at arm's length. "You were supposed to be with him, no matter what, to lull his suspicions. How do you imagine one survives on the Marches, caught in the middle as we are? 'Tis tooth and nail, Ceridwen. Deceit and counterfeit. Lies and treachery. I am sorry to burden you with the truth."

"But I would have been there, Father. I and the other women and children, Welsh and English alike. You would let Alonso take us?"

"Only if I did not bring him down in time."

"You mean you would only kill Alonso once he had slain Raymond for you. Two birds with one stone. You would look like a hero to the prince, and to the English king 'twould seem a shameful quarrel between two brothers—something to be kept quiet."

"Perhaps."

"Raymond's perfidy pales in comparison to yours."

"I never wanted you to know. But it is time you grew up, Daughter."

"Do not call me that. At least my brothers and sisters are now fostered elsewhere, and spared your poisonous influence. If this is what growing old does to one, then I hope I die young." Ceridwen backed away from her father, pierced by the jagged shards of the illusion of him she had cherished. She bumped into the doors, hauled them open and fled into the night.

"Let her go, Rhys." Morgan sank into his chair and put one hand to his brow. "'Twas much more difficult than I thought it would be."

"You had to be hard, she is so stone-pated herself." Rhys regarded his father, with little sympathy. The look on Ceridwen's face would have melted the heart of the devil himself. But not that of Morgan ap Madog.

"Will she forgive him now, do you think?" Morgan's shoulders slumped.

"More easily than she will you. But why do you want her back with him, when Alonso is on his way?"

"Rhys. Are you blind? She loves the bloody Carrog Dhu, to the point that if he were in danger, without her, she would do something seriously stupid in her guilt. Nay, 'tis best she remain where God, and I, have placed her, for better or worse." Morgan clenched and unclenched his fists.

"Then I will see her back safely."

"Why? She has all those enormous Englishmen out there to escort her."

"I am going to wed the lady Blanche." Rhys drummed his fingertips against the oak tabletop, then got to his feet.

Slowly Morgan turned to his son. "You will do no such thing, Rhys. I need you here. I will not allow it. I will disinherit you."

"As you see fit, Father. Blanche but thinks she is fond of Giles. I know better." Rhys drew himself taller.

"Because she gave you her token?"

"In truth, I relieved her of it while she danced at the wedding."

"Rhys, I forbid any more of this foolishness."

"Forbid away. It is not foolishness. 'Tis my life."

"Then leave this place—and do not return with any abducted Norman brides." Morgan stalked away, leaving his son standing alone in the hall.

Rhys took a deep breath and smiled. He sprang to get his longbow down from its place on the wall. He hesitated, then took a second bow as well, after looping several hempen bow-strings around his neck. He grabbed a fistful of arrows from a barrel in the corner and thrust them through his belt before setting out after his sister.

"Psst!"

Ceridwen's fingers paused on the straps of her palfrey's harness. She would let no one stop her departure. "Rhys?"

"Aye. I am coming with you." He materialized out of the shadows of the stableyard and tied his horse to the post.

"Where do you think I plan on going?"

"Back to warn the Carrog Dhu, of course."

"I owe him that much." She struggled with the girth.

"Here, let me do that. Put these on." Rhys shoved a wad of clothing into her hands.

Ceridwen eyed the garments. "Are these yours?" With two fingers she held up the ragged mantle and crusty, knee-length tunic to the lamplight.

"Aye. Be quick about it."

Sighing, she crossed her arms and jerked upwards on her overgown. She had no false modesty before her brother, and to dress as a man would be the wisest course, whatever that turned out to be. She hardly cared. "What about my bare legs?"

"You are a man, remember?"

"Aye, Rhys, just so. Mine are not particularly manly."

Rhys pondered for a moment, then pulled off his boots. "Wear these. At least your puny ankles won't show."

"Are you sure you will not miss them?"

"Aye, my feet are still tough from the summer."

Ceridwen nodded, for in Wales even the nobility went barefoot for as long as the weather would allow. "There is one more thing, Rhys. Here.'' She handed him her dagger. ''Cut off my hair for me. I cannot have it flying about.''

''Oh, Ceri.''

''Just do it!'' She bit her lip as the heavy tresses fell away. It would serve as a kind of penance, as well.

''Not bad.'' Rhys returned her dagger to her and patted the neck of her sleek horse. ''I have brought my old bow for you. It has only a thirty or forty-pound draw. You should be able to make a few shots with it before you tire.''

Ceridwen floundered, trying to find the sleeve openings of the loose woolen shirt. ''Rhys, I can barely nock a bowstring, much less draw and aim properly. What are you talking about?''

''We shall break through the siege. And I shall bring Lady Blanche and her child safely away.'' Rhys leaned happily on his bow, dark, handsome, and casual under every circumstance.

''Oh, heaven help us. Will Alonso simply let us through?''

''We shall arrive as humble volunteers, responding to his call to arms. In the confusion we will make our way to the keep and Raymond's guards will recognize you and let us in.''

''Rhys, I cannot stay, once we have warned him.''

''Of course you will. Do you not understand? Owain was trying as hard as he could to slay Raymond, as was his duty. And Raymond was responding in kind. In his place, I would have done the same to Owain, and honored him with a quick, clean death, as did Beauchamp.''

Ceridwen choked. ''Are you men all in this together? I am sick of hearing about the honor of killing in battle. Why should that be more respectable than a stab in the belly in some remote wayside?'' She rubbed her scar, then realizing what she did, busied herself arranging the folds of her mantle around her head and shoulders.

It felt as though she was reliving her preparations for going to battle with Owain. He had not known she followed him until it was too late to send her back. He had ordered her to lie still, hidden in a ditch. She had remained there, stiff with fear for him, until that last swoop of the knight's sword brought her running. Raymond de Beauchamp's sword.

Ceridwen forced herself to think back, to visualize the field that day. Men shouted and horses plunged, there were bright shields and banners and fresh spring grass. Had Owain only pursued Raymond in order to prove his bravery, knowing she watched? Had her presence truly caused the tragedy?

Owain had been fearless. Bareheaded and laughing, he had raced up alongside Raymond's destrier and taken stabs at the knight with his lance. Provoked him, wounded him, then darted away. Circled around, saluted in her direction—Ceridwen groaned. Da was right. She had killed Owain, right along with Raymond. For in that moment, when her cousin's attention was on her, Raymond had thundered past to deliver the fatal blow.

Rhys shook her arm. "Ceridwen, gather your wits and be guided by someone else for once in your life. You complain about Da, but you are as hardhearted and bloodthirsty as he."

"I am not."

"If you let your husband fall prey to this plot 'twill be proof in full." Rhys thrust the bow into her hands. "Take it. It is of the finest brasell yew to be had. All the way from beyond the lands of the Saracens."

Ceridwen let the weapon slide through her fingers, and relished its satin smoothness. The rich, red-brown heartwood melded against the golden sapwood. So unlike the rustic, knobbed bows of local wych elm, which were powerful enough, but inelegant. This bow held great potential. She had but to decide how to use it.

"Ahem." Giles loomed out of the darkness into the lamplight. "You will need me, if you attempt to return."

"Nay, we do not. We have never needed the English." Rhys stood up to Giles. "We will go alone."

"Please, Rhys. Giles, I have disgraced myself before my father, and my brother is following suit. Will you advise us?"

"I cannot. Nor do I belong here. I and the men with me should be at Raymond's side, no matter his misbegotten orders. He is not thinking clearly. A madness has gripped him."

Giles looked straight at her. Ceridwen thought of Raymond's tormented expression as he spoke those last, unforgivable words. *Begone, Cymraes.* Out of the confusion in her heart a profound longing welled up, to be at peace—with herself, and even with

Raymond. And the only way she could accomplish that end was to confront him, face to face. Before her father had a chance to execute his wicked plan.

Taking her reins from Rhys she swung into the saddle. Few archers rode to war, and it took her a moment to determine how best to carry the bow. She decided to slip one end of it into the cup of the lance-butt rest at her stirrup. Having slung the bow-strings about her neck, she held the reins with her free hand, and looked to her brother. "Let us go."

"Wait. St. Germaine, do you intend to thwart me in regard to the Lady Blanche?"

"I do."

"Would you agree to let her choose between us?"

Giles stroked his chin. "Very well. No abduction allowed. And no dueling. Except with words, and perhaps a song or two."

Rhys smiled. "Splendid." He mounted his black courser and turning to Ceridwen, scanned her up and down. "You make quite a convincing fellow."

"I would be more so if I could indulge in the sort of talk you do. You argue over the terms of acquiring Blanche as if she were a prize mare. 'Tis most likely she will reject you both."

"It is not." Rhys and Giles spoke in unison.

Ceridwen grinned.

"Sister, I think your teeth are a bit bright for a country bow-man. Shall I knock a few out, so you will not give us away?"

"Nay, Rhys. I will not be smiling once I am near Alonso."

Ceridwen crawled through the mud and grass on her knees and elbows, soaked to the skin. "How much farther, Rhys?" She could barely see through the misting rain, and darkness was settling into place for the night, like a raven come to roost. The land and trees and sky blended into a murky gray whole.

"Up there, and we will be able to look down on Alonso's encampment and tell where best to get through."

With a last effort Ceridwen struggled to the top of the rise, and lay panting, shoulder to shoulder with Rhys. All she could make out was the blurry yellow glow of bonfires, burning despite the wet. Smoke flowed in milky rivers along the ground, lending the thick air a sharp tang that bit her throat. "Do you think Giles and the rest are on the other side of the fen yet?"

"We will give them a bit longer. Are you all right?"

"I am cold, now that we've stopped. What do you see?"

"Alonso's men are in the oak grove. Long torchiers are thrust into the ground. They are passing a jug around."

From the sound of their carousing, the soldiers seemed in fine spirits. Then a woman's scream rent the air. Ceridwen's throat convulsed. "What else are they sharing?" she whispered.

"Ah, Ceri, be glad your sight is imperfect."

"Rhys, this must stop. What can we do?" Her fists clenched about the dead, tufted grass.

"Nothing. We will be lucky to save our own skins—and you must not try any heroics. Are you ready?"

"As I will ever be. Kiss me, Rhys. Just in case." Ceridwen hugged her brother fiercely. He kissed her cheeks, left and right, mud and all.

"Remember, Ceri, you are my simple-minded man. Mumble, grunt, or whine, but do not talk. And keep your eyes downcast."

"Aye, Master."

Her legs trembled as she and Rhys stood and began walking toward the siege encampment. Rhys whistled a jaunty tune and every so often called out, "Oy, over here!"

Ceridwen trudged behind him, trying to look the sullen arms-bearer, carrying the bows and arrows.

A sentry stood as they approached. "What fools be these?" He lowered the tip of his pike at them.

"'Tis I, Rhodri of Abergavenny, here for duty, sir."

The burly guard snorted and gave Rhys's shoulder a jab. "What duty might that be, ye good-fer-nothin' Welsh scrap-meat?"

Rhys hauled Ceridwen forward and displayed his weapons. "Lord Alonso's called for men, so here am I, with all I have got. Two bows, two dozen arrows, and this." He shook Ceridwen by the scruff of her neck.

"Urgh," she said.

The man peered at the bows. "Better'n some as arrived with

nowt but a shaftless bodkin to their name. I suppose I'd best let his lordship decide what to do with ye.''

Rhys gave Ceridwen's arm a bracing squeeze as they walked ahead of the guard. She blinked at the light and noise in the center of the encampment. In spite of her brother's comforting touch, fear seeped upwards through her, leaving her legs wobbly and her stomach queasy. Being brought before Alonso himself was not part of the plan.

Giles and his men were to make their way north with the horses until they could go no farther without being spotted. She and Rhys had intended to blend into the lowest ranks of archers, then slip toward the gatehouse of Raymond's keep. There, hopefully, a sortie could be organized to bring Giles and the others in. But Rookhaven brooded, dark and silent in the background, as if empty of life.

They came to a large, open tent.

"That is him, that is Alonso," Ceridwen whispered.

"A grand fellow," Rhys replied, a sneer in his voice.

He was indeed. Ceridwen goggled at the sight before her.

Alonso was raising a sparkling chalice to his lips as they approached. Everard cuffed the head of a lad who turned a spitted goose over the cookfire, and fat hissed into the flames. The soft notes of a harp floated out into the evening, along with the smell of roasting meat.

Alonso had brought every comfort to his siege pavilion. His bed. His musicians. His mastiffs. His mistress. Gwendolyn sat at ease, her long throat exposed as she tipped her head back, laughing at something he had said.

"By your leave, Lord Alonso." The sentry stepped forward and bowed. "These archers wish to serve, milord. Rodney of Burgnabby and his bearer."

The handsome, cruel face of Raymond's brother turned toward them like that of a bird of prey. Ceridwen's skin crawled. What if he recognized her? She tried to make herself smaller.

"Volunteers? How refreshing. The conscripts are less than willing, so far." Alonso strolled in a circle, raking her and Rhys with his sharp gaze. "You." He reached out with his booted toe and tapped Ceridwen's shin.

She kept her head down and did not move.

"Is it deaf?" Alonso asked Rhys, over her head. Alonso was so close she could smell the wine on his breath.

"Nay, milord. Just stupid."

"Hand over that bow—what do you call him, Rodney?"

"Em, *Cud,* milord. He's that thick."

Ceridwen choked back an involuntary snort of outrage. A pox upon Rhys and his clever tongue. Without raising her eyes she held out the shorter of the two longbows, her arm stiff and straight in front of her.

"Cud. An obedient upheaval, at least." Alonso took the bow and examined it. "A fine weapon, but useless in the rain."

"We can change the bowstrings as they stretch, milord, and shoot from beneath the trees."

"Why do you wish to aid me?" Alonso handed the bow to Rhys, his eyes narrowed.

"Vengeance, milord. Lord Raymond murdered our kin, and poor Cud here's not been the same since."

Ceridwen coughed and wiped her nose with her grimy sleeve. As usual, Rhys walked a fine line.

Alonso crossed his arms and tilted his head. "'Tis as sound a reason as any. But the first three days you will serve without pay. After that it is a shilling a week. Your mute here will receive nothing but his share of bread and ale. Report to Brand the Four-in-Hand. He is in the grove, somewhere."

Alonso dismissed them with a negligent wave. Ceridwen breathed a sigh and with a last glance at the encampment turned away to follow Rhys. She hesitated as a jasmine-laced scent wafted past her nose.

"I know *her.*" Gwendolyn's smooth, vicious voice severed Ceridwen's relief like a knife through flesh. She froze.

"What?" Alonso sounded bored—for an instant. "Who?"

"Your little green-eyed blackbird. Remember? Of course you do. And here she is again."

As one Ceridwen and Rhys looked at each other. Even with her back to him Ceridwen knew Alonso's hand was descending toward her shoulder. She bolted into the darkness, stumbling over the uneven ground. Shouts and the sentry pursued her. Her legs pumped and her breath rasped, from fear as well as effort.

She fully expected an arrow between her shoulder blades at any moment, but dared not glance back. Rhys raced beside her, cursing her and women in general. He led her into the maze of thickets and dells that lined Raymond's northern perimeter.

Alonso bellowed orders and horses squealed. Ceridwen's heart jolted in panic. They could not outrun mounted men.

"This way!" Rhys ducked to his left and Ceridwen followed, her lungs searing. Her bow caught on brambles, slowing her down, and she could not see well enough to avoid them.

"Rhys, I cannot keep up with you!" A fresh, awful sense of dread came over her, prickling her scalp. "Stop, Rhys—"

"We will be dead if we do, Ceri—move your arse. Whoa!" Rhys's voice bobbed in volume, suddenly farther away.

Ceridwen struggled forward in her sodden clothes, and she could not breathe fast enough to satisfy her body's need. Then she lurched and stepped into nothingness, somersaulting down a steep incline, her cry echoing that of her brother.

Chapter Nineteen

"I see moving torches." Wace peered through a loophole of the curtain wall. "Horsemen are riding into the fen, milord."

"Good for them." Raymond did not bother to look. He kept his back pressed to the cold, wet stone of the battlement. That was the only reality he could face at the moment.

"Now they have turned. They are halting. I think they have reached the lip of the ravine. What are they doing?"

Raymond moved, but he felt heavy. Like a millstone grinding. He pushed Wace aside and squinted through the narrow opening. "They are staggering drunk, hunting down some poor creature, no doubt. What does it matter? I am going to bed."

"But my lord—"

"What?"

"Should we not do something? Fire a volley of arrows? They cannot flaunt themselves at us and get away with it."

"Save your strength, Wace. When we fight, it will be at much closer quarters. And at a time of my choosing. I am not in the mood, just now."

Wace bore an expression Raymond had never before seen on the lad's face. Defiance. The righteous look of rebellion that every sixteen-year-old boy felt entitled to, sooner or later. The young man bowed stiffly and excused himself.

Raymond wiped his brow with a shaking hand. He was losing the respect of his squire. It was seeping away, along with his own. And every demon he had thought he had battered into numb oblivion—the nameless, gut-wrenching fear, the loathing of Alonso that turned increasingly toward himself—was flowing back to replace his confidence.

There was but one good thing. Ceridwen was far away. Safe, from both him and his brothers.

"Bloody little weasels! They can't have got far."

At the rough voice Ceridwen clamped her jaws shut, to stop the noise of her teeth chattering. Rhys held her hand tightly. They crouched among the dense, dead stalks of rushes in the marsh. The splash of wading horses sounded steadily nearer, and the light of the torches created wavering shadows. A crackling, scything sound accompanied the approach of the search party.

Alonso's men were so close she could hear the creak of saddle leather. Rhys jammed her head under his arm and clamped her mouth with his other hand. For an instant Ceridwen struggled. The dull crackling noise grew louder. She stopped breathing and shut her eyes. The horses crashed by them. Rhys jerked and made a tiny sound, deep in his throat.

"Damn these stumps," a man growled. "The buggers've gone to ground, like the wild animals they are. They'll be out, come the morn—if they've not froze or drowned in the meantime. 'Tisn't as though they can go to Sir Raymond for help."

Amidst general laughter their pursuers retreated.

"Rhys. Let go of my head. Please, Rhys." Ceridwen was doubled over, her nose an inch from the water's surface. His fingers had released her mouth, but his elbow still pinned her head to his side. Slowly, he allowed her to pull free.

"What is wrong? Did you cramp?" Ceridwen straightened and listened for any sound of returning horses. Her racing heart calmed a bit as quiet settled around them.

"Nay."

Rhys sounded tired. She touched his arm. "Giles and the others should be near the northeast postern by now, right?"

"Aye."

They slogged through the icy water and clinging reeds until they reached dryer ground. Ceridwen ached from the bruising she had taken tumbling down the ravine. Her legs were so cold it was hard to keep them moving. But she forced each foot past the other, over and over. "I dropped the bow when I fell, Rhys. Tis a bad omen—I am sorry."

"No matter. The swine must have been slowed when they stopped to retrieve it—perhaps it gave us some time. 'Twas my vanity that chose too fine a weapon, anyway."

Rhys staggered and Ceridwen put out her hand to steady him. "What is the matter?"

"They were cutting the rushes with their swords."

"Oh, Mother Mary." Frantically Ceridwen peered at him, with only the dim light of the bonfires' reflection off the curtain wall to aid her. She checked his body with her hands, and her worry grew when he did nothing to stop her.

"My shoulder, Ceri. They took me for a piece of wood."

She looked and at first could see nothing, as his clothing was dark with mud and water. He flinched as she carefully traced a long rent in his jerkin and tunic, running from below his shoulder blade to the back of his neck. The cloth was soggy and warm, when it should have been damp and cold.

Ceridwen's stomach lurched. "Ah, Rhys, you took the whole stroke upon yourself. 'Tis so deep—I could have taken half for you, at least!" She faced him and clutched his hands.

"Don't be idiotic. 'Tisn't as though I am going to die."

With a sigh he toppled forward into Ceridwen's arms. Her knees buckled. Summoning all her strength, she dragged him into the cover of a thicket, stepping backwards as fast as she could, until she tripped and sprawled, with him on top of her.

For a moment she could not draw breath. When she opened her eyes, she had to blink to make sure they were indeed open. Here the darkness was impenetrable. She lay still and gathered her wits. Reeds hissed in the wind, and soft plopping sounds came from the marsh. The rain-freshened air was spoiled by the unwholesome smell of the stagnant water and rotting plants.

Ceridwen strained her eyes and listened, in an attempt to get her bearings. Her mind raced. A disastrous end, once thought impossible, now grew into a likelihood. She reached for Rhys, and her fingers met his cold, wet cheek.

"Wake up, Rhys, please, please do not die…"

An owl hooted. Then came the low chuck-chuck of a pheasant. Odder still was the cackle of a laying hen that followed. Rhys slowly lifted his head from her stomach.

"Ceri."

She sat up as he eased his weight off her. "Dearling, what must I do to help you?" She cradled his head.

"Follow the birds. Parsifal taught Giles the calls."

Hope kindled within her. "I thought it strange for a hen to be awake now. But how will we find you again, Rhys?"

"Tell Giles to listen for the sound of my lips kissing Blanche…like this." Rhys put his mouth to the back of his hand and produced a sucking, squeaking noise. It was a device they had used in childhood to get the absolute attention of squirrels and other tiny wildlife.

"Sweet fool." Ceridwen's heart caught in her throat and she kissed her brother's forehead. "Ah, Rhys, I would that I had never left home. You would be safe still."

"If it was not this 'twould be something else. Neither of us can stay out of trouble. Go on, now."

"I will return as quick as I can." Ceridwen set out in the direction of the birdcalls, bent low. Her arms swept the darkness for obstacles. The sounds were difficult to follow, for the keep's curtain wall made them echo and bounce. Her hands and knees were raw from falling, but gradually the calls grew louder, and she dared answer. "Miaow!"

"Here, puss-puss," came the reply.

The loud whisper sounded much closer than she expected. If it was not the lieutenant… "Giles?"

"*A votre service, Madame.*" A big hand met her shoulder.

Ceridwen took a great breath. "Oh, thank Mary it is you, Giles. Come, please, Rhys has a terrible wound, he cannot walk far. We must listen for—the sound of an angry field mouse."

"There is a menagerie tonight, I see."

Ceridwen caught Giles's hand and led him back toward Rhys.

Ceridwen huddled, knees to chest, on the leaf-strewn ground next to her brother. His wound was bound in the shreds of a filthy tunic, and he was propped awkwardly against a tree. With them, at the edge of the woods, were the six men of the escort. The rain had stopped and the moon emerged, cold in the night sky. The open field before them was bathed in silver, and the beginnings of frost shimmered on the battered grass.

"We must move on without the horses so we can make for the postern, or scale the cliff-face," Sven the Dane said.

Giles rested at ease, his back to a stump. "I will not abandon my horse to Alonso. Besides, Rhys here must ride."

"Then the only way in is through the barbican gate. Will Raymond have given orders for them to fire upon you, Giles?"

Fear skipped lightly through Ceridwen's heart. "Giles is too dear to him. But I will show myself. They would not shoot at a woman." She hoped not.

"Begging your pardon, but you no longer resemble one," Giles said. "I am going first, and to hell with orders or who they think I am. 'Tis Alonso setting upon us from the rear that worries me most."

"Then a few of us should try to gain entry on foot via the postern, and we will open the main gate for you."

Giles leaned forward and sat cross-legged. "Nay. Everyone shall be mounted. I will go up to the gate, shout the password and Baldric will see my comely face in the moonlight. Then you gallop through—the lady first, her brother second, and the rest of us as rear guard."

"And I naysay you, Giles. You are in my service. Do as I ask." Ceridwen surprised herself with the firmness of her tone. "I will show myself first. You will flank Rhys. Can you ride alone, Rhys?"

"Aye, just let me fall into Blanche's arms once I am in."

Giles scowled. "We shall go by twos then, milady. Like Noah's ark."

Ceridwen decided not to push the issue further. Rhys would still be jesting and irritating folk upon his deathbed. But if his wound was not seen to, and soon, he might indeed die.

Her nerves stretched and frayed as the horses moved through the dark around the marsh. The snorts, rattles and creaks of their progress seemed to make an atrocious amount of noise. Ceridwen's numb fingers tightened on the reins.

Alonso's men were no longer out of earshot, nor so drunk that they had fallen asleep. Now that the mist had cleared, the cold air seemed to make each sound echo like a stone in a drum. They came onto the narrow lane that led to the gatehouse. The moonlight fully exposed them to view.

"Ready, on the count of three…" Giles whispered.

At his signal they burst into a gallop. A shout went up from an enemy sentry to their rear. Then the barbican gate ahead of them flew open. A cavalcade of riders charged forth, lances couched. The warriors uttered no battle cry, but bore down upon them in eerie, voiceless fury. A collision was but a few strides away.

Ceridwen's horse shied, slamming its shoulder into Giles's mount. Their group swerved into a milling mass of men and horseflesh. "The password, Giles!"

"O, valiant knights of Rookhaven—death to traitors!"

The battle party halted, encircling them in a bristling ring of weaponry. "'Tis exactly what we have in mind for curs like you who come slinking and sniffing 'round our gates." The leader's lance tip came to rest at Giles's throat. "The password has changed. Every milkmaid and dogboy from here to Chepstow knows 'death to traitors' by now."

The voice from within the helm was familiar, but deeper than normal. "Wace? Is that *you?*" Ceridwen wrestled with her frightened horse. "Is your vision so dim in that helm you do not see that you have Giles St. Germaine at bay? Put that thing down this instant!"

"Oh, milady! God help me—" Wace groaned.

A man cried out as a volley of arrows from Alonso's archers seethed down upon them from behind. As one, both parties raced toward the gatehouse.

"Porter!"

"Wot's the word, milord?"

"Where is Baldric? Luther, we just came through, now let us back in!" Wace bellowed.

"I 'ave me orders. Who knows what witchery might have changed young Wace into this great hulking—why Lord Giles, 'tis a pleasure now to be seein' ye again."

"Thank you kindly, Luther."

"I do not believe this. *Amor vincit omnia.* Open. Now!"

"Wot's that, Squire Wace?"

"So you do know it is me—*love conquers all,* you idiot!"

Ceridwen was stunned. Had Raymond changed? Had he opened his heart after all, to use the words he had scorned before? Nay, he had probably chosen it as the sentiment least likely to be guessed as a password of Rookhaven. Raymond. The one who had given her a taste of love, then condemned her to starvation.

"I'm only doin' me job, there's no call for abuse." The portcullis rumbled upward, even as the whoops of Alonso's knights grew louder.

She and Wace and the others clattered through, and Ceridwen looked back for Rhys. His horse was right behind hers, but he was not on it. She fought down her panic. There was no room to turn in the passage.

Ceridwen did what she had seen Raymond do, and boosted herself backwards over the cantle of the saddle. She took a deep breath and slid off the mare's rump, praying she would not be kicked when she landed. As her feet touched the beams of the drawbridge, she turned and ran back to the gate.

"Wait, milady, I am coming! Luther, do not lower yet!"

Giles's footsteps thudded hollowly behind her. Ignoring him, she darted beneath the portcullis. Rhys lay facedown in the lane. One of Alonso's men jumped from his horse. He caught Rhys's feet even as Ceridwen grabbed her brother's wrists.

"You want him, laddie, take him!" the warrior taunted.

"Beast! Let go!" Rhys was heavy and Ceridwen's feet slipped out from beneath her in the mud as she pulled. She hit the ground when her foe jerked to break her grip.

Giles bent low over her, but before he could even reach out to take hold of Rhys, something whistled by, invisible with speed. Alonso's man staggered backwards, gurgling, and fell to the roadway. A fletched shaft protruded from his throat.

Giles dragged Rhys into the safety of the barbican. The porter dropped the heavy bar of the gates into place as the portcullis rattled down. Shuddering with cold and anguish, Ceridwen knelt by her brother. Then he moaned, and she wept in helpless relief that he yet lived.

After a moment she realized Giles was gone. He would bring a litter, no doubt. Ceridwen rubbed her eyes dry, and still shivering, peered toward the doorway leading to the drawbridge. A tall figure stood silhouetted by the torchlight. She knew him, by the set of his shoulders, and the tilt of his head.

"I told you to go home." Raymond's voice held no expression.

"I *am* h-home."

"The hell you are. Get out of the way." He brushed past, shoving a crossbow into her hands. She held it gingerly, as if that would protect her from its wicked deadliness. The Pope had banned the use of such weapons long ago. After examining Rhys briefly in the light of the gatehouse torch, Raymond hoisted him over his shoulder and started back to the keep.

"Will he b-be all right?" Ceridwen trotted after Raymond, her frozen thighs rubbed raw.

"I do not know."

Ceridwen looked down at the implement in her hands. "I would not have thought to see y-you with one of these."

"Why not? It performed most efficiently."

"'Tis im-moral."

"A simple 'thank you' would do."

Shame bit her. If Owain had been dear, Rhys was dearer still. "I am grateful. I—I will reward you."

Raymond laughed—a rich, throaty sound she had never before heard. Ceridwen remembered his wonderful singing voice, and for a moment she wished she could run before him and see his face.

"I dare not think what my reward might be."

His sarcasm made her glad to be at his back, after all. In truth she herself had no idea how to reward him. She had already given him everything. Except her forgiveness. They reached the bailey and men hurried out to carry Rhys away, limp and bloody. Ceridwen started to follow, but Raymond blocked her way.

"You are chilled, Madame. He will be well attended while I see to you."

"Oh, 'tis all my fault!" She threw the crossbow down and clutched her arms to herself, sobs catching in her throat.

"Come." Raymond guided her, his arm about her shoulders. She tried to shrug him off. "Nay. I need no seeing to."

"You do. Alys! Blanche!"

A pale Wace appeared as they came through the drapes from the forebuilding. "They are with Rhys, my lord. And Shona is...with...Giles." He grew even whiter under Raymond's silent scrutiny.

"Sven."

The tall Dane, wearing an armored leather hauberk that must have cost him two month's wages, rose from a bench. Ceridwen looked past him and saw the hall was packed with men, women and children, most of them asleep. She breathed her relief that her instructions had been followed in time.

"Escort my over-eager squire below and put him in chains." Sven placed his huge hand on Wace's shoulder.

The young man's freckles showed starkly against his ashen skin. Then he drew himself taller and allowed Sven to take him.

"You are cruel, Raymond. He is but a boy." Ceridwen watched as Wace disappeared down the stairs, his bearing proud.

"He disobeyed me. He risked the lives of four men as well as his own. A night in prison will do wonders for him."

Ceridwen resisted the retort that sprang to mind. Her lips felt stiff. She ached with cold. The trembling that had started in her legs spread until her whole body shook. All she wanted was to lie down by the fire.

Raymond picked up the mazer Sven had put down. He tasted the contents. "Drink this. 'Tis hot mulled wine."

She accepted the cup and swallowed the warm, heady liquid. The deep wooden bowl bumped her teeth, for her hands could not hold it still.

"Do you wish for me to carry you?"

"Nay." She swayed.

"Then move along." Raymond propelled her up the stairs, and she was too weary to resist. He kicked open the door of his solar and made her precede him. She went straight to the hearth and huddled there.

"Get out of those wet clothes."

Ceridwen did not respond. It was as though she were underwater. Her limbs were much too heavy to lift.

"Do not be shy. I have seen all there is of you to see."

She ignored his remark. "How does Hamfast fare?" Her gritty eyes stung when she blinked. Her clothing steamed as she squatted before the fire. She might topple at any moment.

"He is better." Raymond frowned at her. Then, as if she were a small child, he started peeling away the muddy layers covering her. As the mantle fell from her head, she heard the sharp intake of his breath. "What have you done to yourself?"

"What had to be done, my lord."

"A pity." He shook his head, and fingered the chin-length ends of Rhys's handiwork. Then, leaving Ceridwen's torso bare, Raymond went to his bed, pulled off a thick woolen blanket and held it up to the open hearth. "Take off the rest. Hurry up."

Ceridwen slid off the clinging, reeking boots, knowing if she did not, he would do it for her.

"Stand."

She cowered before him. But as he bundled her into the delicious heat of the warmed blanket, it was all she could do not to melt into his embrace, she was that grateful. Ceridwen closed her eyes, not daring to hope his heart would ever be as gentle as his hands were now. With a start she realized she was dozing off as she stood. The room began to whirl. Raymond's arms tightened around her.

"You have my thanks," Ceridwen whispered, relaxing a small measure against his solid frame.

"Into bed we go." He scooped her up.

Her eyes popped open and she stiffened. "We?" Before she could protest he dropped her on the bed and began to strip himself. "What do you intend, my lord?"

"The linens are cold. It will not take long to warm you, if we are skin to skin. 'Tis the best way, short of taking you down to the byre and squeezing you between the milk cows. Ask Giles if you do not believe me."

Ceridwen drew the blanket tighter, as if it could fend Raymond off, and tried not to look at his lean, tawny body. But he merely pulled the quilts over her head, so even the warmth of her breath was not wasted. Then, to her astonishment, he wormed his way to the foot of the bed, under the covers.

He took her icy feet in his hands and pressed them to his bare stomach. She gave a little moan of pleasure and wiggled her toes against his warm skin. There was a muffled hiss. Rogue or not, this man was made of stern stuff.

Raymond curled his body closer around her feet and rubbed her numb calves to a tingling glow. "Better?"

"Aye." She could get used to this. Like a horse being curried. Once again his physical charm felled her defenses. It was wicked to enjoy his touch. But she was so tired and cold.

Raymond gently plucked the edges of the blanket from her clutching fingers. He moved up and wrapped himself inside it with her, spooning against her back. The comfort of his heat was overwhelming. He slid his hand around and briskly chafed her arms and thighs. She felt human again. Then he simply held her against him, and warmth poured off him from head to toe. She could feel his thudding heartbeat. And other parts of him.

"You owe me no kindness, Raymond."

"True, I do not."

"You will not win me over this way."

"Nay, I won't."

"You cannot make me forgive you."

"I know I cannot. Go to sleep, Ceri."

"I sleep better alone." She sounded unconvincing even to herself.

"You had best stick to the truth, had you not?"

Anger flickered, warming Ceridwen from within. His arrogance. It drove her mad. "My father is set to destroy you." She yawned in spite of her alarming words.

"He will have to await his turn," came the mumbled reply.

"Do you not care about *anything?*"

"I have not slept in three days, Ceri. This is the first I have been able to rest since Alonso arrived with his hordes. Let me have this little time, to forget him. And myself."

His arm circled her torso and his fingers entwined through hers. She could not move. She did not want to move. Even with him like this, it was difficult to believe she was actually wed to Raymond de Beauchamp. That he held her in his arms like a precious thing. That his body next to hers made her forget every reason she had to hate him.

"You are too much for me, my lord," she whispered.

But he was already asleep.

Raymond woke and sat up, instantly alert. Then he fell back to his pillow, his head aching. It was as though he had not slept at all. Dawn crept in yellow fingers through the parchment covering the narrow window of his chamber. He looked about, felt the empty bed. He had dreamed…nay, she had been here, she had come back to him. Not to him. To her duty. But to hold her in the night had been like a gift from God.

He found his linen shirt and pulled it on, then his hose, his gambeson, and a now-shabby velvet robe that Meribel had once said made him look like a king…but that was a long time ago. He splashed some icy water onto his face from a basin, and leaned for a moment against the bedpost.

Another day of endless waiting and watching and knowing it was hopeless. Why had she returned to this disaster? Raymond threw open the door and lifted his foot to avoid stepping on Wace. But of course, the lad was below. *I am losing my mind, slowly but surely.*

"My lord." Giles strode toward him, looking well rested. "Things are livening up outside. They are advancing, with a battering ram, and catapults. It appears Alonso has received some reinforcements, and is no longer content to sit idle."

"Have you nothing to say for yourself, lieutenant? Do you simply return and assume you are welcome, that you are pardoned?"

"Ah, my lord." Giles went down on one knee. "I spoke in haste, in heat. Forgive me for being in the right. If I were not, you would not still be angry." He bent his head.

Giles's combination of humility and effrontery broke through Raymond's irritation. "The only reason I am not happy you are here is because it means you will die with the rest of us. And you have brought my lady back. Why? That was the one comfort

I had, knowing she was safely away.'' Raymond clenched his fists.

"She would have come alone, otherwise. Or with that useless brother of hers, who even now is commanding the attentions of every woman in the keep.'' Giles stood.

"Is Ceridwen in the infirmary with him?''

"Aye. With Blanche. Hand-feeding him broth and bits of bread dipped in honey.'' Giles's lip curled.

"That's just as well. I want her fully occupied this day. How did you get past the siege?'' Raymond listened to Giles's telling of events. It took a distinct effort of will not to go and soundly thrash both Ceridwen and her brother for having attempted such a foolish, dangerous scheme. Not that it would do any good. "She said Gwendolyn recognized her? And my other beloved *frère*, Everard the Fat was present?''

"Aye. Alonso has the sanction of both the crown and the archbishop. You are so very wicked, you see.'' Giles grinned wolfishly.

"Of course. Do me a favor, Giles. See if there are any who would volunteer to go out in a sortie with me today. I want to speak to my brothers.''

"At once, my lord.''

Raymond watched Giles's departing back for a moment, then headed for the narrow passage that led down to the bowels of the keep. He picked a torch from a sconce and carried it with him.

Though the dungeon was his own, an involuntary shudder convulsed him as he descended through the living rock, seamed with moss and algae. He hated the dark, close feel of the place. Occasionally he saw pale, almost transparent little salamanders. They took no notice of the sudden light that struck them. Curious. Alonso's dungeon had had no such creatures in it.

A faint drip grew louder, steady and echoing in the rough-hewn chamber that constituted Rookhaven's most dismal aspect. A small glow issued from beyond the next corner. Raymond frowned. He had ordered no lights for his prisoner. He came upon Sven, who jumped to his feet, kicking over a rushlight in his haste.

"What is this, Sven? You have kept him company all night?"

The Dane looked down guiltily. Raymond shook his head and gazed at Wace. "Are you ready to come up?"

Wace's glance flickered to Sven for an instant, then the boy nodded. Raymond raised a brow at Sven. The Dane was now impassive. Raymond decided to ignore whatever it was they were hiding. Secrets would out, sooner or later. He took the keys from Sven and unlocked Wace's manacles and leg irons. "Do you understand why I had to do this?"

Wace rubbed his wrists and ankles, and slowly got to his feet. He pulled his mantle about his shoulders and re-pinned it. "I do understand."

"Are you contrite?"

Wace looked Raymond in the eye, his defiance gone, a clear courage in its place. "I am not, milord. Honor must be met."

Raymond nodded, and his lips barely curved. He rested his hand on Wace's shoulder. "A lesser man would be sullen now."

"Were you ever put in chains, milord?"

"Aye. But I will speak of it some other time. I am organizing a sortie. Do you want to come?"

"More than anything, sir."

"Sven, I thank you for sacrificing your comfort to watch over Wace. But if there is a next time—" Raymond gave Wace a telling look "—let him suffer in solitude."

"Aye, Sven, my thanks for keeping the rats off me."

The Dane graced them with a short bow.

Chapter Twenty

The morning mists lay shallow over the fen, and had already lifted from the meadows occupied by Alonso's army. Raymond rode slowly forward, flanked by Giles, Wace, and Simon the Herald, who carried a piece of white cloth. They halted in the center of the open field, equidistant between Alonso's encampment and the gray stones of Rookhaven's curtain wall. Raymond sat Orpheus, his black destrier, and the animal pawed the ground.

From the window of Blanche's tower, Ceridwen watched squinting in frustration. Her chest grew tight. This was all wrong. She took no pleasure in seeing Raymond ride toward danger. She found no satisfaction in the thought that he might not return. She burned with worry.

"Blanche. I cannot stand by any longer, I haven't the patience. I will burst if I do not do something!"

"You had best stay out of harm's way and give comfort to your people trapped here with you." Blanche looked at her severely and laid aside her sewing. "Have you any idea what it was like here with Raymond while you were gone?"

"Quiet, I would imagine."

"Aye. The kind of quiet that precedes a deluge. The kind that possesses a man before he vents his rage. No one dared even mention your name, such a black mood claimed him."

"Aye, clearly he was not happy to have me back, except—"

"You are an absolute pea hen sometimes, Ceridwen. He fears for your safety. He loves you."

"Nay. How can that be? You are not privy to the awful things he says to me when we are alone."

"What he says is one thing. More telling is what he *does*."

"What he does?" Ceridwen thought about it. He had told her. *My body does not lie.* Her cheeks grew warm.

"Aha! So that is the way of it, eh?" Blanche's eyes gleamed silver in the sunlight. "If you could see yourself! He is a Beauchamp, after all. His hands do his talking for him. I will warrant you cannot help but puddle at his touch."

"I beg your pardon!"

"Oh, Madame, do not act the virgin, when you are that no longer. Do not forget, I *know* what this breed of man is like. I was wed to his cousin for five years. It seems such a long time ago." Blanche's expression sobered. "You are yet fortunate. Bree has no father to turn to, no one to indulge her, and I have no—" She quickly looked down as something on her lap seemed to require her full attention.

Ceridwen knelt by her friend. "Do not feel guilty, Blanche. God did not intend for us to stand alone in sorrow. You have been good and faithful to your husband's memory. If after all this time someone else tugs at your heart, 'tis no sin to respond."

Blanche met her gaze with tear-bright eyes. "I thought I cared more for Giles. But your brother is so full of life. And brave. He makes me laugh…not an easy achievement. But, I am used. Penniless. I am older than he—"

"Those things will never come under consideration in Rhys's mind. He sees what he wants, and he goes after it, no matter the consequences or cost. And he always finds a way."

"I am not unencumbered. My Bree is another man's child."

"You are looking for excuses to deny your true feelings."

Blanche threw her a challenging look. "And what, pray tell, makes you think you are doing anything different?"

Ceridwen studied her hands. "I cannot betray my people."

"Who are your people, Ceridwen? Are they not these folk of Rookhaven, whose babes you have kissed and whose hurts you have tended? Why should they be any less important in God's eyes than those you left behind to your lord father's care? We women are the ones who can help make the peace, Ceri. With our husbands, when the pleasure we give blinds them to the delights of blood and conquest. Forgive me, I speak too much.''

"But you are right, Lady Blanche. I thank you for your vigorous candor.'' Ceridwen smiled and curtsied before leaving.

Breathless from her haste, Ceridwen crept a bit closer through the hedgerow, so she could hear and see the confrontation between the brothers Beauchamp. Hamfast lay beside her and licked her cheek. She rubbed his muzzle absently and kept her gaze fixed upon the scene before her.

The sky was clear and a soft breeze stirred Alonso's flaxen hair. He shifted in his saddle, assuming an air of complete boredom. "I am glad to see you have come to your senses, Raymond.''

As ever, Raymond looked dark despite his fairness. "Aye.''

"Then I had best lay out the terms of your surrender.''

"Nay, Alonso. I have come to tell you this is your last chance. Either depart in peace, or in pieces.''

Alonso stared, then flashed a brilliant grin. "My thanks for your consideration, brother. But I do not understand.''

"Of course you don't.''

Alonso tilted his head, in exactly the same way Raymond did. "I have something to propose. An exchange.''

"Of what?''

"You have married for convenience, have you not, Raymond?''

Ceridwen stiffened.

"Aye.''

Nay, it cannot be true.

"Well, I have a fancy for that black-haired lady of yours.''

"You have *always* had a fancy for my women!''

"Shh—look over there. See those villeins?'' Alonso pointed to a small group under guard near the oak grove.

Ceridwen's heart jolted in fear. She could not see who they were. But she had no doubt they were in grave danger.

"Ten, twelve souls. Women, mostly, and a few brats. What can I do with them? They are such a nuisance to feed. And so uncooperative when it comes to pleasuring my men.''

A dull flush spread over Raymond's neck and face. "Everard. Are you listening? Do you hear the corruption that Alonso's bright manner hides? A wretched beast in the guise of a man, and you follow him like an idolator."

Everard pursed his thick lips. "Raymond, you will surely burn for your calumny."

"Our young brother is an ungrateful cur, Prior." Alonso nudged his horse a step closer to Raymond's. He leaned over, hatred and fury etched on his face. "Meribel was meant for me. *Made* for me, and you *threw* her away! Literally."

The black charger jigged beneath Raymond, who kept silent. Ceridwen chewed her lip and refused to weep as Alonso continued.

"You never loved her as I did—never! And like a spoiled child, even though you did not want her anymore, you destroyed her rather than let anyone else take her from you."

Still Raymond did not respond, but his horse neighed.

Alonso held out one hand. "Give me your little Welsh sweetmeat. You do not want her either, so I have heard. And in return I will spare these prisoners."

At last Raymond spoke. "They are innocent hostages, not prisoners."

"As you will."

Orpheus stamped and half-reared. Raymond calmed the animal with a touch of his hand. "Alonso, you can rot in hell before I will give you anything but the sharp end of my lance."

"I hoped you would say that. Everard, did you not find these unwholesome women guilty of malefice? Witches, one and all?"

"'Twas obvious to one trained in these matters." Everard sniffed.

"Then we shall have a merry fire tonight."

"You have no authority to condemn them, Alonso. Such charges are ridiculous. What do you really want? Their suffering, or mine?" Raymond's mouth set in a grim line.

"You know the answer to that."

Alonso's false smile turned Ceridwen's stomach.

Raymond spoke softly, "Then take me in their place."

Nay! The protest screamed through Ceridwen's mind, and she bit her tongue. A small whine escaped Hamfast.

"Ah, but that leaves out the little blackbird, does it not?" Alonso leered at Raymond, who said nothing. "Why so quiet? Could it be that you *do* care for her? Just a bit? What a frolic, if you were made to watch me with her, and Gwen."

"Ceridwen means nothing to me."

"Liar. Prove it. Give her over, then."

"I will give you nothing, on principle. If you want her, you will have to fight for her. And the same goes for the rest of my possessions."

Ceridwen took a deep breath and ignored his reference to her as chattel. Here he stood before his enemy, offering himself in exchange for the lives of a few peasant women. It was not the first incongruous thing he had done.

She thought back to the night before, and how he had warmed her. And that other night, when he had warmed her even more, and she had thrown his love back in his face. Regret pierced her pride. She was wrong in her judgment of Raymond, and in her condemnation of herself for caring.

He had spoken to her heart long ago, with his first touch. She had no choice. There was but one way to save those women, and Raymond too. She stood and marched from behind the hedge straight out into the open, Hamfast at her side.

Alonso's mouth closed around whatever he had been about to say. Raymond turned a deep shade of brick. Everard dropped the leash of mastiffs. The dogs bounded over, only to stop at the sight of Hamfast, who growled, hackles raised.

"Ceridwen, get over here!" Raymond's voice commanded her, but his eyes pleaded. She ignored him and walked steadily toward Alonso, then froze in fear as the mastiffs closed in on her, snarling and barking in a deafening chorus. Hamfast bared his fangs at them, poised to attack.

"Alonso, call off those monsters! Ceridwen, do not move. I am coming," Raymond called out as his horse leaped forward.

Alonso shouted something and his portly dogs threw themselves to the ground, tongues lolling.

Ceridwen turned to Raymond. "Do not bother, my lord."

When she reached Alonso he looked down upon her with his cold blue eyes. Ceridwen had thought Raymond's eyes pitiless when she had seen them in battle. But she had been wrong. Here was a man truly without a heart.

She dipped in a curtsy before him, and shivered like a leaf in the wind. It was good she had not yet broken her fast, or she would be sick on the spot. Hamfast stared at Alonso as he dismounted, and continued his low growl.

"Ceridwen, what are you doing?" Desperation tinged Raymond's voice.

Alonso caught her arm. Hamfast barked and snapped at the air. Ceridwen turned to Raymond. "I am merely going where I am wanted, my lord." She steeled herself, then took Alonso's warm, dry hand and slipped into his embrace, her head against his shoulder, her hip to his. Her legs began to give way, and he tightened his arm about her waist. She had to convince them both. Rising onto her toes, she slowly put her mouth to Alonso's. He had the sharp smell and flavor of peppery meat.

Alonso startled Ceridwen with his aggressive, bruising response. Someone made a raw sound of pain—it was not she, but fear and revulsion caught the back of her throat. She forced herself to keep her eyes open, to turn and give Raymond a haughty little smile.

Alonso grinned. "The lady both tastes good and has taste, Raymond. You cannot fault her for that. Even your hound will have the sense to join the winning side."

Raymond's face had paled. His blue eyes were narrowed and his jaws bunched with twitching muscle. His deadly gaze moved over Ceridwen, passed on to Alonso, then returned to her, as if he could not make up his mind who he wanted to kill first.

The agony she read in his eyes pierced her to the quick. Metal flashed in the sun. Somehow he had drawn his sword, so swiftly she had not seen him do it.

"My lord, I beg of you, leave her to him," Giles said.

Ceridwen's throat tightened. Giles's loyalty was always to Raymond first. And that was as it should be.

The bright blade quivered in the sunlight. Raymond looked

from Ceridwen to his brother. "Alonso, my lady, you deserve each other. Deliver my people. *Now.*"

"Brand, bring the vermin down. But Raymond, I really do not see the point. Now you have all the more mouths to feed in your miserable little keep."

Relief washed through Ceridwen. At least Alonso had kept his word thus far. The women and children ran and stumbled toward Rookhaven. But what had she done to Raymond? He was to all appearances his usual angry self. But something had snapped within him. She could feel the bite of his anguish mirrored in herself. Ceridwen longed to run back to him, to say she did not mean it. But she had gone too far.

Raymond started to turn his horse. Alonso renewed his grip upon her. He nuzzled her cheek. "I want you, little blackbird. I will guide you to pleasures he has never even dreamt of."

A screech shattered the air. Galloping hooves drummed as Gwendolyn stormed toward them, brandishing an evil-looking falchion. "Alonso, unhand that dirty little wench or I will lop off her head—after I relieve *you* of what you value most!"

Alonso's hold on Ceridwen grew slack. She jumped away, ready to flee his mistress's fury. Ceridwen yelped as rough hands swept her off her feet from behind. Raymond hauled her up and she threw her leg over his horse's rump. "Hold on tight!"

Rippling fear coursed through Ceridwen like the rigors of fever. She needed no command to cling to her husband as Orpheus sped away with them. "Raymond," she gasped.

"Shut up." He galloped with her back to the keep, his men close behind. Alonso was left alone to face his raving lady.

Ceridwen sat on the bed, only daring to glance up every once in a while to check Raymond's expression. He had been pacing for so long, the shadows had moved halfway across the floor. Pacing, muttering and chewing his thumbnail. He paused to glare at her, then resumed his stalking, back and forth.

Hamfast watched contentedly. Of course *he* was already forgiven. But she had done it for those women, and for her lord. How could he think she had really meant it? *He is a man, that is how. And I was most convincing.*

Ceridwen could stand the silence no longer. "My lord. Let me explain, or punish me, but stop this roving to and fro."

"My lady, I am so angry, I had best continue thus."

"I am not afraid of you." It was but a small lie.

"No? Do you not still think of me as the Carrog Dhu?"

Ceridwen stood, and knotted her hands into fists. "I think of you as an ill-humored, overbearing, selfish *man!* And that is something altogether worse than any dragon."

Raymond halted and turned to her. "Do you also think me stupid? How dare you attempt such a sham with Alonso! Your motives are admirable, but your lack of judgment is staggering in its imbecilic immensity."

He took a step closer, his eyes blue and wintry. "I have reasons for my actions. I was not about to let him take you, but I needed him gloating and off guard. *He* believes your overture was sincere. His vanity will accept no other possibility. He will be watching for you. And so will Gwen."

Ceridwen bit her lip. "I was only trying to help."

"When I need your help, Madame, I will ask for it. And that will be a chilly day in hell."

"You would have let him take you instead?"

"I know him, Ceridwen. With me 'tis a game of wills that Alonso plays. He is good at it, possessed of great skill, acquired through long practice. He and Meribel perfected their artful manipulation—on me. I…" Raymond's voice faded into silence. He stared at the chest that held the toys.

"You cannot forget," Ceridwen finished for him softly. "But where does the fault truly lie, my lord?" She trembled at the look he gave her then—perhaps the very one he had given Meribel. Of rage and pain and violence straining to be set free. Enough to quake the bravest soul. But she had to know.

"The fault is right here, my lady." He put his fist to his heart. "This is how she died. Exactly as we are now. But she laughed at me, and I killed her for it, with but a single look." Raymond advanced upon Ceridwen. He loomed over her, but she was no longer frightened.

"Nay, my lord. Looks cannot kill. She did it herself, did she not? To spite you."

Raymond's eyes narrowed, then widened, and he covered his face with his hands. The heartbreak in his voice tore at Ceridwen. "As the arrow-wound to my leg mended, I discovered she had been…led astray. Instead of trying to forgive her, I tried to bring her to heel. And for that she made me suffer."

"Oh, Raymond. What happened?"

"She loved Alonso." Raymond drew a shaky breath. "I felt it. I saw it in her eyes. Every time she touched me, she secretly laughed, thinking I did not know. But I did—from the instant her heart turned away from mine. And she died for it." He stared at the bed, his face a golden mask of pain in the reflected firelight.

Ceridwen wanted him to stop. His confession was too terrible to hear. She did not really want to know how Meribel's death had come about. But she could see he struggled with an overwhelming guilt. "Whose doll is that in the chest? Did Meribel bear you a girl-child? Or…Alonso?"

"Nay." Raymond staggered over to his bed and sank down onto it, his head in his hands.

The sight of his suffering made Ceridwen kneel before him and soften her tone. "Tell me. Ease your burden, Raymond. There is no need to carry such a killing weight."

"Those toys belonged to Meribel. She gave them to me to lock away. She said, as my wife she had no more use for them."

Ceridwen glanced back at the trunk. "Meribel was a child?"

"Everyone was a child, once."

"I mean…how old was she?" Ceridwen was near tears again, to see the hollow, desolate look on his face.

"The same as you, but when we wed she had but eleven winters. Her family was land-rich but needed gold. Father had so much plunder from his campaigns, her people struck a bargain with him to assure themselves safe from future Beauchamp ravagings. Even then I was among those they feared most. We gained a vast territory. And I was at peace, for a little while."

"You got no child on her?"

"I could not ask that of a lass so small." Raymond looked away. "But she never forgave me for it. She said I shamed her, by not treating her as a woman. Then by the time I—" He straightened and gazed into Ceridwen's eyes. "She was seven and ten when she died. She knew I would never set her free. I tried to catch her. God knows I tried. I tried. I tried—"

Raymond wept. The dammed-up sorrow of years spent pretending he did not care was set loose. Ceridwen watched, appalled that she had pushed him to this. But tears would heal his wounded heart. Tentatively Ceridwen put her hand on his shoulder. His body was tense, the muscles hard and unyielding.

"Let her go, Raymond. The choice was hers."

"But her screams, Ceri." He spoke in an agonized whisper. "I cannot forget her screams—she called my name—how it echoed! The doves fluttered up from their roosts when she struck the wall, and the frogs grew silent when she splashed into their midst—I nearly threw myself after her."

"Oh, my lord…you cannot go on blaming yourself. Why do you allow everyone to believe your guilt? It only serves to further the torture you put yourself through."

Raymond rolled onto his back, one arm still over his eyes. "'Twas the only way I could save her honor. And her soul. They would have buried her in unconsecrated ground."

Ceridwen was humbled before him and the burden he had borne. "You are possessed of a truly noble heart…my husband."

He pulled his arm from his face and gazed at her. "Nay, I am possessed by you, who far surpasses me in nobility. But you have no idea what you risked, going to Alonso that way."

"I could have endured his touch, knowing the women and children were safe…that you were safe."

Raymond sat up and his eyes were hard and dry again. "Ceridwen, you still do not see. A woman's body is the least of what Alonso covets. He wants power. To make you weep with the slightest motion of his hand near your face—because he has trained you to fear what will follow. To make you beg for mercy, so you would trade your soul for but a moment free of pain."

Ceridwen felt herself pale. "I do not understand what you mean. Is he not simply a…a lusty man?"

"Lusty? Oh, aye. But his pleasures include other sorts of games. He started with me, long ago."

"My God, Raymond, what are you saying?"

Raymond studied his hands. "Over the years he has acquired a taste for other people's suffering. He has become increasingly expert and subtle in inflicting it, but the stakes must rise each time. That is what he meant, when he spoke of me watching him and Gwendolyn with you."

"I still do not understand."

"Then I will speak no more of it. But mark me, if you fall into his hands, you will wish *I* had slain you before he is done."

Ceridwen swallowed. "But what of Meribel? He said he loved her. Did he hurt her, too?"

Raymond's gaze moved to the window aperture, where a dusty afternoon sunbeam strayed into the solar. "Perhaps he did love her, in his own way. But the two of us tore her apart."

"My lord…" Ceridwen looked at him with longing in her heart and uncertainty in her voice. "…d-do you love me?"

He stared at her, and for a moment she did not know if he would shout at her or strike her or bound out of the solar. Then he released his breath in a soft groan. His hands slid up her arms to her shoulders. He pulled her close, cradling her so that she reclined in his embrace. "You tell me."

Raymond kissed her, and the passion he conveyed through that small area of skin, his lips to hers, left Ceridwen with no doubt. His touch was heady, potent. A magical antidote to her loneliness and heartache, so powerful that it was like being bathed in an elixir of loving strength.

Once again she felt his offering of all the hidden treasures he possessed, of affection and tenderness and deep regard. It was the same kiss he had given to her when she lay fevered and delirious. And she could not resist the silent cry that echoed from his heart to hers.

"Raymond…"

"Do you feel it?" he whispered.

Ceridwen nodded. She fairly hummed with *it*.

"What will you do, lady? I must know, for my life is now in your hands."

She looked into his eyes, no longer cold, nor hard, but glowing from within like flame-lit cobalt. "I will keep your love safe, and cherish it as I do the memory of my mother's dying embrace. As something rare and precious and only offered once.''

Raymond smiled. A warm, genuine smile of happiness, the first she had ever seen from him. It gave her a glimpse of the golden boy he once had been, as Alys had said. Ceridwen put her hand to his dark-stubbled cheek and drew her knuckles along it. When her fingers reached his mouth Raymond kissed their backs.

''I will never hurt you. Not on purpose.''

''I know.''

''But we are running out of time. I have an idea as to how to get you and Blanche and the other women out.''

Ceridwen knew a piece of him was still afraid of loving her, or he would not be reminding her of the siege—of endings and separation. She had to go after that piece, capture it and tame it, while he was open and willing. But oh, so gently. Her fingers interlaced with his. ''Must we speak of it now?''

''Nay.''

''Then let us pretend, my lord, that it is springtime, and the lambs are frolicking…we are in a high meadow, and the clouds overhead are like the full sails of ships in the wind.''

Raymond took up the fantasy. ''The lupine is blooming, and the air has the tang of the sea. We can hear the waves crash from afar. I would sing for you, as I have for no other, and we are utterly alone.'' His mouth was but a breath away from hers, when there came a hammering at the door.

''My lord!'' Wace burst into the solar. ''Oh—forgive me, but—'' The young man's ears bloomed red as he stared.

''What is the matter, Wace?'' Raymond spoke without a trace of anger. Ceridwen sat up and composed herself.

''Alonso's sappers are at work beneath the south wall. Giles says it may be days or hours, depending on their skill and the state of the foundations. We can smell the smoke upon the ramparts, sir, and the men—''

''Listen to me, Wace. Take a deep breath, aye, that is better. Now, have the garrison make their best guess at Alonso's end point and start digging from the inside toward it.''

''But—''

"Wace, go. I will be with you in a while." Raymond gave Ceridwen's hand a little squeeze. "And take Hamfast."

As the squire coaxed the reluctant dog from his warm spot and through the doorway, Raymond whispered in Ceridwen's ear. "Am I forgiven, *Cymraes?*"

"I will hold nothing back from you. The heart beating within me is mine no longer." Her eyes brimmed, and for once she was not ashamed of her tears.

Raymond's response was slow, deliberate, and silent. Ceridwen shivered and smiled. Blanche was right. His hands were most exquisitely eloquent. They skimmed her face, her breasts, her waist and hips, lingering here and there to loosen her overgown. They sang to her, a sweet, subtle song that evoked a rising harmony from within her. Her body resounded to his touch, so that her own hands shook as she drew him close.

"Nay, Ceri, there is no hurry."

In spite of his words Raymond undressed her without pause. Ceridwen let him do as he willed. She wanted him to take away with him whatever he needed in order to face the battle ahead. She only hoped that what she offered would be enough.

Her fingers slid into his warm, thick hair. His robe fell away. Then his gambeson and tunic dropped to reveal his broad shoulders, and a chest with well-defined muscles which worked in concert with his arms to lay her down in the bed.

Raymond's heat quickly put the chill of the bedclothes at bay. He wrapped her in warmth. He made a valiant effort to touch all of her at once, with his mouth and hands and body. Ceridwen glowed with yearning. She knew what he wanted, for his desire matched hers.

He had her utmost attention. Up close, she could enjoy every nuance of his expression, catch the flush of his skin against hers, appreciate the sparkle of moisture that softened his eyes. Her legs twined about him, and what followed was so natural, and so good, that she had not an instant's hesitation. She clung to him and surged with him in an ageless rhythm.

Ceridwen looked up at Raymond's face, and hardly recognized it. His dark-lashed eyes were half-closed, and he wore a look of rapture. Of being completely at one with himself and her and the intimate merging of their bodies. He whispered to her in French, the same two syllables, over and over. Ceridwen did not understand a word.

But she did not need to. His body did not lie.

Chapter Twenty-One

A haze of smoke drifted past the window of the solar. It bit into Ceridwen's lungs as she leaned to see out, and dimmed the afternoon sun. She had not seen Raymond since the previous evening, when he had gone to deal with the sappers. During the night Alonso had torched the deserted village.

Volleys of flaming arrows now screamed over the curtain wall at regular intervals, along with an occasional stinking animal carcass. Wet hides spread over the wooden hoardings of the battlements helped against the fire, but the thatched roofs of sheds within the keep were charred to nothing.

A few of Alonso's more daring men had scaled the walls and fought Rookhaven's defenders along the ramparts, though many more floated facedown in the moat. The steady boom of the battering ram against the gates set Ceridwen's heart pounding harder with each stroke. She could see Rhys, moving stiffly among the archers, shouting praise, and advice, no doubt, whether it was wanted or not.

"There he is, Alys." Ceridwen's heart sped in its beat. Raymond's bright hair streamed as he ran across the bailey to aid the men bolstering the gates. They had wedged great timbers against the iron reinforcements of the cross-members, but pale cracks showed where the wood had begun to split.

As if he sensed her gaze, Raymond looked over his shoulder and up, straight to her eyes. He smiled at her. A confident smile, bright with life and hope. She lifted her hand to him, proud beyond words.

"Ye've brought him back to us, Mistress." Old Alys patted Ceridwen's arm. "'Tis as though he's returned from the dead."

"Mayhap he has learned to leave the dead behind. As I have."

Alys looked out the window. "I could weep to see him whole again, just as wickedness hammers its way closer."

"Do not be afraid, Alys. You must assemble the people and make ready to use the bolt-hole Raymond cleared. Now that Alonso's men are concentrated here at the front gates, you can flee into the mountains, before it is too late."

Alys shook her head. "I'm too old for such a journey."

"Nay, you are strong! Besides, who will lead the others?"

"They'll not go, Mistress."

Ceridwen felt the breath leave her body, and a cold fear took its place. "What do you mean?"

"They will stay with their lord—and lady, to the last man, woman and child."

"I will see about that! If I command them, then they shall depart." Ceridwen turned to leave.

Alys stopped her with a touch. "Pet, they're as stubborn as Himself. They'll not budge until one of you goes with them."

Ceridwen stood, hands on hips, and stared at Alys, a frown creasing her brow. "Then I will send Blanche out with them."

"Nor will I go, Ceridwen," Blanche said.

Little Bree ran to Ceridwen and she scooped the girl up. Ceridwen's eyes asked Blanche the question she did not dare speak aloud before the child.

"'Tis better this way, Ceridwen. There can be no life without love, and all that I love is right here. Besides, I have no doubt that Alonso will be vanquished. Who could stand in the face of men such as these?" With a wave Blanche indicated the fighters ranged along the battlements. All displayed a ferocity that reflected their lord's revived will.

"I pray to God you are right, Lady Blanche."

The fires burned and slowly spread. The very water of the marshes seemed to be aflame, and the glow leaped and ebbed as evening fell. "What evil magic has Alonso wrought now?"

Ceridwen turned from the window of the solar and handed Raymond a brimming mazer of ale. His clothes and skin were grimed with both sweat and soot. He put the bowl to his mouth and gulped the brew down, keeping his eyes fixed upon her all the while. He wiped his face with his sleeve, then closed his warm, strong hand around hers. "'Tis no magic there. Alonso has poured whale oil upon the fen and set it alight. He wants no hiding places left for survivors."

Ceridwen's heart ached with the pressure of his fingers against hers. This new Raymond, tender and loving in or out of bed, was infinitely precious to her, and she had so little time with him. She had wasted too much of it in pursuit of pride and anger. "Raymond, Alys tells me no one will leave, even to save their own lives, or those of their children."

"One close look at my sword's edge and they will go. When death stares one in the face idealism quickly fades. As soon as the first of them feels my blade the rest will run, believe me."

"Not exactly an inspired solution."

"Does it matter, if they live as a result? Or most of them, anyway? Besides, I save my inspiration for other things."

With a growl Raymond caught Ceridwen about the waist and pushed her back to the bolsters on the bed. He devoured the skin of her neck with playful nips and hungry kisses.

"You are ruthless!" She returned his attentions with equal ardor, tinged with desperation.

"I do what I must," he said, around a kiss she would not allow him to break.

At last Ceridwen released him and took a deep breath. Raymond searched her eyes with his. He smoothed back the hair from her face. *"Est-ce que tu sais que je t'aime?"* he murmured.

Ceridwen searched his dark-lashed eyes...like mountain lakes on a midsummer's eve. Deep and blue and inviting. She still did not understand Norman French—but the last two syllables were familiar. "You need not tell me in words what I know from your every touch and glance, my lord."

Raymond closed his eyes then, and crushed Ceridwen to his chest, his face buried in her loose hair. Slowly he pulled away, and they both sat up. "As soon as it is fully dark I will send them through," he said. "The tunnel has only just been cleared and supported. We have strung rope through to the end."

"How did you find the passage?" Ceridwen kneaded Raymond's tight shoulders and was glad to feel him relax under her hands.

"I followed the salamanders." He gave a grunt of pleasure and dropped his head as she rubbed a particularly knotty muscle.

"The what?"

"My dungeon has little blind salamanders in residence. They had to come from somewhere. I thought perhaps once there was a passage to the surface. Then, when we were digging to meet Alonso's sappers, we came upon an old streambed. It must have fed the marsh long ago, but the water has dwindled since."

"What of the sappers?"

Raymond shrugged. "They now have the entire curtain wall of Rookhaven as their grave marker. Milady, many thanks, but I must attend my men. I came to bid you farewell, not to take my ease." He stood and cupped her face with one hand. "Don some sturdy, warm garb. Wace will take you and Blanche out of here."

"Blanche will not leave without Rhys, nor I without you."

"I cannot fight well knowing you are here. You hinder me. But I have no time to argue. Do as you like."

"The deceit that worked before will not work again, Raymond. I will never again believe another declaration of indifference from you." Ceridwen grasped his surcoat in her fists and tried to give him a shake.

Immovable, he ran his hands down to her hips and pulled her close against him. "You know where to look, to see if I lie."

"Your eyes *are* most expressive."

Raymond smiled. "Always the innocent." He kissed her mouth. "When this is over, we will go to that highland meadow."

"Do not try to distract me. I will not leave."

"Wace!" Raymond's arms held her tight and the vibration of his voice flowed from his body to hers. The door opened to reveal Wace, in a mail hauberk. A pair of manacles dangled from one hand. Ceridwen looked up at Raymond in disbelief.

"You would not dare!"

"As I have said, I do what I must, my lady. Wace, if she refuses to go with you, use the irons and drag her. Remember to make sure you put them over her sleeves. Here is the key."

"Aye, my lord." Wace's glance darted nervously from Raymond to Ceridwen. Free of her husband's embrace, she squared herself before the young man.

Raymond paused at the door. "A little Welsh spitfire cannot thwart you, lad. She is a kitten at heart. But do not allow her out of your sight. Even while she is changing into her traveling clothes." He left the solar without a backward glance at Ceridwen. She understood his omission was not out of heartlessness, but it hurt all the same.

The squire blocked her from following Raymond.

"Wace, you shall not lay one finger upon me."

"Not unless I must, milady."

"I am not going to leave."

"You will. I have my orders."

Ceridwen decided to take another approach. She sighed in a resigned fashion. "What is the state of the keep? Tell me the latest news, while I change. Turn around."

"Nay. I will speak, but I am to watch you at all times."

"Where shall I escape to? What weapon shall I spring upon you? Here, hold my dagger." She held it out to him.

"Nay, milady, I would not dishonor you with such mistrust."

"Then why do you stand there with irons in your hands?"

"That is a different matter altogether, milady."

Ceridwen stifled her frustration. Wace was turning into a man all too quickly. "At least my lord wants to make certain of my comfort, with his instructions to you regarding the fetters."

"Em…he gave those orders because otherwise your hands might slip through the manacles, Madame."

Upon hearing this, Ceridwen disrobed with angry jerks. She managed to pull on a heavy tunic and hose without revealing too much skin. But sweat dripped from Wace's chin by the time she had finished. "You were supposed to speak, not stare, squire."

Wace swallowed. "Alonso will breach the gate while the night is yet young. I am to have you well away by then, and we will be cloaked by the dark when we emerge outside the walls."

"Let us collect Blanche and Bree. I would not bring Raymond's wrath upon you for failing in your duty." Carefully, Ceridwen watched Wace's reaction. He took a deep breath. His expression softened, and he ran his fingers back through his hair, in a gesture much like his master's.

She tied her flute at her waist, threw a mantle about her shoulders and preceded him out of the solar. They headed for Blanche's turret. The door was ajar, but there was no response to their knock. Wace stuck his head in through the doorway.

"Lady Blanche?"

With his attention diverted Ceridwen fled down the stair and around the corner. She ducked into a dark alcove and pressed herself against the cold stones, her heart racing. Wace loped on by, cursing and scanning left and right. Again she slipped out and ran towards a tower leading to the battlements.

She raced up the spiraled steps that led to the evening sky. Stars were strewn across it, like jewels on a sea of indigo, and the sight caught at her heart. *They shine in beauty, no matter what atrocities take place beneath them.* Ceridwen crossed a wooden catwalk, easily thrown down in case of pursuit. For an instant she considered doing that, but abandoned the idea, for she did not know what the soldiers needed. Someone could fall to his death below.

She looked down into the bailey, and was gratified to see villagers in the flickering torchlight, filing into the narrow earth-work hole that could only lead to the escape passage. Raymond stood to one side, his sword gleaming, long and lethal.

Ceridwen returned her attention to the way before her. Buckets of foul-smelling stuff were ranged along the walls, and torches burned at regular intervals. She must find Rhys. If anyone could convince Blanche to leave, he could. She halted to listen, and realized that the din of the battering ram had stopped.

Hope surged within her. Perhaps Alonso had decided to withdraw for the night and rest his men.

Male laughter swelled from the next watchtower. A familiar, rough voice rose, singing in Welsh. "This is for you, Giles. I will teach you the words in English, so you may sing your lament. *Her glance has turned cold, her path avoids mine, the lips that once smiled now curl in disdain…*"

Rhys was wearing out his welcome, if he had not already. Ceridwen hesitated, then stepped up to the doorway and coughed.

"Well if it is not my heroic sister, come to be immortalized in verse." Rhys grinned and extended the one arm he was able to freely move. Giles's frown deepened, and the guardsmen nodded to her, looking a bit embarrassed to be found carousing. But she knew what they were about. The enemy would take no comfort in seeing that the defenders' spirits remained high.

"May I speak to you in private, Rhys?"

"A moment, gentlemen. When Ceridwen calls, I must jump to do her bidding." Rhys eased himself to his feet and walked with Ceridwen from the tower.

"Rhys, do not torment Giles! Where is Blanche?"

"Gone. Safe. Awaiting me with her daughter and Alys, beyond the next valley. She is furious, of course."

"Clever Rhys! However did you manage it?"

"Oh, I deceived her. I sent a boy to tell Blanche that Bree had wandered down into the sapper's hole, and was afraid to move without her mother's voice to guide her. Bree and I played a little game of hide-and-seek in the tunnel. The boy led old Alys down, and whilst I told her of Bree's predicament, the lad took the wee thing on ahead to the outside.

"Once Blanche arrived, she and Alys felt compelled to berate me for my carelessness, then go after the child. When they were clear through I locked them out. I had paid a stout farmhand to accompany them, the boy had his father's cart-horse, and he led them away on it."

"I told her you always got your way. Ah, Rhys, I am so glad." Ceridwen hugged him, careful of his wounds.

Her brother's warm grin vanished. "What are *you* still doing here? Raymond said you would be gone by nightfall."

"Well, *he* does not always get his way. I belong here, and here I will stay. I will perform any task you set me to—I can fletch arrows or carry water or—"

An uproar of shouts and curses interrupted her. Men swarmed to the battlements and arrows hissed into the darkness. The sulphurous buckets of Greek fire caused wild screams as their burning contents splashed through the crenellations and onto the men who had crept in silence up the curtain wall.

A hideous shriek announced the failure of the main gate's last beam, under the renewed onslaught of the battering ram. Ceridwen ran toward the spiral stairs. Raymond was below, at the head of the men who would meet the first wave of besiegers. He could expect no mercy from Alonso's soldiers.

"Ceridwen!"

She looked back to see Giles and Rhys starting after her, and sped down the steps. At the second level she stopped. Here was a landing, with a sheer drop to the courtyard. The shattered gate lay in pieces of splintered wood and twisted iron. Alonso had filled in a causeway of rubble to cross the moat. He rode in triumph to take Rookhaven. He might take Raymond's head, as well.

Alonso let his men run before him to clear the way. Rookhaven's archers hesitated, for Raymond fought on foot, clashing with the soldiers hand-to-hand. He swung his red-washed sword in powerful arcs and slew them two at a time, until the rest stood apart from him, afraid.

Alonso rode through the gateway, his fair hair gleaming in the torchlight. He stopped right below her, shielded by the wall. A drop more than double the height of a tall man.

Ceridwen summoned her hatred for him, her love for Raymond, and all the courage she possessed. *Lord God help me!* She jumped from the platform. With a shout she landed partway on Alonso's shoulders and part on his horse's rump.

The breath was knocked from her body and she had a dreadful pain in her middle, but Alonso tumbled to the ground with her.

His mount lunged forward as he fell back. He and Ceridwen rolled onto the stones of the bailey, already slick with blood.

"Bitch!" Alonso hauled Ceridwen to her feet and backhanded her as Raymond ran up to them. Alonso smiled, terrible in his depraved beauty. "Look what I have here, brother. If you want her in one piece, throw down your sword."

Raymond kept his gaze fixed upon Alonso, not her. Ceridwen swallowed, and her stomach gave a queasy lurch at the taste of her own blood. This was her fault. Her own rash stupidity. Because of her, Raymond would die, just as Owain had.

A small noise escaped her as the blade of Alonso's dagger pressed against her throat. Only then did Raymond's stricken gaze meet hers. She hated herself for disobeying him, for forcing him to choose between her and his castle—and for making him watch yet another wife leap from a wall.

But in his eyes the love he bore her and his pain at seeing her captive were all too clear. Slowly, he laid his sword down, and his next words were like nails rending Ceridwen's flesh.

"I surrender my person and my keep unto you, Alonso. I swear upon the blood of Christ that you may do with me as you will. I will offer no resistance, so long as you release Ceridwen, and my people go free and unharmed."

"Why should I, Raymond? I can kill the both of you and them too. Who is to stop me now?" Alonso grabbed Ceridwen by the scruff of the neck and shoved her to the ground.

With a roar Giles jumped down from above. Raymond scooped up his sword. What happened next took place so fast it barely registered with Ceridwen. Alonso spun out of Giles's reach and kicked upward, his leg a blur of motion. The sword flew from Raymond's hands, but he lunged at Alonso to fight barefisted.

Giles groaned and clutched his ankle. Rhys came down by the stairs and tried to stop Ceridwen as she ran to Raymond. He struggled with his brother, delivering punishing blows to Alonso's face and gut. The men of Rookhaven surged behind him.

"Hold!" Alonso's shout brought Raymond to a standstill. Ceridwen was baffled. Another of their inexplicable rules.

"I accept your terms, Raymond. Seize him!" Alonso's knights obeyed his barked order after only an instant's delay.

Held by four men, Raymond stopped the charge of his own mercenaries with a deadly look. As Rhys pulled her back, Ceridwen looked into Raymond's blazing eyes and wished with all her heart she had killed Alonso when she had fallen on him.

"I will honor my brother's request." Alonso spoke in measured tones, then wiped the blood from his mouth. Ceridwen knew his words served only to convince his men that he had some degree of chivalry, and did not come from any sense of mercy.

"The creatures who defend and inhabit this keep may go free, as long as it is not to English soil that they crawl."

"What guarantee do we have that you will not kill Raymond?" Giles demanded.

Alonso smiled. "You have my word that he shall live. Longer than he will wish to, I imagine. His soul must be purged of sin, and we must count his ransom when you bring it, after all. Now, out. Every last one of you!"

The enemy men-at-arms charged, pikes bristling. After a few more scuffles Alonso's men confiscated all weapons and herded the defenders of Rookhaven out into the night, Rhys and Ceridwen among them.

She looked back to see Giles lunge at Raymond's captors, only to be kicked and beaten down with staves until he lay quiet on the cobbles of the bailey. True to his word, Raymond allowed himself to be taken towards the mouth of the dungeon. Alonso and Everard followed, head to head in conversation.

Ceridwen slammed against the pikeman behind her, pounding her fists on his chest. "Raymond! I will come back for you!"

His head snapped up as her voice rang out. Then the pikeman cuffed her temple so hard that spots of white flashed behind her eyes. As she staggered, a knight jabbed his lance-butt into Rhys's wounded back. Her brother gasped in pain and the man looked pointedly at Ceridwen. "Your lord slew my best friend with that crossbow, lady."

She stared back into his eyes, pale against his dirt-streaked face, and nodded. She knew what it was like to lose a friend. And to want someone to pay for the loss.

Chapter Twenty-Two

Raymond wanted to swallow, to relieve his raw, parched throat. But he could not afford even that small effort. In the darkness he focused on breathing, on sucking air in and letting it out…just enough to keep his thoughts coherent. He hung upside down. Perhaps his eyes would burst forth from his head. But so long as he did not have to move he was content enough.

Gooseflesh formed on his chest as a tiny breath of air chilled his damp skin, beyond the cold that already enveloped his body. His heart convulsed despite his resolve. The door. They had returned. *I am here for Ceridwen and the others,* he reminded himself. For as long as he could last, and as much as he could take, until Alonso had spent his blood lust.

Voices sounded faintly, drifting toward him from the stairwell. Gradually they grew louder. Nearer. Red light flickered and intensified. It forced Raymond to shut his aching eyes, even as he tried to close his mind against what was to come. An involuntary shudder made a violent journey through his body, leaving wave upon wave of racking agony in its wake.

Raymond's panic swelled and grew, until it was a wild demon within him, out of control. *Not again, no more.* Frantic screams billowed in his throat. He fought to stop them from rushing out of his mouth to echo in the dungeon.

All his life he had stifled any reaction to the pain Alonso inflicted upon him, and now…he had almost nothing left. Silent tears had flowed, he had not been able to stop them. But it would

please Alonso greatly to hear him cry out at long last. And if
Alonso was satisfied, he would not turn toward anyone else to
find his pleasure.

Giles woke with a groan. His head throbbed. He opened his
eyes as far his bruised lids allowed, and saw the pale gray sky
of dawn. He sat up and grimaced, remembering the disastrous
night just past. Alonso and Everard had taken Raymond. The
garrison could not help. And he was about as much use to his
lord as a spavined jade.

Giles's hands sank into cold mud as sharp pains shot through
his sides. Nearby, Wace dozed, openmouthed, propped against
the wall. They were in the alley behind the stables. And he
himself sat in a reeking puddle of horse piss.

"Wace. Wace de Hautpont! Wake up!"

Wace startled to attention. He wrinkled his nose at Giles.
"Lord God, sir, did you drink beyond your capacity?"

"Even I could not produce such a volume, Wace. And if you
do not wipe that idiot grin off your face I will dunk your head
in this mess. Help me up. Where is Raymond now?"

Wace's expression turned grim as he assisted Giles. "Still
below, in the dungeon. Last night I…I heard him. But there were
too many guards…what if he is already dead?"

"He is not dead. If he were I would feel it in my bones. They
are not likely to kill him, as he is being held for ransom." Giles
spoke with a fierce certainty, but he too was afraid.

"Where do you hurt? Can you fight?" Wace sniffed and
wiped his cheek with his wrist.

"My ankle is bad. A few ribs are cracked. Are my teeth all
there?" Giles bared them for Wace to inspect.

"How can you worry about your teeth when our lord is in
torment and it is we who have failed him?"

"Wace, being miserable does no good in these situations. We
are conspicuous. Unless we are lucky, we cannot do much until
this evening when it gets dark. The longer we wait, the drunker
Alonso's swine will get. And hopefully the fog will set in. Did
everyone else escape? Lady Ceridwen? Shona?"

"I did not see Shona. Our lady is safe beyond the walls, with the garrison. But they are weaponless.'' Wace sucked in his breath. ''Hamfast. Where is he?''

''Let us worry about ourselves first.''

Silently, except for the suck and plop of their feet in the mud, they slipped into the warmth of the stable to wait.

''Rhys, I must go back.''

''Why, so you can die alongside him? Do not be a fool, Ceri. We can only help by retaking the keep, or coming up with the ransom to·buy Raymond's freedom. Since either way looks to be impossible, I will see to your safety instead of his.''

Huddled together in small groups, the remnants of Rookhaven's people had spent the night in a linden grove, on a rise overlooking the now abandoned siege encampment. The smoldering ruins of the village made a dismal backdrop to the field of scattered bones, all that was left of the sheep and pigs stolen and gorged upon by Alonso's army. They had even devoured the few milk cows that had been left behind.

Ceridwen hugged her knees to her chest and rubbed her arms. Her stomach growled and she thought of the children on their way into the Black Mountains. They must be cold and hungry too. But at least they were not here. The memory of the battered lieutenant sprang to her mind's eye. ''What about Giles, Rhys?''

''What about him?''

''He looked to be half-dead last I saw! Do you not care?''

Rhys took one of her hands in his. ''Ah, Ceri, try to understand, will you? This is war. We fight prepared to die, taking as many of the enemy with us as we can. We do not go forth hoping to be rescued at the expense of others.''

''I do not care what you expect! And where is Wace? And Shona? I have to go back!'' Ceridwen lurched to her feet and began a wavering path toward the keep, stumbling in her fatigue.

To the exclamations of the watching men-at-arms, Rhys jumped her from behind and they slid in a tangle down the hill. At the bottom he held her hard, until she stopped struggling. He stroked her hair from her eyes. Chastened, Ceridwen wanted to weep at her brother's gentle touch.

''One thing at a time, Ceri. You must eat, regain you

strength, and then we shall see.'' Together they limped back to
the group. The huntsman, Bruce, had managed to bring away a
sack of grain, another man had a flint. Before long, oatmeal soup
bubbled, some within a dented helm, and the rest in a scorched
brass pot retrieved from the village.

''Alonso expects us to slink away into the forest, never to be
heard from again. But when he emerges, we shall be ready, to
reclaim what is ours,'' Ceridwen said, and the men responded
with doubtful looks.

Some of the mercenaries had gone home, as their chances of
reward seemed nil. Enough remained to form a company of
fighters, but they had no horses, and the makeshift weapons were
more embarrassing than useful. ''Sharpened sticks are better than
nothing,'' Sven said, in an attempt to hearten them.

''Aye, and a kick in the arse is better than a boot in the face,
ain't it, lads?''

''How 'bout a hammer t'yer stony pate is better'n a hot poker
up yer—er, pardon, milady.''

''Never mind—she cannot understand the half of what you
are saying.'' Rhys winked at Ceridwen and she rolled her eyes.

''I know what Giles would say under these circumstances.''
To Ceridwen's discomfiture, expectant silence greeted her statement. She had not meant to speak aloud. She surveyed the tired,
dirty faces surrounding her and rallied. ''Two in the bush are
worth but one in the bed....''

The men looked at each other. Flustered, Ceridwen knit her
brow. ''...or is it the other way 'round?''

Loud guffaws broke the stillness of the morning, amid much
backslapping. Cheeks flaming, Ceridwen turned to face Rookhaven. She clenched her fists at her sides, not wanting the men
to see her falter. Alonso would not wait for any ransom. *Until
you would trade your soul for a moment free of pain.* Raymond's
words haunted her, each moment she was apart from him.

The morning wore on, and the men-at-arms grew restless.

''Rhys, what if you lead a small party to Llyn y Gareg Wen?
Speak to Father. He might help us. 'Tis worth a try.''

''O excellent woman! My brains have softened with all this
talk of love. I can collect Blanche along the way and surprise

Da. We should have left at first light.'' Soundly kissing Ceridwen goodbye, Rhys went to call for volunteers.

After he had left, Ceridwen addressed those who remained. ''You have not known me long, and have no measure of my worth, either as your lady or as your leader. I will not presume to be the latter, not as long as Raymond lives.'' She looked down at her hands for a moment, and cleared her throat.

''Master Bruce will get word to Cruikshank and Lucien de Griswold of our plight. I might suggest something else in the meantime. As the *Cymraeg* have fought the English for many years, I have learned a few things. Lord Alonso, as are most commanders, is used to a head-on battle—to meeting a known enemy, assembled at an agreed-upon place, at a prearranged time. But what if we fight as the Welsh have learned to fight? We make ourselves invisible in the forest, entice the enemy within, and then spring upon them to capture their horses and arms.''

A warrior stood, wide-eyed. ''Invisible, my lady? What manner of charms and spells would that take? Is the moon in the proper conjunction for such an endeavor?''

''Nay, my friends, 'tis not magic. Be invisible by moving subtly and silently. We will climb the trees, and rub our faces and hands with mud. We will wear crowns of leafy twigs and…'' Ceridwen's throat closed. She fingered her tunic. The wool was stiff and stained a dark, rusty red. A blackness had begun to grow within her, as though the enemy blood Raymond spilled had imparted a bitter, dying passion to her, and it had taken root.

She thought of the women who had been raped. Of the half dozen villagers still hanging from the oak tree. Of Owain. Giles. And most of all, Raymond. It was ironic. English blood cried out for vengeance as loudly as did Welsh.

Ceridwen swept the group with her gaze, and it did not matter that she could not distinguish their faces. ''If we are careful, we can drop down upon them unawares. Even without bows we can destroy them utterly, every last one, with slings, stones, and spears. And if Alonso is among them, he is mine.''

She felt them wonder at her vehemence, and knew they remembered the tales of victorious Welshwomen, finishing with their daggers what their men had started, on the dead and wounded of battle. She looked to Sven. He understood. He had the same sort of wild blood within him that she did, despite his calm, mannered exterior.

"Let us try it," he said, and rose to stand beside her.

Ceridwen slipped out of the linden grove while Sven was not looking. They had all practiced and agreed upon who should go where and which signals meant what. But not a moment longer could she bear the thought of Raymond in Alonso's hands. She stepped determinedly along the path leading to the barbican. What she meant to do would only succeed if she went alone.

"Lass! Wait!" Old Alys emerged from behind some brambles.

Ceridwen jumped, her heart pounding. "Please do not try to stop me, Alys."

"Nay, I won't." She held out a leather bag. "Yer burial silver. It might do, to ransom Himself, might it not?"

Ceridwen's heart leaped again at the old woman's frail hope. No doubt it was not enough to ransom a cat, if Alonso was involved, but she took the pouch. "Many thanks, Alys. I will do what I can with it. Go back, and tell no one you have seen me."

"God keep ye." Alys retreated, tears wetting her cheeks.

Ceridwen took a deep breath and tied the bag to her belt. What she needed most was her wits, not coins. As she walked she composed herself for the part she planned to play. Closing her eyes for a moment she visualized Ewan, a boy from Llyn y Gareg Wen. *He cranes his neck and tilts his head so. He hunches one shoulder thus…his right wrist bends at an odd angle, his left leg drags a bit, and he squints.* That part she was quite good at already. She was dirty enough, certainly.

Ceridwen shuffled and limped and gibbered her way closer to the gate. Even "Cud" was not this difficult to impersonate. *Lord be with me now.*

"Oy! Gerroff wi' ye—shoo!" The guard waved his hand at

her as if she were a troublesome fly instead of a fellow human being, however unfortunate.

"Bread, bread." She opened her mouth and struck herself on the forehead with her palm, as she had seen Ewan do with good effect on the ale-wives of Llyn y Gareg Wen. If she survived, she would bring him a pot of honey. Two, if she could get them.

"The thing won't go away—"

"Ach, Mathias, leave the eejit be."

Ceridwen bristled. What did he mean? Ewan was no idiot.

"It's likely to get itself thrown off the parapet, for sport." Mathias scowled at her from beneath heavy black brows.

Ceridwen willed tears to her eyes. Nothing. Where were the wretched things when she needed them? She scrunched up her face and ducked her head.

"Miserable, disgusting piece—a changeling, aintcha? Whyn't yer mam leave you fer fairies to spirit away?" He cuffed her head, hard, and a genuine cry of pain escaped her, for it was already sore from her tussles with Alonso and the pikeman.

"Leave off 'im. Run along, laddie—see if there's owt to eat from the kitchen midden." The other guard glared at Mathias and shoved Ceridwen on through. She could hear them arguing even as she scuttled into the bailey.

Acrid smoke drifted in wisps from cooking fires and braziers scattered along the battlements. Just inside, the bodies from the fight still lay in disorderly heaps. Covering her nose, she eased her way along. The door of the dungeon was nearby, and Raymond had to be down there. Ceridwen crouched in the shadow of the curtain wall and waited for an opportunity to slip past the guards.

Apparently they had not found the key, for the lock was broken and the door ajar. Alonso must not be too concerned about Raymond's ability to escape, for as the hours passed, the watchmen drifted away, until only one man was posted. Perhaps she was too late, after all. Ceridwen's heart ached and pounded in protest at the thought.

Her feet went numb from sitting on them. Stiff with cold, Ceridwen huddled against the stone wall and watched the guard. He yawned and scratched himself, then strolled over to a corner, his back to her. A sigh of contentment and a steady splashing told Ceridwen this was her chance. She darted into the dark maw of the dungeon.

The meager light from the narrow wall openings dwindled as she descended the sloping walkway. When it failed entirely so did her courage. She stopped to get her bearings. The dark closed in, like a suffocating blanket of nothingness. If she took a wrong turn, or fell down a stair…it did not bear thinking about. She felt her way along. Her fingertips skimmed the cold walls and stubbed painfully on the outcroppings.

At first Ceridwen had thought the place silent, but now that she could no longer see, each splatter of dripping water from overhead sounded clear and distinct. Odd rustlings mystified her, until something small scurried over her foot.

Her sharp intake of breath brought with it a musty taste of dank air. Drafts hissed from unseen openings as though they were the malevolent breath of the dismal fortress. A place where one dealt death, or waited to be claimed by it.

She tried to hurry, and a cobweb against her forehead drew a small shriek from her. An irrational desire to run screaming headlong into the blackness seized her, to blot out thoughts of what she might find. *Steady on.* One step, then another.

Ceridwen clutched her flint, borrowed from the garrison, and took a deep breath. She touched the rough granite wall to orient herself. It was moist, and the chill more pronounced at this lower level.

These stairs must lead to a chamber below. To a place that had once echoed to endless screams, so Alys said. Long before Raymond became lord here. But the memory still whispered from the stones, crying out the ancient agonies of forgotten men.

Cold air slid past her face, carrying the faint scent of sweet, rich blood. *'Tis only my overtaxed imagination.* Knowing better, Ceridwen's stomach lurched and her heart battered her ribs. She wanted to call Raymond's name, but fear that he could no longer answer caught her throat and held it tight.

She slid her toes forward to find the edges of the steps, each one a tapered wedge that formed the downward spiral. Down and around, a dozen small descents. Then there were no more, just an empty flat floor at her feet, and blackness all around.

Silence, but for a tiny creak. Weighted metal, groaning against metal. She stood still and held her breath to place the sound, but it had stopped. Her nerves stretched in the darkness, like the feelers of a cockchafer. She caught the burned, greasy smell of a torch. Ceridwen did not want to look, but her fingers searched the wall, passing over rings and icy lengths of chain until they found a sconce.

Her hands shook and she struck the flint wrong. She tried again. With the second snap of sound the oil-soaked torch burst to life. The light of the flame ate up the black space. The brilliance hit her and Ceridwen's eyes clamped shut—too late. She smothered her scream with both hands at the sight of Raymond.

Nothing had prepared her for this.

He hung by his ankles, chained to a thick beam. His wrists were bound, and his hands cleared the floor by mere inches. Caked black pathways, and others still gleaming crimson, coursed across and down his body. Blood had dripped from his fingertips into a puddle, now half-congealed. His flesh shone, taut and raw. Limp strips of skin clung to his charred back and legs.

They had left a flaying knife just out of his reach. There was not a chance of him bringing about his own relief with it. An overturned bucket lay nearby. Horror curled in her stomach as she realized the water had been for reviving, not drinking.

Her heart hammered and a wave of nausea engulfed her. How could Alonso and Everard have done this to their own brother? "Raymond?" she whispered. Merely to touch him now might kill him, if he did yet live.

His body jerked, and the small movement reproduced the metallic creak she had heard earlier. Ceridwen trembled and swayed. Her teeth began to chatter. She knelt and put her face next to Raymond's mouth. Nothing…then his breath, still warm with life, whispered along her cheek. A blue spark lit the crack of his eye. His lips moved, and his voice emerged a hoarse, dry rasp. "I knew you would come."

"I am here, Raymond, I am with you now." Ceridwen fought

her panic. She took up the sticky knife and cut the ropes from his wrists. She kept up a steady litany, as if the stream of words would somehow give him a thread to hold onto, and keep him alive. "My love, do not worry, I will get you out of this place, you will be right again, you'll see, we will lie on our backs in the meadow and watch the clouds overhead, and suck the sweet-grass stems, and I will play my flute into the wind for you to catch the notes and you will sing the harmony and…"

On and on she talked, all the while wrestling a large block of oak closer to him. An old block, with the deep grooves of axe blows in it, the wood stained forever dark. At last she had it in position beside him. After putting the bucket upside down next to his hands, she found a stout piece of a broken stave. She climbed onto the chopping block and tried not to choke at the close-up view of the wounds on Raymond's legs.

His feet were blanched from the shackles around his ankles, attached by a chain to a big iron ring. It hung from a heavy hook, screwed into the beam. Ceridwen slid the stave through the ring and angled it up and onto the edge of the beam. Though she took care, even that small motion made Raymond's body swing, and the irons bit deeper into his flesh.

He groaned.

"Raymond, are you listening? Forgive me for hurting you, but I am going to try and shift you, so you must try too. Put your hands upon the bucket there before you." She looked down. There was no sound from him, no purposeful movement. "Raymond! Show me that you understand."

His arms dangled. The middle finger of his right hand twitched randomly. She gulped air, then a reserve of iron that she did not know she possessed took charge. Biting down hard on her lip, she flicked an area of exposed muscle on his calf until, with a jerk and a moan, he responded. Ceridwen repeated her instructions, and this time he managed to raise his hands and rest his palms on the bottom of the bucket.

"I will lift, and you must try and support yourself from below so you do not break your head when you fall free. Pretend you are a squire again, doing handstands. Can you do that?"

"Aye."

It was a mere croak, which she scarce dared believe, but it sounded like evensong to Ceridwen's ears. The muscles of Raymond's shoulders bunched as he pushed against the wood and took some of his weight off the shackles.

"Ready? Here goes!" She shoved upward on the stave to raise the iron ring, using the beam as a fulcrum. Her arms and legs trembled with the effort of holding him up long enough to slip the ring from the hook. When the ring came free she released the stave and grabbed Raymond's knees as he fell.

He broke his descent with his arms but Ceridwen still tried to slide her own body beneath his as they landed. But her feet slipped in his blood and she grazed her head on the oak block.

Raymond lay facedown on the stone floor. After a few moments a strange, panting, animal sound came from him. Ceridwen scrambled to his head and stroked the tangled hair from his cheek. At the sight of his clenched jaw she realized he was holding back screams. "What is it—oh Raymond, what is it?"

"My feet…are waking…don't touch me."

His voice was barely audible, so hoarse was it. Ceridwen guessed why. In anguish, she could only watch him suffer. He shivered, his muscles contracted in spasms and sweat born of pain dripped from him.

"Let me cover you, at least." Gently, she laid her mantle over his singed, flogged back. Off to one side she saw his clothes and boots strewn on the floor, and gathered them up. "I will get your irons separated and we will go."

Ceridwen, pretending confidence, searched the floor from whence she had moved the oak block. "Where is the axe?"

"There is none."

Her heart sank. "You have no axe?"

"I do not…behead…my prisoners, nor…lop off their limbs." Eyes closed, he rested a few heartbeats before continuing in a halting fashion. "Ceri, go. I cannot walk. They will be back, and I will not…have them take you. Give me that much peace of mind."

"My lord, we have come a long way together, from the worst enmity to the truest love and I will not leave you now or ever, so there is an end on it."

"Ceri, you'll make me weep."

She peered at him. "Your eyes are all purple. Is that how I looked after Nat choked me?" To speak of inanities might keep the awful truth of their situation at bay.

"You were the most beautiful creature I had ever seen. I had to have you." His exhausted smile curved with the little bunches of muscle at either side of his mouth.

"You did not! You took great pains to shun me."

"For your own sake. A Beauchamp's love is an evil thing."

"'Tis a good thing, Raymond. Please, try to sit up now. I will help you."

He righted himself with her aid and sagged against the block. "I am thirsty."

"I will find you something." Ceridwen spotted a small rush-light lamp by one of the cells, and lit it from the torch.

"Nay, Ceri, do not bother. I cannot last." Raymond gazed up into her eyes.

"Be quiet and do not move." She kissed his dry lips. "I shall be back directly."

She looked over her shoulder and saw that he still watched her intently, as if she were the only visible thing in the universe. Ceridwen tore her gaze away and hurried up the steps. Despair squeezed her heart. Even if she could release his shackles he could not possibly manage the stairs. And she could not possibly carry him. He was close to a point beyond which he could never return.

She chewed her lip. Dying or no, Raymond was thirsty. She would find him some ale or wine or even water, if that was all there was to be had. And stay with him until the end.

Chapter Twenty-Three

As Ceridwen progressed up the passage toward the light of the surface, she stopped to set the little lamp in a corner where no draft could blow it out. At the top she emerged into the late afternoon. The sky above the curtain wall surrounding the bailey was rippled pink and orange with clouds underlit by the lowering sun. Mist from the marshes flowed in through the broken gates to swirl about her feet.

The sounds of merry-making floated from the main hall. *That is why so few of Alonso's men remain outside, they are enjoying Raymond's food and drink.* Anger overrode Ceridwen's fear, but the guard spotted her as she stepped away from the dungeon.

Instantly she remade herself into Ewan. "Mercy, lord, mercy on me," she whined as the guard raised his fist. For the blink of an eye he hesitated—and it was enough for her to scurry off toward the kitchens. With a curse and a halfhearted jab of his pike in her direction, he returned to his dice.

Within a few moments, Ceridwen flattened herself into a shadowed corner and gripped the precious vessel of ale she had pilfered from the kitchen shed. The dungeon door was shut, and the guard had seated himself before it. There was no reason for him to allow "Ewan" inside, and she would no doubt get a beating for her effort. She had no weapon, and if he saw the bag of silver, he might just slit her throat and take it all.

What else could she offer him, in return for gaining entry to that hellish place? The answer turned her stomach. But she would get Raymond's drink to him, no matter the cost. Ceridwen scrubbed her face with her sleeve, slid her mantle back, and attempted to smooth her hair. Her heart bounding, she approached the guard, swaying her hips as best she could.

"What do you want?" He jumped up and glared at her.

Ceridwen tried to look guileless. "Lord Alonso has sent me to find out if his brother is ready to be shriven by a priest. Lord Alonso will not have it said that he and Lord Everard denied their own kin a chance at absolution."

"You don't look like any messenger of Alonso's. I can't even tell whether you're a lass or a lad." The guard's pike-tip drifted lower, pointing at her belly.

"Does it matter? Which do you prefer?" The audacity of her own reply made Ceridwen ill, but she had to get his mind away from the thought of idly running her through.

"What do you mean, you filthy creature? Bah—you *are* from Alonso, to talk so depravedly. Stay away from me—if he's cast you off you must have a bubo or the pox." He indicated the pitcher. "What's in there?"

"'Tis vinegar, to slake Sir Raymond's thirst."

The guard smiled without humor. "So Alonso's treating his brother like Christ, now? That's no surprise. Go ahead, then. But if you're not back by sunset, you'll rue the day."

Ceridwen squinted at the sky. She did not have much time. "I will hurry, sir."

The sentry allowed her to step through into the cool dankness beyond the door, then leaned in after her. "Don't make me have to come get you, right?" he called.

Ceridwen opened her mouth to answer, but no words came. Someone was behind the guard. A length of wood rapped his head, and without a sound he slid to the floor. Two scruffy men dragged him out and Ceridwen fled toward the darkness to hide.

"Psst! Mrrow!"

A plaintive cat noise echoed, halting her. She turned and peered at the doorway. There came a tall, powerfully built man with an unmistakable saunter, though he limped, and a slimmer, shorter fellow at his side. With a jolt she recognized Giles and Wace. The surge of hope for Raymond dizzied her.

"'Tis I," she said, joyfully going to meet them.

Giles enveloped her in a highly odiferous embrace. "Oh, my lady, forgive us our shortcomings."

"Do not be ridiculous, sir, just thank God you are in one piece." Ceridwen passed the pitcher of ale to Giles. "Do not drink that. Wace, come to me." She kissed the blushing squire emphatically even as she pulled him along. "We must hurry."

Ceridwen retrieved her rushlight and they descended in haste to the evil place below. "My lord, we are here for you."

Raymond looked at them mutely and blinked. He had donned his tunic, but the effort had apparently exhausted him. Ceridwen insisted Raymond drink all the ale. She issued terse commands on exactly how to handle him, and soon he was cocooned in her mantle, Wace at one end and Giles at the other.

"You are good at barking orders, milady," Giles remarked.

"Thank you, 'tis the sterling example of the lot of you that has inspired me," she replied. "Hurry your arses, now!"

Giles grinned and did as he was told. They topped the stairs and inhaled the cool evening air. The guard was propped beside the door, still unmoving. Ceridwen stared toward the gates, open but patrolled by Alonso's men.

"How are we going to get out of here?" Wace was pale beneath the soot smeared on his cheeks.

"There, do you see that empty cart? Put Raymond in it, with those who defied him." Ceridwen turned to meet Giles's eyes. "Will it work?"

Giles nodded. "Lady, you are too clever. Come, Wace."

Taking care that no one saw, they dragged the cart to the area of Raymond's last stand against Alonso. One by one, they piled the bodies of the men he had slain into the cart with him.

"Someone is coming!" Wace hissed.

Ceridwen heard the heavy tramp of several men approaching from around the corner. "Quick, lie down among the dead!"

Giles and Wace threw themselves onto the gruesome mound, face-up, Ceridwen saw. But she dared not risk being recognized by one of the guards either as Ewan or as Raymond's lady. She got into the wain, and shuddering, lay cheek to cheek with a corpse, her arm over her face.

Opposite her was Raymond, his eyes glittering in the shadows. The soldiers were within a few feet of them. Ceridwen blinked furiously at Raymond, to get him to close his eyes. He winked at her, then, to her relief, he obeyed.

One of the guards, well-loosened with drink, spoke in a low tone. ''There's enough blades and baubles here to buy a lake of Rhenish, lads. Look sharp to it, and we can take what we want.''

Ceridwen could not see, but heard the shift of the stinking corpses, the creak of leather, the snap of bone as someone's death grip was broken from his sword.

''Oy—I think this one's still breathing!''

A big hand grasped her ankle, and she nearly screamed. Ceridwen stiffened herself in imitation of the noisome, rigid men surrounding her, and tried to keep her fingerhold in a crack between the floor boards of the cart. The looter jerked on her leg and met with resistance.

''Pah, must be the bloat settin' in. He's a plank already.''

The soldier let go, and she took a tiny, shallow breath.

''This load is worthless, in rags and not a scrap of brass among the lot, I'll warrant,'' the man said, his disgust evident.

Ceridwen exhaled, slowly. Raymond's eyes gleamed again, then their twinkle gradually vanished. Worry stabbed her that perhaps he was suffocating beneath the weight of the slain men. As the guardsmen picked over other bodies it grew increasingly difficult for her to hold still, for flies crawled on her face, the smell made her want to vomit, and the mere thought of lying with these mangled wretches was more than she could bear.

But she concentrated on keeping her breathing shallow. After what felt like eons, Alonso's men gradually departed, clanking off with their booty of swords and other arms. Ceridwen lifted her head and gave thanks to God, then whispered, ''Raymond, can you hear me? Are you yet with us?''

He did not reply. She began to pull at the nearest body.

Giles's hand stopped her efforts. ''We must away, lady. We cannot help him here. He is better off dead outside than alive in here where Alonso can get at him again.''

Ceridwen nodded, her heart in her mouth. She jumped down

and she and Wace put their shoulders to the yoke while Giles pushed from the rear.

"What're you doing there?" Yet another pikeman strode toward them. Ceridwen froze but Giles spoke jovially.

"Owney follerin' orders, sir. His lordship wants all this lot cleared out. Says the smell puts his appetite off."

"Your smell would put anyone's appetite off. Hurry up."

Wace gave a respectful tug to his forelock as they passed the surly guards. Not Mathias and his friend, Ceridwen was relieved to see. The cart creaked and groaned under its hideous burden. They forced the cart through the mud out the gates.

"Slow down, milady. Save your strength, we cannot rush with him. Wait 'til we are over the rise."

Giles was right. Ceridwen fought the panicked urge to run. The yoke rubbed her skin raw but she tucked her head and kept up her steady push along the rutted track. As soon as they were out of sight of the keep they stopped, hauled the dead men free of Raymond and laid them upon the swale. Breathless, Ceridwen climbed into the cart and put Raymond's face between her palms. "My lord?" She stroked his filthy cheek.

"Ceri...I thought you were about to bury me alive." His blackened eyes crinkled above his effort at a grin. Ceridwen swallowed her tears. The ale must have done him good.

He squeezed her hand. With exquisite slowness, he sat up, and shifted himself to the edge of the cart, shackles rattling. "I will not have you work as oxen pulling this thing any farther."

Wace knelt and tried to kiss the back of his master's hand.

"Nay, Squire." Raymond gazed at the lad's tear-streaked face. "Any fault is mine alone. We shall not speak of it. Ever." He looked at Giles and the knight's smokey eyes gleamed. "Well met, St. Germaine."

"As soon as I break this chain between your feet we can hobble on." Giles set up a large stone to serve as anvil.

"Excuse me, sir, but let me try my hand." Wace spoke, a sheepish look on his face. With a great deal of grimacing and a stout cloak pin, he picked the locks of the irons.

With Ceridwen's shaky help Raymond eased his hose up over his raw legs. "You and Sven hid this talent from me, Wace?"

The young man hesitated beneath the collective stares of his elders. "Em, aye, we put my fetters back on when we heard you coming, sir. But it took lots of practice to get them off."

"You have my thanks," Raymond said, but the vestige of a smile he had worn was gone.

At his desolate look, fear once again lurched into Ceridwen's heart. "What is it?"

His battered face held no expression, but the blue of his eyes flickered like a guttering candle flame. He gave a negative shake of his head. Then Giles and he, supporting each other, began limping away from Rookhaven. For a moment Ceridwen watched, then fighting tears, she trudged after them.

Night had fallen deep and chill upon the encampment. The trees beyond the fields provided shelter for the motley camp Ceridwen and Sven had organized. Small fires glowed in the dense blackness of the forest. They warded off marauding wolves, attracted by the carcasses left behind by Alonso's men.

Raymond dozed fitfully alongside Ceridwen. He was weary beyond exhaustion, but could not stay asleep. Nightmares plagued him, red, searing memories of what Alonso had done. He opened his eyes wide and stared unblinking into the fire.

"Raymond?"

"How is it you know the moment I am awake, Ceri?"

"I feel you stir, somehow, in my heart."

"Go back to sleep."

"My lord, you must talk about it."

"Do not pick at me like a scab! There is nothing to tell."

She pressed his arm with her small hand. "Look what happened the last time you pretended that."

"You do not understand, Ceri. You cannot. It was…" He fell silent, the words ground to bitter dust in his mouth. A broken man. Alonso had succeeded, no doubt beyond his fondest imaginings. Raymond's heart thundered and he felt a flush of shame suffuse his face.

He had cried out. Nay, he had screamed, long and loud—and he was still screaming, inside. It had been a relief to have the excuse that by making Alonso's dream come true, he spared the others his brother's wrath. But once started he had not been able to stop. It had been as though, during that endless, hellish night, he had given voice to all the pain he had suffered before at Alonso's hands without making a sound.

Never again. He looked at Ceridwen, worry and concern on her face. And pity? Was that there too? He could not bear to find out. A familiar numbness began to fill him, like the gray mists that crept up to hide the tor.

"Raymond?"

Ceridwen's hand was cool and soft against his hot skin. He fought not to jerk from her touch, not to close himself off. But the numbing mist was bliss, for now. There was nothing he could say to make her, so bright and full of life, understand.

He squeezed her fingers before turning his back on her, the one he loved. After he had rested, he could at least pretend, for her sake, that he was all right. Then he would wait for his anger to burn away the mist, as it had always done before.

The next day Raymond lay in his makeshift bed of leaves, alternately shaking with chills and burning with fever. Ceridwen tended him as best she could, but in the end the greatest comfort she could provide was simply to hold him close. Helpless as she felt, at least he was alive in body, though his spirit concerned her just as much.

Another evening fell, the second since leaving the keep for the grove. The men spoke little, their morale was as low as food was scarce. Ceridwen wondered how long it would take before Raymond would be able to travel. Then, as she held him, the hairs on her nape rose. Beyond the circle of firelight the brush crackled. "Giles, something is there. Look!"

Eyes glowed green out of the darkness. Giles started to rise. Before he made it to his feet a huge gray shape leaped toward Ceridwen and Raymond. A surge of joy replaced Ceridwen's terror as the blur of teeth and fur resolved into Hamfast. His great pink tongue licked her face, then Raymond's.

Raymond stirred, grumbling at this friendly assault.

Ceridwen's delight redoubled when Shona stumbled into the clearing, scratched and muddy, but whole and smiling. The men shared Ceridwen's astonishment at Giles. His eyes overflowed with tears, and he scooped the maid into his embrace and swung her around. Shona opened her mouth, presumably to speak, but was forestalled by Giles claiming her lips in a kiss that allowed no room for breath, let alone speech. Without a word he carried his prize off to the edge of the clearing.

"What is he doing with her, Wace? I cannot see." Ceridwen peered futilely into the shadows. "Is she all right?"

"Em, I believe so, my lady. It appears that Giles is making some sort of appeal, as he is on his knees, pressing her hand to his forehead."

"'Tis about time he abased himself before Shona. She has put up with him much too long."

Raymond's dry appraisal brought everyone's attention back from the touching drama. Pale skin stretched taut over his cheekbones, his hair hung in tangles, but his eyes shone clear and lucid once again. Hamfast buried his head beneath Raymond's arm, and the dog's long tail thumped the ground without pause.

"My lord, praise God you are back with us," Sven exclaimed.

"Praise too the foul breath of this offal-eating hound. 'Tis enough to raise the dead. And the half-dead."

Raymond's remark warmed Ceridwen's heart. If he felt well enough for a sarcastic jest, perhaps he was truly on the mend. But she did not expect it when his hard hand met her neck, and pulled her down to meet his mouth in a possessive kiss which, by comparison, made Giles's look the picture of decorum. More shocking still was the way Raymond rolled with her, pinning her beneath his body, one leg drawn up to straddle her thighs.

The garrison cheered.

"Raymond, do you mean to ravish me before all these men?" Ceridwen squeaked.

"To move at all is killing me, sweeting, and I am close to losing consciousness, but I must inspire their confidence, prove that I still possess all my capacities. To you as well." He bit her neck below her ear and growled, matching the low rumble coming from Hamfast's throat.

Ceridwen smiled. "If the reason is not that you are overwhelmed by love and a desire to please me, then you had best stop right now." His heart thudded, strong and slow against her palm. "You fiend! You are not in the least excited over me!"

"You want me to stop, then fault me for my self-control?"

She was glad of the smile in his voice, but he winced when he moved, and she knew he was braving the pain for her benefit. "You should rest and let your body heal. Should we not be on our way soon? You are not thinking of something daft again like handing yourself back to Alonso in the name of honor, are you?" Still in Raymond's arms, she shuddered at the thought.

"Nay, Ceri, I have done with that sort of honor. Now I will do what I have always wanted."

Silence surrounded them, but for the sighing boughs of the trees. Ceridwen lifted her head and squinted. "Where is everyone?"

Raymond turned her face back towards his. "My men are the souls of discretion. But Ceri, are you in pain? What was that grimace you just made?"

Ceridwen gazed up into his eyes, the reflected flames of the fire dancing there. "Grimace? Oh. Well, my lord, I do have an imperfection. I cannot see things clearly when they are much more than a stone's throw away. Less, actually. I squint."

Raymond mulled this over for a moment. "Jesu—I've been a fool. All this time, since first I ever saw you, I have assumed your narrowed eyes were an expression of loathing. Now you say 'twas merely to get a better look at me?"

"Aye. I cannot get my fill of you, Beauchamp. Not with my eyes nor my hands nor my—"

"Ah, milady, then surely I must remedy such a sad state of affairs. Thank God for Bruce's oaty gruel this day. It has given me the strength I will need, to satisfy my little *cygne-noire*." He ran his hand along her hip.

"What does that mean, my lord?"

"You, love. You alone."

At this Ceridwen could only swallow, and stroke his unshaven cheek, wanting to soothe every cut and bruise visited upon him by Alonso. "What is it you have always wanted to do?" she whispered.

Raymond kissed her palm. "You might think the worse of

me for it, but…part of me would like to join the students and minstrels who wander the land, playing their music and discussing philosophy. Father always said such people were parasites. Fleas upon the backs of men like him.''

''All fathers have such things to say. To be a troubadour is a dream to dazzle the heart, and with a voice like yours you would soon be renowned. But still, Raymond, should we not first make for a safer place?'' Ceridwen looked at him in concern, for his eyes held a dark expression as he stared into the fire.

''Ceridwen, where is Percy?''

She sucked in a little breath of shock. ''Is he not already at the monastery? Then, oh Mary—I know not. They dragged me away, and then you, but I do not remember seeing him, either among the living or the dead when we brought you out.''

''Then I cannot leave. I will not go without him.''

The next dawn Ceridwen stood alone on the field, hidden in the mist. The garrison was in place among the trees. Giles and Raymond had gone into the woods after a pair of stray horses. They intended to ride up to the gates, challenge Alonso, and demand Parsifal's release. But Ceridwen could not bear for them to take such a risk. Raymond had dismissed her plea to wait for Rhys and reinforcements.

So, she had thought of an alternative. She would attract the attention of Alonso's men ahead of Raymond, and lure them closer in a way that she was almost certain would stop them from loosing their arrows upon her. Then she would alert the garrison, and Raymond's men could spring upon Alonso's.

She had not told Giles of her idea. Nor had she breathed a word of it to Raymond. Only Sven knew. Her plan was not wise. But Ceridwen knew there were two things she could count on. The lust of her enemy, and her own fleetness of foot. She touched the flute at her waist, then loosened the laces at the neck of her tunic. Doubt assailed her. *'Tis these English who are ashamed of their bodies.* That was little comfort. Ceridwen shivered as she shed her mantle.

''Milady. Whatever you are about to do, let me come with you.'' The soft voice belonged to Shona.

Ceridwen smiled sadly at her. "Nay, my dear, for Giles would never forgive me should any harm befall you. This must rest upon my head alone. Are he and Raymond still gone?"

"Aye, Madame. Still, I cannot allow you to go alone."

"'Tis not your place to allow or disallow what I do. Go back to the camp and hide yourself, as I instructed you."

Shona frowned and balked, then purposefully began to unlace her overgown.

"Shona, go this instant!"

"Nay, Madame. You are going to entice them into a trap."

"You have winkled it out of Sven!" Ceridwen reassessed the winsome girl. Shona's jaw was set, her fingers worked at her laces. Her gaze was steady and cool. Ceridwen shook her head. "You are as stubborn as am I. When we return we will face more wrath than has ever before been turned upon either one of us."

"I am ready for that, my lady. I am yet a virgin by virtue of my ability to outrun Giles and every other man who tried to catch me." Shona tossed back her blond mane. "And this helps, too." She patted the hilt of the dagger Raymond had given her.

To face the enemy alone was a terrifying prospect. With Shona at her side, Ceridwen's heart was a small measure lighter. They walked in graceful steps toward the barbican. Emerging from the misty vale, they halted a bowshot's length from Rookhaven. Alonso's men moved along the gray battlements.

Ceridwen looked into Shona's eyes. The maid's resolve helped steel her own. As one, the women pulled away their upper clothing. With such abundant evidence, there could be no mistaking their gender, even at this distance.

Ceridwen put her flute to her lips. Fear and cold made her tremble, but did not stop the song that flowed in visible puffs from the instrument. She played as never before. Every drop of love she bore Raymond colored the notes.

A pair of soldiers appeared at the gate. They stared, turned to each other, then stared again. More of Alonso's men, atop the curtain wall, froze in apparent disbelief.

Ceridwen dropped the flute from her mouth. She backed away a step. Now Shona's eyes reflected her own fear. *This is a ter-*

rible mistake. Alonso's knights would ride out and savage them. A collective shout sounded and the portcullis rumbled up. Foot soldiers pounded across the drawbridge.

Ceridwen turned and fled, Shona a step ahead of her. At the top of a rise they stopped, clouding the air with rapid breaths, and turned to face the pursuit. Alonso's fighters slowed, seemingly uncertain. Ceridwen played the haunting melody once more, hoping Rookhaven's men would hear her signal.

The last note floated away and for an instant, silence lay suspended over them, as if the music had the power to keep the men at bay. Then the besiegers charged. Ceridwen held her ground, just long enough to open the leather bag and fling its contents at the attackers. They scrambled to collect the silver, and she ran as fast as her breath and body could take her. Shona was just as fleet.

Sven leaped, roaring from his hiding place in the trees. Then all the rest of Raymond's garrison jumped down. With nothing more than their fire-hardened sticks and clubs, they burst forth from the grove to clash with the siege army.

"Oh, nay!" Ceridwen's heart was ready to burst. Raymond's men could not hope to defeat the enemy unless they followed her plan. But it was too late. She should have realized the garrison's pride would not allow them to hide for long, however effective a tactic it might have been.

At a small crunch of sound she turned—to meet Raymond's furious gaze. His eyes were not focused upon her face. She gasped, remembering her state of undress. Cheeks burning, Ceridwen clutched the gaping edges of her clothes and hurriedly relaced them. She knew Raymond was outraged not only by her chosen method of drawing out Alonso, but because Giles and Wace had obeyed *her* command and stopped him from joining his men.

Raymond struggled against their restraining arms. "Damn you—release me or I shall slay you both once I am free!"

"My lord—"

"I would rather have Alonso take my life than be held by you within his sight."

Ceridwen hung her head. She angered Raymond at every turn. But at least he was here with her—alive.

"Forgive us, milord." Giles stepped back, as did Wace. "We have no right to detain you."

Ceridwen watched Raymond wince and roll his shoulders as if to remove the feel of their hands upon him. "Madame," he began, and Ceridwen cringed at his use of that title, which of late he reserved only for the most scathing of his remarks to her. "You shall pay for this. Dearly and repeatedly."

She looked to Giles for support. His lips were tight, his breathing hard. He too had fixed an angry gaze upon his beloved. Shona's tentative smile faded. Ceridwen straightened her stance. "My lords, our action was my fault entirely. I beg you to appreciate how this brave lass and I—"

"Please, Ceridwen. No excuses. Well do I know the folly of your good intentions." Raymond turned to his lieutenant. "Giles, I am painfully aware of my current physical limits. Nonetheless, I would fain attend my men."

Giles bowed. "Command me, lord."

Raymond caught Ceridwen's arm. "As for you, be glad I have not the time to give you the attention you deserve." In spite of his stern tone, he pulled her close and kissed her on the lips. "Wace, make certain she and Shona keep out of sight."

At a gesture from his lord the squire brought one of the found horses forward, a roan mare. Accepting a leg up, Raymond mounted the animal bareback, with a rope for bridle. He cantered out to the battlefield carrying a makeshift lance. Giles rode the second horse alongside.

Ceridwen watched them go, an impossible lump in her throat. With Hamfast and Shona beside her, she reluctantly lay flat upon the same rise she and Rhys had used when they first arrived. The chill of the damp ground quickly seeped through her tunic. Wace fumed and fidgeted beside them.

The battle took form. Sharpened tree-limbs against iron-tipped lances. Bare chests against shields and mail. Blood flowed freely on both sides. Raymond and his men fought desperately and pushed Alonso's forces back. But fresh combatants poured forth from the keep. Eventually Alonso himself emerged, his great-horse prancing. Ceridwen's anxiety soared. *How could God allow such a man to live and breathe?*

Then, with one arm about Hamfast's neck, Ceridwen rubbed her eyes in disbelief. "Do you see what I see?"

"Aye," Shona whispered.

A blue-white brightness bounded from the forest onto the field. It stopped, pawed the earth, then stepped regally among the fighters. The white stag. A myth Alonso had turned into the symbol of his own legendary cruelty.

Raymond halted his horse. The fighting stopped. All watched, awestruck, as the stag paused in their midst. Then a seething hiss prefaced a bloom of red on the white stag's neck. Blood coursed down the ermine coat. A peacock-fletched arrow shaft protruded from the wound. The beast staggered and keened, proving its mortality.

Alonso's men fell back, dismay upon their faces. A terrible omen. The downfall of the magical creature which represented their invincible lord was tantamount to their own demise. They faltered, and Raymond's men roared after them.

One after another, Alonso's soldiers dropped their weapons and fled—into a hail of arrows targeting the white emblems of their surcoats. Welsh bowmen lined the ridge ahead of them.

"Da!" Terrified that her father was about to turn on Raymond's company as well, Ceridwen ran to meet the familiar, dark figure who approached, Rhys at his side. "Please, tell them to stop!" she cried.

"They are under orders to shoot selectively, Ceri," Rhys assured her, grinning as ever. "The old man came to his senses at last. He likes Blanche more than he ought. And Raymond."

Morgan scowled at his son, but greeted his daughter tenderly. Ceridwen heard Alonso shouting and turned from her father's warm embrace. Wace, poised to rush onto the field, had his fists clenched around a stout piece of fencing.

"Father, I must go to Raymond, come what may." Without awaiting an answer Ceridwen led Wace and Shona. Down the slope they raced. Ceridwen paused at the edge of the ranks of fighters. Her husband did not acknowledge their arrival on the field. His complete attention was fixed upon his brother.

Alonso stared, unblinking. "So here you are, Raymond. I have missed you. But by what wizardry do you still live?" The elder Beauchamp sat his charger proudly, elegant as ever, but the waver in his voice betrayed his unease.

"I am here by God's grace, Alonso. That, and the love and cunning of a Welshwoman." Raymond faced his brother, empty of emotion. No hatred, no revulsion, nothing. But as if to belie his lack of feeling, a shiver ran through his body, and the constant burn and ache of his wounds increased.

Alonso looked to the ranks of archers now at his flanks. And beyond them to the men of Rookhaven. His tongue darted out and slid over his lips. "'Twould seem we are at an impasse."

"Nay, brother. It would seem you are defeated."

"I had every right to make an example of you, Raymond. If you dare harm me now, you will discover there are even worse ways to die, once the king's men get hold of you. Everard will see to it. He is already on his way to John's court."

"Everard can go to hell. As for you, Alonso, I will be merciful. Get down from your horse and onto your knees. Say your prayers to whatever demon you wish to escort you, and I shall do the world a favor by striking your discourteous head from your shoulders." It was not what Raymond had thought to say, but the words seemed to form themselves without his permission, like bubbles on a stew of rage.

Alonso laughed. "Strike me with what? *I* have the sword."

Dark murmurs welled from the men of Rookhaven. They advanced, clustering around Alonso. His big charger jigged and snorted. At his brother's tone Raymond's anger surged anew, and he did not try to stifle it. "Where is Parsifal, Alonso? Have you fed him to your mastiffs?"

Alonso remained impassive, except for the twitch of one eyebrow. "Parsifal? What are you talking about?"

"He is alive, Alonso, or was a few days hence."

"Aye, I am."

Raymond's heart battered his ribs as Parsifal pushed his way from the crowd of warriors and came to stand beside him.

Alonso paled and crossed himself. "Jesu."

Raymond swallowed hard. Parsifal held the long, crystal-hilted sword, naked in his hand. "Greetings, brothers."

"Where have you been, Percy?" Raymond hid the relief that otherwise would have made him embrace the young knight.

"I have been contemplating my true nature, in the refuge of a bolt-hole. I have reclaimed my sword from that pig of a reeve. And I have come for the vengeance that is also mine. Tell them, Alonso. Tell them about the crusade."

Alonso's gaze darted from Parsifal to Raymond, then to the bloodied garrison of Rookhaven. Parsifal's face colored and his expression hardened. The Beauchamp look, of vengeance sought, of dark vows as yet unfulfilled. "They want to hear, Alonso!" Parsifal gestured widely with his sword. "What did you do, when the Saracens came, and there was but one starving horse left between us? Strong enough to bear one, but not both?"

Alonso spoke not a word.

"I returned for you, Alonso. I came back and you pulled me down and left me to the infidels. Do you know what they did to me, brother? What entertainment I provided?" Tears streamed down Parsifal's thin cheeks, but his eyes were fully open, as if he were not aware of his own weeping.

Raymond extended his hand toward his younger brother. "Please, Parsifal—stop. He will never be moved by what you say. This is what Alonso loves—to have our pain, our humiliation, on display for all to see."

Parsifal turned his tormented gaze to Raymond. "They let me go, sword and all, for I was a man no longer. I gave Lady Ceridwen to you, for I could never be a husband to her. Nor father any child." He spoke in a low voice full of anguish, but such was the silence that every word was audible.

The attention of the whole assemblage shifted to Alonso. Disgust and outrage molded the faces of the warriors. Raymond's stomach churned as his anger built, closer and closer to the killing rage he could but rarely control. "You deserve to die, Alonso, but I fear that if your blood spills upon my soil, the land will be cursed for future generations."

"My progeny or yours, Raymond?" Alonso sneered.

"Let me take him, Raymond. 'Tis my right." Parsifal's blade glinted in the strengthening sun.

"Nay, Percy, would you dirty your soul with Alonso's blood, when you are about to join holy orders? Leave him to me. My soul cannot get any blacker than it is already."

The color drained from the young knight's face. He faltered, and looked at the weapon in his hand as though it crawled with scorpions.

"Give it to me." Raymond reached for the sword, but found that his own hand shook. The prospect of killing Alonso both tempted and revolted him. He breathed deeply, struggling for control. Long ago, when he had still believed in himself, he had vowed never to allow Alonso to provoke him to evil. Once again, he had nearly succumbed. Raymond balled his fingers into a fist.

Parsifal let the blade drop to the turf.

Raymond's hesitation was not lost on Alonso, who grinned widely. "Ah, Raymond, do you try to escape your blood instincts? Your Beauchamp heritage? Do you dream of finding yourself free of the desire to kill?" Alonso looked at his brothers. "You cannot. Nor can Percy. It does not matter whether he becomes a monk or not. The blood will out." He sighed, relaxing into his saddle as if he merely exchanged pleasantries. "And, do you know what is most amusing?"

Raymond could only stare at Alonso, who began to laugh.

"The jest is that I have seeded half the shire. So many bastards, brimming with the same blood lust you and I share. There is no escaping it, Raymond. Once I am gone, they will have only you to rise against."

The men-at-arms stirred. Their mutterings grew to a low roar. A gray-bearded pikeman shook his raised fist at Alonso. "My daughter *died* whelping one of your bastards!"

Alonso maintained a wintry silence.

"You took my Bettina—on our wedding night." A young man brandished a red-stained staff.

"I had every right to her." Alonso sniffed.

"There's laws and there's rights, but no lord should take all that you have and live to boast about it!" The grievances went

n. Each brought a higher pitch of imminent violence. The soldiers stepped nearer to Alonso. He spat at them. As a hand grabbed for the reins Alonso spurred his charger's sides.

The great animal leaped forward, knocking down sturdy men. But the rest were not to be stopped. Many pairs of hands caught at the stallion's bridle and harness. The men braved the animal's teeth and hooves and pulled him to a halt. Alonso was dragged from the saddle. The horse galloped to freedom.

"Hold!" Raymond urged his mount forward. As the roan shouldered past the men, Raymond saw three distinct heads of hair—red, black and blond, ranged at the crowd's edge. He groaned inwardly. Wace had better see to Ceridwen's safety, now that she had dragged him to the fray. Then his concern eased as Giles rode to them and pulled Shona onto his horse.

Raymond turned his attention to Alonso, held fast, his own sword at his throat. Hamfast broke free of Ceridwen and bounded over to stand beside Raymond's mount. The hound growled at Alonso, lips pulled back to reveal sharp teeth.

Sven spoke up. "Lord Raymond, do not naysay us, for we have no wish to disobey you. But there is blood and honor to be avenged. If Alonso lives 'tis an offense to God and man alike."

Alonso's eyes rolled as the sword edge pressed into his neck. Raymond slid down from the roan and approached his brother, the withered grass crunching beneath his feet.

"Alonso. You cannot continue as you have been." Raymond fixed his gaze upon his brother. "Shall I allow you to run into the forest and hide from these men, to freeze and starve and be set upon by wolves—and Hamfast? Or, would you rather I bring you into Wales, where your reputation precedes you? The women will wait with their daggers for you to fall asleep, despite our best efforts to remain awake."

Alonso's throat convulsed. "You will not hold me to ransom?"

"I fear there is no one within a hundred leagues who would trouble himself to spend a farthing to have you back. Where are your loyal men? Your faithful mastiffs? Your loving Gwen?"

Malice narrowed Alonso's eyes. "You have always wanted

this, to have me at your mercy. Here is your chance, why hesitate?'' He curled his lip in a manner all too familiar to Raymond.

Ceridwen had worked her way through the crowd and came to his side. Her hand slipped into Raymond's and squeezed his fingers. His heart lurched, like a foal staggering to its feet. Such a simple thing. The touch of a woman. This woman.

He looked down into her earnest eyes, and made his choice. ''Too often, Alonso, you have made me wish I had never been born. But I have been born anew. Nothing and no one can stop me from living now. I will not be sucked back into your darkness.''

''Give me room then, Raymond, for I will not be touched by the filthy hands of commoners. There is a third choice beyond the two you have offered. 'Tis not without honor.''

''Leave him,'' Raymond said, and the men stepped back, growling with obvious reluctance. Alonso drew his dagger. He contemplated its edge, and its lethal point.

''Taking life is a sin, Alonso, whether 'tis that of someone else or your own.''

''My sin was in not taking yours, that day on the dolmen.'' Raymond's skin crawled at Alonso's vicious tone.

Parsifal moaned.

Alonso's face shone with sweat. ''There is one last game to play, Raymond. One you should enjoy.'' Alonso raised the dagger and aimed the point at himself.

''Nay.'' Raymond's voice caught on the tightness in his throat. He wanted to make Ceridwen leave, but dared not take his gaze from the weapon in Alonso's hand. Alonso slashed open his own surcoat. His eyes gleamed as he placed the dagger-tip below where his ribs converged, and angled the blade upward.

''You have gone soft, Raymond. I can best you at this game as I have at all the others. You haven't the nerve.'' Alonso applied pressure to his skin with the dagger point, and a drop of blood beaded down the blade.

Dread permeated Raymond's limbs and cold fingers of panic clutched his gut. *Upthrust, always.* His own advice. ''Don't.''

Alonso smiled. Even as Raymond returned his brother's gaze the blade flashed. In that instant Raymond recognized Alonso's smile as merely a distraction. Love and fury driving him, he leaped to intercept the dagger's plunge toward Ceridwen. Alonso was fast, but Raymond had always been faster.

He caught Alonso's wrist. His brother was like Spanish steel, flexible, unbreakable. They wrestled and fell together to the ground. Raymond gasped with the impact as his wounds opened. Still clutching the dagger, Alonso broke his wrist free of Raymond's grip and tried to roll away. Raymond countered by leaping atop his brother and forcing him to lie face earthward.

Alonso howled and stopped struggling.

Raymond got up and slowly turned him, revealing the dagger buried in Alonso's chest. The hilt moved a fraction, up and down, its jewels winking with every beat of his heart. Raymond looked on in horror, incapable of movement. Ceridwen ran to his side and he could do nothing to prevent her.

Alonso whispered, "Kiss me, Raymond. Take me into thyself, so that I may live on, in the darkness of thy soul."

"Nay." Raymond began to tremble. He shook his head.

"Help me, then. Finish it. I have not the strength."

Alonso desired the *coup de grace*. He fought for breath while his lifeblood pulsed away, his skin turning grayer as Raymond watched. Raymond's hand hovered near the dagger's hilt.

Alonso's gurgle of laughter penetrated his dilemma. The sound echoed off the walls of Rookhaven then died away, as if the baron were already a wraith haunting the keep.

He mocks me, even now.

A shadow cloaked Alonso's body, as Parsifal joined them. The young man stared, then genuflected over Alonso. "I forgive thee, my lord brother. For everything."

Alonso looked at the young knight, his eyes wide. Raymond took a shuddering breath. He met Ceridwen's gaze. She nodded to him, encouraging him. Aye, his own victory lay in forgiveness. It was the only way to put his pain to rest.

It was the one thing completely beyond Alonso's reach.

He took Alonso's hand. "I too forgive thee, brother. For all

I have suffered at thy hands." Raymond said the words, surprised to find he meant them.

The baron's long fingers twitched, then were still.

Parsifal turned away. Ceridwen put her arms around Raymond. He looked upon Alonso's body in bewilderment. "Perhaps he has yet won. I had not the courage to kill him, nor to spare him pain."

Ceridwen squeezed his waist. "He has won nothing, Raymond. Alonso never broke you. You may have entreated God for mercy, but never him. With his final act he tried to manipulate you into an impossible choice. 'Twas most wicked of him."

Raymond could think of no adequate reply. Then, he caught Ceridwen's hands, and nodded to Percy. "Come, there is one who needs our aid." Raymond led them to the wounded stag, which lay on its side, panting. At their approach it tried to rise, but Wace wrapped his mantle around the magnificent animal's head, covering its eyes. With Percy's help they held the beast still.

Raymond whispered to the stag as he did to his horses when the need arose, indeed to any creature of his acquaintance in pain. He stroked the white coat, and the stag calmed. Awe and pity touched Raymond's heart. "'Tis real. No phantom would bleed, nor feel the hurt."

"Aye. As real as your heart, Raymond. You have healed yourself, and so can you help this stag to go home." Ceridwen's eyes shone bright.

"If I do not kill it in the attempt. I pray your father's arrow is not barbed." With one swift pull Raymond removed the arrow from the stag's neck and pressed the wound with his palm. It oozed, but did not pulse. "He is in God's hands now."

They withdrew. The animal gathered itself and stumbled to its feet. The winter sun haloed the air around the white stag—then he was gone.

Chapter Twenty-Four

Ceridwen took a last look over her shoulder. A wispy column of smoke marked the smoldering, blackened ruins of Rookhaven. She tightened her fingers around her pony's reins. Raymond, his brow furrowed, rode beside her on Grendel. Ceridwen's heart went out to him. He had buried his brother, and with him, she hoped, the past.

The afternoon sun warmed her chilled spirits. Bright sky contrasted against the dark, blue-green masses of forest ranging up the slopes of the Black Mountains before them. The garrison trudged along, and ahead, Shona rode pillion behind Giles, her cheek pressed to his broad back.

Wace proudly led the destrier, Orpheus, rescued from the keep, and Percy was well on his way to Father Torval. Morgan and Rhys had started home with the main body of archers the day before, leaving a dozen bowmen as vanguard to the exhausted English fighters.

From his courser's considerable height, Raymond looked down at Ceridwen. His expression softened as he met her eyes. She discreetly appraised him. He was still pale, and too lean, but his wounds were healing faster than she had hoped. A simple life, good food, and plenty of loving would put him to rights. She returned his smile. "My lord?"

"I was just thinking, of all that I have lost, 'tis my bed I shall miss the most." He stroked Grendel's massive neck.

"Truly?" Ceridwen arched a brow at him. "Not your mail hauberk?"

He groaned. "Cruel wench, do not remind me! But nay, Ceri the greater loss is of goosedown, and thick quilts, and the haven of my bed. 'Twas like a ship I set sail in each night. Sometimes to bliss, and sometimes to terror, but I always returned each morn to a safe harbor."

"I will be your harbor from now on."

Raymond's smile broadened to a wicked grin. "Aye. I will make sure of that. Rough seas or calm, I shall ever sink my anchor into your sweet depths."

"My lord, such scandalous talk should not reach the ears of the innocents surrounding us!"

Raymond made a great show of looking about. "Where? Where among all these knowing souls, is one innocent?"

"Shona, certainly. And Wace. And of course Hamfast. You ever protect his virtue." Ceridwen waved in the direction of the hound, who loped up and down the line of travelers, inspecting the path for anything of interest.

"Aye." Raymond smiled, and Hamfast bounded over, his tail lashing the air.

Ceridwen's breath caught at the sight of Raymond at ease, his golden head unhelmed and sunlit. She swallowed and blinked. He would think her silly for weeping at the mere sight of him.

Hamfast turned from Raymond and began to bark, as a tumult of hoofbeats announced the approach of riders from the rear. Vivid pennants snapped above a mailed knight with a contingent of lancers in formation, cantering closer. Ceridwen looked from them and back to Raymond in alarm.

"Do not worry, love." He reached over and touched her shoulder. "Oy, Lucien! Well met!" Raymond shouted and halted his horse. The remainder of Rookhaven's defenders stopped to rest. So this was Lucien de Griswold, who had been delayed by the rising River Usk. His coppery hair gleamed in the sun, and there was a bemused expression on his striking, noble face.

"What ho, Beauchamp? When I heard of your plight I thought I would find you fighting to the last man, not taking to the hills."

Raymond took a sidelong glance at Ceridwen before answering his friend. "I have different priorities than I once did, Lucien. Can you not see how that might be?"

Ceridwen felt herself blush as Lucien rested his gaze upon her and said, "Indeed, you are a fortunate, if undeserving scoundrel, Raymond."

"Well do I know, Lucien." Raymond grinned. "We are on our way to Llanmadog, where we shall help defend the people against any who dare pass without peace in their hearts."

"Most admirable. But why not rebuild Rookhaven?"

"'Tis dead, in every way that matters. And our lord King Jean-*sans-terre* is bound to confiscate it. Apart from my excommunication, I am an outlaw, now. No doubt Everard shall denounce me for Alonso's death."

Lucien smiled wryly. "I could be denounced as easily, if the number of times I have wished Alonso dead were to count against me. Do you want an additional escort?"

"I welcome your company for as long as it pleases you to ride with us." Raymond reached over his horse's neck to clasp hands with Lucien. It warmed Ceridwen to see that her husband had such a faithful, stalwart friend.

That night found them on a high meadow. Ceridwen inhaled the scents of the sea and the damp, scrubby grass that now lay flat and gray, awaiting the snows of winter. A thrill ran through her limbs. She was on her way home with her beloved. They were together, safe, and in good company.

Raymond held Ceridwen close, cradled between his knees. They huddled before their own fire, a little apart from the rest. Opposite them Hamfast snored and twitched in his sleep. A pocket of sap in the blazing beechwood popped, and sparks swirled up to mingle with the pinpoints of light in the black sky. Ceridwen took another deep breath of the tangy air.

"Raymond?"

"Mmm?"

"How—" Ceridwen hesitated. This was as good a time to ask as any. "How are you going to punish me? I must know."

"Punish you? What a thought." Raymond bent his head and put his rough cheek to her smooth one.

"You said I would pay, 'dearly and repeatedly.'"

"Ah, that. 'Tis simple. If I ever again catch you running about the countryside bare-breasted, I shall lock you away." He firmly placed a hand upon each of the areas concerned.

"Me? Where? And for how long?" Ceridwen's breath came faster as Raymond's warm fingers caressed her in slow circles.

"In our bedchamber, for as long as it suits me to keep you there." He squeezed the rest of her between his thighs.

Ceridwen shivered happily at the thought of again sharing a bed with Raymond. "But I shall escape while you sleep."

"Nay, for I shall make myself prisoner with you, and neither one of us will have the key. I shall give it to Wace."

"Hah! And I was worried." Ceridwen reached back and slid her fingers into Raymond's thick, light-spangled hair.

He drew his mantle closer about her. "Ceri...if I knew how to say it in Welsh I would, but, *Cymraes*...I love you."

Ceridwen stilled. He had used plain words instead of his body alone. She twisted around and put her lips to his. He responded with a kiss that sent a heated jolt right through to her toes. "I know," she murmured.

Raymond's hands slipped along Ceridwen's shoulders and found their haven within her tunic, as she resettled her back to the comfort of his solid body. "You are a wise woman."

"Aye," she admitted readily. "But I wish I had seen the beauty in your Norman heart sooner."

"Any good you see in me is but a reflection of your own."

Still resting against Raymond's chest, Ceridwen looked up at the rising moon. It hung fat in the sky, a hazy ring encircling it. It appeared bigger and brighter than she could ever remember—as did her hopes and dreams. "I disagree. You have your own light, Carrog Dhu, you will never lose your fire."

"Not so long as you are there to tend it, Ceri."

Ceridwen faced her husband, and looked into the glowing depths of his eyes. He caught her in his arms and crushed her against him, in full view of the now silent camp, and she kissed his mouth. His heat poured into her, his male strength surged through her blood and blended with her feminine power. Ceridwen let his fire flow deep, branding her heart, and a certainty came to her. "Owain takes pleasure in our happiness, Raymond."

"Hmm. Then I owe it to him to bring you full joy, as many times as possible, as often as you wish."

She smiled. "I will hold you to that, Beauchamp."

* * * * *

A
Regency
Invitation

to the House Party of the Season

Nicola Cornick, Joanna Maitland,
Elizabeth Rolls

On sale 3rd December 2004

Available at most branches of WHSmith, Tesco, ASDA, Martins,
Borders, Eason, Sainsbury's and all good paperback bookshops.

WE VALUE YOUR OPINION!

YOUR CHANCE TO WIN A ONE YEAR SUPPLY OF YOUR FAVOURITE BOOKS.

If you are a regular UK reader of Mills & Boon® Historical Romance™ and have always wanted to share your thoughts on the books you read—here's your chance:

Join the Reader Panel today!

This is your opportunity to let us know exactly what you think of the books you love.

And there's another great reason to join:

Each month, all members of the Reader Panel have a chance of winning four of their favourite Mills & Boon romance books EVERY month for a whole year!

If you would like to be considered for the Reader Panel, please complete and return the following application. Unfortunately, as we have limited spaces, we cannot guarantee that everyone will be selected.

Name: _____

Address: _____

_____ Post Code: _____

Home Telephone: _____ Email Address: _____

Where do you normally get your Mills & Boon Historical Romance books (please tick one of the following)?

Shops   ❏   Library/Borrowed   ❏

Reader Service™   ❏   If so, please give us your subscription no. _____

Please indicate which age group you are in:

16 – 24   ❏   25 – 34   ❏

35 – 49   ❏   50 – 64   ❏   65 +   ❏

If you would like to apply by telephone, please call our friendly Customer Relations line on **020 8288 2886**, or get in touch by email to readerpanel@hmb.co.uk

Don't delay, apply to join the Reader Panel today and help ensure the range and quality of the books you enjoy.

Send your application to:

The Reader Service, Reader Panel Questionnaire, FREEPOST NAT1098, Richmond, TW9 1BR

If you do not wish to receive any additional marketing material from us, please contact the Data Manager at the address above.

FREE

2 BOOKS AND A SURPRISE GIFT!

We would like to take this opportunity to thank you for reading this
Mills & Boon® book by offering you the chance to take TWO more
specially selected titles from the Historical Romance™ series absolutely
FREE! We're also making this offer to introduce you to the benefits of
the Reader Service™—

- ★ **FREE home delivery**
- ★ **FREE gifts and competitions**
- ★ **FREE monthly Newsletter**
- ★ **Books available before they're in the shops**
- ★ **Exclusive Reader Service offers**

Accepting these FREE books and gift places you under no obligation
to buy; you may cancel at any time, even after receiving your free
shipment. Simply complete your details below and return the entire
page to the address below. You don't even need a stamp!

YES! Please send me 2 free Historical Romance books and a
surprise gift. I understand that unless you hear from me, I will
receive 4 superb new titles every month for just £3.59 each, postage
and packing free. I am under no obligation to purchase any books and
may cancel my subscription at any time. The free books and gift will be
mine to keep in any case.

H4ZEE

Ms/Mrs/Miss/Mr...Initials ....

BLOCK CAPITALS PLEASE

Surname ....

Address ....

....

....Postcode ....

Send this whole page to:
The Reader Service, FREEPOST CN81, Croydon, CR9 3WZ